WHEN FALL BREAKS

Julie Solano
& Tracy Justice

DEDICATION

For our husbands and four children who inspire us every day. Thank you for your unending support and understanding throughout this exciting journey. We did it!

~In the mountains a dramatic fall is a given.
As sure as the river will rage and the billowing winds will blow,
the forces of nature will sweep across the land, altering everything in its path.
Some warmly embrace the turn of seasons, while others cling to the past,
trying to evade the dying beauty.
The guarantee lies herein.
As hard as one may try to blind themselves to the destruction,
no one will escape the inevitable death that comes . . .
when fall breaks~

CHAPTER I

RUFF DAY

I FEEL THE HEAT CREEPING up my face, as I sit on the front lawn of Jefferson High covered with wrappers, crumbs, and gooey tuna droppings. Cringing in disgust, I quiver, as warm, sticky soda runs through my fingers. It's the first day of my senior year, and Chelsea Chapman has already managed to humiliate me by subtly sticking her foot out as I distractedly walked by while texting my boyfriend, Pistol. Her sneaky little stunt sent me stumbling into the colossal, red garbage can that sits at the front entrance of the school. To make matters worse, as I sit picking stubborn bits of sunflower seeds out of my sweater, I glance up to see a group of hot jocks patting her on the shoulders and laughing hysterically.

"Enjoy your trip Twinkle Toes?" taunts the shorter, husky one near the front of the group.

The temperature rises in my face, as the anger and humiliation I'm feeling finds its way to my cheeks. *Darn it, I wish I didn't have to say goodbye to my beautiful, peaceful summer and hello to these merciless bullies. I've played their game for three years now, and I just can't win. I'm over it.* Not wanting to make things worse, I simply send Chelsea's fan club my best "lick my tuna infected outfit" smirk and shrug it off. *Out of the seven guys standing there, not one comes and offers me a hand. I bet their granddaddies would be rolling over in their graves right now. What happened to chivalry anyway?* I shake my head and look back down to finish cleaning myself up. *Well, if I wasn't already seen as Chelsea's punching bag, this little stunt will certainly solidify that golden title.*

When I'm finally crust free, I make my way toward the music room. People hurriedly push their way through the crowded hall, making gagging noises as they sidestep around me. Suddenly, Jenna bounces up next to me and stops dead in her tracks. "Wow BFF, I know you're into the whole philanthropy thing, but did you have to do a stint in the soup kitchen during school hours?" she gags and pinches her nose.

"No Jenna, I just had a run-in with the overloaded garbage can during lunch. That Slouche Chelsea tripped me when I wasn't paying attention." I shake my head, disgusted that four hours into a new school year, my longtime rival, Chelsea Chapman, is already at it.

"That's unfortunate my friend, cuz it's gonna be a looong afternoon smelling like Hobo Bill from the homeless camp down by the creek." Jenna curls her lips into her signature pout and sympathetically lifts her eyebrows. "By the way, my little wordologist . . . what's a slouche?"

"That would be my latest word for a slut who dates a douche," I reply.

"Good one friend, " she smacks me a high five. "I'm not sure Chelsea still qualifies. She's not dating Jackson anymore. Didn't you hear the latest? Over the summer, she dumped him for a one night fling she had at a rodeo over in the valley. I guess he wouldn't ever talk to her again, so now she's back on the prowl."

"Oh boy gentlemen, get your antibiotics ready. You may need them soon," I joke.

The meaning behind my wisecrack is not lost on Jenna. "No kidding. Here comes round two of . . ." rather than stating the unspoken STD Chelsea's rumored to have, she claps her hands together twice, cocking her head back and forth with that funny, open-mouthed, smirky cheerleader face they all use.

As she's clapping, Jenna catches a glimpse of her watch and drops the Chelsea topic. "Oh my gosh, I've gotta get across the street to the gym. It's weightlifting today and I'm gonna try to sneak a peek at Ty through the locker room door before I go to P.E," she winks with a chuckle. "I'll catch you after school and we can go to practice together." She pinches her face and fans her hand back and forth in front of her nose. "Anyway, it might do you some good to jump in that chlorinated water. I'm not sure if regular soap and water will cut through that stench."

"Hey!" I giggle. "Thanks for boosting my self confidence, Bestie. I'll text you later so we can hook up before practice."

Thankfully when I slip into the music room, Brody is there with his compassionate smile. Wrinkling his nose he chokes, "Tough day, Pip?" Coughing out a slight chuckle, he dangles his keys in front of my face and offers to get me out of guitar class a little early. "Mr. S. won't care, and I'm sure *Hotel California* can wait another day to get mangled by your stinky, little fingers."

"Oh my gosh, you're my hero. Thanks for the rescue Bro," I whisper as we walk toward the door. Without saying a word, Brody smirks down at me with those darned, heart-melting dimples, shakes his head, and gives me a little booty bump.

"Any time Pip . . . any time."

Riding to my house in his Abercrombie-scented Rubicon, I can't help but think of how lucky I am to have Brody Tatum in my life. Since the summer after kindergarten, when my twin brother Caden drug the adorable little brown haired, blue-eyed cutie home from the neighborhood Fourth of July picnic, he has been a permanent fixture at our house, our third musketeer, my BGF "Best Guy Friend," and a part of every significant childhood memory I hold dear. One of my favorite of those memories is the day he started calling me "Pip," short for Pip Squeak. Something about Brody's special name for me makes me melt. I don't know if it's the name that does it, or the memory of the way I got it.

It was the fall I turned eleven. Our families went on vacation to Maui for our Thanksgiving break. We were down at the beach and I wanted to go boogie boarding with Caden and Brody. The three of us were giggling and splashing around, as Caden tried to instruct me on how to get inside the tube of a wave. "Just hold onto the board and when I push, kick your feet as hard as you can. You'll shoot right through. It's fun and you can breathe in there. Here comes a good one. Ready, set . . ." With a strong thrust, I felt myself smoothly gliding on the glassy surface. Fascinated by the wall of water surrounding me, I laughed and breathed in the salty ocean air.

For seconds I imagined I was flying through the air, until swiftly, I felt the corner of the board catch and jerk from my hand. With my abrupt release I found myself being pulled farther from the sunlight and into the darkness. My body was unexpectedly inverted, my feet toward the surface, and my head submerged in the swirling surge. Crunch, my chin pounded the ocean floor as my body somersaulted inside out. Again, and again, I could feel the searing pain as my jaw repeatedly smacked the sandy bottom. Panic started to rise and I began to run out of breath. Dizziness overcame me, as I kicked wildly trying to right my position in the water. My mind fumbled for options as I realized my fierce kicking wasn't getting me anywhere. My tiny little body wasn't strong enough to overtake the fierce current. I strained to stop the impending reflex to breathe. The pain in my jaw was shooting up to my ears.

As I began to take in my final breath, there was an unexpected tugging on my suit straps. I felt water rush quickly down the sides of my body, and I torpedoed upward. Relief overwhelmed me as my head finally broke the surface of the water. My nose stung and my eyes burned from the invasive, merciless saltwater. Tears rolled down my cheeks as I desperately gasped for air. I felt strong hands firmly wrap around each of my shoulders shifting pressure back and forth to help me regain my balance. All I made out through my stinging, blurry eyes was the grimace of his face. With a slightly nervous voice he chortled "Wow, you little pip squeak, look at your tiny little self taking on the big, bad ocean. That must've been some ride, huh? Dang, I had to race your bro to get to you, but you're good now. I've got ya. See, I'll always be here to save you Pip. We'd better get you back to your mom and dad. Hop on." He gently propped me up on his back and began to carry me out of the water.

Splashing toward us, Caden frantically ran to our sides. "You got her bud? I'm so sorry Sis, I tried to get to you as fast as I could." At that, I flashed a thumbs up and laid my head on Brody's shoulder. Exhausted, I closed my eyes enjoying the soft breeze gently blowing across my face. I can still remember the gentle rocking of Brody's steps, and the retelling of the epic "Pip Squeak vs. The Big Wave" story as my two favorite boys carried me to safety.

From that day on Brody and Caden were my biggest guardians and I was their keeper. Getting ourselves into mischief at every turn, our neighbors all referred to us as "Stinkerbell" and "The Lost Boys." Together, we defended magical fortresses, hog-tied unsuspecting neighborhood pirates, and slayed late-night bedroom monsters. We were an inseparable force, ready to take on the world.

"Hey Stinky, snap out of it. We're here," Brody chuckles as he flings my door open and pulls me out of the car. Without even realizing it, my feet are off the ground and I have a perfect view of his tight, sporty butt. A split second later, blood rushes to my head and my long, curly hair bobs and swirls uncontrollably as Brody carts me up to the front lawn. My eyes blur momentarily and then begin to regain focus.

And boy do they focus. *Holy Mr. Universe!!! This guy must be doing some serious football training, or the eighteenth birthday fairy brought him a shiny, new hard body over the summer.* I'm caught off guard by the impulse that overtakes me. *Why am I so tempted to grab that thing right now?* I'm stunned that the thought of grabbing Brody Tatum's butt just crossed my mind. *Kaitlyn Elizabeth Woodley, get your mind out of the gutter. You are completely committed to your boyfriend, and secondly, Brody is your best friend . . . What is wrong with you?* The convincing does no good. My heart begins to pump faster, and heat begins to flush across my face. Tingling sensations burst through my chest, and I feel like someone just shook a bottle of soda and opened it inside my stomach. "*I must be getting sick,*" I whisper to myself as I work to analyze the sensation that just started jumping through my body. *Blood rushing to my head . . . check, accelerated heart rate . . . check, warm fuzzies from the feeling of Brody's hand curled around the back of my legs, his muscular shoulder cradling my stomach, his Abercrombie cologne sending shivers through my . . . wait a second . . .* This feeling doesn't come from merely being turned upside down. I've been carted around by plenty of cavemen trying to prove their strength at Dad's football camps every summer. There's something different about this. My heart is literally quivering. Then it dawns on me. This is what I felt the first time I saw Noah kissing Allie in *The Notebook.*

No . . . This can't be happening; not with Brody. My best guy-friend Brody? The guy that taught me how to throw a cow pie like a frisbee, swallow a noodle and pull it back out of my throat, and spit farther than a man? Definitely not! I won't stand for it!

I begin to kick my feet, back and forth, crying out, "Put me down you savage beast!" I'm shocked when the sting of Brody's playful hand smacks my fanny and he drops me to the ground. Stunned into silence, I try to figure out what's going on inside my head. Maybe during the trash incident this afternoon, I accidentally ingested someone's discarded drugs. That, in combination with spinning upside down could certainly do funny things to a teenage girl's brain. Wearing an unfamiliar look on his face, Brody glances at me for an extended moment, shakes his head, flashes his handsome dimpled smirk, and says, "Race you to the door!!!"

My hands are oddly shaky, and I'm completely breathless as I fumble with my key in the front door. *What in the heck is wrong with me right now? Can he see my hand trembling? When did this dang keyhole shrink? Crap.* The keys slip from my shaky, sweaty fingers and hit the ground with a loud thud. I drop to my knees as Brody bends down to grab them. Simultaneously, our hands reach the key and our foreheads come to rest against each other. We are looking at one another through blinking lashes when his fingers barely graze mine and fold in on the keys. A large gulp sticks in my throat and once again, my new internal carbonation machine erupts, sending an intense zing through every nerve ending in my body. The rush of adrenaline thrusts me backward in such a blur that I trip over the porch step, landing right on my dad's favorite dog statue. As it hits the ground, its head snaps from its body, and rolls down the sidewalk, coming to rest at the edge of the grass.

Laughing hysterically, Brody roars "Wow, Kaitlyn! You're truly having a RUFF day, aren't you? What's the lab going to do without his head?" Then in his usual quick wit he chuckles, "Hate to say it, but you're really gonna get a licking when Coach gets home." He clicks his tongue, winks, and chuckles, as he spins around, unlocks the door, and opens it for me.

For the second time today, I find myself down on the

ground, furling my brow, and pinching my lips together in an exaggerated pout. "Wow, Brody, don't laugh too hard, you might pee yourself."

"Oh Pip, I'm just playing. Don't get all feisty on me." He extends his hand in my direction . . . *His tan . . . muscular . . . Godlike . . . hand. The one that's connected to that gorgeous, strong, athletic shoulder . . .* Suddenly, Brody's voice snaps me out of my pheromone induced fantasy. "Here, let me help you up." Mindlessly, I grab his hand, caressing his fingers a little more than I intend to. He pulls me slowly back to my feet. After my gradual ascent, my eyes lock on his full, smiling lips. "Hey Pip . . ." he whispers, so near I can feel his breath on my face . . .

Swallowing the lump in my throat, I reply, "Ya?"

"You've got a little grass on your butt. Do you mind if I get that for you?" *Good grief, even his whisper is sexy today. He's like the male version of a siren.* I'm so entranced by his soft, tenor voice, that I nearly jump out of my skin when he swats at my rear with enough force to kill a mosquito.

"Owww, you didn't have to slap my grass!" I shout and give him a fierce shove as I barrel through the door.

Brody chases me down the hall laughing, "Well, you didn't want me to just grab it did you?"

Blowing him a quick, slobbery raspberry, I throw my bag outside my bedroom door, sprint into the bathroom, strip off my smelly trash-infected outfit, and jump in the shower. *Man that was gross. I can't believe Clappy Chelsea Cat is already at it. When is she going to give up on torturing me? It's not like I'm in direct competition with her anymore. She chose cheerleading, partying, and guys; I chose swimming, academics, and music. We don't even hang out in the same crowd.* Not two minutes after I'm standing under the refreshing stream of water, trying to shake Chelsea from my mind, I see the reflection of a bobbing hand in the mirror. "What the heck Brody? Get out of here! I'm not dressed!"

"I'm only here to bring you your phone, Sassypants! Jenna keeps texting you about practice." With a slight chuckle to his voice, Brody continues, "Besides, it's no mystery what's behind that curtain anyway!"

"How would you know Stalker Boy? Have you been spying on me?"

"I didn't have to Pip. That vision of you streaking through the living room when we were in third grade will forever be burned on my retinas. I'm sure not too much has changed since then." He erupts with laughter as I raise my hands over the curtain and launch a stream of fruity bath gel at his head.

As the heat of embarrassment begins to escape through every pore in my body, steam fills the entire room. "Get out! You bathroom terrorist!" I scream, throwing a handful of water over the top of the shower. "Have some water with your soap!" I pause my one-sided water-war long enough to hear a weird squeaking sound and the scamper of feet fading down the hallway. When I peek out of the curtain, the coast seems clear. I grab my robe from the hook next to the shower and pull it in around me. Fully covered, I tiptoe out of the shower and look around to make sure the little pest is really gone. I peer to the left and right, and when I finally glance forward at the steamy mirror where I had just seen the bobbing hand, my jaw drops. The words So Hot! are scrawled across the steam in Brody's distinct handwriting. Right in front of So, a word has been smudged out, leaving me wondering what it said.

What is that supposed to mean? I wrack my brain for possible explanations. *Is this room hot? Does he think that I think he's hot? Or does he think I'm . . . No!* As my mind scrolls through the possibilities of his cryptic message, a silver streak comes flying through the air and thumps me right on the bridge of my nose. I bend down to see what it is. In front of my feet lies a silver Hershey's Kiss. "What was that all about you Poo Flickin' Hillbilly?"

"If your brother ever gets hurt this year, I have to fill in as QB, Pip . . . just letting you help me with my aim, Buddy," he reaches out and nudges my shoulder with a loose fist. Smirking he adds, "Did I hit my mark, Pal?" He rubs his thumb across my forehead examining the fresh red dot in between my eyes. He leans in really closely and quietly whispers, "From the looks of the imprint on your forehead, I'd say I planted that kiss right where I wanted it."

Confusion overtakes me, as he slowly leans forward and gingerly plants a soft kiss right on the bridge of my nose. No sooner do his lips touch his sensitive target, then he flies backward, leaving me breathless. With a flustered look plastering his face, he winks, double cliques his tongue, chokes out, "all better." He backs into the wall with a thud and stumbles away. "Meet you at the jeep," I hear floating down the hall. All that remains in his place are the scents of peppermint gum and Abercrombie cologne. My pulse races, even in his absence.

Trying to catch my breath, I muster all of the strength I have left in me. I scream down the hall, "Damn you Brody Tatum!"

Where is all of this coming from? What is he doing to me today? I'm so confused. I hope he didn't notice the shakiness in my voice. I don't know when, and I don't know how, but I'm going to kick his butt for this.

"After you." Brody cocks his head toward the passenger seat. Holding the door open, his mouth is curled up in a cocky little grin like he's enjoying the heck out of his assault on my overly-baffled mind. My lack of composure this afternoon must be incredibly entertaining.

"I can do it myself, Prince Charming," I sneer, jerking the

door from his hand.

"By all means, go for it," Brody replies calmly extending his hand, palm up, allowing me to take on the challenge.

I grab the handle of the door with my right hand, and try to get a good hold on the seat with my left. Struggling to find a place to set my hand, my finger pokes through a hole in something hard. Images of sports equipment I've seen on my brother's floor race through my mind. *I don't even want to know what that is.* I shake it off quickly before I have a chance to get too grossed out. I hear it hit the ground.

"Crap," I hear Brody mumble, followed by a few muffled words that include a distinct, "cup." Scarlet-faced, he looks back up at me, "Sorry Pip, I didn't mean for you to get tangled up in my stuff."

"At least I cleared a place to set my hand," I joke, trying to ease the awkward moment. I'm practically doing the splits in attempt to reach the step of his jacked up Rubicon when I feel my booty being gripped, hoisted into the air, and swung away from the Jeep. Brody chuckles as he holds me away from him, barely avoiding my swift punt to his shin.

"Not so fast, you little pip squeak" he laughs. "That just reminded me about something."

I entertain the thought of kicking him again, when I realize there's no use battling this beast of a boy. He sets me down on the ground, pulls his lips into an amused smirk, crosses his arms, and waits patiently for my expected rant. With a flushing face, and gritted teeth I hiss, "You just remembered what? You mean to tell me, you've watched me poke my finger through your . . . your cup and try to claw my way into this thing for five minutes, for nothing?" I quickly point up toward the towering seat, "Why did you just rip me off of there like a stinkin' rag doll?" I am clearly flustered and irritated by the chain of events this afternoon. I'm usually a little more composed when dealing with Brody, but today, I don't feel like practicing maturity, I feel like acting five. I stomp my foot, cross my arms, and stick my chin out waiting for a response.

"Sorry Pip, while you were getting dressed, I ran next door and grabbed my football gear. I was so pre-occupied fantasizing about shower scenes and chocolate kisses, that I wasn't thinking when I loaded it into the passenger's seat. There's no room left; not even for a tiny, little thing like you." He gently pokes me on the shoulder. "We're on to Plan B."

"Plan B?"

"Yep, the plan where you sit right there next to me." He motions with his head to follow him to the driver's side. "Stand back Kaitlyn," he opens the door and pats the four inch clearing to the right of his seat; the only part of his Jeep that's not cluttered with sweaty gym clothes, fast food wrappers, and country music CD's. "Hop on in Pip," he whoops. "It's snuggle time Baby!" His suggestive remark leaves me awkwardly silent. I throw a sideways glance at the cleared section of the seat. Remembering what was just scrawled in the steam on my bathroom mirror, I take a deep breath and slowly release it, trying to regain my senses before I have to half-ass it in his lap back to the pool.

With an unprecedented squeak to my voice, I yelp, "So now we're snuggle buddies, huh? What part of fruity bath gel to the face did you not understand? You, you . . ." I'm so flustered by all of these weird innuendoes, all I can do is shake my head and drop my jaw. I want to argue. I want to scream at the top of my lungs, but despite my best efforts, nothing will come out. For the first time ever, I'm at a loss for words with my BGF.

In the brief second I gain the nerve to glance up at him, I catch a bit of a bobble rise and drop in his throat. At that moment, I swear, I think he's blushing. The way he joins in my silence, tells me that Brody knows he took his frisky, little game too far. We stand there for a moment. The heat of the late August sun is beating down on us. I know it's only about 90 degrees outside, but the searing heat between us feels more like 190 degrees. Sweat begins to roll down my back as I struggle to clear my head.

The silence is finally broken when Brody clears his throat, and in a serious yet gentle tone he apologizes, "Sorry Pip, let me help you up." He pauses holding his hand to me, palm raised. "Give me your hand," he singsongs. *Gosh, I'm a sucker for that crooning tactic.* With some reservation, I position my foot on the step, and place my hand in his. With a quick jump and his helpful lift, I'm suddenly nestled into my four inches of prime shotgun seating. He jumps in, rolls his head toward me, lifts his eyebrows, and smiles down, "Let's get you to practice, Pip Squeak."

"Can't wait," I mumble, breaking my silence as the engine roars to life. Finally, I get to go swim off all of the day's madness. Maybe the pool water will chlorinate every last brain cell retaining an image of Brody's one-sided afternoon tryst with my mind. That would be a relief. As I sit psyching myself up for "Fierce Friday's" workout, I feel Brody trying to shift the jeep into reverse. As he works to pull the gear shift down, he struggles, "Uh. . . this isn't working Girl. You're gonna have to put at least one of those pretty little legs on the other side of my stick."

"Bro? Um. . . That didn't come out right, did it?"

"Oh, it came out just fine," he snickers.

I bite my lip, close my eyes, and cautiously drag my right leg over the stick, trying to find a place to set my foot down. *Think saddle, think saddle. Just like mounting a horse . . .* I repeat in my head trying to save myself the embarrassment of straddling the stick. Brody's seen me ride hundreds of times. This position is no different. Impatiently, I stamp around, trying to find the floorboard with no success. I lean into his side, and push, pull, and twist my leg to clear a spot. By the time I get to set my leg down, I'm practically panting.

"Why you breathing so hard, Pip?"

"Geez Louise!" I grunt. "This is a workout, just digging myself a place to sit! I don't know if I'm gonna have enough leg power to get through the pre-set."

"Well, keep working on that hole," he smirks. "Eventually, you'll make it big enough to burrow into comfortably." His smile widens even bigger. "Hurry up though, cuz I'd kind of like to get a jump on it." He erupts in laughter.

I glare at him trying to figure out what's so gosh darned funny. *Oh Wow.* "Ha . . . Ha." I draw out. *Boys . . . they all have one thing on their minds.* "I get it now . . . Alright, you turd. Pull your mind out of the gutter." *I thought we had moved past this craziness, but I guess not. Brody is not acting like himself today at all. What has gotten into him?* "I'm just gonna sit here and keep my mouth shut so you have nothing else to twist into your sick fantasies."

"Just playin' Pip, but seriously. We've gotta get going cuz I really don't want to be late for practice. Coach will make me run extra plays, and I've gotta bale tonight with Caden and Mason."

CHAPTER 2

FRIENDS?

DURING THE SHORT RIDE DOWN the oak-lined road toward the pool, I notice students leaving the school. *Phew, I'm not late for practice.* Crowds of teens are migrating across the street toward the football stadium, pool, and local park which lie adjacent to one another just across the street from the high school. "Don't hit that guy!" I point, when I think Brody doesn't see the cell-gazing freshman crossing the street. Seeing the little scrub with his phone reminds me that I never texted Jenna back. I slap my hands up to my cheeks and pull down on my face. Taking a deep breath, I look at the clock on the dashboard. "Oh no, Bro. Jenna's gonna kill me. I was supposed to meet her before practice," I whine through gritted teeth. I drop my hands from my blanching, stretched face and grab my swim bag. "I'd better shoot her a quick text." I reach into my phone pocket, and it's empty. *Shoot, I left it on my bathroom counter.* "Oh man . . . Bro, can I use your cell?" I beg.

"As long as you can reach it," he says with a playful nudge to my shoulder.

"Ok, is it in your gym bag?"

"Nope."

I'm getting frantic, and don't have time for anymore of Brody's games this afternoon. I know he's just trying to be playful, but Jenna's going to unfriend me if she thinks I'm ignoring her. Last time I didn't respond to her texts, she wouldn't speak to me for three days. She's been really moody lately, and I don't want to add to whatever it is that's bothering her.

"Where is it Brody? I'm running out of time here," I whimper. My anxious legs bounce like a jackhammer.

"Where does a man usually hide his goodies?"

More guessing games, great. Okay, I'll play. "Um, in his glovebox?"

"Nope."

A twinkle of mischief lights his eyes as Brody points his bobbing finger to his pocket. "Oh my goodness Bro. Why can't you get it for me? I am not going to stick my hand in your pants!"

"Pip, I need to keep my hands on the wheel. There's kids everywhere. It's fine with me if you don't want to get it yourself, but you're gonna deal with Jenna when she doesn't hear from you. And don't come crying to me. I already tried to bring you your phone, and you blasted me with your foofy bath gel."

I bite the inside of my lip and roll my eyes before I bravely attempt to drive my hand into his pocket. "I can't get it Brody! Your gosh darned pants are too tight!"

"Work for it, Pip," He pushes back into the seat, lifting his hips and shaking them back and forth.

"I'm digging as hard as I can Magic Mike! I can't get it! Is it even in there?"

"Oh ya. You'll know when you hit it. Trust me. They always know," he's practically snorting with laughter.

Why is he messing with me so hard today? This is not like him. He usually saves this kind of teasing for the Kitty Krew. My face contorts and my muscles quiver as I burrow my hand as far as I can into his deep pocket. *Two can play at this game; that little turd.* The urge to inflict a bit of pain to remind him just who he's messing with, suddenly strikes me. When I finally feel the phone, I dip my hand under it, giving Brody's inner thigh a quick twisting pinch.

"Holy Crap, Pip! Your fingers are as strong as needle-nosed pliers!" Brody shrieks, pulling his foot from the gas and swerving toward the curb.

"Never mess with someone who plays three instruments buddy!" I laugh.

Simultaneously, I free the phone from his pocket. A millisecond later, Brody slams on the brake to avoid going up onto the sidewalk. The phone flies from my hand, and lands under his feet. "Get it Pip, it's stuck under the brake."

I plunge down into his lap, reaching between his legs for the phone. I slam into the steering column when we abruptly come to a stop. While I'm feeling around on the floorboard, I hear Brody start to snicker. "This is really funny to you, isn't it big guy?"

"Oh, you have no idea how much pleasure this is bringing me right now."

When I finally grab the phone and come up to the surface, I see an amused grin plastered across his face. He looks like the cat who just swallowed the canary. Elbow propped on the armrest, and eyes forward, he puts his thumb to the side of his mouth and his fingertips to his temple, his pinky dangling loosely. "You may not want to see this Pip," he murmurs half under his breath.

"See what, Bro?"

"Uh, look up there," he shoots a sideways glance over his left shoulder.

"OH! HELL!"

Veins pulsing, nostrils flared, eyebrows lifted, and arms crossed, my boyfriend stands glaring down at me through the driver's window.

With my eyes scrunched closed, I whisper, "This looks really bad doesn't it Bro?"

"Uh, huh . . . you may want to fix your hair and pull your shirt down a little Pip," Brody whispers back through the side of his mouth.

Facing forward, I work to straighten myself up as I hear three long, drawn out thumps drum on the window.

"You ready to face him Pip? Cuz I can handle this if you need me to."

"No, no . . . I got this. Please, please . . . just stay out of it."

"I'll try Pip . . . no promises."

My heart is racing as adrenaline courses through me. I can feel the color drain from my face when I think of how this must look. I know how jealous Pistol gets over other guys. He can barely stand when I hang out with my own brother. Not knowing if he actually saw me between Brody's legs, makes me really nervous. I can't gauge his reaction. I plaster on a fake smile, clench my fists to try to control my shaking, and tell Brody to go ahead and open the door.

We're met with Pistol's fiery words, when he hisses, "Well, well, well, you look awfully chummy today, best buddies," making sure to enunciate the words "best buddies." His eyes narrow and his strong glare is intensely aimed at our overlapping thighs. I begin to quiver inside as I notice him shaking his head while he surveys my disheveled appearance. "You're one sloppy mess Kaitlyn; you been wrestling around with this mama's boy all afternoon?"

"I'm sorry Pistol, this isn't what it looks like. Really."

"Oh, really?" he crosses his fingers atop his head, cocking it slightly backward. "Where are you two coming from anyway?"

"My house."

Shaking his head he adds, "Nope, it takes a lot more bumpin' and grindin' than a quarter mile neighborhood road trip to make a woman's hair that crazy. Last time I saw that kind of hair on a girl, we may have been riding, but it certainly wasn't in a Jeep."

I glance up to see Brody's white knuckles, clenching the steering wheel with enough force to snap it right off the column. He pinches his mouth shut and takes in a deep breath through his nose. I know Brody is not Pistol's biggest fan, and it's taking every ounce of restraint he has in him, not to say something.

I reach up to smooth my long, ruffled, hair, hoping it's not as bad as Pistol's making it out to sound. His last comment brings stinging tears to the back of my eyes. I know exactly what he's doing; reminding me that there's a hot cowgirl lurking around every corner, and he has a lot of options outside of me. I've tried so hard not to believe rumors of one-nighters with all of his wild rodeo girls, but those kinds of comments make me doubt all of his stories and alibis.

I start to speak, but Brody interrupts, "And how recently was your latest FIVE-SECOND ride asshole . . . and don't even tell me you're talking about Kaitlyn like that you pile of . . ."

I try to quiet him with a quick unnoticeable nudge to his side.

" . . . cuz she's not that kind of girl! You hear me?"

"Please Brody, you promised," I whisper.

"Oh, so now the two buddies are keeping secret promises to each other?" Pistol pipes in.

"What are you implying Dip Wad?"

"Please Brody," I beg as I feel him slowly move from under my leg and toward the door.

He turns toward me. In a firm voice he says, "Kaitlyn, I promised I'd try. But enough is enough. I can't stand aside and watch this cocky little cowboy bully my best friend. You didn't do anything wrong!"

"Just let me talk to him alone, Brody. Maybe I can explain. I know you're just trying to help, but I can see he's just getting angrier. I mean, think if you walked up on your girlfriend like that."

"Okay Kaitlyn, but I don't like this one bit. I'm right here if you need me."

Brody slides over and helps me out of the jeep. As he releases my arm he looks Pistol in the eye and spits, "I'm watching you."

"Oh, I'm shakin' in my boots, preppy boy. Why don't you butt out and let me talk to my girlfriend. I drove all the way from the valley to see her."

"Make it fast. She's almost late for practice and she doesn't need anybody else yelling at her," Brody throws his hand toward the pool, where I'm sure my coach is waiting impatiently for me to join them. I can see the stretch circle starting to form out on the pool deck.

"Who made you her daddy? Kaitlyn's a big girl. She can manage her own time."

I've got to stop this or we're both going to be having late practices today. "Okay boys, Bro, you should get to practice now. I know you have a commitment tonight that you can't be late for." I pat Brody on the arm and let him know it's okay to go. I walk toward Pistol and try to explain. I've got to soften him up so Brody knows it's okay to leave.

"Ya, sorry about that, Dimples." I gently grab the bottom of his shirt, twisting it around my finger. "I know this doesn't look good, but it's really nothing. I kinda tripped over the garbage can at school and Brody took me home so I could take a shower."

"Oh, so he was with you, while you were showering?"

"Nnnn. . . .no!" I stutter. "We're neighbors Pistol. He ran home to get his gear. I just had to get the garbage off of me before I could get in the pool."

"Damn it Kaitlyn. You can be such a klutz." He grabs at the back of his head, frustration evident in his voice. "You always get yourself into these predicaments. And every cotton pickin' time, who comes to your rescue? Brody Tatum! It's starting to make me question your, "Friendship," he aggressively curls his fingers into his famous air quotes, then drops his hands back to his side resignedly. He shakes his head and looks at me with hurt in his eyes.

I feel horrible that I've gotten him so riled up. I need to make him feel better. Draping my arms around his neck, I look into his eyes, and whisper, "Pistol, please don't worry about Brody. He's my brother's best friend; my next door neighbor. You know he's been in my life since we were little kids. He thinks of me as a sister."

"Oh, he thinks of you as more than a sister, Baby Cakes. With that tight ass and firm rack, you think he's not looking at you as more than a friend? I can guarantee he wants you." His face begins to soften as he looks me up and down. His speech slows, "I mean the first time I saw you on this side of the hill, I damn near lost it. I practically drove my truck off the embankment watching you jog down the road with Jenna. Bouncing, curly blonde hair, cute little smile, round blue eyes, tight, tan swimmer's body . . . I honked and waved my rebel flag at you. You didn't even know who I was yet. Remember that Babydoll?" He pulls his strong arms around my lower back, "Come here girl." He slides his hands around my waist and wraps me in a strong bear hug. "Look at me Babydoll," he gently tucks a loose tendril of hair behind my ear and I begin to disintegrate at his tender touch.

Now this is the Pistol I fell for. The sweet, sexy bull rider who always made me laugh and told me I was beautiful. "I'm sorry I got so upset. You know I don't like to share my Babydoll with anyone else." His cute little dimples begin to appear, and that captivating sparkle returns to his eyes. Goodness gracious, this handsome boy is enchanting when he starts getting all snuggly and cute. "Baby, look at me. If you really want to convince me that you're just buddies, you're gonna stop hanging out with him."

I look up into his deep, chocolate eyes and softly reply, "I can't do that Pistol. Our families hang out together. He's my brother's best friend. He's at my house all the time. You've got to trust me. We're just friends."

Again, he stiffens, releasing me from his embrace. I drop my arms to my side, clenching my fists in preparation for his response. "Damn it Kaitlyn; that's so convenient, isn't it?" he bellows. I see his mood intensify and I begin to back away. He grabs my arm. "I tried to play nice guy, but you listen to me right now . . . You are mine. If you want this to work out between us, you're going to stay away from Brody Tatum. It's disrespectful to me, and I don't like the way he looks at you."

I tug at my arm, trying to discreetly release it from his hold. He doesn't let go. I feel a bruise forming as he digs his fingers tighter around my forearm. "Owww, Pistol . . . that hurts," I try to wiggle my arm free of his grip.

"Tell me you understand Kaitlyn! You keep your distance from that guy. I'm not messin' here," he groans, gripping my arm even tighter.

As I'm standing there trying to process Pistol's intense rage, and the emotional roller coaster he just took me on, I hear my brother's truck engine roaring up behind me.

His brakes screech as he pulls up on the curb nearly taking off Pistol's backside. He drops my arm instantly. The door flies open as Caden jumps out and barrels toward us. "What the hell are you doing holding onto my sister that way?" he screams in rage, shoving Pistol in the chest and cocking his fist back.

I step in between the two tensed boys. "Caden, it's okay. We were just talking." I put my hand to Caden's chest, signaling to stop. In a blink, Brody joins us.

"Awww man. I'm sorry. I only took my eyes off of them long enough to get my football gear together. I heard you pull up like a bat out of hell. What's going on? What did I miss?"

"I was stopped at the crosswalk when I saw this asshole shaking my sister by her arm."

"Guys, I'm fine, really." I turn toward my boys. "It was a misunderstanding. Brody, it's just like the Jeep. It looks worse than it is. We're just talking. Really."

"Kaitlyn, get in here, you're late." I hear my coach shouting beyond the cyclone fence, not far from where we're standing. "And boys, Coach Woodley is gonna have your hides if you don't get over to that field right now. I don't want to see us lose to the Lions cuz our best offense is sitting the bench to second string!"

I look at all of the boys, and try to give them all gentle goodbyes. Shaking my head apologetically I whimper, "I gotta go! Text you later Pistol. Sorry about everything. Brody, thanks for helping me out today; Caden, I'll see you right after practice."

"Ya, I was about to leave anyway. I just came to tell you that I have to break our date tonight. CJ's in town, and we need to practice."

"CJ?" I question.

"My new team roping partner from the valley. Kaitlyn . . . I don't have time to explain all this. Your coach looks pissed." Sarcastically, he whips his head toward the football field and adds, "And you panties better get to practice. Don't worry boys. I wouldn't do anything to hurt your precious sister . . ." he pauses, glares at Brody, and snarls "or best friend."

Caden turns to Brody, "I'll take care of Coach Dad. No worries, we'll get out of practice on time." Brody nods back to Caden in agreement.

"We stay til she goes," Brody and Caden stand firmly in place, arms crossed.

I lean in to give Pistol a hug goodbye. He turns away and heads to his truck. Walking away from me, he growls, "We'll

talk later Kaitlyn." His rejection stings. Pistol's hard headed-
ness about Brody's and my friendship has my mind drowning
in a raging sea of helplessness. I can't give up my friendship
with him just because it makes Pistol jealous. He's stood by
my side for over a decade. He's seen me through the ups and
downs of my entire adolescence. I wish Pistol could see that
we're nothing more than friends . . . I drag my hand across my
forehead, and I'm reminded of my crazy afternoon with Brody,
teasing, giggling, spanking, chocolate kisses . . . *yes, we're just
friends . . . the thought of Brody sends that warm fizzing sensation through my body . . . aren't we?* My body goes cold, and I
feel the color drain from my face.

CHAPTER 3

HAMBURGERS AND FRENCH FLIES

I GRAB MY SWIM BAG, fling it over my shoulder, sprint up the sidewalk, and into the locker room. No one is in there, so I know I'm on Coach's "Hamburger List." That would be the list of people he plans on eating for dinner tonight. *Darn it, I was hoping to get out of practice by 5:30, but I know I'm going to be pulling lane lines and working tarps for this one.* I run into the dressing room and grab my cap and goggles from my cubby, snap up my towel, kick my shoes into the corner, and take off for the deck. "Here coach!" I choke out, winded from the mad dash into the pool. I start spreading my towel on the deck, hoping I can blend in with the rest of my teammates.

As I work to straighten my towel, I see a shadow circling my feet. "Nice of you to join us today, Ms. Woodley," Coach says with a hint of sarcasm. A shiver runs down my spine and a bit of adrenaline finds its way through my chest. I'm not used to getting in trouble; when it comes to school and sports, I'm one of those rule followers. Besides, I've seen Coach Hendryx eat a couple of my teammates for slacking, and after what I've already been through today, I'd rather not endure the pain of his sharp teeth. I give him a pleading look, hoping he won't call me out about the scene in front of the pool. The last thing I need is for everyone to start asking about Pistol again.

"Sorry Coach Hendryx, it won't happen again," I stammer, looking down at my feet hoping that we can just move on with practice. While my eyes are focused on the ground, I spot Jenna's feet. I hesitantly lift my head, waiting to make eye contact. "Ahem," I fake cough, but she won't look over. "Jenna," I whisper. Still no eye contact. A little louder, I whisper again, "Umm, Jenna, I need to talk to you." She turns her back to me and starts talking to McKenna. *Oh my gosh, I knew I was in trouble if I didn't text back. I can't believe I didn't get ahold of her before practice. This is such a mess. She won't even look at me. Could this day get any worse?*

"Excuse me," I'm pulled from my troubled thoughts by Coach Hendryx's harsh tone. "Everyone else is getting in the water Woodley, where the heck are you? We're short on lanes today. The senior citizens are having a water aerobics class in lanes one through three. I told you to grab a partner, a kickboard, and do ten one-hundreds . . . moderate pace. Now go you Hamburger!"

"Looks like it's you and me," the French exchange student, Daemon, walks up beside me and snaps my suit strap. The sting of the snap against my already frayed nerves makes me jump and I ball my hands into fists. I throw my head back, and let out an audible sigh. *Do I really have to share a lane with Dipwad Daemon, whose sole purpose in life is to pester people? This day just got so much worse.* I shake my head in disbelief at my run of bad luck, grab my gear, and head over to the last lane, rushing over as quickly as I can to create some distance between Daemon and me. I think I'm farther than I am when I feel the back of my heel being trapped between two large pincher toes. "Darn it, Daemon! Not today, please!" I screech, begging the relentless French dip not to mess with me during practice. I whip my head around and send him my "Go die in a rat-infested gutter" glare, when I catch a warped smirk spread across his face. All I can think to myself is, "This jerk is gonna eat my bubbles today."

I jump in and take off instantly, kicking furiously through the first 500 meters. Daemon doesn't have a prayer of catching me. I goggle stalk him for a few laps and no longer see him anywhere near my feet. To my surprise, as I cruise into the wall ending my first set, I feel a pinch to my inner thigh. Shocked, I gasp in enough toilet water to drown an army of ants. I spit, cough, and gag; my eyes bulging in my tight goggles.

"What the hell, Daemon?" I hiss, splashing a tsunami of water into his eyes. He opens his gigantic mouth to take in as much water as he possibly can and spits it right back in my face. "You're disgusting," I snarl, wiping his spit water from my nose and mouth. Before he has a chance to respond, I turn away from him and use his groin to push off for my next set. I kick him hard enough to knock his nuggets up his throat and hear a high screech permeate the water and find its way to my satisfied ears. When I hit the end of the first 25 meters, I feel a hand stop my head. Adrenaline rushes through me when I feel myself being tugged up by the suit straps. *Crap.* It's coach Hendryx, and he does not look happy.

"Woodley, you Hamburger!!! What the hell did you do to your teammate back there? He can't even pull himself out of the pool."

Seething inside, I try to hide the snarkiness in my voice. With a little grin I simply say, "Not sure the French teach their athletes to SWIM during practice. He can't seem to stay off the wall. Sorry Coach; he got tangled up in my feet. It won't happen again."

"You're right Ms. Woodley; it won't happen again. You're going to have a 1000 Fly to think about how we don't treat our "less skilled" teammates. I want you to see how it feels to need the wall, Kid. Just think of it as a "French Fly; you Hamburger!"

As I begin my Fly set, I work extra hard, concentrating on my technique. I want to forget about this terrible day, and swim my way out of my depressed mood. I push all distractions out of my overly agitated brain . . . *chest press, hip pop, chest press, hip pop* . . . I repeat in my mind over and over again. *Think about the swim Kaitlyn, think about your breathing pattern, let everything else go . . . chest press, hip pop, press that T . . .* The rhythm becomes so automatic, that despite my best efforts, my mind begins to drift. I'm taken back to late spring.

Brody, Caden, and I were looking for some country fun, when we decided to hit the "Jefferson Round Up," a great little rodeo out in the valley. Bro took us back behind the corral to visit his cousin Mason, who was getting ready to take on Saddle Bronc. Laughter and competitive banter filled the air surrounding the stalls. Harrowing tales of scars and other battle wounds were being tossed back and forth. The boys were definitely rowdy, getting pumped up for the event. Stetson hats, Justin boots, and Wrangler butts lined the fence, and even more were packed tightly in our small circle. I was enjoying every second of this little country girl's cowboy fantasy when I looked up to see the hottest dimple-laden smile I had ever set eyes on. Holy hotness, my breath hitched as I took in the full view. Pearly white smile . . . check, chocolaty eyes . . . check, clean cut shave . . . check . . . Mason coughed, "Ahem . . . Earth to Kaitlyn, I was trying to introduce you to my friend, Pistol, here."

I glanced over at Mason and realized he was talking about Dimples. I graciously extended my hand, practically whispering my name. A huge smile spread across my face as I felt the flush of red hot adrenaline race up my cheeks and jump out every pore in my scalp. This was the best looking cowboy I'd ever seen, and Mason was introducing us?

"Honored, princess," Pistol chuckled, "But I don't do handshakes with pretty little ladies such as yourself. Come on in here for a good luck hug."

"If you insist," I laughed out.

He scooped me up and swung me around. His captivating woody cologne wafted around us and left my head spinning. "Just for being a good sport, I'm dedicating tonight's ride to you Babydoll." He tipped his hat and gave me a wink. As I melted in a swirl of hormones, he grabbed his riding gear and walked toward the chutes.

I remember gaping at Mason in disbelief, "Holy hell Mason, you didn't tell me you had the most adorable cowboy friend in Jefferson County . . ."

"He's actually been trying to get me to introduce you two ever since he saw you at his sister's last swim meet. Said you looked like the live version of Ariel from The Little Mermaid. Glad I could finally make it happen. I can give him your number if it's okay with you."

"First let me see if he can go the full eight seconds," I joked. "Just kidding, friend. Go ahead, but I'm sure after seeing me up close, he'll change his mind. Besides, I'm no Ariel . . . not to mention, I have blonde hair; he probably mistook me for someone else."

"Goodness Kaitlyn," Brody piped in. "The guy probably just soiled himself being in your presence, and you think he's not gonna want to text you? I wish you could see yourself through anyone else's eyes but your own. You're a walking, talking, Athlete Barbie. I mean, if you weren't my best friend, I'd go for you," he chuckled, shook his head, and suddenly turned to Mason. He raised his eyebrows, and said sternly, "You better not be setting her up with a jerk Cuz. I know how these rodeo cowboys are, and from what I've seen, they don't make very good boyfriends."

Mason looked at Brody and shook his head, "Okay, Bro. I'll keep an eye on it." The seriousness in Brody's voice melted away and he wished his cousin luck before we headed up into the stands to watch the event.

I was riddled with nerves and anticipation, not only for the fact that I might hook up with the hottest cotton pickin' cowboy I'd ever seen, but for the impending ride in my honor. When the horn blew, I saw Pistol fly out of the chute, one hand on the rope, the other in the air, perfect mark-out, and the bucking began. The horse shot across the arena. Up down, up down, Pistol's legs bounced in perfect rhythm with the bucking. This boy could ride. As the eight second horn blew, he dismounted beautifully and took a few running steps toward the fence. He jumped up on the crossbeam and paused scanning the crowd. He stopped looking around and fixed his eyes right on me. When our eyes met, I saw his gleaming teeth flash through an enormous smile. He extended his arm, pointing right at me and mouthed, "That was for you."

I never felt that kind of rush before in my life. Even after he saw me up close and wrapped me up in his arms, he still wanted to dedicate his ride to me? Me? This was too good to be real . . . but when a text came across my phone with an unknown number, saying, "Ya, that was for you," I suddenly found a new reality, and his name was Pistol Black.

Suddenly the memory begins to fade from the back of my mind, and the pool wall comes back into view. I've lost count of my laps, but figure I've done at least eight while I reminisced about how great my relationship used to be. Heaviness begins to cave in on my chest as I think about this afternoon, Chelsea's bullying, my dad's dog statue, skipping out on meeting Jenna, Brody's disarming flirtation, Darned Grab-Ass Daemon, and how upset Pistol is with me. On top of the embarrassment, confusion, guilt, anger, and sadness, exhaustion begins to overtake my muscles. I push myself harder and harder trying to shake the uneasy feelings invading my spirit.

By the time practice is over, I can't even pull my arms out of the water. While my teammates have all left for the evening, I finally drag myself into the locker room twenty minutes after the slowest swimmer has gone. I look through the glass doors leading out to the sidewalk in front of the pool to see Jenna standing there arguing with Caden. I strain to hear what is being said, but all I can make out is, "Lay off Jenna. Cut her some slack."

I open the glass door and stumble down the path to Caden's 4x4. I'm met with silence and stares, as I shake uncontrollably. I struggle to hold back the flood of tears that are pounding at the backs of my eyes; mercilessly, one escapes, and rolls down my cheek, stopping at my top lip. I suck it in and a breath catches in my throat. Jenna shakes her head and throws her arms around me. I collapse onto her shoulder and the floodgates break open. Tears stream down my face, and continue to roll down Jenna's shoulder.

"Are you okay, Sis?" I hear Caden in the distance. It's hard to hear him through my sniffles and broken gasps for air. "It's been a rough day for you, hasn't it? How about you guys come with Brody and me tonight and try to forget all about it? Let me call him and see if we can come up with a little distraction for you while we bale out at his grandparents' ranch."

I listen as Caden pulls out his phone and dials Brody. The phone rings several times when I see him whisper, "voice mail." I can hear a faint beep and Caden begins to leave a message. "Hey Bro, this is Caden. Call me when you get this message. There's a change of plans tonight. We're bringing the girls to the ranch. Come up with a plan for something they can do while we bale. I'm heading out to the store to pick up some coffee and a thermos. Let me know if there's anything else you want me to get."

We make final plans to pick up Jenna before we head to the

valley. Caden helps lift my shaky body into his massive truck. "Thanks Twin," I say, knowing good and well there's no way I would make it into the truck by myself. My muscles are torn down to nothing after that grueling workout. Caden begins to drive down the road blaring Florida Georgia Line on the stereo, when *Cruise* cuts out, interrupted by the ringing of his phone. I can hear Brody's voice come across the speakers, "Hey Dude, sup?"

"Before you talk, know you're on hands free and my T over here can hear every word that comes out of your mouth." I can tell my brother is feeling bad for me because he's using my nickname. T is the endearing nickname I got when I was just a toddler. Caden couldn't say "twin" when we were babies, so he just called me his T. The name kind of stuck. It's been my nick-name ever since. Nowadays, he mostly uses it when he's trying to be all sweet and brotherly.

"Good to know . . . wouldn't want her to hear what a douche bag I think her boyfriend is. . . or how she could do so much better. .haha."

I pipe in, hoping he can hear, "Thanks for your concern . . . Buddy." I put extra emphasis on the "B" in "Buddy."

Caden interrupts our bickering, "Okay, okay, so did you come up with anything for tonight pal?"

"Oh, ya, after the day we had, I thought of a way to blow off a little steam. I came up with a list of supplies that I would personally find quite entertaining for tonight. Kaitlyn, if you hear me, grab a pen and paper . . . We need a shovel, axe, rope, and rake to start with; then throw in some marshmallows, Her-shey's, and graham crackers . . . Oh, and don't forget a lighter and hot chocolate."

"Whoa Bro," Caden chokes out surprised. "That's a very interesting list of supplies. Would you mind letting me in on your little plan? It sounds somewhat criminal."

"Don't worry Caden, I'm sure you're thinking of a million

ways to get rid of Pistol, but this isn't about him tonight. It's all about the girls."

All that is running through my mind at this point is an axe, shovel, rake, and rope. I'm glad to hear it's not for Pistol, but I am definitely at a loss for words. *What in the heck is he planning? Why do I need a rope and axe?*

"I'll see what I can come up with," are the last words Caden speaks in the conversation. Then he turns to me with a huge grin and laughs, "Sounds like this is gonna be one helluva party, Sis."

CHAPTER 4

YOU BET YOUR SPLASH

"IT'S 7:30 KAITLYN! WE'RE SUPPOSED to be at Jenna's by now!" I hear Caden's voice bouncing down the hall toward my room. I'm using my face make-up to try to cover the small bruise left on my arm from earlier today, but since my summer tan has slowly begun to fade, it's not matching my skin as well as I'd like.

"I'll be right there!" I raise my voice, and then let it fall, frantic to make this go away as fast as I can. *Maybe I'll just wear long sleeves; the nights are getting cooler anyway.* I give up on trying to hide the bluish-red imprint of Pistol's thumb. *I can't believe the hold he had on me earlier actually left a bruise.* I raise my arm to my face, and upon closer inspection, I can see two more tiny circles where his index and middle fingers had held me so tightly during his escalated temper tantrum. *I guess I understand why he got so bent out of shape. Maybe if Brody had just stayed in the Jeep, this wouldn't have happened. Pistol has a difficult time wrapping his mind around the fact that we're just friends, and Brody's mere presence gets him completely fired up. Last week it was an embarrassing hickey that Pistol slyly planted when we were having a "make-up-make-out." Brody had surprised me with my favorite Butterflake Chill coffee after swim practice and it sent Pistol reeling. Now it's this. It's almost as though he wants to physically mark me as "his" every time Brody comes around.*

I finally give up on trying to cover the bruise and throw on my black hoodie. I barrel down the hall to see Brody and Caden waiting close to the front door. There's some muffled banter flying back and forth between them. Their low conspiratorial chuckling pierces through their amused grins. I can tell they're up to something, but when I ask what's going on, they just shake their heads and say, "Nothin.'" However, when those two little rascals get together, there's always some impish adventure waiting to happen.

I shake my head and click my tongue, not knowing how else to respond to the awkwardness of whatever they've got up their sleeves. "Do we need to let Mom know where we're going?" I ask Caden before we head out to pick up Jenna.

"Don't worry, we'll see her in a few. She's already with Cinda having their weekly reality show date night.

"Oh crap, those two and their reality television. What's it tonight?" I ask, *Bachelor, Little People, or Adoption Story?*"

"My bet's on *Bachelor,*" Brody says, throwing a smirky little sideways glance at Caden. "Every cotton pickin' time I see your mom, she's drooling about that hot new season pick, Theo."

Caden begins to bob his head up and down and bites his lip to stop the smile that's beginning to overtake his entire face. "Oh, are we making this a bet?" he chuckles, like he's already in with Brody on some conspiratorial plan. "Cuz, I'll take *The Adoption Story.* Those ladies love getting all torn up on wine and crying over heart-wrenching fertility struggles."

I elbow Caden, "Dude, be sensitive. You know it's their

way of connecting to Jenna's adoption story. Besides, it's a kick ass show . . . By the way, since you've left me no other choice, I'll take *Little People.*"

"So you're up for the bet then?"

"You guys have known me long enough to know I never shy away from a bet; so, what are we betting?"

"The two losers jump off Kelsey Creek Bridge," the boys laugh.

My stomach drops. *Holy crap.* That's the only right of passage I haven't ever had guts enough to participate in. In Jefferson County there are only two things that solidify you as a bona-fide country badass. One is riding a bull and the other is jumping off Kelsey Creek Bridge. Most of us have ridden at least some kind of rodeo beast, but Kelsey Creek is a different story. You either have to be drinking or crazy to plummet off a thirty-foot bridge into a ten-foot diameter swimming hole, surrounded by jagged boulders and a fluctuating water depth. *Well at least I have a thirty-three percent chance of getting out of this. And I'm not giving them the satisfaction of thinking I'm a wuss.* I put my poker face on and hesitantly say, "Let's do it boys."

Within ten minutes, we pull up at Jenna's house. Brody jumps out and opens my door for me. He grabs my hand and I leap to the ground. As we walk up the pathway to Jenna's beautifully illuminated Lindal Cedar Home, I can't help but gawk at the gorgeous snowberry plants and blue flax lilies interspersed in the Asian inspired garden. *Goodness, this property is breathtaking.* I take in the vivid, contrasting colors of the native plants and flowers that line the perfectly manicured lawn, and listen to the bubbling fountains that boldly stand on each side of the stairs leading up to the wrap-around deck. As I stand atop the deck, I look out over the hills surrounding the property. They are lined with rows and rows of perfectly spaced green, leafy grapevines which supply their private vineyard. This house is very different from most of the homes in our town, which are small, tract homes that have seen their fair share of weathering.

Jenna's parents are obviously city transplants. Her dad made a fortune at his family business in Napa Valley and came north to begin a new vineyard, bringing her mom to the tip top of California so she could continue her teaching career. She wanted to be in a place where the kids were raised with an iron fist and still had respect for their elders. The faculty room at Jefferson High was where our moms met and became best friends. Needless to say, Jenna's family now lives comfortably on their private hilltop vineyard, surrounded by twenty-four acres, with a pristine, unobscured view of Mt. Shasta. To top it off, the historic Blue Goose train, runs around the base of the hill twice a day. This home is any small town teen's dream party house. It's a good thing for her parents, that the wild child has no interest in sharing her toys.

After our lovely late-summer night stroll through Jenna's fortress, we knock on the door. There's no answer, so we try again and hear two voices choke out, "Come in! Come in! Quit your knocking!!! We can't hear through all your ruckus." As we pass through the grand foyer and enter the family room, we see Jenna's mom, Cinda, giggling hysterically with tears running down her face.

"Hey Cinda," I greet. "Laughing and crying at the same time without the snort? That's talent. Must be a doozy on tonight." I glance over at the television to see what's causing her mixed emotions. *Oh crap. It's the Adoption Story again.* My stomach drops because I know I have just lost the bet. I plop onto the plush couch in mental agony. "Where's my mom?" I ask Cinda.

"Going in for a refill," she giggles. "Hey Jacie, get out here. Your kids came to see you!" She calls to my mom.

Mom saunters out from behind the wall, holding up her favorite wine glass, the one decorated with a yellow feather and a slice of chocolate cake. "Present!" she shouts.

Oh, wow. The boys and I all look at each other. "Are you guys okay?" Caden questions.

"Perfect!!!" shouts Cinda, raising her matching wine glass. At that, they clank their glasses together and start laughing again.

"Oh goodness, you two are so embarrassing. Are you still on your Alison G. Bailey kick?"

Distracted, by the homecoming of the latest adoptee, the mom's are no longer looking in my direction, and leave my question unanswered.

"Look, this little girl came from Moscow . . . just like Jenna," Cinda points to the television.

"I thought they put a stop to Russian adoptions," Brody says quizzically.

"Hmmm . . . You're right, Brody, this must be a re-run." A puzzled look flashes across Cinda's face and she becomes slightly somber.

"By the way, where is Jenna?" inquires Caden. "We're taking her with us to bale tonight, if that's okay with you."

"She's up at the pool waiting on you kids. She already filled us in on Kaitlyn's day, so you guys are welcome to take her as long as you have her back in the morning." A contemplative look, crosses her face, and she speaks a little more slowly and softly. "We need to head down to Sacramento tomorrow to take care of some unexpected paperwork." I hear a nervous edge to her voice and see my mom's hand come up to her shoulder.

"It's gonna be fine. I'm sure these things come up all the time." Cinda shoots a strange look toward my mom and shakes her head back and forth just enough so I catch her signal.

Sensing their need for privacy, I stand up and we move toward the door. "Okay guys, we need to head out, and we're gonna grab Jenna on the way," I say, breaking the heavy silence in the room.

"Be safe, and remember we need her back before noon."

We shuffle out the door and head up the hill toward the pool. The night air has become a little brisk, but I enjoy walking along the lantern lit path and listening to the crickets chirp in the distance. We find Jenna sitting poolside on an oversized lounge chair. She's illuminated by the glow of her laptop. As the pavers end, the gravel begins to crunch beneath our feet. At the sound, Jenna quickly fumbles to close her computer and her face goes dark. I sense a nervous energy about her, and quietly ask if she's okay.

"Yep, everything is fine," she responds quickly as her toothy grin lights up against the darkness. "Are we ready?"

Rather than questioning her further, I take her at her word and squeal, "Ya, let's get this party on the road!"

Jenna throws her laptop in her bag and we excitedly skip back down the path where Caden's big black monster of a truck is waiting for us. We all jump in, buckle up, and take off toward the valley. Wild boy, Caden pumps up the stereo and the lyrics to *You Know I'm Here for the Party* blast through the cab of the truck. Jenna and I are in the backseat and start bouncing up and down to the rhythm of Gretchin Wilson's party pumpin' anthem. After a few minutes, Brody reaches toward the volume and the song suddenly begins to fade. Looking over his left shoulder toward the back seat, he laughs. "So, Jenna, we made a little bet with Kaitlyn on the way to your house. We're gonna need you to help us see it through."

"Why's that boys? What kind of trouble are you getting my friend into now?"

"Kaitlyn here, agreed to jump off Kelsey Creek Bridge to-night!"

"Tonight??? In the dark??? Oh no!!! No, no no . . . You're kidding me right?" I shake my head back and forth as my teeth begin to clatter and my stomach flip flops at the thought of jumping off that bridge in the dark.

"Don't worry pal, I'll do it first; make sure all is clear for you. Don't forget, I lost too," Brody tries to comfort me.

"Good luck boys! Do you know how many years I've been trying to get Kaitlyn to jump off that bridge with me? You guys are delusional if you think you're gonna actually make this happen," Jenna playfully jokes.

She turns to me with her eyes wide and whispers, "You seriously agreed to that bet?"

"Well, I didn't want to come across as some lame wussy girl. Besides, I'm having a tough time forgetting all the stuff that happened today. Maybe a thirty foot free fall will help knock all this crap out of my head."

"Having done this a few times before, I can definitely tell you, when you hit that water, it will most certainly wash out every single piece of crap you have from today . . . and yesterday . . . and maybe even the day before that. And if you're lucky, you might end up with a free enema to clean out all the other crap you have built up below the waist." Jenna breaks out in laughter.

"Wow, thanks Jenna. As if I wasn't already pooping my pants about this ordeal. Thanks for the little nugget of support," I laugh nervously trying to be a good sport despite the fact that I'm terrified beyond belief.

"So, it's 9:00; we have a few hours until bale time," Brody interrupts Jenna's hysterics. "The dew won't be in til midnight, so I think we hit the bridge first."

"Why so late Bro?" city-girl Jenna asks.

"We've got to wait for the dew to hold the alfalfa together. It helps with leaf loss. On top of that, Mason won't be there til later, and we need all the muscle we can get. Those puppies weigh like eighty pounds each."

"Ah, the mysterious Mason Brooks," Jenna spouts. "What's he up to these days?"

"He's staying out of trouble. He's hitting the rodeo circuit pretty hard, keeping up with chores on our grandparents' ranch, and trying to stay away from fast cars and fast women," Brody chuckles.

"Ya," Jenna giggles, "I hear his name flying down the halls of Jefferson like every day. Apparently, he excels at using his natural talents. It makes me want to get to know him better."

"Wait," Brody responds. "You want me to hook you up with him or something?"

"Ewwwww. No. It was a joke. That would be weird. You're like my brother, and he's your cousin. It would be like illegal. . . gross," she shudders.

"I guess I get your point," Brody responds, "But, I thought you were like the other two thousand girls who ask for hookup requests every weekend. They all say he is one of the hottest guys they've ever laid eyes on."

"Well he is," I accidentally chime in a little too enthusiastically.

Everybody knows that Mason Brooks is gorgeous. It shows his picture right next to the word HOT in the dictionary. I've known Mason since we were kids. When his mom took off and left him alone with his unreliable father, he moved in with his and Brody's grandparents out in the valley. Over the years, I've watched him grow from a raggedy, sandy haired twig, into a tall, lean, sexy centerfold cowboy. On top of his stunning appearance, he's witty and sharp as a tac. The girls love him because he's got confidence, but he's not cocky. He's nice to everyone. It's funny, he could have any girl in the county, but he doesn't ever seem to have a steady girlfriend. I guess he's holding out for someone special.

"Hey, hey . . ." Caden interrupts, "You guys talk about him like he's a God or something. I mean, I didn't exactly fall out of the ugly tree, and I don't have two-thousand girls a week asking to hook up with me."

Jenna snorts and starts to laugh.

"What's so funny about that? I was awarded 'Sexiest Man in the Junior Class' last year. Check the yearbook!"

Brody, mid sip, blows water all over the truck, and laughs, "Dude, that's cuz no one knew about the vote that day and you were the only person to participate in the election."

"Whatever . . . You saw all the girls lined up to vote for me. Jealous much?"

Just then I see the bridge come into view. I feel the nerves seize in my stomach as we begin to slow to a stop. I jump out of the truck and stretch my tensed, shaking legs. The gang follows closely behind me as I walk toward the bridge and peek over the edge. My pulse begins to pick up and my voice has been chased from my body by the storm of anxiety building inside me. I swallow the lump in my throat, and everyone turns toward me.

"Holy, hell, that was a loud gulp. Are you going to be able to handle this T?" Caden looks a little worried.

"I told you, I'll go first and check it out. That way we can be sure it's clear." I can feel his warm breath against my ear and goosebumps rise on my arm as Brody comes up behind me and whispers, "Besides, I'd hate to see anything happen to that rockin' little body." He raises his eyebrows and I see a dimple pop with his gleaming white smile. He plants a tiny peck at the bridge of my nose as he begins to climb over the rail where the words *Jump Here* are painted on the edge of the bridge. "Wish me luck Pip." At that I watch his moonlit silhouette drop from the bridge and free fall down, down, down til all that's left is a big white surge of water circling the center whirlpool of bubbles blasting up from the depths below.

I hold my breath as I wait for Brody to surface. Dizziness begins to settle upon me and I tip a little to the side. I feel my brother's strong hand grasp my elbow and he leans me into him for support. "It's fine T," he reassures me. "Brody has done this a hundred times. Look, you can see him coming up now."

When I see his muscular frame begin to emerge from the water, I release the breath I've been holding and gasp for air.

"You're literally blue from holding your breath, T. You're

the best swimmer I know; are you really that scared?"

"What if I jump too far? What if I breathe at the wrong time? What if I go too deep? I don't take risks like this Caden . . . I'm not scared of the swim; I'm scared of the fall."

Silence surrounds us as Caden contemplates the depth of the words I've just unleashed on him. I turn around and walk off, leaving him alone at the edge of the bridge. I grab my bag from the back seat of the truck and head off behind a giant cedar to change into my swimsuit. Fumbling through my bag in the darkness, my back brushes up against the bark of the towering tree. *Owww . . . that hurt.* I slip off a flip flop, working to maintain balance on one foot. Again, I fall backward into the tree and my bare foot slams down onto the pokey pine needles that blanket the ground. The scratches and stabbing are painful, but the physical pain is stifled by the mental terror plaguing my mind. I somehow manage to get myself changed and rejoin my brother at the edge of the bridge.

Looking out across the forested landscape, I see jagged cascading boulders, narrowing into a small body of water. The drought has left the river narrow, but the swimming hole below the bridge still has a pretty good girth thanks to a couple of recent rains. Silhouettes of giant pine trees drape the army of mountains. Stars dance in the darkness overhead. Tonight's sky is so clear, I can see the wispy, white milky way meandering among the stars. From where I stand, the moon is barely visible, but its glow blankets the valley, giving off just enough light to see the surrounding beauty. This incredible view has temporarily calmed my nerves.

I jump when Brody comes up behind me unexpectedly and grabs my sides. I'm pulled from my reverie instantly. "Dang, you're cold!" I bellow and wince at the feel of his icy hands on my bare belly. His hands stay a little longer than they should and I begin to feel the surge of electricity from earlier resurface. I'm surprised at myself for wanting his hands to stay right where they are. I like his touch, and I'm finding comfort in it as I look down into the dark river.

Still holding my sides, he moves in a little closer. Though he sets his icy chin down on my shoulder, everything inside me begins to heat up. "Do you think you can do this Pip?"

I can't even think of his question. All I can focus on is his cold, wet skin pressed up against my back. I feel the water from his body, escape him and run down onto me. I'm frozen in place, at the feeling of this strong, handsome boy draped around me, trying to comfort me in the middle of my nervous breakdown.

"Kaitlyn? Are you still with me? Why aren't you saying anything?"

I'm standing there, staring down into the green water. *Am I dumbfounded because of this jump, or because my best friend has just created an electrical storm in my body that is beyond my comprehension and my control?* I'm a smart girl. I mean I plan on majoring in science. I should know better than anyone that water and electricity don't mix well. I already feel the sparks popping between us just from his proximity. As I stand facing impending electrocution, my breath begins to quicken. I struggle to find words to answer him. "Ummm. . ." I utter. But nothing else comes out.

Brody's chin continues to rest on my shoulder as he moves in even closer behind me. "Kaitlyn?" he whispers.

"Ya?" I whisper in return.

"Breathe . . ."

Again, I feel his warm breath, spread across my shoulders, and I can smell his mint gum wafting around me. My senses begin to heighten from his touch and his smell, and I look back at him over my shoulder. Shakily I mutter, "Bro, I'm not sure I can do this."

He slides his hand off my side and finds my hand. Gently, I feel his fingers curl in around mine and he whispers again, "Pip, I've got you. You know I won't let you do this alone. I'm going with you. Here, I want you to step over the rail with me."

I'm shaking so badly I can barely move when Brody helps me over the guardrail. I let go of his hand and extend my arms backward, putting a death grip on the metal support behind me. Brody, however, doesn't let go of me. He somehow sneaks into the small space behind me, holding onto me again. I hear him say, "On three Pip . . . one, two . . ."

"No, no no! Not yet." I freak out.

"Kaitlyn," he giggles "Have I ever let anything happen to you?"

"Well, there was that one time when you convinced me to let you push me on the old rickety swing set and it tipped over on me."

"Oh ya, that . . . But . . . but I pulled it right off . . . and you said yourself that that was the first time you truly felt like you could fly," he lifted his eyebrows apologetically.

"Brody, the only reason I felt like I could fly was because I was so dizzy from knocking my head on the ground that I passed out." I let out a small, yet audible huff.

"Pip, I know I messed that one up, but we're not six any-more. I can promise you, that you are the last person I'd ever let anything happen to. I will protect you with my life. We've got this. Besides, you've never backed out of a bet. Now let's jump," he implores.

Brody moves off to my side and grabs my hand once again. Feeling his strong grip, and letting his reassuring words sink in, I get a sudden burst of courage. I blow out a deep breath and stammer, "Okay, on three."

A big grin grows wide on his face, "One, two, three," he counts. It's no longer a choice. Brody has taken me by the hand and projected us out into the open air. I'm falling, falling; time stands still. I feel the wind swooshing up through my toes, nose, and hair. The wind works in harmony with Brody's protec-tive grasp to wage a full assault on my senses. He snaps his face toward mine and quickly says, "Last breath before we hit. Breathe."

I take in as much air as I can and feel my feet break through the frigid water. I plummet into the dark, green abyss, still gripping Brody's strong hand. Like bullets, we dart downward, enormous bubbles dancing between us, until we begin to slow. Kicking our feet with as much force as we can muster, our momentum begins to shift upward. We ascend toward the surface, and I can feel the pressure of the water lift from my shoulders. After several seconds we hit the surface and pull cool mountain air back into our parched lungs.

I wipe the water from my eyes, and the first thing I see is the soft moonlight cascading over Brody's silhouette. He shakes the water from his hair and screams a cry of victory. "Yes!" he shouts pumping his fist high into the air. I answer him with a hysteric laugh of my own. I reach up to give him a high five and he grabs my hand, pulling me into a strong hug. He raises me up above the surface looking toward me with admiration. "You did it Pip!" he beams up at me. I look down at him with a smile and he gently slides me back down his body. My stomach flips a little as my skin slowly glides against the ripples of his wet, muscular abs.

Brody hasn't let go of me since we left the bridge. He suddenly gets quiet and a serious look begins to replace his wide smile. Our eyes are fixed on each other as he holds me in a close hug. I can feel his pride, but I can also feel something in myself too, a sensation I've never felt before with Brody. I can't explain it, but it's driving my body to respond to him in a way a friend would not respond. I'm tingly, nervous, and confused, as I wrap my legs around his waist. He leans in and I feel his hot, minty breath moving up my neck. He moves his face up toward mine, and everything around us goes silent. Our eyes meet again, and he slowly lowers his gaze to my mouth. I bite my lower lip as I take in a deep breath in anticipation of . . .

SPLASH. Cold water drowns our faces and the intensity of the moment comes to an end. The shock of the cold water rushes over my belly, when Brody flies back, and releases me from his embrace. I whip my head in the direction of the splash, and there stands Caden in between us looking as though he's just seen a horror movie. "What the hell was that guys?" We are both silently stunned, not knowing how to answer. *I think I almost kissed Brody Tatum.* We simply look at each other, eyes wide, eyebrows raised, jaws slack. I watch Brody pull a handful of water over his face, turn away from us, and swim back to the river bank.

CHAPTER 5

FIRED UP

I T'S A QUIET RIDE TO the ranch. Caden's eyes are locked on the road, while Brody stares out the passenger window. Tension fills the cab of the truck. Being the light hearted girl that she is, Jenna keeps popping off unanswered jokes trying to lighten the mood. Unlike Caden, who had a front row seat to Brody's and my close encounter, Jenna obviously missed the intimate scene in the swimming hole. I'm a little tongue-tied right now, not knowing what to say to either of my boys. *I wonder how much Caden saw.* I try to replay the moment of the missed kiss in my head to see if I can get any clues as to when my brother showed up.

Reliving the moment raises some unexpected reactions in my body. My heart skips a little and I feel my pulse quicken. I really don't understand what's been going on between Brody and me today. I've never been drawn to him in this way, and all of a sudden I have the need to be as close to him as possible. Surprisingly, I like the way he's joking with me, carting me around, and looking after me tonight. Thinking about him is making me light and fluttery inside. It's making me feel all of the things I've been missing with Pistol. *Pistol.* I can't help but think of my boyfriend. *I am so confused. How can I have these feelings for my best friend? Besides, I'm not a cheater.* My strong attraction to Brody is really playing with my mind. I hope I can stifle these irrational urges before I do something unforgivable.

I snap out of my trance when we pull up to Mason Ranch around 10:00 p.m. It's pretty dark now, and the gravel drive is dimly lit by the lights shining through the windows of the ranch hands' house. As we get out of the truck, Mason comes bouncing up to the truck with a huge smile on his face. "Howdy, guys!" he greets with enthusiasm, shaking Caden's hand and giving his cousin one of those manly "handshake with the left, one-armed hug on the right" combo greetings. "Glad you could come hang out for a bit before we get to work. So, what kind of fun did you boys come up with for our baling pre-party?"

Caden heads to the back of his truck to pull out the stock-pile of supplies he brought for whatever their little surprise was going to be. As he takes out the rope, shovel, axe, and rake Mason starts laughing. "What in the heck are you boys planning to do with that?"

"I have no clue Pal. This was all your crazy cousin's idea. He won't let us in on the big secret. I don't know what it's for," Caden shakes his head, with a frustrated look on his face. He still has an edge to his voice, which tells me that he's not very happy with Brody right now.

"Hey, lighten up Caden; I thought we came to get Kaitlyn's mind off this horrible day," Jenna pipes in.

"You're right Jenna, we all need to lighten up." Brody turns to Caden. In a contrite tone he explains, "It's for a bonfire down by the river. I thought it would be fun for the girls. We're gonna be roasting s'mores on the rake. Our grandpa used to do it with us when we were little. We could make like a dozen at a time to share with all the ranch hands. It was just a good memory, and I know how much your sis likes s'mores. I thought it would cheer her up."

Amusement fills Mason face. He laughs, "Well I'll be darned . . . I forgot all about that. That was the coolest trick ever! Ok then, how 'bout we load up the Ranger with all of the gear. I'll drive a couple of you. Brody, you can take your four wheeler and one of the girls."

Jenna jumps up and moves toward Mason. "I've never ridden in a Ranger before. Can I ride with you Big Guy?" She bats her eyes and sidles up next to him, jokingly pouring on the flirty charm like only she could.

Mason puffs out his chest and tips his head toward Brody. "Guess this means you've got Kaitlyn, Cuz. My heart jumps and my eyes grow wide when he looks over at me and smiles. I take a deep breath as the smile induced quake moves through my chest and quivers in the pit of my stomach. *Crap on a cracker; this is just what I need . . . more alone time with Brody. Time to put on my acting panties again and try not to let him feel my nerves trembling.* I see a dimple pop in Brody's cheek as his grin widens. He walks over to me, puts his hand on my back, and silently guides me toward his four wheeler.

Once the gear is loaded, the gang hops in the Ranger. Brody is already seated on his four wheeler waiting for me to jump on. He looks up at me and pats the seat behind him. "Come on now," he chuckles. I take a deep breath before I slide on behind him. I'm very cautious about leaving a gap between Brody's behind and my thighs. The closeness between us has my stomach tying itself in quadruple knots; simultaneously, electric tremors shoot down my legs. My nervous system's hyperactivity is leaving me a little weak. The trembling has begun, but I definitely don't want him to feel that he's getting to me again. Rather than holding onto him, I lean back, gripping onto the bars behind me. "Are you even on here Pip?" he questions before he starts the machine.

"I'm here, let's go Bro. They're leaving us in the dust. We've got to go before my brother starts to wonder what's taking us so long." Nervousness is evident in my voice. The ATV roars to life, and we head across the road into the wide open alfalfa fields. The wind in my face and the smell of freshly cut alfalfa is awakening my senses. To my right, the deep green of the field is barely visible under the moonlight. Enormous water wheels line the field. The sprinklers are on and I can feel the mist of water against my face as it blows in the gentle breeze. As the soft spray dusts my eyes, I turn my head left and see a small barn nestled in front of a second field. Off in the distance, a herd of cows dot the landscape. They aren't too close, but I can still hear the faint ringing of their bells.

We continue along the dirt path and make our way deeper into the fields. The road is becoming increasingly bumpier, yet I try to maintain my distance on the four wheeler without holding on. As we hit an unexpected rock, I am jostled forward. Before I can stop myself, my bottom launches into the air and I plummet right into Brody. The four wheeler comes to a sudden stop and I try to peel myself from his back. "Sorry," I apologize, crinkling my nose and biting at my bottom lip.

He twists his body around toward me, glancing down at my lip pinned between my teeth. In response, an almost painful look crosses his face. I hear him inhale deeply. "Careful Pip," he warns. "I don't want to throw you off. Now hold on."

"I'm okay," I respond. "I just wasn't paying attention."

Brody turns back toward the handles and flips his hat backward. "This is gonna get pretty bumpy, and I'm not up for your stubbornness tonight." He reaches back until he finds my hands. He takes them into his and pulls them gently around his waist. "Scoot in Pip Squeak. I'm not gonna let you fall." He pins my hands beneath his until he can feel me begin to hold on by myself.

I scoot forward until there is no longer a gap between us. As his warmth begins to spread over me, my body begins to betray me once again. I tremble as I feel his rippled abs beneath my sensitive fingers. I feel him let out a small chuckle and shake his head back and forth. "Are you nervous, Pip? I can feel you shaking." *Perfect! He thinks I'm shaking because I'm scared. I'm glad he doesn't suspect the real reason.* "Just don't let go." He covers my hands once again with his, as we start to accelerate. I can't be sure, but I think I hear Brody's soft whisper float back to me, "Ever."

A rush of adrenaline spikes through me. *Did I just hear him right?* I push the thought from my head and try to focus on the path speeding below my feet. I watch the blurred fields as we fly over bumps and bounce through ruts. I keep rocking into Brody, but still, I maintain strict focus on the landscape. We hit another rut, and my hold tightens against his stomach. As my grasp tightens, I feel a little burst of shivers run beneath my fingers. "You okay Brody?"

"Whoa, that enchilada must've been bad last night!" he quickly replies.

"Well that explains that!"

"What?" Brody questions.

"The little quiver I just felt beneath my fingers. Glad it was just gas." *Phew. I can finally relax. Maybe it is all in my mind.*

As we slow, the gravel of the riverbank begins to crunch beneath the tires of the four wheeler. We come to a stop just beside our circle of friends. Brody jumps off first, and takes my hand, not letting go until I gain my footing. We join Mason, Caden, and Jenna, who've already set out chairs and built a fire pit near the water. Caden is working to chop wood as Mason places it in a crisscross pattern in the center of the pit.

Jenna watches Brody walk me toward the circle. The way she's looking at me with her brows pulled together shows that she's suspicious about something. "Sheesh Kait, I thought you'd never show up. Did you guys forget something, or was Brody driving slow on purpose?"

"Ya, he's a bit of a Mama's Boy on that thing," barks Caden with a hint of sarcasm in his voice. "Never could push a machine to its limit," he chuckles.

"We'll see who's a Mama's Boy later pal. It's on!" Brody quickly challenges Caden to a race. Those two have always been competitive when it comes to guts and glory.

"Enough boys! Quit your bickering. I really want a s'more. Get busy already." Jenna works to calm the boys and restore peace to our circle.

"Shoot!" I hear Mason huff. "We forgot the lighter."

Jenna's eyes roam back and forth between Mason, the boys, and me. She has an insistent look on her face when she suggests, "I think all of you guys should go get it. I need some time with Kaitlyn, and it will do you boys some good to go work out whatever is eating at you tonight."

"You're right; let's go guys," encourages Mason. "We'll be right back," he turns and walks toward us. "You can use this flashlight til we get back." He hands me the flashlight and shuffles back toward the Ranger with the boys, leaving Jenna and me with a little alone time.

I shine the light around, looking for a good place to settle down for a chat. We decide to pull the chairs down by the river and listen to the babbling brook while we wait for the boys to return. "So what's up with those guys? There's a lot of tension between them tonight. Everything seemed fine until we went to the bridge." I don't respond. I can't. I bend over in my chair, pick up a twig, and drag it through the sand, making zig zag designs around my feet.

"I know, you know what's going on Kait. I can tell by the way you're acting. Let's hear it."

I have to talk to Jenna. I work to convince myself to open up. Come on. She's your best friend. She can help. "I'm not sure, but there's some weird energy between Brody and me today, and I think Caden's picking up on it. You know, it's a twin thing."

"Weird energy?" Jenna asks. "Are you fighting? You guys seemed pretty cozy to me."

"Ya, that's the problem. I don't understand what's going on between us. He's been flirting with me all day, saying suggestive things, brushing against me, holding onto me, giving me zingy feelings, and the problem is. . . .I really like it. I don't know what to do with this, Jenna. I've never felt like this with Brody before. He's always just been my best guy friend."

"Well, geez Kaitlyn. It's about time you opened your eyes to Brody Tatum. It's pretty unnatural that you've gone this long without noticing his jaw dropping looks. I was actually starting to wonder if you swung the other way . . ." Jenna laughs. "Just kidding. But, seriously, think about how gorgeous he is; tall, adorably wavy brown hair, blue eyes, flat abs, and that sweet dimply smile, you'd seriously have to be dead not to notice him."

"Kaitlyn, I've been watching this unfold for weeks now. Don't tell me you just noticed. I mean, don't you find it curious that Brody is there every time you turn around? How did he know you needed help after the garbage can? He found you in Mr. S's room and he doesn't even take a music class. And how do you explain fun little treats like unexpected Butterflake Chills? He's trying to make you notice him Kaitlyn. I was secretly hoping you'd get rid of that jerk Pistol when you finally caught on to Brody's feelings. I just didn't know if you ever would."

"So, you knew about this? And you think it's okay?" I ask incredulously. "It's not like incestuous?" I giggle in disbelief. I am thoroughly confused by Jenna's reaction. I shake my head back and forth. "This can't be right. He's been my friend since we were five. Not to mention, I do have a boyfriend. Jenna, what do I do about these feelings? He flipped on the switch, and now

I can't shut them off."

Jenna completely bypasses my question and fixates on Pistol. "That Asshole? I can't believe you're still with him after the way he's been treating you. He breaks dates with you constantly . . . and . . . and you hear the rumors about how he is with other girls at rodeos. You just don't seem like happy-go-lucky Kaitlyn anymore. You're sad all the time because he's so dang possessive he's almost ruined your social life. I mean, he has a hard time letting you talk to your own brother. Don't you see it? He's not good for you."

I start to draw inward as I feel the air suck out of my lungs. I want to defend him, but deep inside, I know Jenna's right. I haven't truly been happy for months. I continuously doubt myself, wondering why I'm not good enough to keep his attention focused on me. He always drops hints about other girls and how they call, text, and flirt with him. I'm not sure if he likes making me feel insecure, or if he's just reminding me about how "wanted" he is. I just wish we could go back to the first month when it was all excitement and butterflies. He used to be so sweet. He always made me feel like I was the most important girl in his world.

My thoughts are interrupted by a text alert that sounds on my phone. "Just a sec.," I tell Jenna. "This could be the boys letting us know what they're up to." I work to get my phone out of my pocket and see an unknown number at the top of the screen. It doesn't say anything; it's just a picture message. I open it, and my stomach drops at what I see. It's a picture from the back. I see Pistol lifting a blonde cowgirl onto a saddle. I drag my fingers across the screen, zooming in to see if I recognize her face. I don't know who it is, but what I do see, is his hand planted firmly on her butt; and from the look on her face as she's looking down at him, she really enjoys it. I shove my phone back into my pocket while I decide how to cover this one. After what Jenna's just said, there's no way I want to add to her misperception of Pistol.

"So, who was it?" Jenna asks.

"Oh, just my mom making sure we got here okay," I fumble for a rational explanation.

"Well, I didn't see you text back," Jenna accuses, like I'm not being honest.

"I just sent her a thumbs up. That only takes a half of a second. Why are you questioning me?"

"You're just acting really weird. You know if something's wrong you can tell me," she tries to change the direction of our conversation.

Just then the boys pull up. Mason walks over with the lighter. "Hey, before they get over here, just a word of advice Kaitlyn . . . Whatever is going on between you and Brody needs to be toned down in front of your overprotective brother. He may be over-reacting about whatever he saw at the bridge, but he just had it out with my cousin. Whew . . . glad I'm not Brody right now."

I am stunned by Mason's warning, and I decide that I don't want to cause any more problems tonight. I pull my chair back up to the pit, where a low fire is beginning to spark and pop. The boys have the rake out, and Brody begins to pierce marshmallows through the metal prongs. He has ten marshmallows lined out and begins to roast them over the fire. A grin spreads over his face as he begins to slowly circle the pit. The rest of us begin to shoot perplexed glances at each other, when we hear him chanting "duck, duck, duck . . ." until he finally says "goose," and plops down in the empty chair right next to me. I look across the fire to my brother who shakes his head slowly back and forth and shoots ninja daggers out of his eyes toward Brody. Brody smirks back in his direction and asks, "You okay over there Dude?"

In the most sarcastic tone I have ever heard him use, Caden snarls out, "Actually, I'm getting a little bored. I'm about ready to go grab my gun and do a little goose hunting."

Oh crap. Mason is right. Caden is fired up tonight. Hopefully they settle this before they go work. I really don't want anyone to end up stuffed inside a bale tonight.

"They're ready guys," Brody completely ignores the hunting comment and lets us know that our marshmallows are done. "Get your graham crackers and chocolate ready, I'm bringing 'em around. Ladies first." He stops at me and lets me pull the first marshmallow from the rake and slide it between the graham cracker and chocolate.

"Thanks Bro," I smile, and watch him continue to serve the others. I take a bite, and all of the crap from the day slips from my mind when I taste the sweet chocolate and gooey marshmallow melt over my tongue. I'm a few bites in when Brody sits back down next to me. He looks at me and smiles, leaning into me a bit. He begins to move his finger toward my face and I draw my eyebrows in and track his finger, wondering what this is about. I feel his finger gently swipe the left corner of my mouth and watch him grin at me with amusement.

"Well look what we have here Pip," he holds up his finger with a swirl of chocolatey-marshmallow. "We can't let this go to waste now. Are you eating it, or am I?" he laughs, wagging his finger back and forth right in front of my face. I look down at the blob, bouncing like a metronome before me. I tip my head back and start to laugh. No sooner do I open my mouth, then he plunges his finger right in. *Oh my goodness, being a germaphobe, this would typically gag me . . . but for some reason, with Brody, I am not grossed out at all.* I close my lips around his finger sucking off the marshmallow as he gently pulls it from my mouth.

I look up to see Caden glaring at us from across the fire. "Let's go bale boys. Dessert is over. Girls, you seem to be pretty good at keeping fires burning. Make sure you don't let this one die."

"If you need us, just call. We have our phones, and the key is in the quad," Brody reassures us before they leave.

"Ya T, make sure to call ME if you need anything," Caden interrupts as the three boys walk off toward the Ranger.

"Holy hell that was hot," Jenna gapes at me in disbelief. "If that was any indication of this 'weird energy' you speak of, I can see why Caden is ready to go all "Fireman" on Brody. I'll try to work on him, but until I can get through to your brother, someone needs to spray down the sparks that are exploding between the two of you. Lord knows we don't need any more wildfires this summer."

Again, I have to catch my breath before I can respond to Jenna's keen observation. "I told you Jenna, there's more to this than Brody flirting. I don't know what's going on, but it's been a hormonal ping pong match between us all day. I'm just as into it as he is."

"Well, you'd better get a handle on it til you decide what to do with Pistol, cuz whatever's been set ablaze between you two, is not going to be easy to smother; and it's way too intense to hide." Jenna raises her eyebrows and looks back toward the fire. "Speaking of blazes, we'd better get some wood on this thing. The boys will be pissed if we let it go out."

It's around midnight when we set the last piece of wood on the fire. We can hear the baler off in the distance and know the guys won't be done for a while. After a brief discussion, we decided to go down by the river and try to scrounge up some more wood. I find a few pieces of dry oak lying close to the bank, while Jenna heads off into the surrounding brush. Several minutes later, she comes back with a huge armful of twigs and branches and plops half of it down onto the dwindling flame. "This will keep it going until we can find more wood," she grins.

The fire roars back to life and she looks incredibly pleased at her accomplishment. We sit for a while in front of the newly blazing fire and chat about the upcoming Homecoming week and ideas for the swim team float. When the fire begins to die down, Jenna tends to it again, plopping on the remainder of her stash. She brushes her hands together saying, "I think I've got this country girl thing down."

Just then we hear the boys walk up behind us. "How's it going ladies?" Mason's charming voice breaks through the crackling of the freshly stoked fire. "We're taking a break and thought we could make some hot chocolate . . . Sure glad you kept that fire going."

"Jenna's been taking great care of it," I reply. "Have a seat and we'll get the water going."

The boys gather around, laughing and joking. Clearly, they've worked things out, and have moved past the earlier events of the evening. As Brody tells the story of nearly being baled because he couldn't pull his pants up fast enough to dodge the baler after going to the bathroom, the water begins to boil and Jenna helps me get the hot chocolate ready. The boys take their cocoa and lean back in their chairs to rest. "Looks like the fire's almost out guys. Do you want to let it die or should we keep it going for the girls?"

Jenna jumps up. "I'm not ready yet, Kaitlyn and I are still discussing Homecoming plans." She walks down to her secret brush stash again and comes back with another armful.

"Jenna? What have you got there?" Mason walks toward her to inspect her armload. An amused look crosses his face before he decides to speak, "Ummmm . . . By any chance, is this the first load of that you've used?" he cringes.

"No the third!" Jenna smiles proudly as she looks around at the boys. "It works like a charm; you'll see!"

Mason's expression intensifies and he brings his hand up to his face. Shaking his head he chuckles, "Oh Good Lord boys. We've got a problem. . ." silence fills our little circle as we lean in to listen to Mason.

"What?" Jenna freaks. "Don't just tell us we have a problem and not say what it is!"

"Well, I was thinking if there was an easy way to break this to everyone, but I guess I should just say it. Boys and girls be prepared . . . Jenna, that's Poison Oak."

I close my eyes and shake my head in disbelief. "I know we've got unfinished work in that field, but we'd better get that fire out so these girls can get home and take a shower. This could be bad."

"Oh heck . . . I'm so sorry guys. I had no idea." Jenna pauses momentarily, cocks her head toward the sky as though she's thinking, then walks over to the Ranger and begins rifling around through our supplies. When she finds whatever it is she's looking for, she mumbles, "Gotta do something, be right back."

We're all left feeling a little puzzled, and a lot worried as she scurries back into the brush. "What is she doing?" Caden asks in disbelief.

All I can say is, "Who knows . . . With Jenna, anything is possible."

CHAPTER 6

ITCHES IN OUR BRITCHES

IT'S BEEN THREE DAYS SINCE Jenna's infamous bonfire and I've never been so miserable in my life. I work to paste the medicated ointment all over my swollen, splotchy, red face. I guess I shouldn't feel so bad; at least it's limited to my face and hands. Poor Jenna got the brunt of it. Not only did it get her face and limbs, but that sneaky little booger crept its way through her whole system, popping out in the most delicate of places . . . places that you can't necessarily scratch in public. Despite my incessant misery, it has been very entertaining to watch Jenna grinding back and forth in her chair during pre-calc. She tries to disguise her personal scratching by putting her arms in the air, snapping her fingers, and singing out whatever concept Mr. Anderson has just lectured about; however, I don't think he is too amused with her new arm routine for point-slope form. Our classmates, on the other hand, are certainly enjoying the daily sideshow.

After my face is covered in white goo, I plop the tube of ointment in my drawer. Simultaneously, I hear a text alert come over my phone. I don't generally get texts this late on school nights, so I'm curious to see who it is. Walking back into my bedroom, I reach for my phone on my computer desk and see a text from Pistol.

Pistol:
Hey Babydoll. I'm back from my rodeo in Hat Creek. Hopin' to see ya before I head back to the valley.

Thinking about letting him see me like this, has my stomach turning inside out. My incessantly contracting nerves have my brow sweating beneath the goo. I'm a bit nauseous as I sit down on my bed, trying to figure out how to respond to his text. I haven't told him about Friday night and he's going to want some kind of explanation when he sees my face. On top of my Friday night secret, I'm still angry with him. The issue of the picture with the hot cowgirl wrapped up in Pistol's happy palm, has been weighing on my mind, and I haven't worked up the nerve to confront him about it.

My head is spinning and anxiety grips and twists at my belly. I know I look really bad right now, and I'm not sure if I want his friendly, little visit while I'm both mad and ugly. All I'll be able to think about is how I don't compare to that blonde rodeo girl from the anonymously sent picture. If I'm going to have enough confidence to confront him about it, I'm going to need to be on my "A" game . . . and I know I'm not going to be able to move forward in our relationship if I let that disturbing text slide. Letting him see me in this state might make me a little too vulnerable. I really can't put myself in that position. I decide to send him a quick response, hoping to postpone his visit.

Me:
Are you thinking about coming to

```
town?
```

```
Pistol:
I'm already waiting outside your
window ;)!
```

DARN HIM! Everything's always on his terms. It's not a choice of whether I see him. He's already made the decision for me. I have to let him in. What can I do? Think, think . . . Oh, Mrs. Doubtfire moment! I remember the scene from the Mrs. Doubtfire movie when Robin Williams covers his face in a mask and throws on a robe to disguise himself as an old woman. Since I'm already wearing the robe, I run down the hall to grab some leftover cucumbers from tonight's dinner salad. As I run to the kitchen to grab the veggies, I shoot Pistol a quick return text.

```
Me:
Give me just a sec. I'm getting
dressed.
```

```
Pistol:
No need for that Babydoll. I've been
dying to see you with your clothes
off. Just let me in already.
```

I run back to the bathroom and fumble through my supply drawer. Luckily, I find my green gel mask and wrap the band behind my head, securing it in place. I grab the two cucumber slices I plucked from a plate in the sink, stick them onto the goo surrounding my eyes, and fumble my way to the door.

"Hellooooooo. . ." I open the door and greet Pistol, just like Mrs. Doubtfire did in the movie.

"Well hello Mrs. Doubtfire." Pistol takes my hands and pulls them out from my sides. "You're looking AWFUL . . . 'ly' good tonight," he corrects his small falter, and drops my arms back down. Though I can't see a thing, I can feel his movement, and sense him looking me up and down. "So what's up with your new look? This is not what I was expecting when I decided to stop by to see you. Do you even have eyes behind those cucumbers?" I hear him chuckle as he taps at my eye cover. I dodge to the left, keeping him from knocking off the small round barrier that separates him from the truth. "Go fix yourself up! I was thinking we could grab an ice cream, but there's no way I'm going anywhere with you looking like Yoda from *Star Wars!*"

"I was kinda thinking about kickin' it at home tonight," I fumble for a spur-of-the-moment excuse so I don't have to go through with the 'Big Reveal.' *Think, think,* "My skin is pretty messed up from all . . . the chlorine and I was working on a new moisturizing regimen."

"Well I'm sure you have enough of that gooey stuff left over to try it out tomorrow night." Pistol is relentless in his insistence that I get ready. "Kaitlyn, we haven't seen each other for three days. I'm only here for one night. We have school all week and you know I don't have any extra time to give you."

I feel Pistol's warm, over-sized hands wrap around me. He begins running them up and down my legs and thighs, up my back and around the front toward my stomach. I can feel him trying to find his way under my shirt, so I slide my hands over his and slyly curl our fingers together, adding some resistance to stop his movement. The slithering and groping from every direction reminds me of an octopus, but I don't say anything. I can tell I'm already upsetting him with my lack of cooperation in the "getting ready" department, and I don't want to add to his frustration.

"Babydoll, I really need to do something with you tonight. I can't handle being away from you this long. I missed you. Now take off that hideous mask and get yourself presentable."

"Okay, let's make a deal . . ." I joke. "Would you like to see what's behind door number one?" I slightly hinge the cucumber away from my left eye and set it right back down, "or door number two?" I repeat the gesture on my right eye.

"I choose door number three." Before I have a chance to react, Pistol pulls the mask right off my face. The cucumbers drop to the floor, leaving my face completely exposed. His mouth drops in disbelief. "Aw hell Kaitlyn! What happened to you?" He pushes the mask back over my face. "Ummm . . . Let's not make this deal tonight," he chokes out. "Okay, I get it. I'm not taking you anywhere looking like that. What is on your face? Cuz it sure doesn't look like chlorine burn."

"Ok," I fess up. I drop my head, and focus on his boots rather than looking him in the eye. I take a deep breath and let it out. "The other night, we had a bonfire and Jenna kinda used a little poison oak to keep the fire burning. She didn't know what it was, and I obviously wasn't paying attention to what she was using. I guess that stuff can make its way through your system when you inhale it. We both have it pretty bad."

"So what? You and Jenna had a bonfire alone? That sounds a little out of the ordinary for you two girls. Don't you usually spend your weekends driving up to Oregon to shop at the mall?" Pistol pauses in contemplation.

The uncomfortable silence pries my eyes from his boots and forces me to drag them up to meet his eyes. I can read the look on his face. It's telling me he knows there's more to this story. He huffs out a quick breath, "Bonfire's are more of a country thing . . . a guy thing Kaitlyn! Where were you, and who were you with?" belligerence begins to overshadow his formerly tolerant tone.

His aggression brings out my defensive side, and I decide now is the time to bring up the image that's been burning at the back of my mind. "Why does it matter? You were having plenty of your own fun out in Hat Creek," I hiss back.

"What are you talking about? I was at a rodeo; exactly where I told you I'd be. You, on the other hand, never said you were going anywhere! Where were you, Kaitlyn?"

Pistol grabs my arm, "Answer me!"

"Loosen your grip Pistol. I already have bruises from your minor assault in front of the pool on Friday. People are going to start getting a little suspicious if you don't stop doing that." He doesn't let go.

"Fine," I respond. "I'll tell you where I was as soon as you explain THIS to me!" I raise my voice, grab my phone from my robe pocket, and shove it right up to his face, revealing the cowgirl picture.

He slowly releases his grip on my arm and chuckles a bit. He shakes his head for a second and pulls his hand up to his chin, curling his fingers around his jaw. "Who sent you that? You got spies out on me? I thought you trusted me more than that." He pulls his hand away from his jaw and tilts his head back. Shaking his head and pinching his nose he mumbles, "That's just Candie. I already told you about her. She's my new roping partner."

I'm not backing down on this one. "I thought your new partner was a guy named CJ . . . and why is your hand cradling her butt like that?"

"Cradling? Nice verb choice Kaitlyn. You can be so dense sometimes. I'm surprised they let you into all those advanced classes." Pistol clicks his tongue as he grabs my phone from my hand and looks closely down at the picture. "For one, CJ is short for Candie Johnson. She happens to be an excellent roper. That's all. End-of-story. And secondly, her saddle was slipping. We were short on time, so I helped her tighten it, and gave her a boost. Haven't you ever seen a guy help a girl mount a horse before? It's called being a gentleman."

"By groping her like that? And look at the smile on her face! Wow, Pistol, I can practically see her heart skipping in the picture." I pull the mask from my eyes, so he can see the full extent of how livid I am about a cowboy named CJ turning into a hot blonde named Candie Johnson.

"Well, I didn't come here to fight. I think I'm gonna head out. Text me when you're looking. .I mean feeling better . . . and when you can be honest about what really happened Friday night."

He chucks my phone at the wall and marches out the door, only to be met by Caden and Brody. When he sees their red, swollen faces, he shakes his head and clicks his tongue. Scowling, he turns back to me and spits out, "Never mind telling me about who you were with on Friday. I just figured it out. And you're mad at me about my roping partner? Huh." He turns away and stomps down the hall.

The boys brush past Pistol and come in to check on me. At the sight of my appearance, a slight chuckle escapes Brody, but he quickly stops when he sees the seriousness on my face. "I'm not sure whether to laugh or ask if you're okay, Pip. I heard a bang. What just happened?"

I release the breath I've been holding and slowly reach up to my head. As I pull my fingers through my hair, the sleeve of my robe slips down to my elbow exposing the very spot where Pistol had just grabbed me. Caden slides his hand under my elbow, bringing it closer to his face.

"Why's your arm all red, T?"

Brody squints his eyes, focusing on my arm, and then does a speedy about face and runs down the hall.

I can hear the rapid thumb of his feet and the door quickly creak open and slam shut. A spike of adrenaline shoots through my entire body and buzzing fills my ears. I can't even respond to Caden, wondering where Brody just went.

"Don't worry about Brody! Sis, what's up with your arm?"

Staring silently back at Caden, looks of realization and then anger quickly replace his concerned expression. He lets go of me and sprints down the hall to join Brody. *Oh no. They're going after Pistol.* I stand frozen in place, wondering how I let this happen.

I hear brakes screech, a door slam, and muffled voices flying outside my window. I can't make out their words, but the voices stop and I hear metal crunch. It sounds like someone just threw a potato sack on the hood of a car. I'm terrified to see what's happening outside, but I find the nerve to creep down the hallway and turn the handle, cracking the door open just enough to hear what's being said. I press my ear up against the hardwood and strain to hear the argument.

Brody's deep voice carries through the surrounding silence, "You'd better NEVER touch her again you Son of a . . . !" A slam vibrates through the darkness.

"You think you're really going to stop me from seeing her? I don't know what you think you saw, but whatever it is, you're over-reacting!" Pistol spits back, followed by another thumping sound.

"The last two times you've been around her, she's ended up with bruises! That's no accident! You think your tough man-handling a tiny, little girl?" Brody barks back. "Why don't you try bullying someone with a little more muscle, Tough Guy?"

I hear a thump and momentary silence, followed by Pistol's groaning voice, "You know better than anyone that she's a klutz! That girl can't stand on her own two feet! I caught her when she was falling you idiot! Now you're coming after me for helping her out?"

The sound of shuffling replaces Brody's and Pistol's heated argument.

I cannot believe he just put me down like that and then lied about what happened. A surge of anger shoots through me and I open the door to get a better view. I can't believe the scene that's unfolding before me. Brody has taken Pistol from behind and has him in a headlock. His fist pumps rapidly into Pistol's face.

Caden must've heard the door creak, and he suddenly swings his head toward the house. He yells, "Stay back T. You don't need to get in the middle of this."

Fear wells up inside me and I don't know how to react. I'm worried that Pistol won't be able to take this kind of beating, but I'm also afraid that Brody is going to get himself into huge trouble. He has a good shot at a football scholarship. I can't let him mess that up. I'm not worth this. I contemplate how to stop this mess when Brody screams out, "Don't you ever insult her like that again! She's too good for you!" I hear another thump, followed by more yelling, "Had enough?" Brody finally drops Pistol to the ground. "And if I ever see another mark on her after being around you . . . Let's just say this is gonna feel like a gentle massage!"

Pistol scurries to his feet and jumps inside of his truck. His tires screech as he peels out down the street. Brody and Caden grab the hose and begin washing down the front sidewalk. I'm standing there watching them clean up, unsure of how to talk to them about what just happened. I feel horrible about all of this. I know they were defending me, but I can't help but feel bad that Pistol just got the living daylights beat out of him. My stomach turns, thinking about the pain he must be in right now. He's gonna hate me. I decide to pull out my phone and text him.

Me:
I'm so sorry Dimples. I just caught the tail end of that. I'll talk to the boys. Please don't hate me.

There's no response.

I turn around and head back into the house. I am so shaken up, I don't even know how to react. This is all so new to me. I mean, these guys have always defended me, but not against someone I care for so deeply. It has created a storm of conflicting feelings, which have left me stunned and speechless. When Caden and Brody walk through the door, I avoid a possible confrontation by sneaking through the living room and taking a seat in the dark corner. I silently crawl onto the couch and listen to their conversation. They don't see me sitting there when they begin to open up about what just happened.

"I really appreciate you taking care of my sister like that, Bro," Caden says with sincerity.

"You know how I feel about her, Caden. I know it's caused a little drama between us lately, but that girl means the world to me. I'm just so incredibly drawn to protect her these days. The thought of that jerk with his hands on her tears me up inside."

"Brody, you've got to be straight with me Dude. Is it just protecting her from Pistol? Cuz it seems like it might be something more," Caden questions. "I mean, I watched you with her at the bridge. Pistol wasn't even around. What was that?"

"Well, don't kick me in the balls or anything, but I'm kinda feelin' it for her lately. She's so darned funny and witty, and I can't get past how beautiful she is . . . The way she doesn't take my messin' and she throws my bull right back in my face, just gets me right here." Brody double fist bumps his chest. "I just want to be around her all the time. I'm so confused. It's been keeping me up at night with this kinda sick feeling; knowing you're gonna kick my ass, and she's gonna kick my ass, but then while I'm lying there thinking about getting my ass kicked, I realize, I'd totally risk that for her. She's everything I've ever wanted in a girl. She's smart, funny, athletic, gorgeous . . . The best part about her is, she doesn't even know it. She's amazing, and she doesn't throw herself all over me like these other hoochies we go to school with. It's so . . . so intriguing. Caden, I think I'm falling for her."

"Dude, you're right . . . You should put on a nut cup before saying stuff like that to me. That's my sister; our best friend! Don't you think getting involved with her could screw up our friendship for life?"

"You're right, that's what's making me so sick inside. I'm gonna work on this buddy. Don't worry, I'll figure it out."

Oh my, I can't believe I just overheard that conversation. If I wasn't feeling butterflies before, Brody has just unleashed an entire swarm inside of me. I pull myself into a ball to try to tame the whirring tsunami of nerves thrashing around in my stomach. At the sound of my feet brushing against the leather, both boys turn toward me. Brody's jaw slackens and I tuck my head between my knees. Looking down at my feet, I slowly raise my hand in a gesture of hello. "Hi guys, I guess I wasn't supposed to hear that, huh?"

"Nope," Brody pops the *p* sound when he responds in a slightly elevated tone. A gulp shatters the silence. "I think I'm gonna go now, Caden."

I never look back up, when I hear the door shut behind him.

CHAPTER 7

PETTING ZOO

"**D**ON'T FORGET ABOUT DRESS SHOPPING after school today," Jenna jumps up next to me as we head into our honors chemistry class. It's our favorite period of the day. For one, the whole gang is together, which makes it super fun. Then, there's the teacher, Mr. Pine. Not only is he a brilliant scientist, but he knows how to use his skills to create explosive chemical reactions in all the girls. I'm not sure how I even keep my head on straight when he's in front of the room. He's a former pro baseball player, current coach of the Mighty Miners, and if Michelangelo's David could walk and talk, they'd be mistaken for twins . . . well, minus the out-of-style, curly, marble hair. Okay, let's just say he's cut.

We take our seats, and I look up to see the lioness Chelsea, pawing her way up toward Mr. Pine. She's baring her sharp teeth at the group of girls currently surrounding him. Her dominant presence and possessive tendencies, send the other girls hesitantly meandering back to their seats. When everyone has cleared, leaving her alone with Mr. Pine, Chelsea leans into him and hands him a Starbucks Coffee. "I just wanted to thank you for helping me out with that whole bonding thing yesterday." She bats her eyelashes up at him, while a guarded expression spreads across his face. "Who would've thought that the balance of attractive and repulsive forces could cause such a strong connection. It's like Beauty and the Beast or something."

"Get a load of Cha Cha Chelsea up there flirting with Mr. P. again," I roll my eyes and look at Jenna, who clues me in to his repulsed reaction.

"Look at his face Kaitlyn. He's dying inside. She's trying to bag him like he's an eighteen year old guy. Good thing he has all that practice fending off voracious Detroit Tigeresses."

We're still watching the Chelsea show, when we see Mr. Pine raise his eyebrows, shake his head and walk away to set the coffee on his podium. He doesn't say a word in response, but only clears his throat and walks back to the front of the room.

"Alright class. It's time to settle down and get started. Take out your lab journals and turn to your notes on covalent bonds," Mr. Pine tries to get the class on track. Even though it's an honors class, everyone is so jacked up on Homecoming spirit that it's hard to calm them down. Rather than raising his voice, he returns to the front of the room, stands in back of his podium, raises his eyebrows at us, and patiently sips his coffee while surveying the scene unfolding before him.

Leaning into me, but still looking toward the front of the room, Jenna whispers, "I'd be careful with that coffee if I was him. That little predator probably slipped him some Roofies."

We both giggle and grow silent as we watch Puss n Boots slink her way back toward her seat. Brody is sitting in front of me when she stops unexpectedly at his desk. It's spirit week, and Chelsea has gone all out donning her home-crafted spirit attire. Her little gold t-shirt is cinched up the sides in red and black bows, and she's had it autographed by most of the football team. When she bends over his desk she purrs, "Hey Brody, I saved you a special spot."

Drawn away from his conversation with Caden, he looks at Chelsea and replies, "Huh?"

"I was trying to ask you to sign my shirt." She bends down allowing the V of her neck to drop low enough to see the naughty little kitty designs covering her Victoria's Secret push up bra.

"ME-owwww," I hear Jenna's spunky little purr, fly through the room. I'm not sure, but I think I might even hear Mr. Pine laugh a little.

I glance over to see Caden's look of disbelief when Chelsea reaches into her bra and pulls out a hot pink Sharpie. "Right here, she points to the open space front and center over her heart. I saved you the best spot."

"I think I'm gonna be sick," I whisper to Jenna as I watch Brody's left hand wrap around her waist to secure the shirt in place. His right hand moves slowly across her chest leaving his famous signature and one smiling, little Cheshire Chelsea. I can feel the heat rising in my face. I don't know why I'm getting so mad, but I'm incredibly agitated that Brody is petting her like a kitten. He has his hands all over her . . . And in chemistry of all places!

My brother is gaping at the spectacle before him. "Holy Crap," I hear Caden mumble slowly under his breath, right before he lifts his hands toward Chelsea and grunts, "I'm on the football team too! Where do I get to sign?"

"Anywhere you want, Big Guy. You pick the spot," she giggles back at Caden, pouncing over toward his desk and handing him the pen.

"Wow, Cade, let me grab your jaw from the ground for you. You look like a salivating pound puppy, ready to pounce." Chelsea Cat's insidious pheromones have definitely overtaken the back corner of the room, and both of my guys are under her spell.

As my brother works to slather an extra large signature just below Brody's, she watches me with a smug look on her face. "I know it's pretty bumpy," she grins. "Though they are nice and firm, so it shouldn't be too much of a problem to sign them . . . I mean . . . it . . . my t-shirt . . ." Her face lights up and she cocks her head a bit. Giggling she adds, "You probably don't have to deal with that, right Kaitlyn? Swimmer's chest and all."

I try to bite my tongue, but she has my boys pawing all over her like nursing kittens, and I can't help when I blurt, "Ya, ummm, it's not an issue. There's only one petting zoo in this school and it doesn't belong to me. You know you should really start selling tickets. You could probably pay for college if you charged admission every time you let someone knead those things."

I don't realize I'm talking loud enough for Mr. Pine to hear, but apparently he does, because coffee begins to spray from his nose and mouth. He pulls his fisted hand up to his face to stifle his uncontrollable choke-laugh until he has to take a brief exit from the room.

Caden is gaping at me, slowly nodding his head up and down, "Wow, T . . . impressive. Feeling a little feisty today? Pretty sharp tongue you've got there."

I scrunch up my face, not saying a word.

While Mr. Pine is out, Chelsea takes the opportunity to lure Brody in once again. "Hey Brody," she singsongs sweetly. "Are you going to the Homecoming formal this Saturday?"

On no, she is not going there.

"Not sure yet Chels. The girl I was hoping to take is already going with a real 'Piss' Ass.'" He emphasizes "piss" and whips his head over his right shoulder. Our eyes meet. "She hasn't re-alized that the man of her dreams is sitting right in front of her."

Yep, that sudden, sharp pain would be spikes of adrenaline again. I try to ignore his, not so subtle, toying with my emo-tions. I know I overheard him talking to Caden about his attrac-tion to me, but he said he was going to work on getting past this.

I need to help that happen. It's what's best for both of us. I can't give his remark any attention. I begin humming to myself to drown out the sound of the annoying conversation happening in front of me. As I hum Taylor Swift tunes in my head, I drop my eyes back to my desk and try to *shake it off.*

The talk of the dance reminds me to check with Pistol to see if he still wants to go with me. I haven't talked to him since last night, and seeing that the boys roughed him up a bit, I wonder if our Homecoming date is still on. I hide my phone beneath my desk and type out a quick text.

Me:
Sorry again about last night. The boys can be a little overprotective sometimes. Are we still on for the Homecoming dance? If so, I need to get a dress.

I see little bubbles come across the bottom of my screen, so I know he's read my text.

Meanwhile, I catch Chelsea's continued seduction of Brody, "So if you haven't asked anyone . . . You should know I've been holding out for the perfect date. Would you want to go together?" She leans in closer. "It could be fun." She bites her bottom lip and raises her eyebrows. "I'll make sure it's a night you'll never forget." She rubs her hand up and down his arm and gives him a wink. "If you're lucky, I might even bring snacks."

"Oh great," Jenna pipes in, "seduction and snacks. There's no way a boy can refuse that."

"Ya, no need to shop for snacks. She should already have a stockpile of Fancy Feast." I mumble under my breath.

I see Brody sink down in his chair and hear a deep gulp when he swallows. He turns to me slowly and mouths, "Should I?"

I can't believe Brody's asking me for advice about a date with Chelsea. He knows how much I despise her. I mean, didn't he just hear me refer to her as a petting zoo? "Don't ask me! You can handle this little kitty on your own Great Ringmaster," I hiss with disgust.

Jenna bursts out in laughter, "Don't forget the whips buddy. You're gonna need them to keep that mountain cat under control. And here's a fair warning for you; it looks like she's in heat, and I'm sure she's got a whole bag of kitty 'tricks' just waiting to lure you in."

I can't even describe the look on Brody's face, listening to Jenna's warning. He looks like a twelve year old boy sneaking a peek at his big brother's Playboy magazine for the first time. "Oh and Bro," she snaps her fingers at him to try to break his gaze at Chelsea's chest. "Watch out . . . she's been circling all day. When she backs up to you and raises her tail, you may want to run for the hills."

At the words "whips" and "tricks," Caden peels his eyes from Chelsea's chest and joins in the banter. "Whoa, where do I sign up for this circus? Do you have any hot feline friends who need taming?" he jokes.

Through Jenna's sarcastic remark, I can hear Brody talking to Chelsea, "Well, since Plan A isn't panning out, I guess I can take you, Chels. Text me later so we can make plans on when and where to meet."

I cannot believe he just accepted her invitation to the Homecoming dance. I feel a surge of anger come over me. I stand up, stomp my foot, and shout, "Yay, let's all *CLAP* for Brody." I clap my hands together furiously over my head. "He just got himself the Purrrr-fect date to the Homecoming dance!"

I don't know what's gotten into me today. I'm not usually bold enough to stand up to Chelsea, but right now, I feel like that little feline is pouncing on my territory. I pick up my binder, pat Brody on the shoulder, snark, "Good choice," and walk out the door.

Out in the hallway, Mr. Pine is wiping the coffee off his coaching shirt. I'm shocked to see him there, and jump when he questions? "Where are you going Ms. Woodley?"

I fumble for a believable excuse,"I'm headed out to the quad. I have to sell pretzels during the bazaar. Am I okay to go?"

"Ya . . . uh, just remember the test on unstable compounds tomorrow."

"Ya, no problem, got that one covered." I excuse myself and begin to walk over to the pool. All I have to do to pass that stupid test is think about how I'm feeling right now. As I saunter across the street, I review the test definition in my head. *Unstable compound: highly reactive, can condense, decompose, or become self-reactive quite easily due to pressure or temperature. Yep . . . I'm an unstable compound, that's what I am.*

When I get to the pool, I make my way to the dressing room and pull the curtain shut. I'm sulking, angry, and confused. I can't believe Brody is going to Homecoming with the one girl that has bullied me mercilessly since fifth grade. Well, I guess being that he is an eighteen year old boy, he would rather have a "Post-date Guarantee," than respect our lifelong friendship.

I become increasingly upset as I think back on everything we've been through together. He knows how hard Chelsea is on me. My throat tightens, and tears sting at my eyes as I feel the stabbing pain of Brody's betrayal jab at my heart. I'm taken back to the summer of seventh grade.

"Someone's here to see you," my mom opened the door to my room. I lay crying on my bed, head buried under my pillows. It was the worst day I'd ever had. I was at the top of my game and set to compete at the North Valley Championship Swim Meet. During practice, Chelsea managed to get into my head and break me down. She was enraged that I'd beat her out, knocking her off the "A" Relay team that would compete at the Championship meet. She had somehow made it look like

I was to blame, and gotten everyone in our lane to gang up on me. During warm-ups, they kept mowing me over with the kick boards. Throughout the main set, they would slow down upon my approach and kick furiously to drown me every chance they got. These girls were working double time to beat me down and make my practice miserable. After two hours of choking on water, being scratched by toe-nails, and kicked in the head, my spirits were low and I was feeling a bit defeated. By the end of practice, I shakily climbed out of the pool; tears filled my goggles. Chelsea, walked up next to me and said, "You think you're so much better than everyone else, don't you? Let today be a lesson to you. You're only as good as I let you be. Nobody here likes you, Kaitlyn. I'm surprised you even want to go to Championships. It's not going to be any fun for you anyway, Loner."

With no response, I solemnly hung my head and pulled the loose ends of my towel around my back and up into my face. I stood momentarily in silence, when I felt a hand come up to my back. "Are you okay, there?" I heard a sweet, soft voice come from behind. "You know those are all lies right? She's just jealous."

I didn't want to appear weak. I nodded my head a little, but a traitorous squeak escaped me as I struggled to hold back a cry. "I'm okay," I whispered and lowered the towel to see who was talking to me. It was the new girl, Jenna, who swam in the lane right below me. It was her first year on the team, and she'd quickly made her way through the ranks, showing great potential in all of her strokes.

"Thanks Jenna," I quietly sobbed. "It's good to know that there's one person here who doesn't hate me."

"Well, those catty girls make me sick. Who needs them, right? She stuck her pinky out to me. "Give me your pinky," she said.

I held out my pinky and she intertwined hers with mine.

"As long as I'm here, you've got a friend. Got it?" She

tugged down on my pinky and gave me a wink.

A small smile spread across my face. "Thanks . . . friend."

I remember her putting her arm around me and walking me to the car, where I began to melt at the sight of my mom.

A couple hours had passed and I wouldn't look up when my visitor entered the room. I didn't feel like seeing anyone, and my eyes were heavy and tired from crying. That's when I heard Brody's comforting voice.

"Hey there Pip Squeak," he said softly.

I raised my hand to say hello, leaving my face buried.

"I just wanted to come and wish you luck before your meet tomorrow."

"Thanks, Bro . . ." my muffled voice tried to claw it's way through the obstacle course of bedding surrounding my head.

"I can't hear you buddy. Please look at me."

I shook my head back and forth, and felt the bed sink as he sat down beside me. His hand came to rest gently on my back.

"I brought you something," he jostled me, trying to get me to turn over. "But you have to look at me before I'll give it to you."

My curiosity got the best of me. I guessed I could quit being stubborn long enough to see what he brought. "Okay," I slowly rose from the bed and sat up facing him.

Brody gave a little chuckle and peeled the tear-plastered hair from the sides of my face, finger-combing the loose, wet strands behind my ears. Holding both of my cheeks in his hands he said, "Pip, you and I are best friends. It kills me to see you so sad. Your brother told me about your practice with Chelsea, and I want you to go down there and beat her ass for the way she treated you. I wish, so much I could go and watch you swim in that meet. I was saving this for your birthday, but I decided I wanted to give it to you today.

"Awww, you don't have to give me anything Bro."

"I want to. It's for luck." He pulled a small silver box out

of his pocket. He held it up to me and opened it, revealing a sterling silver horseshoe necklace with two small, pink birthstones embedded at the curve.

"Oh Brody, a lucky horseshoe; that's adorable, thank you," I reached in and gave him a huge hug.

"Well, I saw it right after you clobbered me at horseshoes during the Fourth of July picnic. Horseshoes are supposed to bring you luck, you know. I couldn't help but get it when I saw I could personalize it with your birthstones . . . and you're welcome. Here, let me put it on you." He brushed my hair away from my shoulders and strung the dainty necklace around my neck, securing the clasp. He smiled, dropped his hands to my shoulders, and whispered, "I'll always have your back, Pip. Good luck this weekend."

That was the first real gift a boy ever gave me. I still wear that lucky necklace every time I compete.

The chime of my phone shatters my bitter-sweet memory. I've begun to calm down, but the thought of Brody and Chelsea together stings more than I care to admit. I thought he was always going to have my back. I guess that was before he started liking cats.

Jenna:
Hey, where are you? You never came back.

Me:
I couldn't stomach any more. That girl made me so mad, I wanted to make her choke up a hairball.

Jenna:
Ya, she's gross. Just so you know, Brody hasn't said a word since you

left the room. I think he knows he messed that one up.

P.S. That was quite a scene friend, I'm proud of you for turning the tables on her for once. She was working her tail off to get to you. It was funny when you left her speechless with your petting zoo metaphor.

P.P.S. We're still dress shopping after school, right?

Me:
Not sure . . . haven't heard back from Pistol. Kinda worried cuz I know he read it. I saw the bubbles pop up :(

Jenna:
Ass Munch . . . Let me know when you hear. If he doesn't follow through, you can join our girls' group.

Me:
Thanks Pal. We'll shop no matter what.

CHAPTER 8

TODDLERS AND TIARAS

WE'VE GONE TO SEVERAL DEPARTMENT stores and tried on dozens of dresses, when we finally stop at a fun boutique that has some good prospects. "This one is decent," Jenna holds up a short, black, one-shoulder glitter dress, pinning it against her body as she spins around."

"Ya, it's cute. You should go try it on," I encourage. "We've been looking everywhere, and that's the best one I've seen for your body type. You're so petite. It won't drown you like some of those long gowns you've been looking at."

I rifle through the dresses until a cute sequined gown, with a heart-shaped bodice catches my eye. "I like this coral one." I pull it off the rack. "I think I'll go to the dressing room with you."

After a few minutes in the dressing room, I hear Jenna giggling.

"What's going on in there?" I laugh.

"I look like a cupcake in this dress."

"Hang on a second. Don't change yet. I'm zipping up and

then I want to see." I finish zipping my dress and look in the mirror. I love it so much. It fits perfectly and the color brings out my summer tan. I feel like a princess. "K, done . . . Be right there."

We open our doors at the same time looking each other up and down, "Oh, Kaitlyn . . . You have to get that dress! It's perfect!" Jenna jumps up and down in excitement. The ruffles of her cupcake dress bounce wildly up and down.

"Ummm . . . thank you . . . ummm. .your dress is cu. . ."

"I know, I know," Jenna interrupts. "I look like a cake topper. This is definitely not going to work."

Now that she's said it herself, I feel like it's an appropriate time to laugh, and of course take a picture to post on Instagram so that everyone else can get a good laugh too.

I'm playing around with hashtags for the hilarious picture when my long awaited text from Pistol comes across my phone.

```
Pistol:
I've been thinking about it, and I
guess we can still go.
```

Wow, he still wants to go? Yes! He doesn't hate me! I'm so happy that he's coming that I quit working on my "#bestie#home-coming#cupcakedress" post and respond enthusiastically.

```
Me:
Yay, I'm so glad you could forgive
me for everything that happened. Are
you doing okay?
```

```
Pistol:
I've looked better, but at least now
our messed up faces will match for
the pictures. How's the poison oak,
```

btw?

Me:
Still there, but starting to fade a little. I'll try to cover it with make-up if it's still there for the dance. I want to look good for you.

Pistol:
You didn't get your dress yet did you?

Me:
I think I just found it. It's super cute.

Pistol:
Well, I hope you don't dress like a mom. I want to see those killer legs. Make it short, tight, and preferably red or black. Those are the colors I look best in.

Wow! Now I have to dress in the colors HE looks best in? What ever happened to Homecoming formal being the girls' night? Disappointment tackles my excitement when I realize the gorgeous, coral dress I just found isn't going to fly with Pistol. Red is way too slutty for me, so I guess I'm going to try to find something in black. It's a good thing the cupcake dress didn't work for Jenna. At least we won't have to go as twins.

Me:
Okay, I'll see what I can find.

```
Thanks again for going with me.  I
miss you Dimples.

Pistol:
I miss you too.  You owe me doll.  I'll
collect Saturday night;)!  I'll pick
you up at your house around 7.
```

I put my phone back in my purse and take off the gown. Jenna is already dressed and waiting for me. "Hey Jenna, I think I changed my mind on this." I open the door and hand her the dress. "Will you go see if they have it in black? And maybe shorter? And possibly tighter? And not so flowy?"

"So basically, the opposite of this dress? Like maybe something Chelsea would wear?"

"Ya, just think I might try a little change."

"Okay; but that one's amazing. Give it to me and I'll go look while you get dressed," Jenna is hesitant to take the dress.

Just as I finish buttoning my jeans, I hear the rush of feet and a quick tapping on my dressing room door. "Shhhh, let me in, let me in . . . quick."

I swing the door open and pull Jenna inside. She shoves two beautiful little dresses into my hand. "Here . . . these are perfect for us . . . black for you, and coral for me since you didn't like it. . ." A sense of urgency dominates her tone.

"What's going on? Is there a stick up in the lingerie department or something?" I joke.

Jenna throws her hand over my mouth and holds her index finger over her lips whispering, "Lower your voice, I don't want them to know we're here."

"Who?"

Whispering so softly it's barely audible, Jenna smirks, "Chelsea and some cowgirl sidekick. They're out there looking at dresses for the dance. I got an idea." The look of mischief creeps its way across Jenna's face.

"Oh, goodness Jenna, you and your ideas." I'm a little scared, cuz there's no telling what that girl has up her sleeve. Or in this case, in her purse!

"What is that?" I accidentally speak with a little too much volume, when I see Jenna pull out a plastic baggie of shiny green leaves. "Are you crazy bringing that in here?"

"It's not what you think it is. You know I wouldn't do that. Look closer."

She holds the baggie up to my face and I see the very familiar three-leaved bunches of tiny oak-looking leaves. "Holy crap, Jenna! What are you doing with that? Haven't you had enough britch-itch lately?"

"It's not for me, Dingbat. I grabbed some from the bonfire to show my parents what it looks like, and never threw it away . . . thought it might come in handy sometime. Looks like today's the lucky day."

An incredulous look grows on my face as I question her, "So what's your plan? Smoke her out of the boutique so she can't get a dress?"

"Better . . . we hide in the dressing room and figure out how to get this," she shakes the bag, "all over the inside of her perfect dress!"

I'm in shock at Jenna's audacity. This might be a little over the top, even for her.

"Shhh . . . I think I hear them coming . . . Kaitlyn, jump up on the bench so they only see one pair of feet."

We can hear Chelsea and mystery cowgirl approach with the assistant.

"Okay, girls, if you need any more styles or sizes, just let me know and I'll see if I can find them for you," the assistant unlocks the door allowing Chelsea in.

I see a huge bundle of dresses fling over the dressing room wall right into our stall. Jenna gets a huge smile on her face and gives me a thumbs up, "Perfect!" she mouths, trying to stifle a giggle.

"I don't know Jenna," I grimace, "I'm not sure I can go through with this."

"Oh, grow a pair, Kaitlyn," Jenna sneaks a peek through the crack and looks back at me, "Come here . . . I want you to see this dress her friend is holding up. It's hideous," she's bobbing up and down muffling a fake, quiet laugh.

I quietly sneak down off the bench and tiptoe over to the door. Peeking through the crack, I see a voluptuous, blonde cowgirl holding up a sleazy, satin, red dress, with just enough fabric to cover a toddler at a beauty pageant. The girl holding the dress looks vaguely familiar, but I can't place her. I hear them begin to speak.

"I found the perfect dress for you, Chelsea. It just screams Queen. Didn't you say you love red?"

"Awesome," she claps her hands, "That's my favorite color; bring it in here CJ."

CJ? Oh my gosh . . . Is that Roping Partner CJ? That's where I recognize her from . . . the picture. I'm stunned. *What is she doing with Chelsea?*

I see the red dress flop on top of the pile encroaching on our stall.

"Here, take this back. It's too cutesy and flowy . . . reminds me of that annoying Goody-Two-Shoes, Kaitlyn Woodley."

"Like, Pistol's Kaitlyn? I've heard she's a little on the conservative side. Ya, you wouldn't want to wear that dress . . . it has virgin written all over it."

My brow lifts, mouth drops, and then I slam it shut. I'm searching for words as I nod my head and shake my finger in the air. The first thing that comes out of my mouth is, "Game on Jenna . . . Give me at least half of that darned bag! I'm ready to give that cat something to scratch!"

"Now you're talking," Jenna gives me a soft high five, and

we get closer to the crack in the door to see if we can figure out how we're going to make this happen.

While we're huddled next to the crack, we hear the girls continue their conversation. Chelsea's annoying voice speaks up first, "Speaking of Kaitlyn, I hear she's taking Pistol to the dance. If you decide to go on a double date with us, it could be your chance to make your move . . . You know, let him see you without your boots and hat."

"But I don't even know this guy, Ty, you want me to go with . . . It's kinda weird," CJ whines.

"Well, you're not really going to have fun with HIM. He's a typical jock. He's gonna be grinding with tons of girls. The plan is to get Pistol," Chelsea schemes. "Look, I know you guys have been messing around a little, but wait til he sees you looking all sexy standing next to Kaitlyn in her nun habit. He'll drop her for sure."

"You're right . . . I'm in," CJ replies.

"What a hellcat! Did she really just say that? And Ty? Like my Ty?" Jenna mouths back to me with an incredulous look plastered on her face.

I'm standing in disbelief, shaking my head, ready to hit something. "I'm going out there right now!" I mouth, pointing to the door.

"Stop! As much as I want to go with you, we can't." She mouths back, shaking her head "no" and moving her hand side to side in a "cut it out" gesture. "It will ruin everything. We're going to get them good Kaitlyn. The only ones who are going to be sexy Friday night are you and me. They're going to look like they were on the receiving end of a cat's scratching post! I don't care who ends up with poison oak, I'm taking this bag to every freakin' short, tight, barely-there, slutty dress I see . . . starting with all of the ones laying right here."

"Well, let's try ours on first. We need to make sure that stuff doesn't touch them." We try on the cute little dresses Jenna threw at me. They are tight, gorgeous, and accentuate our impeccably sculpted swimmers' legs . . . Perfect to combat C.ow J.aw and Mufasa.

"We'll see who looks like a nun . . . Let's do this," Jenna, opens the baggie, and begins to carefully rub the inside of each dress invading our stall. She works from top to bottom, making sure her hand doesn't touch the contaminated fabric.

"I get to do some too," I take the bag from her hand. Knowing it's probably her final choice, I make sure to rub the red dress thoroughly inside and out."

We quickly make our way out to the slut-dress rack, and slyly begin to rub the inside of the baggie on the first victims. I hold each dress up, pointing out embellishments and cute details, while Jenna slides the exposed leaves across the chest and skirt of each one nodding her head and saying, "Oh ya," and "Mmmhmmm." After several minutes, our mission is accomplished, and we head to the clerk to buy our dresses. It's a quick transaction and Chelsea Cat and Daisy Duke never even see us in there.

When we break free of our little crime spree we double over laughing. "I'm gonna pee my pants!!!" Jenna snorts.

"You're brilliant Jenna, but we're taking this one to our graves. This Homecoming dance is going to live in infamy."

CHAPTER 9

HOMECOMING

IT'S BEEN FOUR DAYS, AND most of our poison oak has cleared now. We're looking pretty decent, unlike the cheerleading squad and the rest of Chelsea's litter, whose faces all look like diaper rash. Yes, it's quite a mysterious epidemic that's plagued the halls of Jefferson this last week. No one has been able to figure it out. The principal finally got Mr. Pine to collect some cultures to see if he can pinpoint what it is. Chelsea, happily volunteered for the swabbing by Mr. P. Fortunately, I have a great, poison oak-free poker face, and Jenna got called out of town again, to finish whatever it was she had to do in Sacramento. There's no way she would've been able to conceal our secret. She totally would've claimed the glory had she watched Chelsea and the Cha Cha girls using the guys as human scratching posts and grinding in their laps at lunch and snack breaks. Hopefully, no one will suspect the dresses before the dance. However, right now, we're completely preoccupied getting ready for the "Miner Pit" party.

We are pumped for tonight's game. Our swim coach has

never let us out of practice early for Homecoming, but since the majority of the team are seniors, he decided he'd cut us some slack and let us enjoy our last one. It's the first year we'll actually have enough time to dry our hair and put on make-up. "I can't believe we finally get to go to Homecoming on time! This is so exciting! I'm not going to look like a poodle this year!" I cheerfully call to Jenna who's going through my closet to pick out a cute red, black, and gold outfit. When she emerges she looks adorable. She's got on a black t-shirt with a red Miner's logo, and a gold sequined headband. It's basically the same outfit I'm wearing, but in the opposite colors. We laugh when she steps out of the closet looking like my twin.

Caught up in the spirit of the evening, we dance around the room and make faces at each other in the mirror as we put the final touches on our makeup. We've slathered our cheeks with red and gold glittered spirit streaks, straightened and curled our hair, and we both look smokin' hot. We are jumping around and acting like dorks, when I pull my hair brush up to my mouth. I can never resist singing into my hairbrushes and curling irons. It's one of my signature moves while getting ready. Changing the lyrics to the *Party Rock Anthem,* I sing to Jenna, "Poison oak is in the house tonight . . . but you and I are gonna have a good time, this itch will make them lose their mind, Mountain Kitty has to scratch her behind. . . hahahaha," we start cracking up. As the song continues, we both start bouncing up and down in the mirror, singing, " Every day they're itching, itching, itching."

Jenna adds, "Now we see them twitchin' . . . twitchin' . . . twitchin.'"

We've been having so much fun having a curling iron concert and re-writing lyrics, that time has flown by. When Jenna looks at the clock, she's a little shocked. "You may want to stop singing into your brush and use it on your hair. We only have five minutes til they open the gates. We are not missing the mine-shaft entrance this year. I love the part where the boys carry the pick axe through the shaft and plant it center field for luck. It's so hot."

At Jefferson High, it's become tradition to keep a wooden mineshaft near the visitor's bleachers. It acts as an entrance for the team, which comes running up from the locker room, through the shaft, and out to the field. The entire cheerleading squad, pep band, and pit crew, which would consist of all the crazy teenagers that rock the game, all form two long single file lines that guide the boys to the center of the field. They run through the shaft and crowd, giving high fives, hollers, and chest bumps to get them pumped up and ready to kick booty. It's a fun way to begin the game; however, Jenna and I typically miss this tradition due to our strict swim coach. We are stoked that we get to be there tonight.

"Ya, I can't wait to watch the Caden-Brody dream team. Dad says they are unstoppable. They are so in tune with each other; it's obvious they've been playing together since their Pop Warner days. This should be really fun to watch. . . though, I'm still super aggravated with Brody," I add. "I can't get over the fact that he's taking Hello Kitty to the dance tomorrow night."

"It's not like he wants to take her, Kaitlyn. It was pretty obvious to me that she wasn't his top choice. You really didn't give him another option," Jenna defends Brody. "Have you even talked to him?" she asks.

"Well, I got a couple missed calls, but I haven't responded. I'm avoiding him til I can figure out what to say."

"That's not very nice." Jenna reprimands.

"Wow, Jenna. Mom always taught me that if you don't have something nice to say, don't say anything at all. Whose side are you on anyway?" I pick up a pillow from my bed and playfully toss it at Jenna.

She dodges the pillow and lets it fly through the open door. Giggling, she responds, "I'm not on a side Kaitlyn. I just want what's best for both of you. And to me . . . that would be . . ."

"Don't even go there," I slam my hand across her mouth. "I have a boyfriend. Brody and I could never work." An image of Brody and Caden using my first training bra as a sling shot comes to mind. "Ummm, we know way too much about each other. Besides, you've seen how Caden feels about Brody and me. He would lock me in a closet and then go and snap Brody in half. I don't want to be responsible for breaking up the dream team and derailing the road to sections this year. I don't want to hear another word about this."

She shakes her head at me, "Fine, it's time to head out anyway, but this is not a closed topic."

We are almost at the field, when we stop the car for a litter of cheerleaders crossing the street to get to the game. Once they're across, we watch as they rub all over each other, walking back to back, and stopping every few feet to bob up and down. If they could only see how weird this looks to the random observer. "I'm sure they're scratching, but lord knows if I'm right," I chuckle at Jenna. "They may just love skin to skin contact."

As we drive past the field, I peek through the chain link fence to see that the crowd is insane. We have to park all the way down at the high school parking lot across the street, and walk up to the game. When we get to the crosswalk, the football team is jogging from the high school over to the field, but I try to avert all eye contact as they pass by us, just in case Brody is among them. I am relieved when they cross to the locker room without incident. "Good luck tonight, Dad," I shout as I see my dad trailing behind them as he looks over plays.

"Thanks Honey, you know if you want to come down, you can always help with stats."

"Thanks Dad!" *HECK No, I'm not going to miss Homecoming pit for anything.* I think to myself.

Once we're inside, we get our free Miner cowbells, buy some pom poms and bangers, and head for the pit. Even if the cheerleaders are so preoccupied with scratching that they can't get the crowd pumped up, we're gonna make sure we bring the party. There's only fifteen minutes til kickoff. Word spreads that it's time for the boys to come out. Our entire pit crew stands and moves like a large ameba toward the field. Led by the pep band and cheerleaders, we line both sides of the mine shaft, leaving a large aisle for the boys to run through. We're screaming and cheering down on the field. Cowbells are ringing. People are popping each other over the heads with bangers, pom poms are flying, and voices are roaring through megaphones.

I have the sense that eyes are glaring into the side of my head, so I look over to see rashy Chelsea Cat standing right beside me in her cutesy little cheerleading uniform. Fortunately, the red in her uniform highlights her swollen, scarlet face. When I notice our proximity, I let my bangers clap together with exceptional intensity. She's pinned between me and the rest of the crowd with no escape route, as I continuously bonk them into the side of her head. I look forward, not letting on that I know exactly what I'm doing. Her hands flail fiercely trying to bat the bangers away, but I'm relentless, kind of like she is when she's on the prowl. I beat harder and faster, screaming and yelling, pretending I don't have a clue what I'm doing. Jenna stands directly across from me on the other side of the mine shaft watching me knock the crud out of Chelsea with my bangers. She is doubled over laughing hysterically, shaking her finger at me.

The crowd is roaring as the pep band begins to play the *Miner Fight Song.* Swiftly, the Miners approach the shaft. The first out, carrying the Mighty Miner's pick axe is Brody. The boys are jogging at a good pace. Even though I'm still mad as heck at the kid, my eyes are locked on Brody in that sexy uniform. I can't help it. The team is dressed completely in black tonight, and the guys look sharp. I know Brody is a wide receiver, but if I had anything to say about it, he'd definitely be the 'Tight End.' As I watch him jogging through the tunnel, I notice his eyes scan the crowd. When our eyes meet, a grin spreads across his face. I know we haven't spoken in days, so I'm shocked when he slows, runs right up to me, and grabs my hand. "What are you doing Bro? You're supposed to lead the team out there."

"I am, Pip. It's just that it's a special night, so you're gonna help me."

I shake my head in disbelief. "What are you talking about?"

"I get to choose someone to help me for Homecoming. It's a tradition, don't you know? Oh ya, you never get to come this early. Just come on, let me show you. It will be fun." He gives his head a quick snap toward center field.

I am not a crowd person, and definitely do not want to be the center of attention. I hesitate momentarily until I feel Chelsea's eyes try to decapitate me with her laser sharp glare. "If she doesn't want to go with you, I will," her whiney voice permeates our little safety bubble.

I look over to her and scowl, then look back at Brody, "Let's go."

He bends down and scoops me over his left shoulder. "Careful of the axe," he cries, resting me on his left shoulder pad with the axe tucked in closely with his right hand. The crowd erupts with cheering as we make our way toward center field. As we run, Brody huffs out, "Pip, sorry about earlier this week. I have to know you're not mad at me so I can concentrate tonight. All I can think about right now is how I've messed up our friendship. It's killing me that you won't talk to me. I need your luck for my first league game. You need to plant the Miner axe for me." He slides me down, grabbing me at the waist, and gently sets me on the ground.

"Well being that you just managed to sweep me off my feet, you're forgiven. And about that luck, uh, I'll see what I can do." A grin spreads across his face as he hands me the axe. The crowd grows silent.

I hear a player shout, "He's got Coach's daughter!" It echoes through the stadium as the crowd erupts once again.

I hold the axe over my head and pause momentarily looking Brody right in the eyes. The crowd starts chanting, "Woodley, Woodley, Woodley."

"Good luck Brody Tatum," I whisper, slamming the axe down into the ground with as much force as I can manage. The crowd erupts in cheers.

"Thank you," Brody grins and turns to run back toward the team.

"Wait," I grab his arm, spinning him back toward me. I pull my lucky horseshoe necklace from beneath my blouse and unclasp it from my neck, "Touch this . . . it's always brought me luck."

He slides his hand over mine, trapping the horseshoe in between our clasped fingers. "You still wear that?"

"Of course I do. My best friend gave it to me. It reminds me that we've always got each other's backs. Now go kick some booty Cutie!"

He gives my hand a tight little squeeze, smiles, and runs back to the team.

Luck is obviously on our side when the Miners win the coin toss and choose to receive the kickoff. It's the first play of the game and Brody is not only starting at wide receiver, but he's also playing special teams. He's deep in the field to receive for the Miners when the ball is launched into the air. He watches the kick and swiftly positions himself directly under the ball. It's a perfect catch. He stealthily maneuvers through the first two Lions and heads down the field. He's at their 40 yard line when he spins through another defender, breaking his tackle. He's almost down when he catches his balance and continues down the field. Brody is too quick for the opposing team. He makes it to the 40–30–20–10. . . and he's in for a touchdown. He's put the first six points of the game on the board. The crowd cheers wildly. Chelsea screams from the track, "That's my boy!!!"

Jenna looks at me and gags, "Dude, get over it! He didn't

even let you plant his axe tonight!" she screams down at the cheerleaders. Chelsea obviously didn't hear over the newly erupted *Miner Fight Song,* but the people in the pit around us start patting Jenna on the back and shake their heads in agreement.

My mouth is still hanging open from Jenna's bold outburst. "I can't believe you just yelled that. Give me five, Sista!" I raise my hand and slap her a high five. I turn around to see I've just missed Jenna's current crush, Ty, boot the ball through the goal post for the conversion. These boys are on fire tonight. What an incredible start to the game.

The Lions gain possession of the ball, but squander their downs away in no time flat. I'm so focused on trying to send the boys lucky energy that I don't even notice that Douche-bag Daemon plants his skinny French butt right in the middle of Jenna and me. He's dressed in an outdated tuxedo that hits him just above the ankles. "What's up Daemon?" I grumble, shooting him my, "What makes you think you can separate my best friend and me with your scrawny butt?" glare.

"Zhust getting ready for ze halftime show. When I came to pick up my escort I noticed zomething. All of ze girls down there wiz Mizz Chelzea have red, blotchy faces . . . All of her friends in ze stands have zem too. You and Jenna just had zis problem . . . Is it not a strange coincidenz?"

"What are you insinuating?" I question.

"Oh, nozing . . . just a little curious. I'm trying to help Mr. Pine wiz ze investigation."

I'm caught off guard that he has sniffed us out in his pursuit of the mysterious rash. I fumble for a response. "Well, Detective Daemon, perhaps they're all suffering an allergic reaction to the same tray of kitty litter . . . or maybe they rolled around in a field of bad catnip . . . They have been acting pretty aroused for days. Now, move along, you're in the middle of my Pit Party."

He stands up, and makes his way back through the crowd,

writing something on a small notepad as he leaves. "What was that about?" Jenna asks guardedly. "Do you think he's onto us?"

"I don't know, but that is the last guy we need to find out our secret. Promise me, that no matter what happens, we deny, deny, deny," I whisper with wide eyes.

"Oh, I am the Queen of Denial," Jenna chuckles. "Speaking of queens, I'm looking forward to the halftime show. After the crowning of the queen, I hear those cheerleaders have a pretty special routine they've put together.

"Seriously? How special could it be with the Cha Cha Crew?"

"Well, I don't know what they have planned, but while you were caught up talking to Dumb Ass Daemon, a few of the cheerleaders just came and sat down in front of us. I'm pretty sure I just caught them passing around a flask with the rest of the Aristocats. Can't wait to see looped up Chelsea claw her way to the top of the pyramid tonight. This should be good."

We look up just in time to catch Caden running through the goal posts with a quarterback keeper. The crowd goes wild once again, and I swear I hear Chelsea's backwoods friend Lexi point to my brother and shout in her hillbilly drawl, "You may not be able to do it, but I'm gonna 'sack' that quarterback tonight, Baby!" I catch a glance at Peyton, another member of the litter, sharpening her claws. Word is, she has a huge crush on my brother and wants to hook up with him at the dance tomorrow night.

I turn to Jenna in disgust, "Are you flippin' kidding me?" I pull my hand to the side of my face. "Oh no no no. This is not happening. Not if I can help it. It's bad enough that Brody has gotten involved with the Cha Cha's; now they're all going after my brother too? Unacceptable."

Jenna appears to be just as mortified as I am, though she fumbles through arguments she can use to make me feel better. "Oh, Kait. I'm sure Caden has more sense than that. He's not going to give Hoedown Lexi the time of day. Whatever she thinks she's going to do with your brother is all in her head. She's obviously been sipping from the same moonshine as Chelsea. The only sack she's gonna be hitting tonight is the one she shares with her cousin-grandpa."

Jenna starts humming a backwoods twang and pretending she's picking a banjo when she's interrupted by the announcer, "Ladies and gentleman, I'd like you to focus your attention to center field, where the Homecoming Court will be arriving shortly. This year, we have nine couples, including our honorary princess and princesses who are on exchange from France and Sweden."

I am completely uninterested in the Homecoming Court. The faculty decided to try something new and choose the court for us this year. That way people who don't typically have a chance of being nominated, can have an equal opportunity to participate in Homecoming. Our senior class didn't even have a vote on who was a part of it. Needless to say, every prince or princess is either a member of the nerd herd or the brown nosing elite. The only person I really associate with on the court is Dipwad Daemon, and I don't need to stick around to see him lose. "Let's go to the bathroom while they're doing this so we can get a closer view when the cheerleaders come out.

"Sounds good to me," Jenna agrees.

As we step down to leave for the bathroom, I make sure to step right next to Lexi and accidentally let my banger smack her right in the face, "Hey!" I hear her yelp.

"Oops, I'm such a klutz," I chuckle, and never turn back.

When we leave the bathroom, rather than returning to the stands, we go down to the track to get a better view of the cheerleading halftime routine. The girls are stumbling around, giggling, and making weird faces at each other. Audrey and Courtney have their noses pulled up with their index fingers, oinking at each other like pigs, while two more sets of girls are stacked on top of each other having chicken fights. Their coach is working fiercely to try to get them lined up for their routine. Even from a distance, we can hear the click of her black stilettos as she runs around in her little black pants and tight tank top trying to wrangle her girls together. She is furiously chomping her gum, screeching, "We perform in 45 seconds girls! Get it together!" She double-claps her hands as she screams in vain, "Girls, you're making me look bad! Come on!"

Jenna and I are cracking up and can't wait til the music starts. "This is gonna be good! I've got my phone on video," Jenna bounces up and down excitedly. When the music begins, the girls start heading toward the field like the zombies from Michael Jackson's *Thriller.* Some are headed left, some are headed right, while Coach Priscilla shrieks, "Left, Left! No . . . Left!" They are completely out of sync and giggle wildly as they ooze all over the field.

The cheerleaders are finally set in formation when the music, *Can't be Tamed,* by Miley Cyrus begins.

"How fitting," Jenna laughs when the music starts.

"Meow," I chuckle back.

Jenna holds up the video camera on her phone, and lets it roll, capturing the first blunder of the routine. Just as the girls lower into a crouch and begin to spin their heads around in circles, Ami ceases, and begins to vomit, splat down Chelsea's leg. Instantly, we can hear Chelsea growl, "Gross!" She stops dancing and begins pawing the ground, trying to clean the vomit off her shoe.

"Wow . . . looks like she's digging in the litter box," Jenna snickers.

Chelsea finally stops pawing and tries to catch up to the rest of the noodle-armed cheerleaders. I've never seen a bigger circus act in my life. They bounce around awkwardly as they try to figure out the next move. Peyton, actually bends over giggling in defeat, no longer even trying to follow along with the rest of the girls. Finally, as the chorus begins to blare through the speakers, the girls try to back their way into formation. Only their backs are visible to us, when Carley steps up on Taylor's hip. As she climbs to her shoulder, one foot slips, catching in the waistband of Taylor's skirt, proving once again, that cheerleaders do not wear underwear. I hear the crowd gasp, and a little boy standing in front of me points laughing, "Daddy, I saw her booty."

Chelsea trips over Taylor, who's currently out of formation trying to adjust her bloomers; but she manages not to fall. Once they are in place for the basket toss, Chelsea jumps into the bases' hands. They look like they're feeling pretty chipper tonight because they give her an extra high toss. I recognize fear in her eyes as Chelsea soars to new heights. She begins flailing like a cat falling from a ten story building. Arms and legs everywhere, claws out, I watch the bases work extra hard to try to position themselves under her landing. As she re-enters the Earth's atmosphere, her right arm pokes through the open elbow of one base, and her left leg pokes through the open elbow of another. Luckily, they catch her head, but overall, it's a miss.

BAM! She crashes to the ground. She's lying in the background as the cheerleaders move around and finish their routine, oblivious to the fact that they have a girl down in the backfield. "Yay," they shout, kicking their legs in the air, screaming, and clapping for themselves, high-fiving as they run off the field. They take off, leaving Chelsea on the 50 yard line, rolling around and holding her leg up in the air.

"Dude, is she actually licking her wounds?" I turn and ask Jenna.

"Well, she does need to clean the puke off her leg. Just glad I have it all on video," she holds her phone up giggling. Jenna is so proud of her foresight.

We look up to see Coach Priscilla, try to run out to Chelsea. We are cracking up watching her heels sink into the moist ground with every step. When she finally reaches the 50 yard line, she motions to the ambulance. I'm not sure, but I think I see her mouth the words "*Oh Shit*" in slow motion. I turn back around looking into the stands to see the faces of the crowd in utter disbelief. People are shaking their heads and leaning into each other whispering. I actually see one guy stick his thumb up to his mouth, pinky extended, and tip his head back as a sign that he thinks they've been drinking.

As we watch the entertaining crowd, the ambulance leaves with Chelsea, and the boys come back to the gridiron. Some are shaking their heads, while others are holding their foreheads in embarrassment. It doesn't last long. Dad calls them into a huddle, I hear a loud cheer, and they run back onto the field to play some ball. The mortifying halftime show clearly has no effect on the players. In the first play that the Lions have the ball, their quarterback's pass is picked off by our defense. We run it in for a touchdown. The Miners dominate the second half, and the game is pretty much a shutout.

We're forty seconds away from the end of the fourth quarter. The Miners are up 42 to 6, when we see the assistant coaches, Mike and Jeff, begin an early celebration. They grab the Gatorade coolers and head for Caden and Brody who are relaxing on the sidelines after their nearly flawless game. When the buzzer goes off, the Gatorade finds its way all over the boys. Cheering ensues as Caden grabs the enormous Miner flag and runs it around the track in a victory lap. The band plays the fight song as we all make our way out of the stadium.

"Well, that was certainly entertaining," Jenna smirks, "I wonder if Chelsea Cat will still be going to the dance tomorrow."

"Oh, I'm sure she will. She still has eight lives left." I reply, knowing full well that cats always land on their feet.

CHAPTER 10

EXPECTATIONS OF AN OCTOPUS

JENNA HOLDS MY ARMS OUT to my sides, giving me the once over before Pistol arrives at my front door to pick me up. "We did good," she nods, proud of her handy work. "You can look in the mirror now."

Standing in the mirror, I barely recognize myself. Jenna has definitely polished this rough stone to perfection. We've straightened and curled my long, blonde hair into loose waves and Jenna has lightly brushed the remaining poison oak rash with powder and light coral-hued blush, giving me a nearly flawless complexion. She has perfected my eye-makeup, accentuating my deep blue eyes, and has used her magic mascara to make my lashes look super long. My face and hair help boost my confidence a little, though I'm still on edge because I'm not used to wearing a dress that hits quite so high or hugs quite so tight, but a girl's gotta do, what a girl's gotta do. Those rash-faced man prowlers will not be calling me a nun tonight.

As I spin away from the mirror to give Jenna a "Thank You" hug, the doorbell rings. "It's probably him," Jenna whispers in my ear. "Go kick some booty. Make him drool. When he sees you tonight, he'll know that you're the most beautiful girl in this county. He's not even going to remember that goat roper, CJ," she double clicks her tongue and gives me a wink. "I'll meet you there in just a bit to check on you."

Jenna walks me down the hall. I look up to see Pistol standing in the doorway next to my parents. My heart stops when I see him dressed in sexy-as-hell black wranglers and a crisp white button down dress shirt. It's slightly open at the top, drawing attention to his muscular, clean shaven jaw line. *Holy heart throb. My own personal Luke Bryan. . .* I gulp; heat shoots to my face when he holds out his arms and says, "Wow," pausing to look me up and down. "I need to get me a little hug, Babydoll. You look stunning tonight."

He pulls me in for a tight hug, and doesn't let go. He smells amazing. I am so thankful he looked past the incident with the boys and found it in his heart to take me to the dance tonight. I've missed my handsome cowboy, and can't wait to show him off at the dance.

My trance is broken when I hear my dad clear his throat "Well then," he coughs out, breaking our hug. "Twelve o'clock curfew Missy." He gives me a stern look and then directs his attention to Pistol. "I trust you'll take good care of her young man." My dad says firmly, shaking Pistol's hand in a gesture of good faith.

"Yes sir," Pistol smiles and nods at my dad. "Have a good evening Mr. and Mrs. Woodley . . . No worries, Kaitlyn is in good hands." He loosens his hold, and goosebumps cover my arms when he bends down and whispers into the top of my head, "Let's go Babydoll. I want to see what that sexy dress looks like under the moonlight." He slides my hand into his and walks me out the door.

We get to the bottom of the steps, just out of my parents' line of sight, when I feel Pistol's hands start to slink up and down my thigh, pull my dress up my leg, and grope at my behind. I feel overly exposed and uncomfortable standing out under the streetlight. "Ummm, did you grow a couple extra arms in the last thirty seconds?" I giggle jokingly, trying to brush his hands away and pull down my dress. "Pistol, my parents might be watching us . . . I think we should get to the dance now."

Pistol grimaces and whines, "Damn it girl, you're so high strung all the time. Don't worry about your parents. I told them you were gonna be in good hands and they seemed fine with it," he winks, sliding his hands around my hips again.

"Pistol, you and I both know that this is not what you meant when you were reassuring my dad that I was in good hands."

"Oh, loosen up and have some fun for once. We've been dating for like three months and you haven't even let me go past second base. Am I so unattractive to you that you don't want me to touch you? Cuz I know there's plenty of girls who would jump at the chance to have me as their date . . . and I'm sure they'd be just fine with a little snuggling."

At his harsh words, I feel myself start to stiffen and pull back a little. *Kaitlyn, be nice. You know you've missed him. Give him a chance. Besides, you spent all this time getting ready. You actually look hot for once. This is going to be a great night.* I try to convince myself not to walk away right there. When I tune back into what he's saying, I hear Pistol continue on.

"I mean, doesn't it make you feel kind of weird that I've done more with girls I'm not even dating than I have with you?" He wraps his hands around my shoulders and holds me out at arms length, grimacing down at me like he's trying to solve a complex calculus problem. "I thought things would be different tonight being that I'm still taking you to the dance . . . even after what your brother and his sidekick did to me the other night." He shakes his head looking bewildered, "I thought you'd at least try to make this a little fun for me. Don't you want me to have a good time Babydoll? Come on . . . you owe me that much . . . let's get to it."

His approach with me right now has me off balance, and I'm ready to turn an about-face and high tail it back to my house. I can't believe he's trying to guilt me into acting like one of the Cha Cha girls. I don't even know how to respond to him at this point. Good grief, this guy can turn from romantic to sleaze bag in five seconds flat. Despite his handsome appearance, I'm completely turned off by his presumptuous attitude and incessant groping. *What happened to hand holding and sweet kisses on the forehead? I guess I should've stuck with a nun dress.*

Despite my hesitation, I get into the truck with Pistol and we head to the dance. Once again, I find myself combatting his fondling hand. He's managed to slip it around my left leg, and has worked his way up to the point where I am getting way too uncomfortable. I'm just not feeling it with him after the disrespectful scene on my front porch. His fondling is getting under my skin, so I cross my legs and turn them toward the door.

His tongue clicks with frustration, and I try to distract him by turning up the radio and shouting, "I love this song." *Really Don't Care* by Demi Lovato is blasting through the speakers, and to be honest, I really don't care what song it is, as long as it gives me a reason to bounce around and fend off his attack. I begin to snap my fingers and flail my arms down low by the stick shift to block his ever-growing tentacles from making their way back to my leg.

"What are you doing, Kaitlyn? You're bouncing around like a yo-yo."

"You told me to loosen up Pistol," I laugh. " . . . just trying to do what you said." I plaster on a fake smile and continue snapping my fingers and springing up and down in the seat.

After a few minutes, we come to an abrupt stop in the gym parking lot. The jolt forces me to slam my hands to the dashboard and stop my dancing.

"We're here," he mumbles.

I don't acknowledge the hard landing, or the fact that I almost flew through the windshield. All I want to do is get out of this car and get a little distance between those hands and me. "Cool," I shout, hopping down from the truck and shutting the door too quickly for him to make another move. I practically run up the stairs, letting Pistol lag behind a few steps. My shoe slips off and I have to pause for a minute to put it back on when I hear the patter of his boots rush up behind me. As I stand up, he grabs my waist and spins me into him.

"So, Cinderella, are you going in there without me or something? You didn't even wait for me to lock the truck." A look of defeat spreads across his face, "Look Kaitlyn, if you don't want to be here with me, I can take you home right now," he whines, then pauses with a look of contemplation. "Look, I'm sorry I came on too strong. I just thought with the way you dressed tonight, you were open to a little more . . . action."

Guilt overcomes me. I guess I did go out of my way to try to shatter the nun image tonight. It's my fault he wants to touch what he can almost see. I mean, this thin layer of fabric stretched around me is pretty revealing. Not to mention, I am his girlfriend. I at least owe him some physical contact. I know we're in an awkward place in our relationship right now, and normally I'd be fighting my hormones to stay in the "Good Girl Zone," but tonight it's just not there.

Off in the distance, I hear the laughter of Chelsea's friend, Peyton. When I shoot a quick, side glance in that direction, I can see a group of girls surrounding her. Among them is CJ in all her hog-tying glory. She's standing next to her date, Ty. Her long, silky hair falls down to her elbows. She shakes it back and forth, whipping it out of her eyes and off her shoulders. I recognize her shimmery, silver dress from the rack of skimpy dresses at the boutique. Her matching stilettos give her height over the other girls in the crowd, especially Chelsea, who's slumped over on crutches, as a result of last night's cheerleading fiasco.

I don't know why, but jealousy suddenly overtakes me. There's no way I want this cowgirl to sink her spurs into my boyfriend anymore than she already has. Instantly, I grab Pistol's hand. "Sorry if I gave you the wrong impression. I'm really excited to be here with you tonight." I plant a huge kiss on his plump, pink lips, and draw it out long enough for Chelsea's group to catch the whole show. I can hear the clicking of their high heels getting louder as they move in our direction. The clicking takes a momentary pause, then continues on toward the gym. Pistol doesn't even notice them walk by. *Mission accomplished.*

After a couple minutes, we stop to come up for air. Though I don't feel the intense electricity that once rocked every nerve ending at his touch, his kisses are pleasant, and I still find him incredibly attractive. We pull away and Pistol shakes his head back and forth, shooting me his crooked grin, "Whew, now that's what I'm talking about, Babydoll. I think we're finally on the same page with where we want this night to go." He holds me out, both arms extended, looking me up and down. He releases the caged breath he's been holding, interlacing it with the words, "You are so hot." He reaches to the back of my head and runs his fingers through my hair, giving it a little grasp, and pulling me into his chest. Pistol leans in with another passionate lip lock that fills my core with heat and leaves me gasping for air, " . . . and let that kiss remind you that you're all mine. Now that you know who you belong to, we can go inside." He takes possession of my hand and we enter the dance.

The music is blasting, and people scatter among the room checking out the decorations. Someone has obviously gone to a lot of trouble to bring the feel of the stadium inside. The gym floor is decorated in green AstroTurf and lined out like a football field, with towering balloon goal posts adorning the North and

South ends. Red, Gold, and Black stars dangle from the ceiling. Huge blow up footballs are interspersed among the stars, suspended on invisible lines. The East and West sides of the gym are lined with benches that have been brought in from the field. Large Gatorade coolers sit on the food table, and football helmets are overturned, holding chips and other snacks. Off in the corner sits a photo booth, which is getting its fair share of attention. Lights whip around and splatter against the walls as the disco ball shoots their reflections in every direction.

The music is loud, which doesn't make conversation easy. That doesn't seem to be a problem, since Pistol isn't talking much anyway. He's scanning the room checking out the surroundings as he tugs on my hand, pulling us through the crowd. As we make our way to the other side of the gym, a bit of nervous energy has overtaken me. It seems as though Pistol has high expectations of me tonight; expectations beyond what I can deliver. On top of that, I know that I'm not all that fun as a dance date. Unlike the majority of my classmates, grinding isn't my thing, so I try to dodge the dance floor whenever fast songs play. Luckily, a slow song comes on first. As the lights dim and music slows, Pistol pulls me into the middle of the floor. He holds me so close I can barely move my legs. I struggle to find a place to set my feet. I try to create a little distance so I can maintain my balance, but he clings tighter. "Just work with me here, Babydoll. Relax. I want you to feel what you do to me. I'll do the work." I try to loosen up, just enough that I don't trip and fall.

Again, I feel his hand creeping up the back of my leg. My face flushes with embarrassment as I feel the bottom of my dress slide up. I really don't want to upset Pistol, so I hope that the protective cluster of people surrounding us blocks the view of his hand moving way too high up the back of my thigh. As we sway back and forth, I scan the gym to see if any of my friends are here yet. *Please be here Jenna.* I think to myself, hoping like heck she will come to my rescue. This is way too close.

It's making me feel slutty and I don't like it one bit. As I scan the crowd, I see the Cha Cha girls over by the Gatorade. Even in the dimly lit gym, the reflection of the disco ball illuminates their blistered faces. I'm not sure how many girls are afflicted, but by the looks of them rubbing up and down on the goal posts, I know there's at least fifteen. They're doing their best to mock strippers on a pole, but I know the true story. Those girls are scratching a nasty itch.

"Crap," I jump as Jenna runs up behind me and pokes my sides.

"Gotcha!" she laughs. "So, are you having fun yet?"

I give her the "My Best Friend Already Knows the Answer to That" look.

"Ahhh. Ok." She turns toward my boyfriend smiling, "Hey Pistol. I hear they spiked the Gatorade on the far side of the gym. Would you mind investigating to see if that's just a rumor?" she flicks her head in the direction of the farthest cooler where the Cha Cha's are standing.

"Seriously?" he looks excited. "Sure, I'd be happy to go check them . . . I mean . . . IT out." He looks at me asking, "Are you okay here for a minute, Babydoll? I'm going to see if I can hook us up with a drink."

I smile at him and give him a nod of approval, "I'll be here with Jenna."

He leans in, giving me a soft kiss on the top of my head and meanders across the room.

"Okay Kaitlyn, what's going on?" Jenna asks after Pistol heads off toward the crowded cooler.

"Okay, I know he's really hot, and I'm incredibly attracted to him, but I can't handle him tonight, Jenna. He's expecting me to take our physical relationship to the next level, but I can't go there with him. Letting him kiss and hold me the way he has been tonight is sending him the wrong message, and I don't know how to draw that line without pushing him away. Not to mention, I don't want to upset him. He's my boyfriend and date, and I owe him a good time . . . especially after the boys beat the heck out of him the other night; but gosh darn it, it's like fending off an octopus. His hands are all over me, pulling up my dress, holding me so tight I can't even breathe. I've only been here for twenty minutes, and I'm already exhausted." I let out a deep sigh, and try to catch my breath while I still have a chance.

Jenna crinkles her face, the way she does when she's thinking really hard. "Well, first of all, you don't owe him anything. However . . ." she looks over toward Pistol, "if you're done with him, I can see someone who's willing to take on the challenge." She points in the direction of the Gatorade cooler by the far door.

I look over to see that Pistol has made his way over to the girls. He's definitely locked eyes with CJ who is giggling mercilessly, and holding him on the shoulder. Seeing CJ with her hand on my boyfriend's shoulder ignites some conflicting feelings. I might be confused about putting my own hands all over him, but rage bursts through me when I see another girl trying to steal my guy.

Heat blanches my face as I watch the interaction between CJ and my boyfriend. They look awfully comfortable together, so I can tell they've been this close before. A surge of power shoots down my arms and I reflexively ball my hands into fists at my side. I feel like Popeye after swallowing a can of spinach. I gaze toward them anxiously, wondering how to react. There is obvious chemistry between my boyfriend and his roping partner, and it looks as though she's willing to give him what I am not. However, I resist the urge to stalk over there and peel her hand from his shoulder. My eyes are monitoring the scene unfolding by the cooler when I peer to the right and catch a glimpse of Brody walking toward the group. He's accompanied by one dangling Chelsea Cat, who appears to have fettered herself to my best friend.

I momentarily shift focus from Pistol and CJ to Brody. At first glance, my stomach does a little flip, and I feel a burst of adrenaline launch into my limbs. I'm surprised at the intensity of my body's reaction to Brody. He looks stunning, dressed in slacks, a light button down shirt, and slender tie. He's incredibly handsome and classy looking, but appears mis-matched holding onto Rashy-Chelsea in her uber-revealing, trashy, red, toddler dress. Though my handsome cowboy stands right next to him, I'm drawn to Brody, and feel a tinge of jealousy that I'm not the one on his arm. I struggle to understand why I have completely dismissed Pistol and CJ, and my mind and body are absolutely entranced by my best friend. Though I've tried to beat it away, my attraction to Brody has gotten stronger since the bridge . . . even if I have been beyond angry at him for accepting Chelsea's invitation to this dance.

I see Pistol do a sudden duck and turn out of CJ's hold as Brody approaches with Chelsea on his arm. I can see Brody address him, but I don't see Pistol respond. He turns back toward the cooler and begins to fill two cups. Brody's eyes follow Pistol as he comes back toward Jenna and me.

"Here you go, Babydoll. Sorry it took a while, the line was really long." I take the cup from Pistol, disregarding his little fib about the line, and look beyond him to meet Brody's distant gaze. I've watched him track Pistol's movement up until the moment he reaches me. Once he is at my side, Brody's eyes drift from Pistol and lock on mine. He gives a tiny smile and nod, tipping his cup in my direction. Pistol takes a drink from his cup, releasing a smacking sound. "Well, no need to worry about spiked punch, this stuff is pure sugar water," Pistol sighs with disappointment.

I'm becoming overheated with emotion, and I'm relieved to hear that the punch is safe to drink. As I take my first sip, *Pop, Lock, and Drop It* by Huey begins to blare through the speakers. A flurry of people fly out to the dance floor, including Jenna, who has found her way to Ty. The gym is inundated with grinding teens. I stop looking at the faces of my rubbing, pulsing, dangling classmates, and examine for a moment the dresses; the dresses that Jenna and I had so mischievously rubbed with our brilliant revenge. I'm ecstatic to observe that it's The Cat Club who are mostly wearing the infected attire. As I watch Kiersten grind up and down on Blake with unfathomable flexibility, all I can think is, *Oops, that's gonna get his face.* Next I turn to see Kayla with her legs wrapped around Jesse and I don't even want to think of where he's going to end up with the itch.

Just as I watch Melissa slide down the speaker onto Justin's shoulders, I'm interrupted by Pistol, "Ahem," he fake coughs. "Come on Babydoll, I said I wanted to dance." Pistol tugs on my hand trying to pull me out to the floor.

"Let's catch the next slow dance, Dimples. I'm really not into the grinding thing." I say as sweetly as possible, wrapping my arms around him and sending him my cute puppy dog smile.

"Kaitlyn, come on. I came all the way over here. Just grind with me." He looks down at me with imploring eyes. "You have on the perfect dress for it." He slides his hands down, grabbing the back of my tight little, black dress and snaps it back at my thigh. "It will be fun." Pistol begs, tugging at me once again.

I'm feeling a little stressed out. I don't want to upset Pistol, but I've made it clear from day one that I'm not a marinade. I don't rub myself all over guys, especially not in public. I just wish he'd stop pressuring me. He clicks his tongue, "You're boring as hell at dances. This is stupid," he groans, tilting his head back and closing his eyes. The guilt of not grinding with him strikes me hard when I watch him pinch the bridge of his nose and suck in a deep breath.

I can't take it anymore. I want him to have a good time. "Pistol, if it means that much to you to grind, go ahead. I'll be here finishing my drink."

"Really?" Pistol opens his eyes wide, and looks down at

me with surprise.

With resolve in my voice, I whisper, "Really."

A smile spreads across his face when he chuckles, "I'll be back in a bit."

Not even three seconds have elapsed from the time I give him permission to the time I watch him saunter across the room to Chelsea, Peyton, and gang. He leans over to CJ putting his face right up against her ear. She nods; he grabs her hand, and pulls her out to the dance floor.

Holy Hell! I can't believe my eyes. He's out in the middle of the floor grinding with CJ right in front of me. Her dress is pulled up above her thigh, and I'm pretty sure I just saw him spank her. She's riding his leg like he's a flippin' saddle bronc, bucking, grinding, and sliding all over him. Her hands are holding onto his knee like a bareback rigging, and she's throwing her head back into his chest giggling. When I told him he could grind if he wanted, I didn't think he'd really take me up on it. And I sure as heck didn't think he would go straight to CJ.

Rage overtakes my mind. I set my drink on the table and I bolt like lightning across the dance floor, straight to the feet of the securely tethered "roping team." With everything in me, I push CJ off of Pistol, roaring, "I believe you're riding my cowboy." CJ stands gaping at me in shock as I raise my eyebrows and say, "You're eight seconds are up . . . now, buck off."

With the most exaggerated movement I can gather, I throw my leg over Pistol's, mounting him with an execution that even outshines CJ's. I start grinding up and down on his leg. "Is this what you want, Pistol?" I boom, throwing a glance over my right shoulder. I watch him as his face brightens. He thrusts against me and gropes at my hips, butt, and chest until I am disgusted with myself. After a full minute of grinding, I shake him off and run to the girls' bathroom, where I hide in shame. I don't even look back to see his reaction to me leaving. I cannot believe I stooped low enough to push a girl and get in her face, and I'm completely embarrassed that I had a full audience watching my entire performance. As I hide in the bathroom stall, a tear slips out and rolls down my cheek. I just made an ass of myself, and I ruined everything with Pistol. I never want to leave this bathroom again. Ever.

CHAPTER 11

VICTORY DANCE

AS I STAND IN THE corner of the stall sobbing, I hear a soft, gentle voice make its way from around the corner, into the bathroom. "Pip? Are you in there buddy?"

It's Brody. I can't let him see me looking like this. I work to wipe the tears from my face, trying not to smudge my makeup. I tiptoe out to the mirror to check my face . . . *not too bad . . . The waterproof mascara actually works.*

"Pip, I know you're in there." I hear his tender voice coming from the edge of the doorway. "I can hear your squeaky little mouse steps scampering across the floor. Please come out and talk to me. The girls out here are kinda waiting for me to let them in . . . no pressure or anything."

It's no use putting him off. Brody can be awfully stubborn and I don't want to be responsible for bursting any bladders at the Homecoming dance. As it stands, I've already done enough damage to their dresses. I slowly tiptoe around the wall toward the doorway. When Brody sees my glossy eyes, he opens his arms wide and pulls me into him. With his comforting embrace, control slips away, and a soft whimper escapes me. "Come here buddy, let's move away from the bathroom." Brody drops one arm, keeping the other tightly secured around my shoulder as he walks me into the foyer. The lights are dim in the corner of the room, where we go to talk. I can hear *My Eyes,* by Blake Shelton softly playing in the background. "Good song," he smirks with a little twinkle in his eyes. He sways with me to the music while I try to calm down.

We stop swaying, but Brody leaves one arm on my shoulder, continuing to cradle me against him. He slips his hand under my chin and gently raises my face. He wipes the tears from my eyes and I continue to look down at his hand. I can't face him right now. "Look at me, Pip," he whispers. I pull in a tiny sniffle and raise my eyes to meet his compassionate stare. "I saw your little performance, and I can't deny that it made me a bit uneasy." He pinches his face and shakes his head, "Who was that out there, Pip? Cuz it sure wasn't my best friend."

I shake my head, look down, and begin to cry as shame blankets me once again.

"Aw Pip, listen . . . you don't have to dance like that for him, or for anyone. You're the most beautiful girl in that gym for God's sake. There's not a guy standing behind those doors worthy of your mesmerizing bull-riding moves; especially not a donkey like Pistol Black," he giggles, and squeezes my shoulder trying to lighten my mood.

I give a little chuckle as I visualize the stellar saddle bronc performance I just gave on a jackass. I begin to feel ridiculous, but try to rationalize my behavior. "Brody, it's just that, I feel like I'm not enough for him. I'm not gorgeous and popular with the guys like Chelsea, and I'm not a rodeo princess like CJ. I'm just the little swimmer girl next door, who everyone thinks of as Mother Theresa. Meanwhile, somehow, I've managed to rope this incredibly, gorgeous cowboy, who can have any girl he wants. I try so hard to keep him happy. I don't question rumors or where he goes on weekends. I never put him on guilt trips . . . but I feel like he needs more from me. All I'm doing right now is holding him back from having fun. Brody, if I don't step up my game, he's going to dump me for a truly, beautiful girl who will give him everything he wants."

Brody takes a deep breath and lets it out. He releases my shoulder and gently turns me into him. He softly places his forehead on mine and interlocks our fingers; our arms dangle in between us. He gives my hands a gentle squeeze and his penetrating stare pierces me. His eyes have taken me captive. My heart skips, my breathing shallows, and the air escapes my lungs, soon to be replaced by a rush of fluttering butterflies.

"I want you to listen to me . . . No, don't just listen; hear what I am saying. Kaitlyn Woodley, you are the most beautiful girl I have ever laid eyes on. You shine from the inside out. You are smart, witty, athletic, musical, and downright irresistible. If fate had allowed us to be more than best friends, I would wrap you up in my arms right this second and carry you out of this gym to the magical ballroom you deserve. I wouldn't let anyone remember my beautiful princess riding an ugly ole, undeserving Ass.

I start to giggle, at the image of grinding on an ugly donkey. "Thank you Brody," I sniffle, and reach up to wipe away the last of my tears.

I wrap my arms around his heavily muscled neck and give him a heartfelt hug, burying my face in his chest. As I breathe in my favorite scent, calm overcomes me. It's soothing to feel Brody's warm breath slowly spreading through my hair. It carries his whisper down to my ears, "Pip, you're the most beautiful, best friend a guy could ever have. I'm always here for you." He presses a gentle kiss to my forehead and releases his tight hold on me, taking me by my left hand. He swings it back and forth as though he's not sure if he should let go of me yet. "Hey, I've got an idea," he says excitedly.

"What's that?" I ask curiously.

"We're gonna erase the memory of that last dance performance with a little country swingin,'" he winks at me and smiles. "I can't let you leave here with that silly donkey grinding scene burned into everyone's minds."

"Brody, what about Chelsea? She's your date, remember?"

"Chelsea can wait. She's used to being in line behind you anyway."

Whoa, my eyebrows lift and I take in a quick, sharp breath as my mind tries to grasp what he just said. I'm not exactly sure what Brody meant by it, but the thought of Chelsea waiting in the wings while I swing with Brody makes me light up inside. A rush of excitement strikes me.

The image of watching Chelsea's face during our upcoming performance quickly shatters when I hear Caden's voice behind me. "Hey guys . . . is everything okay?" he asks, with a look of confusion. I'm sure he's wondering where our dates are and why we are together in a dark corner.

"We're all good Dude. Where have you been?" Brody distracts my brother, who is staring at our adjoined hands. "Peyton's been looking for you, I think she's got it pretty bad for you, Dude," he chuckles.

"Well, it was a last minute decision to come." Again, he looks at our hands, shaking his head a little. "If everything's good out here, I guess I'll go find Peyton. She's been texting me since the ball game last night, trying to get me to the dance. Catch you two later."

Caden heads into the gym, leaving us alone once again. "So, you still want to dance?" Brody grabs my hand and twirls me around his finger.

"Sure . . . Let's find Jenna," I whoop. "DJ's love that girl. He'll be sure to play a good swingin' song if she requests it."

I'm feeling a lot better after Brody's pep talk. I'm not sure how he does it, but he's always had a gift for building me back up when I'm feeling small. He takes me by the hand and pulls me back into the gym to search for Jenna. We make our way through the crowds of grinding couples, back toward the food table where the Cha Cha girls are standing. Caden and Peyton are close, sharing a plate of food, as they carry on an apparently, very funny conversation. Just feet from them, I see Pistol in the center of Chelsea and CJ's circle. Chelsea and Pistol are grimacing as they stare down at her glowing phone. *Of course he's made his way back to CJ. I should've expected that.* I'm so upset with him right now that I couldn't care less if he looks pissed . . . *If CJ's the kind of girl he wants, he can have her.*

I peel my eyes from Pistol and spot Jenna over by the speakers dancing with Ty. "There she is Brody," I point enthusiastically through the thick crowd. A mischievous look spreads across Brody's face when he bends down and scoops me off my feet. He throws me over his shoulder. Running toward Jenna, he uses me to knock everyone out of the way, like he's going in for a touchdown. I giggle hysterically as people fly to the left and right, trying to dodge his rushing game.

When they see us, Jenna and Ty stop dancing, and shake their heads in disbelief at the play Brody just made. We are laughing as he spikes me down to the ground and performs his famous touchdown victory dance.

Jenna is grinning from ear to ear when Brody finally stops dancing. "Hmmm . . . was that punch spiked after all? I thought you were going for the goal post for a second there Big Guy. When did your fairy Godmother turn Kaitlyn into a football? And where are your dates?" she asks surprised.

"Ummm . . . where are our dates? We're wondering the same thing." I turn toward Ty, "I'm guessing my date kinda got ahold of yours, huh Buddy?"

"We have ours on a time out. They're all over there by the bench trying to figure out how to get back in the game." Brody answers, pointing toward their huddle. "Let's just say Pistol's had enough personal fouls tonight, and if I have anything to say about it, he's been ejected from this game." He claps his hands together, "Okay, so we need a little favor."

"I'm your girl," Jenna throws her hands in the air.

"Since D.J. Ry Dog seems to love you, we need you to request a song for us. We're done with this grinding stuff; I'm ready to have my childhood dance partner back. More than anything, I want to show that jackass over there that this girl knows how to dance."

Jenna laughs, then pauses in contemplation, "I've got the perfect song for you two." She forms finger guns with both hands and draws them from her hips, double clicking her tongue, as she shoots them toward us. "Get ready friends, I'll be right back."

Brody and I prepare, for whatever song Jenna has in store for us. I'm ecstatic at the opportunity to erase my earlier performance, and to get some dance time with my favorite guy. The thought of our dates briefly crosses my mind, but I dismiss it almost instantly. If Pistol can grind with CJ, then this certainly shouldn't be a problem. As for Chelsea, I'm sure she'll find another dance partner to tangle her crutches around. There never seems to be a shortage of guys where she's concerned.

When the new song starts, the grinding comes to a halt and the dancer's begin to melt away from each other. "What is this crap?" I hear Schuler's voice permeate the country twang. Everyone stands frozen on the gym floor like they've landed on another planet. They're looking around at each other, shaking their heads with confusion. Upturned eyebrows and scrunched up faces glow under the twisting lights.

Brody and I look at each other and laugh, when we recognize the tune Jenna has chosen. As *Country Girl Shake it For Me,* by Luke Bryan blasts through the gym, Jenna jumps up on the speaker at the left of the D.J.'s stage, while Ty jumps up on the right. They start clapping their hands, stomping their feet, and shaking their booties, drawing attention to Brody and me, standing front and center.

Brody sends me a little nod, and grabs my hands. I give my heels a quick kick and accidentally, on purpose, flip them right into the middle of the Cha Cha girls. *I think I've got their attention now.* Brody pulls me in, pushes me away, and pulls me in again, in two quick movements to begin the country swing. We swiftly glide away from the stage to give us some room, when Brody spins me out and spins me back into a dip. The crowd begins to spread away from us giving us space. I can hear Jenna and Ty clapping to the rhythm, and working to get the crowd to join them.

We begin swinging faster and faster as the beat picks up. Brody puts his hand behind his back, letting me know that he's ready for the Pretzel. In a fluid, rapid movement we twist and turn in a circle, spinning in and out, back and forth, arms remaining connected over our heads, around our backs, and back to the front again, throughout the entire dance maneuver. We end the stunt as Brody holds me behind his back, his strong arms extended, bending me into a back dip. He draws me back to the front of him, swinging me a couple more times, releasing one hand and holding his arm out to spot me on a back flip.

I can feel all eyes on us now. The crowd is clapping along and hooting at us, which injects me with a boost of energy. I fly into an exceptionally high back flip over his arm. The crowd goes wild, and I can see an even brighter spark in Brody's eyes. *He is enjoying the heck out of this show.* We perform one more captivating pretzel, and a couple more animated swings, when he lifts his eyebrows and mouths, "Death drop."

"Not sure I remember that, but I can try." I grimace.

"Don't worry Pip, I've got you. Just hang on. You'll definitely feel the drop, but I promise, I won't let you fall. Let's leave this crowd with something to remember," he smiles as he pulls me in for one last swing.

As he releases me, he swings me behind him so we're standing back to back. He gives a quick bend forward, shooting me straight over the top. I roll quickly over his back, landing on my feet so we are facing once again. Again, he releases one hand and holds me out forming a stiff "T" with my body. I plant both feet together, and drop forward to the ground like a crashing airplane. His strong arm keeps me from colliding into the floor, as he steps over the top of me and flips me back into his arms. He throws me up over his head, catches me like he's cradling a baby, and carries me off the dance floor.

Everyone erupts in cheers. I catch a glimpse of Pistol and CJ standing together as Brody carries me past them, never stopping once. I peek over Brody's shoulder and glance back at Pistol as we walk by. With a little smirk, I send him a "Stick that in your Pipe and Smoke it" wave. I mouth, "Bye Bye," and squeeze Brody's handsome neck.

"Where are we going without our dates, Brody? I ask with a giggle.

"To the photo booth, Pip. I never want to forget the look on your face after that little victory dance."

When we get into the booth, Brody sets me on his lap and says, "Let's have some fun with this." He presses the button to begin the sequence of shots. At the first flash, I'm completely shocked when he licks my neck like it's an ice cream cone. I throw my head back in hysterics. I turn around and grab his face, squishing his cheeks into Mr. Chubby, and turn it toward the camera for the next frame. Meanwhile, I turn myself into a blowfish and tilt my head into him. In the third picture, we both stick our tongues out and make rockstar fingers. For the finale, Brody grunts, "Quick . . . twisting-swing position!," just as the flash goes off I spin around on his lap and face him chest to chest, wrapping around him like we used to when we rode doubles on the schoolyard swing. He plants a kiss on my forehead. "Perfect profile pic, Pip," he whispers.

I start cracking up . . ."What's that?" I laugh. "Try saying that ten times fast."

"Okay," he works to restate his perfect alliteration, "Perfect Profect Pip Pip. . Perfect, Pic Pic . . . Perfect frofile fic pic."

I can't help it when I darned near blow snot out my nose laughing. He starts cracking up right alongside me. In the midst of our laughter, the pictures begin to flow through the slot. I reach out to grab the strip of photos, just as I hear the screeching of metal across metal. Light drowns the booth. Chest to chest, and locked onto Brody, I turn my head over my shoulder to see what's going on. Chelsea is standing there, white-knuckled, gripping the curtain.

"What the hell are you two doing? Did you forget you came here with me you jerk? First your hillbilly stomping all over the gym floor with Woodleg Woodley, and now you're molesting her in the photo booth?" she screams. "And if that's not enough, you made this a two-day event by carrying HER across the football field last night and letting HER plant your axe! Well, at least I got to show Pistol your little stunt." She pulls out her phone and holds up a video of last night at the football game. "Ya, he knows all about you two. If you think I'm pissed, take a look around. He already left without you Kaitlyn; you two-timing Floozie!"

Before we can defend ourselves, Chelsea smacks Brody's face with such intensity that I can see the red finger marks outlined on his cheek. She stomps off leaving us both stunned. We look into each other's eyes, straight faced, and then we lose it. We are laughing so hard we begin snorting. The line waiting for the booth joins in the laughter. Brody leans into me and whispers, "Do you think they're waiting to take pics, or watching our show?"

No sooner does he ask, then we hear Schuler bellow, "Holy Hell Dude," we turn to see him slam both hands against the wall of the booth. He leans in, shaking his head. "If this is how shit's shakin' in the booth tonight, sign me up."

CHAPTER 12

LIT

AS WE PULL UP TO my house, I see my bedroom light turn off. "Are your parents still up, Pip?" Brody must've seen my room go dark too. "That's funny," he jokes, "I thought they went to bed at like 9:00 these days. I'll walk you in and let them know you're here safe."

My mind runs through possible scenarios of why my parents may still be awake. "Ya, they're not usually up so late, but they might've waited up to see how the dance went. Or maybe it's because Dad set a midnight curfew, and I'm about a half hour late." *Shoot. I hope I'm not in too much trouble.*

"He gave that jackass a curfew?" Brody laughs . . ." I always knew that man was a good judge of character." He pauses for a moment, clearly getting a kick out of the fact that my dad slapped a curfew on my time with Pistol. "Hey Pip . . ."

"Ya?"

"Wanna know something funny?"

"What Brody?"

"He's never given the two of us a curfew before." He gives

me a little wink and nudges my arm. The smile on his face is glowing as he jokes, "Guess we know who he does and doesn't trust with his baby girl."

We take our time teasing and elbowing each other up the walkway. By the time Brody and I get into the house, all the lights are off. He turns to me looking a bit puzzled. "It doesn't look like anyone's up. I wonder who just turned off your bedroom light," he muses. We walk toward the stairs, and I tiptoe halfway up to see if my parents are awake in their room. Their door is shut and the lights are out. I can hear the ping pong of their snoring, so I know they're not awake.

"Maybe Caden's home. I'll go check." I start to head to my brother's bedroom.

Brody pulls back on my arm and whispers, "Not so fast. I'll go first. Stay behind me." He pulls me behind him and makes his way to Caden's room. He looks back at me. "Nope. I didn't think he was home, yet. His truck's not out front, and it looked like he and Peyton were having a pretty good time at the dance," he grins.

A feeling of unease begins to creep through me. "Didn't you see the light go off in my room?" I ask him nervously.

He pinches his face and nods his head yes. "Let's go check it out," he whispers.

A sudden sinking feeling hits the pit of my stomach, and the hairs stand up on my arms. "I'm not going in there . . . I'm not going in there." I shake my head furiously back and forth, and pin myself to the wall.

Brody pauses for a moment, and looks me up and down. One corner of his mouth turns up in his endearing smirk. I know he is assessing my frantic state, and probably laughing inside at my obvious phobia of the supernatural. "Are you still sleeping on your parents' floor?" he asks incredulously. "Don't tell me you still think there's a ghost in your room?" He chuckles.

I smack his arm. "Shut up Brody. That stuff's real, and it's not funny."

"Pip, there's nothing in your room. Do you need me to sleep on your floor tonight to protect you? Cuz, you know I will. Come on," he takes my hand, "Let's go check it out."

We walk through the dark hallway hand in hand, feeling our way to the light switch. As we approach my bedroom door, I trip over something, jump, and let out a yelp. Brody grabs me. "It's okay, Pip. That was just my foot. I've got you." When we hit the light, I hide behind him, searching my room for anything unusual. Scanning the room from right to left, everything seems to be in place. My clean clothes are still stacked neatly on my desk. My report on teen driving is still face up in the printer. My oversized polka-dot beanbag still sits neatly in the corner with my current novel nestled in one of the folds. My bed is still unmade . . . *wait . . . my bed is unmade?* I take a second look, knowing full well I made it before I left . . . having a clean room was one of the conditions of leaving the house tonight. As I look up toward the pillows, I notice something looks a little off. My giant, fluffy teddy bear, the one that Pistol gave me on our one-month anniversary, doesn't look so big . . . or fluffy. I tiptoe over to my bed, pick him up and gasp. His head has been partially severed from his body, and white stuffing protrudes from his neck. I walk around the bed and look down on the side nearest the wall. My eyes widen as I see his stuffing strewn all over the floor leading to my window. My attention is diverted upward when I feel the cool fall breeze blowing against my face. The window has been left open, and the blinds smack gently against the frame. I am instantly frozen with fear.

My throat goes dry and it becomes increasingly difficult to swallow. *My bed is unmade? My window is open? Someone has been in here.* Fear continues to grow inside of me; my blood runs cold and I can feel it prickling through my limbs, stopping short of my hands and feet. I pull my hands up to my face, covering my nose and mouth, trying to capture a pocket of air so I can breathe. I begin to hyperventilate into my hands. The thought that someone could actually get past my parents and break into my room at night terrifies me. I struggle to find my voice and squeak, "Brody, someone's been in here."

"Stand over here, Pip," he whispers, gently grabbing my shoulders and guiding me up against the wall. "Don't move. I'm gonna check out your closet and bathroom."

When he returns from the bathroom, he holds a photograph of Pistol and me. It's been torn down the middle. "This was stuck to your bathroom mirror." He hands me the torn picture that once hung in the decorative initials above my bed. Pip, you don't have a ghost. You have a deranged boyfriend. I'm gonna castrate that ballsy asshole for putting you through this."

I did not know a heart could shatter so quickly. Seeing my favorite picture of Pistol and me torn in half, hurts more than I care to admit. The breath I've been holding empties from my lungs, and my lips curl downward. I fight the urge to cry. I can't let Brody see me lose it over Pistol again tonight. I turn away from him so he can't watch the battle between my heart and mind playing out on my face. I walk toward my bed to sit down when I hear a text chime from my phone. When I pull it out of my purse, Pistol's name is still flashing across the screen. Before I even have a chance to open the message, Brody is at my side holding his hand out. "Give me your phone Kaitlyn."

I shake my head, "No." Fatigued by the nights roller coaster of events, I begin to succumb to my raw emotions. I'm trying to hold it together, but the first traitorous tear escapes and begins to crawl down my face. "I don't want to make this worse, Brody." I clutch my phone tightly, refusing to give it up. I shake my head thinking back on the events of the evening. "I was already mean to him tonight. I mean, I pretty much flaunted you in his face. He saw the video of Homecoming, and he watched us dancing together, Brody. Then I left the dance without him."
How could I be so cruel after he came all the way over here for

me? The flow of tears increases as I realize how disappointed I am in my behavior. "He's already jealous of our friendship Brody. I just made it so much worse. He's gonna kill me."

Brody comes close and puts his arms around me. "Come on Pip. You know good and well that I am not going to let anything happen to you. Now give me your phone." He wraps his hand around mine, and I hesitantly release the death grip I have around the phone. He takes it from my hand.

An enraged look crosses Brody's face as he reads the text message. Without saying a word to me, he bites his cheek, sucks in a deep breath through his nose, and hits dial. He is breathing hard, and I can see the rage pulsing through the veins in his neck. I have never seen Brody look this angry. His face is red and his nostrils are flared. . . he waits for an answer. He is still holding me, and I can hear Pistol's raised voice booming through the phone.

"What's up slut? Did you finally realize I left you at the dance? Cuz I'm sure as hell not coming back to pick your cheating ass up."

I watch the intensity grow in Brody's expression.

"You listen up, you saggy little ball sac. I've already got Kaitlyn. We're standing knee high in stuffing right now, thanks to your sneaky stunt. If I ever see or hear of you coming close to her again, I will stick my fist down your throat and pull those tiny, little pellets you call balls, up through your mouth, and cut them out like tonsils."

Without waiting for a response, Brody hangs up the phone. He turns into me, "Pip, I am so sorry you had to hear me talk like that . . . but I'm even more sorry this happened to you." He slides his hands to my shoulders and looks me straight in the eyes. "No matter how mean you think you were tonight, you do not deserve this." Brody glances down at the phone in his hand and then over to the teddy bear on my bed. He continues to shake his head as he speaks in a slow soft voice, "Something is off about this guy, Pip. You need to move on. What do you think we should do now?"

I stare at him dumfounded. I search for clarity of mind, but all I can think about is what Pistol said to make Brody so angry. I need to see what that text was about. "Well, for starters, I'll take my phone back," I hold out my hand. He glances down at my phone and quickly deletes the text from Pistol. "Hey, I didn't even get a chance to read that!" I snap.

"Some things are best left unread," he scowls. Contemplation spreads across his face as he stares down at the blank screen and tosses the phone to my bed. Again, he holds my shoulders, and looks me in the eyes. Worry darkens his expression. "Kaitlyn . . . maybe we should call the police, just to be on the safe side."

I stare at Brody, speechless. I can't fathom the thought of getting the police involved over one bad night with Pistol. *We haven't even broken up, and this teddy bear murder might not even be him. Maybe it's CJ or Chelsea. I'm sure they're both a little upset with me.* I finally manage to speak, "And what are they going to do Brody; ask me if I got in a fight with my boyfriend and ripped up the bear he gave me? There's nothing here to prove it was even him." My mind races with questions. *Does Pistol deserve to be turned into the police? I mean how much of this did I bring on myself? Was it even him? Not to mention, that was a very serious threat Brody just made on my phone.*

After sorting through the flood of conflicting thoughts, I continue, "I'm just afraid if we get the police involved, you're the one who's going to get in trouble . . . for threatening to cut his balls out like tonsils." I can't help but give a little chuckle.

A small smirk grows on Brody's face. "I would do it for you, you know . . . cut 'em out." He raises his eyebrows, "You really think I could get in trouble instead of Pistol?"

"I don't know." I shake my head "But, I don't want to take that chance. Your season is going so well, and scouts are going to be looking at you soon. I don't want to draw any negative attention to you. And, I need to focus on Masters. I don't need to lose any training wrapped up in police investigations and court cases. Brody, can we just keep this one to ourselves? I'll talk to Pistol. I'll figure it out." I shake my head latching on to any bargain that will make this go away. "I don't know how to explain all this to my parents . . . and I really don't want to make things worse."

Brody stands there looking down at me with upturned eyebrows. He pinches his lips into a straight line and takes a big breath, "You know, Pip. I'll do this for you, but we need to tell Caden. And, until we get this resolved, you need to have one of us with you everywhere you go. That cowboy is crazy, and this . . ." he picks up the unstuffed bear, dangling it in front of me " . . . is proof."

Brody pulls out his phone and takes a picture of the dangling bear.

"What are you doing?" I ask, worried he may have changed his mind.

" . . . taking a pic . . . evidence to use against this crazy bastard. . . you know, just in case we need it later."

Brody puts his phone away and helps me clean up the stuffing from my dead teddy bear. I'm still shaking as I work my way through my room checking for any more damage. When I pick up the picture, I hold the jagged edges of the two pieces together. While staring at the two of us side by side, the memory of that night floods my mind.

This was the picture we took on the Ferris Wheel last month at the county fair. I reminisce about the soft breeze whipping through my hair, as Pistol took me in his arms and whispered in my ear about how lucky he was to be dating the most beautiful girl in Jefferson County. He was such a gentleman all night, and made me feel like I was the greatest thing that ever happened to him. As we walked around the midway hand in hand, other girls gawked, and some even followed us, but his eyes never drifted from me. He just pulled me close letting everyone know that he was taken. It was the perfect night.

The memory stabs at my heart. The realization that nothing is the same, and we will never be that couple again, hits hard. Pain begins to sear my throat. Knowing that our relationship is probably over, and this is the last time I will ever see this picture, I begin to cry again, not because I want him back, but because the Pistol I thought I cared about so deeply, never even existed. That Pistol was merely made of bits and pieces of a good day here and there. The real Pistol, the one I have come to know, is a self-centered, hedonistic jerk. He might be the hottest cowboy in Jefferson County, but his beauty is clearly skin deep.

As I drop the picture down into the trash, Brody's hand gently brushes mine. I feel his soft grip wrap around my fingers. "Don't waste your tears on this guy. You're too good for him anyway." He takes me into another hug. We begin to rock back and forth, swaying for several minutes. The silence is broken when Brody starts to hum one of my all time favorite songs, Keith Whitley's *When You Say Nothing at All.* He has such a beautiful tenor voice. My mind begins to drift away from the heartbreak of the evening and focus only on Brody. My neck relaxes when I rest my head on his welcoming chest. His sooth-ing hum, and the warmth of his embrace spreads through me, blanketing me with peace. My new sense of calm has made me keenly aware of the comfort of his warm touch against my lower back. He gently sets his smooth cheek next to mine. My heart skips, and I swallow a little gulp as the heat in my body begins to rise. His voice has me captivated and entranced as he begins to softly sing in my ear . . "the touch of my hand says I'll catch you if ever you fall. Ya, I know you best, shhh," he holds his finger to my lips, "now don't say nothin' at all . . ." His soft whisper into my ear has scattered goosebumps up and down my body.

"Heyyy, you changed the lyrics," I giggle, looking up at Brody, who is smiling down at me with a new twinkle in his eyes.

"Yep, you make me want to change the lyrics to a lot of songs, Pip. You know what . . . come over here." In one motion, he pulls his arm from behind my back and slides my hand into his. He tips his head in the direction of my bed, and tugs for me to come with him. His face flushes a subtle shade of pink and he becomes unusually quiet. *He's not talking . . .* His extended pause worries me. *Why does he seem nervous? Is he about to tell me I'm too much work? Or maybe I'm scaring him off with my clinginess tonight. He's had enough of me and my Pistol problems, I know it. I can't lose him . . . not now.* I take a deep breath and let him pull me down onto his lap.

With my arms wrapped around his neck, we sit for a moment more in silence, listening to our syncopated breathing. I'm holding onto him with everything in me, wondering if this will be his goodbye. For a second, I think I can hear Brody's heart beating; I can certainly feel it thrumming against mine. He pulls his hand up to my back and sets the other one down on my lap. When the silence becomes unbearable, he takes in a deep breath, "Pip, we need to talk."

I draw out the word "Okayyy," trying to stall the impending conversation. *This is it.* "You're scaring me Brody. What do you need to talk to me about?"

"I think you know what I'm talking about . . . this . . . this," he moves his hand back and forth between us, "this thing that you and I have been doing . . . the playful flirting, subtle yet intentional brushes of our skin, oh and my favorite . . . trying to sneak glimpses of each other in the hallways at school. And don't say you haven't noticed, because I've seen you looking when you think I'm not paying attention."

I begin to smile and flush in embarrassment. I can't believe he's caught me watching him.

When he sees my smile, and the redness filling my cheeks, he pulls my chin into his hand. He returns my smile and says with renewed confidence, "The thing is, Pip, even if you think I'm not, I am paying attention. It's hard not to."

Whoa. I think to myself. This is not where I thought this conversation was going.

Brody continues, "I wake up thinking about you, and I go to sleep thinking about you, and all I want to do is put myself wherever I know you'll be during the day. My happiest hours are the ones when I get to be near you."

"You actually try to see me during the day?" I smile. "I thought you were trying to avoid me . . . since . . ."

"Look, I know you heard your brother warn me to stay away from you. Believe me, I've tried. I even took Chelsea to the dance . . . but there's nothing there. All I did the whole time was watch over her shoulder looking for you. Pip, you're it for me. I can't seem to feel with anyone, the way I feel when I'm with you."

I'm not sure how to respond with anything except for a disbelieving smile. He leans in and sets his forehead against mine.

"What are we gonna do, Brody?"

"I know what I want to do," he smiles; his mouth is so close I can feel his warm breath against my face.

"What's that?" I whisper back, slowly biting my lip.

"I can't tell you," his lips curl up into a cute, little grin.

I release my lip. "You can't?" I raise my eyebrows, looking him right in the eyes.

"Nope." He shakes his head, not breaking contact with my forehead. "I have to show you," he whispers.

Our eyes are locked, staring for what seems like an eternity when he pulls his forehead away from mine. Slowly, he tilts his head to the side and leans back into me. His warm breath carries the scent of spearmint. That minty smell, combined with his Abercrombie cologne, swirls around my head, sparking my senses.

Fireworks ignite inside of me as I feel his soft lips gently brush against mine for the first time. Without pulling away, he pauses momentarily, as though he's waiting for permission to continue. I sit still, spellbound, entranced by his scent, and memorizing the feel of his perfect lips. He pulls his head away and looks down at me, lifting his eyebrows. I can't help but smile. I am completely lit up inside. "Oh, that smile . . ." he whispers. "Aww what the hell . . ." he shakes his head. "I give up."

I feel his arms wrap me tighter as he brings his soft, warm lips back to mine. He opens his mouth slightly, pulling my bottom lip back into his. He tugs on it with a tiny nibble, giggles, and lets it go, looking down at me again. I don't know what he has done to my senses, but I can't let this stop. I lean back into him, and cover his lips with mine. At the first brush of our tongues, I become breathless. The butterflies take flight, and work themselves into a swirling cyclone inside my belly. They pound at my stomach and chest, fighting to escape. I've never been kissed like this, and I can't help but wonder if I've been doing it wrong up until now. It is so easy with Brody, our mouths move in perfect rhythm. As our tongues lightly brush back and forth, and begin to swirl, I become light headed. I'm completely intoxicated by his scent, the natural ease of our movements, and the comfort of his embrace. Brody slowly pulls away, placing gentle kisses up my neck until he reaches my ear. My skin is on fire from the tiny trail of nibbles he's left along the way. The thumping of my heart is soon drown out by his soft whisper tickling my ear, "Wow, Pip . . . I think I just had my first real kiss."

I am speechless, breathless, and my mind has been invaded by an army of hormones. I've never felt ANY-THING like that in my life. "So, can you remind me how to breathe, cuz I can't seem to do it right now?" I gasp in a whisper.

"I would . . . but you just left me speechless," he gasps. Breathing heavily, he sets his head back on my forehead, and pulls his hands back around me. "Did that really just happen?"

"I think so," I giggle.

Brody leans into my ear and whispers, "Pip, you have no idea how long I've been holding that one in . . . I've thought about it; imagined it since we were in junior high, but never, in my wildest dreams, did I ever think it could feel that incredible to kiss my best friend."

I'm stunned at his admission, and sit quietly on Brody's lap, while we work to calm the aftershock of our first kiss. Our breathing is still labored and we maintain our tight hold on one another. Again, he leans into me, gently resting his forehead on mine.

Comforting silence surrounds us, when suddenly, the pressure of a set of praying hands comes down between us, dividing our heads like a music conductor cutting off an orchestra. We look up to see Caden standing over us. He holds our heads apart, shooting us a searing glare. Silence continues to fill the room, but it's not so comforting anymore.

CHAPTER 13

GAMES

"SO THE RUMORS ABOUT THE two of you turning the photo booth into a love shack are true?" he spits out. "It's time to come clean guys. Holding hands in the dark corner, putting on a show worthy of *Dancing with the Stars,* and now I walk in to find my sister, our best friend, sitting on your lap? Look at you two! Your heads are glued together like a damn peanut butter and jelly sandwich! What is going on between you two? Do not play games with me. I want the whole story."

"It's not what it looks like, Cade. Kaitlyn's had a super rough night, and I'm just here helping her through it."

I watch the anger building inside of Caden when he shouts, "Ya, I've seen you 'helping girls through things,' Brody. My sister doesn't need your kind of help."

Brody looks a little insulted, when he replies, "Just listen for a second, Caden. Kaitlyn is not just some girl. She's my best friend, and your sister. Dude . . . she's our Stinkerbell, remember? We're her Lost Boys. I'd do anything to protect her, and she needs me right now . . . No, she needs us!"

Confusion shrouds Caden's face. "Dude, you're losing it . . . That was a game we played when we were like eight . . . What are you talking about?" Caden shakes his head and rubs the side of his face.

"Well for starters," Brody holds up the half-decapitated bear. "Pistol got mad at Kaitlyn at the dance, snuck in her room tonight, and left her this nice surprise. We found it when we got home. Its neck was slit, and the stuffing was all over the floor. He also tore their picture in half, and left it pinned to her mirror like a sweet little love note. She was pretty shaken up Dude. He got in here while your parents were sleeping upstairs. That guy has some serious balls."

Caden scans the room, shaking his head. "Well what did you do?"

"I called him and threatened to castrate him . . . He does not need to be carrying around balls that big. You know I'll do it too . . . and if you saw the way he was treating your sister tonight, I'm sure you'd bring the knife and help me."

"So, he broke into our house?" Caden asks incredulously. "That seems pretty serious, Bro. Why did you clean up the mess? Now there's no evidence to show the police when we call."

"That's the problem. We decided not to call."

"You are kidding me. My sister is in danger and you decide not to call the police?" Caden shakes his head in disbelief. "I'm really starting to question your judgement here."

"Well, we can't prove it was him. A lot went on tonight, and since I threatened him, we think I can get in trouble."

"Seriously?" Caden grimaces, and releases a deep breath.

"It will mess up everything for our football season, Caden. Plus, Kaitlyn doesn't want to take time away from swimming tied up with legal issues. She has a really good shot at qualifying for Masters this fall, and it would distract from everything she's been working so hard for."

"Ya," I chime in. "If I know Pistol, it will just stoke the fire. He'll be furious. I mean, I don't even know for sure if it's him. Caden, if we let it go, he'll probably just stay away, and this could be a one-time temper tantrum. He's probably just mad and jealous. He'll get over it. He always does."

"Well, who's gonna protect you if he doesn't get over it, T? Or, if it's someone else, then what? Have you really thought this through?" Caden stares at me with a look of concern.

Brody sets his hand on Caden's shoulder. "I think we can handle this, man. We just need to stay with Kait and make sure she's protected until this jackass calms down. He doesn't even go to school with us. He's not around that often. It shouldn't take long if we just leave it alone."

"Ya, besides, I think he's into CJ anyway. He's probably already over me. If it was him, he was just getting revenge for bruising his ego at the dance."

Caden pauses in contemplation, and then shakes his head in resignation. "Okay, guys. I'll trust you on this. But it better not come back to haunt us. And Brody . . . sorry I lost it when I saw you and T together. I should've know you wouldn't cross that line with my sister . . . especially after our talk the other night."

Brody sends a quick glance my way and takes an audible breath. I can tell he's not ready to talk to my brother about "us" yet. He turns his head toward Caden and gives him a slight nod. "Well, now that you're here to take care of our girl, I'm gonna head home. My parents are going to start wondering where I am." He gives me a hug, "Night, Pip . . . stay safe, huh?" He lifts me off his lap and sets me down beside him. I feel the bed rise and a part of me empty, as he stands up, gives my hand a tight squeeze, and moves toward my bedroom door. He looks back at my brother, "Take care of her Dude." He gives Caden a fist bump and retreats down the hallway. His footsteps become faint as he nears the front door. I hear it creak open and then close.

I sit in silence looking at my brother, who is glancing around my room shaking his head in disbelief. I am full of mixed emotions. An odd combination of fear, anxiety, and butterflies swirl inside my stomach. Caden turns toward me, "Are you gonna be okay T?"

"Ya, I'm fine."

"Are you sure, Sis? It seems like you've been through a lot tonight. Is there anything you still need to talk about? The dance? Pistol? Damages to your room? I'm all ears you know."

"I'm okay Cade Monster . . . We can talk in the morning. I'm sure you have just as much to tell me as I have to tell you. Besides, you look tired. You should probably get to bed."

"Well, if you're sure . . . everything looks clear in here. I'll check the doors and make sure they're locked. Let me know if you need me, Sis. I'm just down the hall."

"Ok, we'll catch up in the morning. I want to know all about your night with Peyton." I smile, raising my eyebrows up and down.

He gets his goofy little grin, and I know he is smitten. "What happens at the Homecoming dance, stays at the Homecoming dance!" he winks, taps the door jam, and heads off to his bedroom.

Alone for the first time tonight, uneasiness begins to crawl inside my mind. With my parents asleep, Caden off in his room, and Brody gone, dead silence seeps through the house, finding its way into my bedroom and into my head. I try to take my mind off of the eerie feeling by busying myself with the task of getting ready for bed. I slip into my bathroom to brush my teeth and change into my pajamas, when I hear the floor creaking just outside the door. I freeze and hold my breath, listening for any more movement. The creaking stops, and I whip around when I hear the clanking of the blinds against the window. My heart is racing, and I begin to panic. I sense movement outside of my door. I grab my phone and run into the shower, pulling the curtain shut. Slumping down into a ball, I work to stifle my panicked breathing. *Oh my goodness. What was I thinking getting in the shower? Now I'm stuck here with no escape.* I hope I'm just imagining this. . . but, I hear footsteps.

My phone chimes. *Crap! That was loud.* I fumble to turn it to vibrate, when I see the text that comes through.

Brody:
Pip? Are you there?

I'm sweating and shaking so badly my fingers slip when I try to text back. I freeze again at the sound of more footsteps. I grab my shaving cream to use as a weapon, and bury my head in my arms. I'm huddled in a ball shaking when I hear the shower curtain pull back. My automatic reaction is to raise the can and shoot right into the face of. . .

"Howy cwap Plip, you got it in my mouf!" Brody, flails his arms trying to stop the projecting stream of shaving cream. I'm so terrified, and flustered at him for scaring me, that I hold my finger down until I've emptied the entire can into his face. He finally turns around, gagging, spitting, and hacking into the toilet. I watch in stunned silence as he moves toward the sink to rinse his mouth and wash his face. A nervous laugh escapes me when he turns around after several minutes of suffering. "Well at least I'll have fresh, citrussy breath tonight, *kaahhkkk,*" he chokes.

Even after the bit of comic relief, my nervous system is still shot. Trembling, I try to push myself to my feet. My legs and hands are shaking so badly, I drop the empty can of shaving cream to the floor. Brody reaches under my arms and helps pull me up. Once I've gotten my footing, I smack him on the arm. "You scared the crap out of me Brody!" My high squeaking voice, squeals, "What are you doing here?"

"I didn't feel right about leaving you alone tonight . . . and judging from your appearance, I was right. You look terrified, and," he says grinning, "Obviously, I need to come protect you since shaving cream is the best weapon in your arsenal."

"What was I supposed to do? I was stuck in the bathroom when I heard my floor creaking and the blinds rattling."

My heart is still racing with fear from the second break-in of the evening. This night has completely shredded my composure, and I feel myself start to break. Overwhelming anxiety, sends a nervous tremor through my core, extending into my limbs. Dizziness, faintness, and nausea, overtake my body. Stinging tears pound at the backs of my eyes. Tears stream down the sides of my face, and I find it hard to breathe.

As I gasp for air, Brody takes my shaking body in his arms and holds me tightly. He bends down, scoops me off my trembling feet, and carries me across the room. He sits down on the edge of the bed, pulling me close onto his lap. As I sit there whimpering, he pulls my face into his chest. He kisses the top of my head, whispering, "It's okay Pip. I couldn't let you be alone. I know how scared you are. I didn't mean to make it worse. I should've texted you before I snuck in. Shhhhh . . ." He rubs his hand up and down my back. "You're okay, I've got you now," he whispers, "You aren't alone. I'm gonna stay with you as long as you need me. Shhhhh."

He cuddles me into him, rocking me gently until he feels my body calm. When I finally relax, he stands me up with him. "Let's get you tucked in my little pumpkin," he chuckles, tugging at the cute Jack O' Lantern embroidered on my pajama top. He pulls back the covers and helps me into bed. "I'll be right down here next to you," he says as he slides down to the floor, resting his back against my bed.

I lie in silence for a few minutes. I still feel uneasy being so close to the window. And, I can't help but feel like someone will come jumping out of my closet any minute. I stare at the dark corners of my room, and know I won't be falling asleep any time soon. I know this would be so much worse if he hadn't come back, but Brody's mere presence in the room is not helping my anxiety. He is too far away to make me feel safe. After a few minutes of unrest, I can't help but reach out to him, "Brody?"

"Ya?"

"I'm scared."

"I know, Pip. I'm right here."

"Brody?"

"Ya?"

"I can't see you . . . I need to be able to see you," my voice is still trembling.

I hear the rustling of his clothes as he stands up and looks down at me. "I'm here, Pip." He holds out his hand, and I reach out for him. As he curls his warm fingers around mine, electricity shoots through my hand and straight to my belly. I can't be positive, but I'm pretty sure he feels it too, when he gives my hand a quick, tight squeeze. Then he loosens his hold and begins tracing his thumb around the palm of my hand.

"What're you writing Bro?"

"It's a secret message. You have to figure it out," he softly whispers down to me.

"Okay, do it again." He begins to trace. The soft tickle of his touch is soothing and calms my nerves. I like his little game. It's taking my mind off my fear. I concentrate on the movement of his thumb and I almost swear he's writing words, not drawing pictures. I concentrate really hard as he repeats the pattern . . .

D
R
E
A
M
O
F
M
E

Wow . . . he wants me to dream of him. A new spark of electricity pops inside of me as I contemplate what to do. *Should I?* After a few seconds, I lift the covers, then I give his hand a little tug, pulling him down onto the bed.

"Get in here," I whisper as I pat the mattress next to me.

"Are you sure, Pip?"

"I cannot have my best friend just standing around while I dream of him."

"Well, I will do anything to keep you safe and make you feel better . . . even if it means getting my ass kicked by Caden."

"I'll lock my door, and we'll make sure to get you out before he gets up in the morning. I just won't be able to sleep tonight if you're not right beside me."

I wonder if he can feel me trembling lying next to him.

"I've got you, Pip. You can stop shaking now."

I can't believe he feels it. The thing is, I no longer think I'm shaking because of my fear of the break-in. I'm shaking because the most handsome, protective, best friend a girl could ever hope for, is lying right beside me in my bed. Brody pulls me into him, slipping his arm beneath my neck, and tucking me into his side. He combs his fingers through my hair, holding onto me tightly, and whispers, "Everything's gonna be alright. I've got you my little Pumpkin."

We lie there for a moment, when I hear his whisper, "Pip?"

"Ya?"

"Follow your dreams . . . wherever they lead, you know I'll be there waiting for you."

A smile spreads across my face. We lie there listening to our soft rhythmic breathing breaking the silence of the night. A sense of calm comes over me and I drift off to sleep in his arms.

CHAPTER 14

SECRET GLANCES

MY EYES FLUTTER OPEN AS the brisk, fall breeze drifts in through my window. When I turn my head toward my nightstand, I catch a glimpse of the bright red numbers blaring from my alarm clock. I rub the blurriness from my eyes, and take a second look. "Holy crap Brody," I whisper, jostling him back and forth, "It's 9:00 and my door isn't locked! Brody. . . Brody . . ." I rock him back and forth, until a low grumble comes bellowing from deep in his throat.

"Pip? What did you just say? I couldn't really hear you," he whispers back.

"I said, it's 9:00! You're still in my bed! I fell asleep before I locked the door . . . We've gotta get you out of here!"

Brody's eyes pop open and he jumps up startled with the realization that we could be seen by my parents, or even worse, Caden. In his panic to jump out of bed, Brody knocks the lamp off my nightstand. It falls to the floor with a thud. Within seconds, I hear footsteps coming down the hall. "Quick . . . hide!" I whisper frantically.

Twisted up in the sheets from my bed, Brody clumsily scurries toward the closet. He dives to the back, out of view from my bedroom door, just as it creaks open. My mom peeks her head into my room, glancing around, "Everything okay in here? I heard a thud."

I can feel the color drain from my face. *Quick think . . .*" Ya, I just went to hit my alarm and knocked over my lamp instead. Sorry about being so loud."

"You needed your alarm? Geez, it's 9:00 on the Saturday morning after Homecoming. Your brother's still sleeping. It's okay to sleep in every once in a while Kait. Life's not a race you know."

"I know. I just want to go for a morning run."

"You're not going to wear yourself down now, are you? Didn't you have a late night?"

Trying to catch my breath, I gasp, "Mom. I'm fine. I've got to cross train. Masters are coming up. And. . . no, not really. I came home just after midnight." Mulling over last night's events, I try to play it cool and hide the disappointment in my voice.

"Well, how was the dance? Did you have a good time with Pistol?" my mom asks, smiling inquisitively.

"It was okay, nothing worth talking about. We went, we danced, and Brody gave me a ride home."

"Really? Our Brody?" she asks surprised.

"Ya . . . It just turned out that Pistol needed to leave early and Brody was coming this way. Since I didn't have my car with me, he gave me a ride."

"Oh, okay . . . I love that boy. We are lucky to have him you know . . . He's just like a second brother to you."

"Uh huhhhh," is all I can say in response to the "brother" comment. Lord knows that is not what I'm thinking about that gorgeous closet monster, who has my heart skipping a few beats right now.

"Well . . . if you need to talk about it, you know I'm here."

I can sense the disappointment in her voice, and know she would like to hear more about the dance, but I really need to release my handsome hostage. He must be suffocating about now.

"Thanks Mom. I'm gonna change so I can run, okay?" I say, trying to get her out of the room so I can figure how to sneak Brody out of my house.

When she turns to leave, I shut the door behind her, locking it this time. I tiptoe across the room to the closet.

"Brody," I whisper. "Brody, you can come out now."

When he resurfaces, I am in awe of his non-brotherly appearance. He is shirtless, and I'm astounded by his chiseled abs. I actually find myself counting them until I'm distracted by the sight of his gym shorts hanging low on his waist. I can't take my eyes off of his perfectly toned, hot, body.

"Pip? Are you enjoying the view?" he chuckles. I raise my head quickly, just in time to find him cocking his head back and looking at me with pleasure. His lips curl up in his endearing smirk, and his eyes are sparkling with amusement.

I feel the heat rise in my face. *Oh my goodness . . . he caught me staring again.*

"Did you hear your mom?" he questions playfully. "She loves me, like a son . . . that's so sweet." Then he stops and looks at me with intrigue. "But, you're not looking at me like a brother . . ." he snickers, then lifts his hand gently up to my chin to push my mouth closed. He smiles down at me and lets go, "That's better."

I'm mortified, that once again, I've been caught gawking at my best friend; not to mention, my subliminal fascination, left my mouth hanging wide open. I am so embarrassed that I've been rendered speechless.

"It's okay, Pip. I love when you look at me like that. Come here." Brody pulls me into a hug. We stand there for a short while holding each other loosely. His chin rests on the top of my head.

He finally breaks the silence. "I would love to stay here with you like this all day, but I'd better get out of here before we have some explaining to do. Listen Pip, if you need anything today, I'm just a text away. Make sure to let me know. I'll keep my phone on me."

"Thanks, Bro. I appreciate how safe you make me feel. Thanks for staying with me last night. You're the best, best . . . ffffriend a girl could have." I give him the biggest hug I can manage. I love how strong he feels when he holds me tight. I could stay in his arms forever.

"So we're still in the ffffriend zone, huh?" he chuckles, ribbing my stuttering over the word "friend."

"Bro, you're more than a friend to me. You know that right?"

"I know Pip . . . It just feels good to hear you say it. You're more than a friend to me too. If you haven't figured it out by now, you should probably know that I like you. . . like a lot."

"Well, you should know that I like you back . . . like a lot," I giggle.

"We're gonna have to figure out what to do about Caden. He's not gonna take this well," I whisper softly.

"We'll work on that . . . for now, I'd better get out of here."

We hug one more time, pull open the blinds, and I send him quietly out my window.

He hasn't been gone for two minutes when I hear knocking on the glass.

"Brody? What are you. . . ?"

"No it's not Brody!" I hear Jenna's sassy voice make her way into my room. I walk over and look down to the ground. "So are we not using the front door anymore, Bestie? I just saw Brody using this secret escape route! Jenna says, pointing at my bedroom window. "What is going on?" she squeals with curiosity. "Was there a fire, or was someone taking the walk of shame this morning? Never mind," she shakes her head, "We'll get to that in a minute; we have a lot to talk about. Help me in, I want to try out the new entrance, but I'm not quite burly enough to make it all the way up there."

I reach down grabbing Jenna under her arms. She climbs up the siding, catches her foot on the windowsill, and falls through the window, plummeting onto the floor. She sits giggling on all fours looking up at me as I hold up four fingers on my right hand, judging her highly acrobatic entrance.

"Gotta say, Brody's entrance was a little more graceful." I laugh, "But I guess he couldn't afford to be that loud at one in the morning."

"Shut up! No Way . . . What was Brody doing in your room at one in the morning . . . and . . . why did he come back this morning?"

I can't answer. Silence fills the room for several seconds when I finally see recognition in her eyes. Her mouth drops in awe.

"Nooooo, he stayed the whole night in here?" she pauses, widening her stare, and looking back and forth between my door and me " . . . and he made it out alive? Holy crap, you'd better start talking. And, you can't leave ANYTHING out."

I proceed to tell Jenna about my night with Brody, my dead teddy bear, my ripped up picture, and Brody's threat to Pistol. She seems shocked when I tell her we decided not to call the police. "The thing is, I'm not sure if it was even him. It could've been Chelsea or CJ. I think we may have made a lot of people mad last night."

"Well," Jenna replies, "I can tell you one thing; after you left, a lot went down. That's what I came over to talk to you about. I saw them making out, Kaitlyn."

"Who?"

"Pistol and CJ. After your stellar performance with Brody, which by the way, was the talk of the dance, Pistol ended up with CJ. They disappeared for quite a while, but then resurfaced grinding out on the floor. Her dress was all the way up to her waist! Gross! I wanted to puke . . . Then I saw them make their way into the corner, where he proceeded to shove his tongue down her throat. They were all over each other, Kaitlyn. They took off right after . . . together."

I stare at Jenna, not knowing what to say. She's just confirmed that my boyfriend is cheating on me with CJ. A pang of jealousy and anger start to swirl inside of me. I know I overheard Chelsea talking to CJ about messing around with him, and I had my suspicions, but it feels terrible to hear my best friend was an eyewitness to them grinding and making out . . . on our date. I start to wonder how long this has been going on. Judging from her response, I'm sure Jenna is reading the disgusted, yet puzzled look on my face.

"Oh, sorry. I hope I'm not being insensitive. I just figured with the way you danced with Brody, and him staying the night in your room, that you're pretty much done with Pistol. Are you okay?"

"Ya, I'm okay, just thinking." Another haunting notion pops into my mind, "Jenna, if Pistol was with CJ, who do you think broke into my room?"

I can see her mind reeling, "Well, I know it wasn't Chelsea. She and Peyton were with your brother until after I left. They were having a helluva time. I think Caden really likes Peyton. There were lots of sparks last night. It was actually kind of cute."

"Sparks?" I'm very curious about my brother's newly developing relationship with Peyton.

"Ya, like I could see fireworks shooting off their noses from the friction of their eskimo kisses. It was kind of intense." Jenna suggests, biting her lip and shrugging her shoulders.

"What do you think of Peyton?"

A look of contemplation spreads across her face as she pauses a moment before answering, "Well, I don't think she's like the rest of her crowd. She's actually pretty sweet. Caden wasn't even grinding with her. I think he truly respects her, Kaitlyn. He was so cute. After he watched you dance, he was trying to swing dance like Brody. She didn't even give him heck when they got all tangled up and fell to the ground during the Pretzel. She just went with it. I could tell they were having a great time."

"So watching her and my brother for one dance has you convinced she's alright?" I ask incredulously.

"No, Ty and I hung out with them a lot, and she's pretty cool. She has a sense of humor. There's a brain in there. You might actually like her."

"Ya, I guess I've never heard anything bad about her. It just scares me because she's so close to Chelsea, and we both know *HER* character. I just think the company a person keeps, can say a lot about them. Well, I trust your judgement, but I'm keeping a close eye on that relationship. I will not have my brother's heart clawed out by one of those prissy kitties."

"Na . . . I think she's okay . . . let's give her a chance. Ty seems to think she's decent too."

"Ahhhh, so you and Ty, huh?"

Jenna smirks and becomes a little starry-eyed.

"You look a little smitten. I know you didn't go to the dance with him . . . so how did you end up together?"

"Kaitlyn, he is the most handsome, sweetest guy I have ever met. So you know how I've been sorta stalking him at school, hanging around the gym, and peeking into the locker room? Well, I think he's kinda been doing it back. Anyway, I was dancing up on the speaker scanning the crowd. Every time I spotted him, I caught him watching me. As soon as our eyes would meet, we'd both look away. But we knew we were watching each other. And then, every time I saw a girl go up to him, she'd walk away with her head down. Finally, our eyes met, and locked. When we didn't look away, I could see his huge dimples pop out from across the room. He smiled, and didn't take his eyes off me. Then, he pointed at me, and motioned for me to come over to him. My heart just about fell out of my chest. Do you know how long I've been working to get his attention? Anyway, when I finally got up the nerve to go over and ask him to dance, he said, '*I knew if I sent enough of them away, the right girl would show up eventually. You know, Miss Jenna, I don't like to dance, but I've got a special one in me that I was saving just for you.*' Kaitlyn, he was waiting for me!" Jenna squeals. "I felt like I was in a fairy tale. I'm pretty sure I could feel Fairy Godmother sprinkles zapping me when he grabbed my hand, and pulled me out to the dance floor. And for not liking to dance, girl you should see him move. That boy can shake it."

I am so excited for my best friend. I know she has liked Ty since we all hung out at my house last year when my dad had the end-of-season football barbecue. He is a pretty great catch, I have to say. He's the center on the football team, handsome as heck, and has the best heart of any guy I know. In his spare time, he helps take care of his little diabetic brother, and is a volunteer counselor at some of the Kelsey Creek Children's Camps.

"Kaitlyn, we danced together all night, and he asked me if we could set up a movie night this weekend with the whole gang. I think he might actually want to get to know me!"

Our conversation is interrupted by the chime of my phone. I pick it up and look at the message, thinking it's Brody checking on me. "Hold that thought," I say holding up my finger and looking down at my cell.

> Pistol:
> I saw you last night. I didn't know you were allowed to have those kind of sleepovers. How long has this been going on Kaitlyn?

"Oh my goodness, Jenna it's him," I hold out my phone so

she can see the text from Pistol.

Jenna's jaw drops in disbelief. "That's creepy Kaitlyn. How did he see you?" She sounds worried.

"I'm not sure. I thought I shut my window and my blinds after Brody came in. Holy Hell . . . What do you think he saw? Do you think he was in my house?"

"Think Kaitlyn. Is there a way he could've seen you from the outside? Could he have seen Brody sneak through your window? Maybe he's just making it up, to see if you confess to something."

"No, I'm positive my blinds were shut. I had to open them for Brody to climb out this morning . . . and Caden made sure to lock all the doors after the break in."

I'm in a panic, my breathing has accelerated, and I can feel heat spreading into my face. I pull my cool hand to my warm forehead, and wipe away a bead of sweat. There is no possible way Pistol could've seen Brody and me. Fumbling for an explanation, I ask, "Wait, Jenna, you don't think he saw Brody leaving my room this morning, do you?"

"I don't think so. There was nobody around when I saw him climb out your window. It's the Saturday morning after Homecoming, Kaitlyn. That's one of the latest nights of the year. Everyone is sleeping in."

The thought of Pistol sneaking around my bedroom late at night or early in the morning scares the heck out of me. I mean, I know he's possessive, but creeping around and spying on me takes it to a whole new level.

Jenna purses her lips and points at my phone. I focus on the lines in her brow as she shakes her head back and forth. "Do not respond to that text. You need to tell Caden and Brody. They might be able to figure this out."

"Noooo. We can't tell my brother. He doesn't know Brody was in here last night. You know that Caden will kick his ass if he thinks Brody and I have a thing. I can't imagine what he'd do if he found out Brody slept in my room. And, like you said, maybe Pistol's just messing with me by pretending he saw something he didn't."

Jenna takes a deep breath and blows it out. I pull my fingers through my hair. We stare at each other, contemplating what to do. Tension plagues the room. We both jump when my phone chimes again.

Pistol:
I think he likes your Jack O' Lantern
pajamas as much as I do ;(

I drop my phone and my legs give out on me. I start shaking, and collapse to the ground. Jenna bends down next to me and grabs my phone.

She picks it up and reads the latest message. "Oh hell, those are the pajamas you're wearing right now. Has he ever seen them?" Jenna asks in shock.

"No, I just got them . . . and he's never seen me in pajamas before. I don't know what to do," I whimper.

Jenna scrolls through my phone and begins to text.

"What are you doing?" I demand.

She whispers, "I'm texting Brody. He has to help us with this. This just reached a new level of scary."

"No. You can't text him. You know Brody. He might get himself in trouble trying to deal with this. I don't want him to ruin his chance for a football scholarship. I know this will go away if we just ignore it. He's messing with my mind. Pistol has CJ now. After last night, his big, fat ego is bruised and he wants to get his last dig in. He's gonna be done after this. I know it." I work to convince Jenna to drop it.

Jenna's face is solemn and resolute. "Okay, but if you get anymore crazy Peeping Tom texts you need to tell me right away. I know you're caught up in trying to protect everyone

Kaitlyn. But, you're the one who needs to be protected. And, you can't keep these kind of secrets from your best friends. I'm worried for you. This is seriously scary. Promise me you'll say something if this continues, or I will hit "send" right now."

I look at her and shake my head back and forth, "I don't think you need to worry, but okay," I say hesitantly.

"Okay, what?" Jenna demands.

"Okay, I promise."

CHAPTER 15

FIGHT OR FLIGHT

I BOUNCE MY WAY TO my locker in the student union of Jefferson High. I've got to grab my swim gear. I'm so excited that I get to leave school at lunch today. I'm headed to the qualifying meet, and after putting countless extra hours in at the pool, my coach thinks I have a shot at qualifying for Masters in the 100 Fly and 50 Free. I'm in high spirits as Brody jumps out from behind his locker and pulls me in for a secret "good luck" hug.

"Careful Bro, someone might see us," I warn as he tugs at the Miner Mascot logo on my team sweatshirt.

Protectively, he slides behind me, drapes his arms over the tops of my shoulders, and shuffles me through the crowded area and into the janitor's closet. "Is this private enough for you My Little Lady Miner?" he grins, spinning me back around to face him. His forehead lowers gently onto mine, and he gazes at me with interest. His eyes drop to my lucky horseshoe necklace. He slowly raises his hand and lifts the horseshoe to his lips. "Now you can wear this good luck kiss all day," he grins. "Sometimes

I wonder if I should've gotten you wings, you little Flyer."

"I think this horseshoe has done just fine for me all of these years, thank you very much. It's not the charm hanging from the necklace that brings me luck, it's the charmer who gave it to me."

"You think I'm a charmer?" he grins playfully.

"Well, I would never hang out in a dark broom closet on my own, so you've obviously got me under some kind of spell . . . unless it's just the bleach and cleaners messing with my good senses. Something's making me a little delirious . . ."

"Ya, we'd better get you out of here. You probably shouldn't be searing your lungs with all of these chemicals. I just wanted to wish you luck at your meet today." Brody kisses me on the forehead, and pulls away. An unsuspecting grimace plagues his face, when he looks down at me and questions, "Hey, I don't mean to bring this up, but I'm bummed that our playoff game clashes with your meet. Are you gonna be okay down at Shasta without Caden and me there? It's going to be the first time you haven't had us around since Homecoming, and it kind of worries me."

I hadn't thought about my vulnerability without the boys, but the moment the thought sinks in, I hold my arms tight to my chest to control the shutter that fights to break out of my body. I put on my best poker face, but there's no way I'm going to be able to hide this from Brody. It has been two full weeks, and though I haven't actually seen Pistol, I've gotten frequent texts, that I haven't responded to. In one text he'll apologize and beg for me to take him back, and when I don't respond, he becomes aggressive and insulting. I don't see too much harm in the texts, so I haven't told anyone about them, not even Jenna. If she finds out I've been keeping these texts from her, she's going to kill me. She made me promise, but I know something's going on with her right now. Her mom keeps pulling her out of school early . . . I don't want to cause any more worry than necessary.

Despite the fact that I don't think Pistol will do anything to me, panic works its way into my mind every now and then. It may just be my overactive imagination, or the lingering paranoia caused by the Jack O' Lantern pajama text, but I swear there have been times when I feel like I'm being watched.

"Pip? What's going on?" Brody puts his hands to my shoulders, "You look like a butterfly caught in a net. You know you're shaking right?"

"I'm fine Brody, really. I was just remembering that night. I'm okay."

"Kaitlyn Woodley, it's been two full weeks. You are still shaking at the thought of him? Has anything else happened to you?" Brody pinches the bridge of his nose and pulls his lips into a straight line.

"Nope, nothing Brody."

"Pinky swear," he holds out his little pinky.

I start to extend my pinky toward him, but drop it. I can no longer cover the truth. "Well I've gotten a couple texts," I mumble. I drop my eyes and cover them with my hand.

"Wait . . . Did you just say he's texted you? You haven't told me about this?" concern overtakes his tone.

"I'm pretty sure they're drunk texts since they come in at like three in the morning. They just say stuff like he misses me and he wants me back."

"Come? Say? Is this still happening? When was the last text, Kaitlyn?"

"Well, I found one on my phone this morning. It's no big deal."

"No Big Deal? This dude broke into your house and slit your teddy bear's throat. Give me your phone. I want to see it!" he commands, holding his hand out to take my phone.

"I deleted them . . . all of them." I pause for a second, looking at his somber face. "I haven't responded to any of them. There's nothing to show you."

Brody takes a deep breath and releases it in a huff as he throws his head back. "What am I gonna do with you Kaitlyn Woodley? How am I going to keep you safe if I don't even know what I'm dealing with?"

Trying to break the tension ricocheting between us, I pinch his cheeks in between my hands, just like we used to do when we played "Chubby."

"Look at me Brody." I tug down on his face so his eyes gaze right into mine. "I'm a big girl now. I'm not that little Pip Squeak anymore. You don't have to protect me from Pistol's big, bad texts. Besides, if I thought I was in any kind of real danger, you would be the first person I would call. You know that, right?"

He pauses for a moment, biting the inside of his cheek. "I hope you'd tell me. I couldn't live with myself if I let anything happen to my best fffriend," he chuckles. Instantly his tone becomes serious. "You have to tell me if he texts you again. Got it?"

"Got it." I solute, accepting his command.

He grabs my hand and pulls me in. "Come here you little Smart Ass. Let's snuggle it out."

Our bear hug is interrupted when the lunch bell rings. "Oh man. I've gotta go grab my stuff. The vans leave in ten minutes."

"Same here, the guys are probably already loading onto the bus. Wish us luck Pip. If we win this one, it's Championships baby!"

As I squeeze him hard, not wanting to let go, an idea comes to me. "Give me your best catching hand," I whisper. Without hesitation, he holds out his left hand. I pull a pen out of my pocket, set my necklace on his hand and outline my horseshoe on his palm. Around the outside I write, *Catch the lucky one.* Then I kiss it and squeeze it shut. "I'm sharing my luck with you today. Now, go pick axe those Panthers."

"You're something else, Girl." His dimple pops when he

smiles down at me. As he opens the door to the janitor's closet, Brody insists that I text him about my races. "Kick some booty, now," he cheers as he steps out of the closet.

Knowing we are in full view of everyone, he leaves me with a high five and a wink.

"You've got it ffffriend," I say, giving him a discreet fist bump. Both of our faces are lit up from the rush of our brief, secret encounter. As I watch Brody walking away toward the door, I notice Caden glancing my way from across the room. He has a suspicious look on his face, but just shakes his head as his eyes drift from mine. When he catches a glimpse of Brody headed out toward the quad, I watch him jog over and slow to a stop. They walk out the door together. I can tell something is up, and I can't help but wonder if he saw us coming out of the janitor's closet together.

I don't have time to think about my brother's overprotective nature right now. I've got to get out to the vans before I miss my ride. I grab my gear from the locker, and jog out to meet my teammates in the parking lot. We load up quickly and hit the road for the two hour ride south.

I jump in the van and crawl back to the third row next to Daemon. I'm not happy about my seating assignment at all. It stinks that the coach assigned seats, since no one will voluntarily sit next to a couple annoying kids, and our French exchange student. I really want to sit by Jenna right now, but she has to sit up front next to the most irritating, squirrelly girl on the team, Miley. Jenna scoots as far over toward the door as she can get. Fidgeting back and forth, trying to peek around Jake, who's sitting in the middle row, she glances back over her shoulder, and opens her mouth, air gagging herself with her finger. She holds up her phone and mouths "text me."

I mouth back, "Saving my battery . . . Have fun up there." With those parting words, I send Jenna a sarcastic grin, slip on my headphones, and settle back into my seat. I close my eyes and lean back, trying to avoid any interaction with Daemon. As I sit peacefully, listening to my music, the smell of rotten eggs starts drifting up my nose. *I knew this ride was going way too smoothly.* I roll my head to the left and pop my eyes open, "Really? You're gonna sit here and crap your pants right now?" I ask incredulously.

Daemon smirks back at me wiggling his eyebrows. "Don't worry Princess, there's a lot more where that came from," he growls in his sappy French accent, winking at me and pinching my side.

At his touch, a stinging pain shoots through the skin covering my ribcage. It feels like I just got stung by a wasp. "Ouch, you Asshole! What was that for?" I scream.

"Miss Woodley, watch your French, you Hamburger!" I hear Coach Hendryx shout from the driver's seat.

I twist my face into a sour grimace and glare at Daemon. He's chuckling when he says, "We can do a lot better than just "watch" your French. Why don't you let me show you how it's done?" He sticks out his tongue and swirls it around in the air, directing his fantasy make-out session right at me. My gag reflex kicks in as I watch him move his hands around and wiggle his fingers, like he's holding onto the back of my head.

"That's disgusting Daemon . . . Enjoy your little fantasy, cuz that's all it's ever gonna be."

I start to gag as a fresh dose of gas enters the atmosphere. The smell begins to creep its way around the van. My teammates seated around us start bouncing up and down and waving their hands in front of their faces. Windows start popping open left and right,

"What the hell did you eat today?" Jake turns around and yells back toward our seat.

Daemon laughs, "Lactose intolerant, Dude. They served free chocolate milk and taco boats for hot lunch." He turns toward me and belches right in my face. I swear I can feel my hair blow back over my shoulders. "Why fart and waste it when you can burp and taste it?" he laughs.

Disgusted, I curl up in a ball and turn away from Daemon. I take out my phone to text Jenna, when I see an unread message.

Pistol:
Nice pic inside the janitor's closet today. Why are you putting me through this Kaitlyn? You know what? I'll see you soon. Next time you hook up in a private place, it'll be with me . . .

Oh my goodness. My heart skips a beat from the fresh shot of adrenaline. *How in the heck did he get a picture of me inside the janitor's closet?* My mind races for an explanation of how Pistol could've gotten a picture of me at school. *Did someone else see us in there? Is he following me? It's been over two weeks . . . Why does he still care?* Anxiety is beginning to claw at my stomach, and I wonder if I should talk to Jenna after all? I know I haven't told her about any of his texts, but it's kind of starting to feel like Pistol's a creeper . . . like the stalking kind . . . and I did promise that I'd let her know if anything else happened. I decide to text her.

Me:
Jenna, you've got to figure out a way to get back here and talk to me. Pistol is starting to scare me a little.

No sooner do I hit send, then I hear Jenna's voice arguing with Coach Hendryx, "Look at her back there! She's doubled over ready to puke. I have to trade places with Daemon, or she's not going to have a chance of qualifying today. She's green!"

Relief washes over me when I hear Coach's reply, "You've got a point, Kid. Why don't you have Kaitlyn come to the front. She can squish into the middle. No one should have to smell that French Taco Boat the whole way there."

I take a deep breath of relief, forgetting the aroma that is currently surrounding the back seat, and wretch in response. "Ohhhh, get up here Woodley!" I hear Coach grunt to the back.

I throw my head back, "Praise God!!!" I groan, grabbing my stuff and heading up to the front of the van.

I settle into the four inches of middle seat, sandwiched in between Miley and Jenna. Miley wiggles back and forth, elbowing me slightly, just to let me know that I'm crowding her. Already on edge, I glare at her and shake my fist, "Knock it off, or you'll find yourself at the other end of this wrecking ball, Miley! Are we clear?" I swear I can hear Coach chuckle, as I watch Miley cower away, and turn back to her book, *The History of Video Games*.

Once Miley is off my lap, I pull out my phone and whisper, "Don't kill me for not showing you these earlier." I click on Pistol's name, and start scrolling through his messages. I start with the last one I showed her.

Pistol:
I think he likes your Jack O' Lantern pajamas as much as I do ;(

We never even broke up, you at least owe me a conversation.

I miss you.

I know it's 3:00 in the morning, but I can't stop thinking about you.

Text me.

I miss being in there with you, I love watching you sleep.

Kaitlyn, please text me back. I need you.

God, you suck! Text me back, Bitch!!!

Ok, sorry, I'm just frustrated cuz I love you.

I'll be in town tomorrow . . . call me.

How was your Butter-Flake Chill? You sure looked like you were enjoying it.

DAMN YOU GIRL!!! TEXT ME!!!!! ;(

I saw you in the parking lot today. That skirt is amazing with those cowgirl boots! I'd do anything to get those toned legs wrapped around this cowboy.

We need to talk.

I have to see you!!! Up close!!! I'm not going to keep begging!

Good luck at your meet today. I'll

be cheering for you. ;) haha

Nice pic inside the janitor's closet
today. Why are you putting me through
this Kaitlyn? You know what? I'll
see you soon. Next time you hook up
in a private place, it'll be with me
. . .

I guess there are a lot more than I thought, and when read
consecutively, they sound pretty creepy.

With each new message she reads, Jenna's head bows a
little farther forward, and her mouth slightly drops. "Holy hell
Kaitlyn, this boy is really hung up on you. Have you shown
these to Caden or Brody . . . or better yet, your parents?"

"I told Brody today, that Pistol's texted me a few times, but
when he asked to see them, I said I'd deleted them," I confess. "I
just can't get him in the middle of all of this. He needs to focus
on his playoffs right now anyway. I know he'll get himself in
trouble, and I'm not willing to risk his future over an ex-boyfriend, who's going to be over me by next week."

Jenna studies the texts again, then shakes her head in disbelief. "Look at the pattern of these texts Kaitlyn. See this text,
this text, and this text . . ." she points to the messages, " . . . they
have stalker written all over them! It's almost like he's following you."

"Lower your voice," I whisper, as I see Coach Hendryx
cock his head to the side. His quick movement reminds me of a
puppy, listening to an unrecognizable sound. "We'll discuss this
later," I say, tipping my chin toward Coach. Then I mouth the
word, "listening," and point my finger toward the driver's seat.
At that, I hear Jenna let out a deep breath. Now that I've re-read
his texts, I know I've made a mess of things by not telling my
closest circle of friends. The disturbing thing is, I don't know

if I'm keeping this secret more to protect them, or Pistol. My stomach turns thinking about the whole situation. I bury my face in my hands, and comb my fingers through my hair. When I look up, I'm surprised to see we are pulling into the parking lot of Shasta. Taking a deep breath, I try to calm myself before getting out of the van. The meet is intense, to say the least. I have to get a handle on myself. As I walk through the gates, I glance down at the large concrete steps and into the crowded lanes of the warm up pool. They are dotted with distinguished swimmers from all over the north state. I feel butterflies shooting through my stomach as I make my way down the steps, scanning the pool deck. I feel a little intimidated as I scope out the larger teams, picking out familiar faces of swimmers I've met behind the blocks over the years. I look back to the pool, and psych myself out as I recognize many of the top swimmers in the league. Watching them loosen up, puts me a little on edge, as I convince myself that their warm up pace looks faster than my sprint. I've got to get out of this frame of mind. I'm defeating myself before the meet even begins.

I work to shake off the nerves by reminding myself that I only have to swim two individual events, and two relays today. I have to push everything else out of my mind. Those races need to be my focus. I slip my headphones over my ears and crank up the music to drown out all of the distractions. I bounce up and down a couple times, pop my neck back and forth, perform some arm and leg stretches, and decide to head over to the warm up pool. Swimming the first few laps helps with the nerves. It calms me down and eases the anxiety brought on by Jenna's and my conversation about Pistol's texts. The water feels pretty fast, and I begin to regain confidence. I'm at the end of the lane, when I feel a hand come down on my head. It's Jenna. "Hey, heat and lane assignments are posted. Come with me to look," she says, tilting her head in the direction of the east wall.

Knowing it's about time to get out anyway, I stop my warm

up and join Jenna. When I check heat and lane assignments for the first event, I see that I'm seeded in the second heat. *Ugh.* This is not good news for my Fly. I know I have to win my heat to even have a chance at qualifying for Masters. I don't think that's even possible. I'm pretty sure I've already hit the fastest time I'm capable of this season. I study my competitors posted times. According to this sheet, I have to drop two full seconds to even make it into the top five. *Oh, well.* I shake it off, and go back under the pop-up tent with the rest of my teammates.

About an hour into the meet, it's time for my 100 Fly. I'm standing behind the blocks, looking to the opposite side of the pool. The yard pool looks short, in comparison to the meter pool where I train at home. When the long whistle blows, I step up, and raise my head to examine the distance one more time. *Oh, my God!* My heart stops, when I swear I catch a glimpse of Pistol standing at the end of my lane. I recognize the boots, follow them up to a prize buckle and quickly catch the side of his face. He disappears behind the crowd before I can actually confirm that it's him. Adrenaline shoots through my entire body, and the sound begins to blur from my ears, I faintly hear a muffled, "Swimmer's take your mark." I automatically drop to the block in response. Panicked, I manage to lock myself into position. As soon as I hear the buzzer, I reflexively fly from the block. The adrenaline from the sight of Pistol courses through my veins. I don't even think about the movements. My body is on auto-pilot. There is so much fear running through my mind, that I'm not sure I'm even using my breathing pattern, let alone breathing at all. Before I know it, I've swum all four laps. I hit the wall, pull my cap off, and tilt my head back into the water, allowing my hair to flow back over my shoulders. My lungs are tight, my breathing is labored, and I'm shaking. I'm not sure if it's from the swim, or the panic that's coursing through me. I look up, and see Jenna standing next to the block, looking down at me with her mouth hanging open. I stay in the water, waiting for the fly over start. I don't see anyone at the block, so I look back toward the water to see that the rest of my heat is just now coming in. *Hmmm. I had no clue that I was that far ahead of them.* After the next heat takes off, I crawl out of the water, where Jenna is still waiting to greet me.

"Holy hell Kaitlyn. What got into you?"

I have no idea how Jenna has picked up on my anxiety. I've been in the water ever since I saw Pistol. I continue to tremble, as a warm tear runs down my cheek.

"Kaitlyn, why are you crying? You're already the fastest flyer on our team, and you just completely obliterated your own record." She grabs my arms and turns me around to face her, "Did you see the time on the Colorado? You dropped three flipping seconds, Kait!!!"

I stare back at her blankly, unresponsive to what she has just said.

She shakes her head, looking at me with confusion. "Did you hear me Kait? You dropped three . . . seconds . . . and creamed the entire heat!!! Wait, are you hurt? Are you okay? Why are you crying?"

I finally work up the nerve to speak, "I. Saw. Hhhim. Jenna. He's here."

"Who did you see? Who's here?" she asks in alarm.

"Pistol . . . he was standing at the end of my lane before the race," my voice quivers.

"Are you sure?" she takes me into her arms and hugs me. "You're stressed. Maybe you're just seeing things," she rationalizes.

"It looked just like him, Jenna. But he ducked into the crowd before I could make sure."

"There's no reason for him to be down here right now. His sister doesn't even compete in high school swimming. The valley doesn't have a team, remember?" Jenna reassures. "I'm sure you just saw a look alike." Then Jenna holds me back at arm's length. "Listen to me Kait; I will search this entire facility, to make sure he's not here. Stay next to Coach and help him time. Do not leave his side."

Jenna walks me over to Coach Hendryx, and takes off on her mission. A forty-five minute search, and a solid 50 Free later, Jenna returns to the Coach's table. "Kait, there's no sign of him. I looked everywhere. If he is here, he's doing a darned good job of hiding. I even had Jake, Fisher, and Hadley helping me. The meet's almost over. Let's just stay here til it's finished."

Despite the fact that my search team turned up nothing, I can't shake the weird feeling that I'm being watched. I know it's probably just my overactive imagination, so I work exceptionally hard to block it out and focus on the upcoming events. The rest of the meet goes surprisingly well. We take first in our Medley Relay, winning a division patch, and third in our Free Relay, which is not too bad considering the level of competition. I end up placing first in my Fly and second in my Free, qualifying me for Masters in all four events. I'm ecstatic that our entire relay team gets to advance to Masters. We've worked so hard for this, and I'm ecstatic that we'll be there together.

We celebrate the whole way back to school, singing, joking, storytelling, and dancing in our seats. The ride flies by with the after party that's happening in the van. When we pull up at the school, it's ten o'clock, and pitch black outside. The brisk fall breeze begins to kick up, and a chill works it's way through me. I'm so glad I have my car here. I'd hate to have to wait for a ride on this dark, autumn night. I throw my stuff in the car, and check my phone before I head home.

Brody:

"Pip, are you home yet? We won!!! Thanks to you I caught the lucky one!!! I want to come over and see

how it went for you."

I grab my necklace remembering the luck we shared today. *Brody is so thoughtful.* I text him back before I pull out of the parking lot.

Me:
Leaving school right now. Be home in
a few. Can't wait to hear about your
game and tell you about my meet!!!

I drive the three minutes up the street to my house, turn off my car lights, and open the door. I get out of the car and pull my gym bag to the front seat, fumbling through it as I work to find my house keys. There is no moon visible tonight, and the darkness of the street makes it darned near impossible to find them. I dig down below a layer of clothes, goggles, and hair ties, and finally feel the ring at the bottom of my bag. I wrap my fingers around the keys, when I feel myself being forcefully tugged away from the open car door. Panic fills me, when a hand covers my nose and mouth. I struggle to breathe. I start kicking and stomping my feet, trying to break loose of whoever has me in this tight hold. Panic shoots through me when I realize this isn't Brody playing a trick on me. The hold is getting tighter, and it really hurts. A spike of adrenaline rushes through me, causing me to pick up my foot and slam it back into my attacker's shin. "Owww, you Bitch!" cries the familiar voice.

Oh, hell . . . It's Pistol. "I told you I'd be coming to see you! Now are you going to cooperate so I can let you breathe? No screaming; got it?"

Gasping for air that I can't seem to find, I nod my head up and down. He finally removes his hand from my nose and mouth, and I strain to breathe. The air barely seeps in, overpowered by a fierce groaning sound. I'm so dizzy, that I can't think straight.

"Look at me, Kait-lyn," he yells.

I don't respond. I'm just too dizzy. I bend down and put my hands on my knees, trying to regain my senses.

I feel hair rip from my scalp, and my neck pop, as he pulls my head up to face him. "I said look at me!" Pistol screams again.

As I look up at his face, I can feel the heat of prickling tears forming behind my eyes. I have never seen Pistol look this scary. His eyes are bloodshot and I can smell alcohol coming from his breath. He pulls me close, and angrily slurs, "I told you I miss you, Babydoll. Why haven't you answered my texts?"

"Pistol, I'm not your Babydoll anymore," I gasp.

I feel the sting of his fingers smack my face. It's such an unexpected response, that I'm not prepared for the impact of his strong backhand against my lips. I feel warm liquid roll down the side of my mouth. I reach up to my face and wipe it away. I see blood smeared across the back of my hand, and know my tooth has gone through my lip. *If I don't get out of here now, this could get really bad.*

Fear overtakes me and I gather enough courage to try to run. I make it about two feet when he catches my right arm and yanks me back to him.

Oh . . . My . . . God!

I hear a pop, and feel searing pain shoot from my shoulder, down my back and out to my fingers. I have never felt anything so excruciating in my life. Fighting not to pass out, I roll my head and look over at Pistol. He begins to blur, but I see his mouth moving in slow motion, "Ohhhh, Shhhhhit," as he lets go of me. Ringing drowns out all sound, and blackness slowly closes in, until there's . . . nothing.

CHAPTER 16

SECRETS UNVEILED

I FEEL THE COOL, SOFT breeze blowing across my face as I strain to open my eyes. At first glance, my vision is a swirling kaleidoscope of shapes and colors. The incessant turning makes me slightly nauseous. As I squint my eyes to try and focus, I can feel the tension in the tightly stretched skin that covers my pounding forehead. I'm facing upward, and I can faintly identify the outline of falling leaves drifting across the evening sky. The distant streetlight has illuminated the night, just enough for me to recognize my neighborhood. I feel like I'm floating on a cloud as I move slowly beneath the streaks of stars. When the stabbing pain starts to make itself known, I come back to my body and recognize his smell, and the trembling arms cradling me. The buzzing in my ears slowly fades away, and I hear the whisper of Brody's voice, "Please be okay Pip, be okay . . . It's okay Pip, I've got you . . . Please be okay."

I know Brody's worried. I hear it in his voice. I struggle to lift my hand and touch his cheek. I let out a shriek from the pain that shoots through my injured shoulder. When he looks down, his eyes are glazed over in tears. I wipe the one I see rolling down his cheek, "I'm okay Brody. I'll be okay. Don't worry."

"Pip . . . I should've been there waiting for you when you pulled up. This is all my fault. You told me you were coming home. I shouldn't have waited. I knew I left you alone too long today. I'm so sorry, Pip."

"Brody, it's not your fault," I cry.

"I'm supposed to protect you, Pip. I promised," Brody's voice begins to shake as he kicks at my front door.

He can't get the door open, and leans in to push the doorbell. He yells, "Open up guys . . . It's Brody. I have Kaitlyn!" He continues to kick and yell.

I hear steps quickly approach the door, and it flies open. The first thing I see is Caden's terrified face, "Oh my God Brody! What happened to my sister?"

"Call 911! I don't know what's happened . . . She was unconscious lying in the street when I found her. There was blood on the ground, coming out of her mouth. She just woke up!"

The agony from bouncing and jarring, has me slipping into another spell. I hear the ringing again, as blackness begins to circle in, covering my vision. I fight to maintain consciousness, but it's no use. My body feels funny, almost tingly. My breathing slows. The voices become faint. The last thing I hear is my brother's voice shouting, "Peyton get out here! Run upstairs and get my parents!" I'm fading away into that calm, peaceful darkness, where pain does not reside.

It's late spring of seventh grade. We're out in the valley at Mason Ranch visiting Brody's cousin and grandparents for the weekend. It's an unusually hot day. The sun is beating down, bees are buzzing around the freshly blooming flowers, and I can hear the chatter of the boys, as they work on finding something entertaining to do. Brody's cousin, Mason, has a brilliant idea for a fun way to cool off. He wants to take the horses for a run through the alfalfa field that he's irrigating. There are four of us, but only three shod horses. Caden instantly attaches himself to Smokey, and is hell bent on not riding double with me; especially since we're riding bareback. After a brief argument with my brother, Brody offers to take me with him on his favorite horse, Cheyenne.

"Hey, Pip Squeak, I was hoping you'd want to go with me anyway. Riding with your best friend is always better than riding alone." He smiles down at me, making me feel like he'd have taken me even if there were four horses. "Follow me, and I'll help you get on." He hops up on Cheyenne, then tilts his head in the direction of the fence. We make our way across the lawn where he has me climb up to the top rung. As I balance with one hand and one foot, he brings the horse next to the fence, and reaches out toward me. "Let me give you a hand, Pip." A strange tingly sensation shoots through my arm as he clutches my hand and pulls me around behind him. I don't know where that feeling came from, but I'd never felt anything like it. "Hang on tight, Girl," he chuckles, as he clicks his tongue and gives the horse a little kick. The sudden jolt has me grabbing on tightly, so I don't fly off backward.

As we make our way across the road and over to the field, we pick up speed. The breeze blows my hair off of my shoulders. I have my arms wrapped tightly around Brody's waist, as we trot through the spray of the water. Brody creates his own equestrian water park using the wheel lines. His timing is perfect, reigning Cheyenne in, so we run with the turning of the sprinklers. We laugh wildly as we rush through the water, slowing to wait for the next surge. Again, he kicks, making Cheyenne bolt through the next stream.

"This is the awesomest ride ever!" I giggle, pulling in closer, and resting my chin against Brody's neck.

"You think so Pip? Wanna go faster?" He looks over his shoulder toward me.

"Let's do it!" I squeal.

Without warning, Brody gives Cheyenne a sharp kick. My chin is still resting against him. I haven't had enough time to readjust my hold for the intensity of the impending buck. Before I realize what's happening, I feel myself somersaulting backwards over the horse's hind end. Her coarse tail slaps my face, as I fall to the ground. There is a sharp pain in my knees and shoulders as I land on my head and come up on all fours in a puddle of mud. I raise my throbbing head, looking to see where I am. Suddenly, the air is punched from my lungs, and my upper chest burns with the fresh brand of Cheyenne's hoof.

I see boots running toward me, as Brody bends down, "Pip, are you okay? I saw the horse kick."

I think so, but this really hurts," I say, peeling my tank top over to take a look at my quickly bruising flesh.

"Oh my Goodness Pip, I can see the print from the horse-shoe under your collarbone!" As I'm looking down at my battle wound, I hear Caden approach.

"Caden, look at her shoulder. We should get help. Pip, are you okay?"

"Caden, look at her shoulder. We should get help. Pip, are you okay?" I hear Brody's voice whispered in my ear. When I come back around, my parents are standing over the top of me. My mom is kneeling beside me, holding a washcloth on my forehead. My dad is fanning my face. "Kait?" I hear him say . . . "Kait? Can you hear me, Honey?"

"Daddy, my arm . . ." I cry, as another tear rolls down the side of my face. I focus on the warm liquid crawling slowly toward my ear. Brody's hand comes up and wipes it away, just before it makes its way inside. "I felt it rip, and heard a pop."

I turn my head toward my parents, and see my mom look up at my dad. I watch her lips move, "Her arm?" Then she turns to me. "Kaitlyn, you mean your head, right? How did you get that knot . . . and your lip . . . it's swollen, and bleeding."

The thought of Pistol backhanding me hard enough to send my tooth through my lip, has me crying again. I gasp for a breath before I try to speak. "It was so scary Mom. I couldn't get help." I begin shaking, as panic starts to kick in. Then I completely lose control of my emotions. "He was smothering me and I couldn't breathe," my voice trembles.

"Who Kaitlyn? Who did this to you?" my dad growls.

"Ppp . . ."

"Son of a Bitch!!!" Caden screams, cocking his arm back and throwing his bowl of popcorn like he's trying to drill his wide receiver. As the plastic bowl bounces off the wall, popcorn scatters across the carpet. "I'm gonna kill that Bastard!"

I watch the veins grow in Brody's neck as he yells back, "Not if I get to him first!"

I see my boys look at each other. Their fists are balled. Their breathing is rapid. "I'm out of here! Are you coming with me?" Caden shouts.

"Whoa, whoa, whoa . . ." My mom shakes her hand up and down three times like she's trying to stop traffic. "Not so fast boys, we're going to let the police handle this. Settle down . . . The ambulance will be here any minute. You need to be here for Kait right now. She's in a lot of pain. Our first priority is to make sure she's alright."

There's a knock at the door, and Peyton moves to open it. Within seconds, two E.M.T.'s step up to the couch. One holds a notepad, while the other kneels down in front of me. "Hi there. We're here to make sure you're okay. Can you tell me your name?"

"Kaitlyn," I answer softly.

"Can you tell me what year it is?"

Sweat starts beading on my forehead. I can't focus on the question. My stomach begins to turn, and my cheeks quiver. My mouth starts to water, when I gag out . . . "Ummm . . . I think

I'm gonna throw up."

Brody grabs the popcorn bowl from the floor and runs it to me. Instantly, my stomach begins to wretch, and I lose its contents in front of everyone.

"I know you're trying to follow protocol here guys, but I think we need to stop with the questions and get her down to the hospital, now. She's got a knot on her head, there was blood coming from her mouth when we found her, and now she's throwing up."

"It's my shoulder Daddy . . . I don't care about that head stuff," I cry. "My arm hurts so bad, it's making me sick."

I can hear one of the E.M.T.'s on his radio letting the E.R. know that they'll be bringing a patient into Entrance 3.

Within minutes, I'm up on the gurney, and being wheeled into the ambulance. My mom jumps in with me, and the doors quickly close behind her. The movement of the ambulance has my head spinning in circles. I close my eyes trying to block out the disorienting lights and movement. The sirens drown out the beeping equipment and scratchy voices that continue to blare over the radio. Thankfully, the noise and lights work together to chase the scary images of Pistol's attack from my mind. Before I know it, the ambulance slows to a stop. The doors swing open, and Caden, Peyton, Brody, and my dad are standing at the back, waiting as I'm lowered out on the stretcher. I can't believe they actually beat the ambulance to the hospital. In their haste, they haven't even changed from their football and cheerleading uniforms.

I hear the sounds of pattering feet and rolling wheels rattling beneath me. I cringe at the jolting of my shoulder when the gurney crosses the threshold and makes its way in between the big glass doors on the way to the Emergency Room. The fluorescent lights glow along the expanse of the vast, white ceiling. The smell of the hospital crawls through my nose and ties my stomach into a new bundle of nerves. A low raspy voice speaks with the paramedics, "Based on your initial assessment, we've got the M.R.I. ready. Come with me guys."

Walking alongside the gurney, the doctor goes over a series of questions with the E.M.T.'s. He finally looks down at me and begins to speak, "Kaitlyn, we're going to take some pictures to see what's going on inside of there that's making you so sick. There's pain in both your head and shoulder?" He questions.

I give a slight nod, not wanting to speak for fear I'll throw up again.

"Have you ever had an M.R.I. before?" his brow crinkles, as he looks down at me to read my non-verbal response.

I shake my head *no,* envisioning the big, white space shuttle-like machine, I've seen on movies and documentaries.

"Are you claustrophobic at all?" he asks with hesitation.

"Just a little. Umm . . . I'm more worried I might puke in there. I'm not feeling so hot. Do you think we could hurry? I might be able to hold it just a little longer."

We roll up to the M.R.I. and a team of nurses and other assistants work to carefully move me into the machine. They gingerly place my head on the neck rest and put a pillow under my knees. They tell me to stay really still and that they're going to put headphones on me to help block out the loud noises. My mom gently holds my leg to let me know she's right beside me.

"You about ready to go in, Kid?" the handsome young resident smiles reassuringly, as he wipes a tear from my cheek. "You're gonna do just fine. Stay still and don't be afraid." His voice is calming, and helps ease my nerves as I feel the bed glide into the machine. I close my eyes and listen to the soft elevator music coming through the earphones. I try to stay still and not jump, but the stabbing pain shooting through my shoulder is becoming unbearable. Another tear rolls down my cheek into my ear, and I'm sad that Brody isn't there to wipe it away like he did before.

It seems like hours have passed. I'm lying in a hospital bed surrounded by my family, Brody, and Peyton when the doctor comes in with his notepad. "So we've looked at the images from your M.R.I. Would you like me to have the kids step out before we discuss the results?"

"They can stay." I yelp, before anyone else has a chance to answer.

The doctor glances up at my parents, as if to give them the final word. I can see my mom nod, yes, and he begins.

"Well, Kaitlyn, there are a couple of conditions you're going to be dealing with over the next several weeks. We've stitched up your lip, and it shouldn't scar too badly, but you've suffered a mild concussion from hitting your head on the ground when you fell. You're going to have to be really careful to limit some of your activities, both physical and mental, until it heals. I'll give you a complete list of your restrictions, but I'm going to tell you that it's really important to stay away from any complex reading, texting, using the computer for longer than thirty minutes at a time, and listening to loud music. You need to stay calm and quiet."

My jaw drops at the insane list of restrictions. I want to raise my hand to ask how I'm supposed to get through AP English, but the pain stops me . . .

"Now the second thing we found concerns that right shoulder. You've torn your rotator cuff, and the only way to fix that is with arthroscopic surgery."

The doctor's voice fades out as my ears begin to ring again . . . *Surgery? Surgery?* "What about Masters?" I belt out, "Can I still swim in the meet?" I stutter, turning my head toward my mom and dad.

"Well, that depends on when the meet is, Kaitlyn. I can schedule surgery as early as tomorrow morning, but there is a six week recovery period," he says shaking his head. "Not to mention, you will need some intense physical therapy following the surgery. You may not be able to compete for up to six months."

I say nothing else; the sound of a dying cat claws its way out of my throat. The back of my eyes sting, and I find it hard to breathe. "I'm suffocating . . . I can't breathe," I cry out to my parents. More alien noises escape as I try to draw in breath. Then the hysteria sets in. I cry like a child who's just landed on a desert cactus after being thrown from a horse. I plug my ears and close my eyes. "I just want to wake up now," I cry rocking back and forth in the hospital bed. I work to breathe through my stuffy nose and feel a snot bubble pop above my lip. I snort again, trying to pull in more air.

I feel the bed dip and a tissue come up to my nose. "Blow Pip," I hear Brody whisper. He holds the tissue in one hand and brings his other up to my back, slowly rubbing it in circles. "Shhh . . ." he whispers into my ear. "It's gonna be okay. It could be so much worse. At least they can fix this, Pip."

"This is horrible, Brody! My swimming career is ruined! And the team . . . They're counting on me! Some of those girls only qualified for our relay Brody! They won't be able to swim either! All that work down the drain!" I cry hysterically, shaking even harder.

"Honey," I hear my mom say, "The girls will understand. It's only one season. You can get back in the pool again this spring and start training for summer. We'll help you get back on track." Her voice sounds shaky and hesitant, like she's not sure if she even believes the lines she's feeding me.

Anger begins to overtake the pain and sadness. "I hate him! I hate him! He ruined my last year on Varsity!" I grunt, kicking the covers off my feet. "I'm gonna kick his ass!" I thrash around trying to get out of the bed. Surprise fills the room, at the shock of my wild kicking and uncharacteristic language.

"Don't let her move," the doctor sternly orders. "She needs to calm down with that concussion. Nurse, please get me this pain sedative," he whispers, handing her a slip of paper.

I continue to kick wildly. I shriek again from pain, when I accidentally push down on the bed, trying to work my way up.

"Calm down Baby Girl." My dad says slowly. "You don't need to damage that arm any worse. The doc already has his work cut out for him."

"Ya, calm down, Sis. Don't hurt yourself," Caden says holding onto my feet. He holds them tightly, not in a way to restrain me, but more as a reassurance that he's still with me. He gives them a loving squeeze, "I've got this T. You don't need to worry about kicking his ass. I'll take care of it."

As the boys hold me and try to calm me down, the nurse comes over with a needle. "Hold still, Honey. You're going to feel a little pinch." Just as the injection enters my skin, I hear a ding come from Brody's direction. I look over at him and see a glowing light coming out of his sweatshirt pocket. He pulls out the familiar cell, with my name and treble clef on the cover, and I softly ask, "Why do you have my phone? Who is it?"

"It was on the ground by your car. I picked it up before I carried you in the house." He looks down at the message and looks back up at my brother. Then he looks back down at me. "It's Jenna. She's worried about you cuz you didn't text her when you got home. Don't you worry about it, Pip. I'll fill her in. You need to rest."

I am beginning to feel groggy from whatever the injection was that the nurse just shoved in my arm. I fight to stay awake, but my eyes flutter closed. I may not be able to keep my eyes open, but I can still hear the voices filling the room.

"I think she's asleep," I hear Caden say.

"Good Dude, cuz you guys need to see these texts."

I can't speak, and I can't move, but I listen intently on what the boys are saying.

"The first three are from Pistol. He's apologizing for hurting Kaitlyn tonight. He says he's sorry he left her on the ground but he saw me coming and knew I'd take care of her . . . says he was drinking and just wanted her back. He didn't mean to hit her in the mouth and tug her so hard."

"Let me see that," I hear my Dad's voice.

Before handing him the phone, Brody sighs, "Look Coach, I just scrolled up and there's a lot more. I can't believe this. There are so many. She told me she deleted them. Why didn't she tell us about this? I asked her . . . I asked her Coach."

I can hear the pain in Brody's voice. He's genuinely hurt that I've kept him in the dark about Pistol.

The sounds are beginning to blur. They are becoming more and more faint. Off in the distance I hear Doctor Smith say, "This is serious. I've had a few of these teen violence cases in here before. I think it's best to get the police involved before the situation gets worse."

Relief overtakes me, and I drift off once again.

CHAPTER 17

RESTRAINED

I'M RESTING IN THE HOSPITAL post surgery. When I wake up, I feel like I'm floating about three feet beside my actual body. I'm weightless and hollow inside. I can barely make out my family and friends, who are gathered around my bedside. My head is cloudy, and when I gaze up toward the ceiling, I swear I see fluffy, pink teddy bears floating over my bed. I raise my good arm and point, with a drunk-like slur, "Did you see that guys?" I giggle and start to sing, " . . . this is the day the teddy bears have their picnic . . . Hey! Why are you guys laughing at me? This is a serious matter." I roll my head to my left and focus in on Caden and Jenna. *Oh good.* I'm relieved to see my best friend has found me.

Their faces are all screwed up like they're trying to solve a mystery, "We're not laughing at you, Kait."

"Not you! Them!" I whine, pointing back at the bears that are now jumping from star to star. I turn my head back toward the crowd and wonder why they are not wearing their space suits. "Heyyyyy . . . You guys need to put on your helmets. You won't be able to breathe . . . Where's that Dr. HOTronaut that stuck me in the space ship today? Did he come too?" I scratch my head reliving my entry into orbit. I'm still floating and spinning, "Mom? Can you buy him a Milky Way for taking such good care of me during lift-off?"

"Is she okay?" I hear Jenna whisper under her breath.

An unfamiliar husky voice responds, "Yes, she's just experiencing postoperative delirium. She'll be okay soon enough."

Then I hear Caden laugh, "Hey T, we might not have on our space suits, but you have on nothing at all!" he continues to chuckle.

My face flushes with embarrassment. *Oh my gosh. I can't have Space Commander Centerfold see me like this.* I shuffle around trying to pull the blankets over me.

"Caden, don't mess with your sister," I hear my mom again, followed by the sound of a soft smack.

I forget why I'm struggling so hard with the covers when I realize one of my arms doesn't work. I don't understand why it's pinned and I can't move at all. "Help Mom! I think the aliens put me in a strait jacket!" I begin to panic.

"It's okay Honey. You just got out of surgery. Remember? The doctor fixed your shoulder. You need to calm down."

This is all very confusing to me. I pause and try to focus in on my surroundings. Raising the arm that's not glued to my body, I rub my eyes and squint back toward the ceiling. The teddy bears vanish, the stars float away, and I'm back in the sterile, white hospital room. Things are becoming much clearer as my senses begin to sharpen. A quick burst of adrenaline rushes through me, and I glance down quickly, to make sure I have on clothes. To my relief, I find I'm covered with a hospital gown and blankets. I shake my head and look up to see a seemingly amused crowd dotting the room. "Ha ha brother! Good one," I grimace. "Way to take advantage of my vulnerability," I smirk. "You'd better hope you never have your wisdom teeth pulled.

I've seen videos of that stuff, and I'll be standing by waiting with my camera. Payback's a bitch, you know."

"Kaitlyn Woodley, watch your language. Surgery is no excuse for potty talk," my mom giggles in disbelief of my uncharacteristic cursing.

I hear a knock penetrate the room, and peer out the window, trying to see who's standing outside my door. I can see the shoulder of a black uniform, shifting back and forth.

"I'd better get that." My dad's face turns serious and he walks toward the door. He peeks through the window and turns toward my brother and Brody, lifting his eyebrows and taking a prominent gulp. He forces it down his throat as he slowly turns the handle.

"Cccome on in officer," my father stammers and clears his throat as he opens the door. *Geez; he can't even talk.* I'm surprised he doesn't just come out with a fox call, as Officer Ohmygawd strolls in. I'm glad my mom is secure with who she is. Any lesser of a woman, might take off right about now. I can hear my brother and Brody take deep breaths, and let them out too. I peer over at them to see their eyes glued to the exquisite officer. They're practically drooling at the sight of Angelina Jolie turned JPD.

"Restrain yourselves boys," I whisper. "Your pheromones are jumping onto my bed. It's kinda creepy."

"Is this our victim?" I hear her ask in the background.

Victim? I'm in shock that I've just been referred to as a victim. Where did this go so wrong? I can't believe I'm lying in a hospital bed after being attacked by my boyfriend. I feel like I'm the star of some cheesy after school special. I'm mortified and embarrassed. I'm having a hard time grasping the fact that my whole family and my closest friends are witnessing the aftermath of a situation that I've been hiding from them for so many months. I'm sure none of them saw this coming. I'm not even sure I saw it coming.

The officer walks toward the bed. "Kaitlyn?" she asks. I give a nod, not wanting to talk in front of an audience. "I'm Officer Marnia. I have a few questions for you." Officer Marnia pulls out her notepad and pen.

I'm so embarrassed that my relationship with Pistol reached this point. Besides, I never told Brody or my family about all of his texts. They are going to be furious. *I can't answer questions now . . . not in front of them.* I feel my stubborn pride begin to pump through my veins, and I make a conscious decision to go mute. I turn my head away and look out the window. This is just not a good time for a police interrogation.

"Kaitlyn, I know you hit your head pretty hard. I understand you're suffering from a concussion. Can you recall the details about what happened to you last night?"

An uncomfortable silence fills the room, but I can't let myself answer these questions.

"Kaitlyn, can you answer her question?" my mom pleads.

I just shake my head slightly.

"Kaitlyn. We can't waste time here. The bastard that did this to you could be getting away. We need to find this guy. He's obviously dangerous. What if he hurts someone else?" My dad begins to work on my conscience.

I really do not want to give details, but I don't want to put anyone else in danger. Maybe if I just confirm who it was, they can get him and use the physical evidence my face, head, and shoulder are providing.

"It was Pistol," I groan reluctantly.

"So you know the perpetrator, personally?"

I don't answer. The silence is broken when Jenna huffs, "It's her ex-boyfriend. He's a slimy, Douchebag."

"Let's be objective here," Officer Marnia raises her hand to silence Jenna. "So what time did the slimy, Douchebag attack you last night?"

On the opposite side of my bed, I hear Caden whisper to

Brody, "Damn, a hot badass cop." I'm pretty sure I sense Peyton smack him before I hear the dainty huff come from her direction.

I look back over to Officer Marnia. Judging by the way she's looking at me, I can tell she's frustrated with my lack of cooperation. I decide to help her out with a few minimal answers; but I'm not giving away everything right here and now. "I'm not sure. Brody, do you remember when I came home?"

"It happened right after you texted me from the school." Brody's eyes light up and he gloats, "Wait, I have your phone."

I gulp and feel a burst of adrenaline shoot through my face. *Ohhh crap. This is not going to be good.*

"I think Officer Marnia would be quite interested in seeing this." Brody pulls out the phone and walks over to the officer.

"Here you go Ma'am," he hands it over, and I about lose my mind when I realize all of the information she's now holding. Secret after secret, and months of emotional abuse and stalking, are right in the palm of her hand. I wonder if she's going to read between the lines, or take the texts at face value. Pistol is smooth. She may not catch hidden meanings. I take a deep breath, hoping she doesn't decode his messages in front of my parents. They would be so disappointed in me if they knew I was keeping this from them. They would never trust my judgement again.

The room stands still as Officer Marnia scrolls through the texts. I watch her long eyelashes move up and down in slow motion, as she reads. She pinches her perfectly groomed eyebrows together, and runs her hand along her long side braid shaking her head back and forth. I feel like I'm stuck in a time void, watching and waiting for her to say something . . . anything. I take a deep breath in, trying to calm my nerves when she finally moves her head up to look me in the eyes. She holds out the phone, slowly shaking it back and forth. "You realize, you are a lucky girl?" she raises her eyebrows, "I've seen a lot of messed up teen-relationship abuse cases in my day, and this Douchebag tops them all." I can hear the boys snorting through their noses, trying to hold back their laughter.

"This guy is a pro at manipulation. I bet you feel like this is your fault. You want to protect him right now, don't you?" She shakes her head. "It's okay. I get it. I'll tell you what, I'm going to hang onto this for evidence, but for now, I'm going to start the process of getting you a restraining order. I know you don't want to talk right here, but I'm going to catch you privately to get more details later."

Relief overcomes me. Maybe Officer Marnia isn't just a princess on patrol. She actually understands the situation. She's not treating me like a naive little girl. She's not even making me feel like I did anything wrong. "Okay, I'm going to head down to the office and file an emergency protective order until we can get a restraining order." She holds up the phone one more time, reminding me that it's out of my hands now. "Do you have any idea where we can find Pistol so we can serve him the temporary order?"

"I'll talk to my cousin Mason and see if he knows anything," Brody answers. "I'll contact you if we find him, but you can start your search out in the valley."

"Okay boys. We'll work from our end too. Thanks for your help." Marnia looks down at me, "Rest up, and let these handsome boys take care of you." She looks over her shoulder and sends them a little wink.

I look at the boys, whose chests are puffed out like Tarzan. They're wearing proud smirks on their faces, and congratulating each other on their masculine prowess. They're acting like they just got hit on by Miss America.

"Oh please. Don't make their heads any bigger, they may not be able to fit through that door when I kick them out," I chuckle.

She hands me her card and walks out the door. "If you remember anything, and I don't care what time it is, you call me. We'll talk soon about the details, and some resources that other girls in your situation have found very helpful. Hang in there kid."

I've been out of the hospital three weeks. In that time, a lot has happened. After beating Pistol sober and hog-tying him to a wheel line, Mason called Brody to let him know where the police could find him. He told Brody he didn't care if he got in trouble for it, because he felt so badly about being the one to set us up. Officer Marnia overlooked Mason's involvement, and left it out of her incident report. That made her an instant hero to the boys, who will probably decorate their rooms with her pin-ups soon. At the very least, they will be starting a campaign to make her the centerfold of the "Women in Black" police women calendar this year.

I may actually join their bandwagon. Officer Marnia has been great. She's eased my nerves about having to face Pistol in court, and once my concussion heals and my shoulder gets better, she's going to get me into a self-defense class. She's also set me up with a support group for teen girls who have been in abusive relationships. I'm a little hesitant about that one, be-cause I don't really consider myself "one of those girls," but I may decide to check it out.

In the meantime, I am a fish out of water. I am miserable without my sport. It's always been my therapy and my release. I swim away my aggression and refill my happy tank with chlo-rine. It's just the way I've worked since I was six years old. Needless to say, my first week of recovery, was disheartening. I sat at practice, cheering on my teammates, but I could feel myself losing muscle tone and putting on weight. It was so depressing I wanted to cry. To burn calories, I sat on the steps, kicking my feet like a three year old in swim lessons. It was humiliating. I kept wondering why Coach Hendryx didn't just put floaties on me and send me into the shallow end with a snorkel and flippers. After a week, my frustration got the best of me.

I was daydreaming about kicking Pistol in the face for putting me in this position, when French Daemon swam up out of the blue. He was swimming well outside of his lane, so I'm pretty sure he was trying to mess with me. I swore to Coach that I didn't see him when I kicked him right in the mouth and split his lip open. Coach Hendryx, however, didn't buy it. He decided I needed to take a few more weeks off of practice so I didn't put any more of his swimmers on the injured list.

At this point, my lack of activity makes me want to crawl in a hole, but my friends and family have been relentless about keeping me out of my gloomy bat cave. Since I'm no longer welcome at swim practice, I've been hanging out with the football team. I've helped my dad keep stats for the last two games. Unbelievably, we won our second playoff game and we made it to Championships. This was an incredible feat for the Mighty Miners, as they usually don't go too far in the postseason. The last time our school saw a team this strong, was two decades ago when my parents were freshmen in high school. Unfortunately, we saw the end of our great run when we were stung by the Hornets last Friday night.

The excitement of playoffs eased some of the bitterness of not being able to swim at Masters. Though I was sad that I missed my last Varsity meet, I was ecstatic for my dad and his team. Making it to Championships put the spotlight on the boys, and both Caden and Brody got a lot of recognition for their stellar performances. The dynamic duo played exceptionally well in the Championship game. The Miners were actually up by three points until the very end of the fourth quarter, when

Braden Williams fumbled the ball. It was picked up by a speedy little Hornet, who carried it all the way to the end-zone for the game winning touchdown. Despite the unfortunate outcome of that game, both Caden and Brody have been getting phone calls from various colleges in the region. Choosing where to play next year could be a tough decision for the boys. The Ducks are looking like a pretty strong possibility. I'm not so happy about that. Let's face it, they have an awesome football team, but I'm not sure I want my boys playing for our greatest rivals next year.

The night the boys told me about the Duck's recruiter, I didn't take it well. I went straight to my room and put on all of my Beaver's gear, hoping to convince them that beavers are much cuter animals than ducks. I always thought we'd be going to college together, and I certainly never dreamed that we'd be attending rival schools. Needless to say, I couldn't let the topic die. I even got a little argumentative and aggressive.

I thought my attitude finally got the best of Brody, when he rushed off and told me he'd talk to me later. I sulked and pouted for hours in my room, thinking I'd finally driven him away for good. The hardest part was keeping my disappointment out of Caden's view. He doesn't know quite the depth of feelings I've developed for our best friend. Brody's been doing a pretty great job of downplaying this thing we've got going on too.

After two hours reflecting on what my life might be like next year without the boys right beside me, I was on the verge of a teary breakdown. That's when Brody showed up on my doorstep with a surprise. He took the time to bake me chocolate chip cookies from scratch, and brought them over just to make me feel better. He reminded me that Corvallis and Eugene aren't even an hour apart . . . that's less time than I spend at swim practice. He told me he could bake me cookies every weekend if I wanted and hand deliver them on Saturdays. He always knows the right things to say. That boy is really starting to tug at my heartstrings.

I'm reminded about his thoughtfulness almost every day. For Caden's and my eighteenth birthday at the end of October, he has enlisted the help of the gang to have a barn dance out at the Mason Ranch in the valley. He talked to his grandparents and got it all set up. My parents offered to kick in some financial backing as long as they can join in and make it a big country birthday bash for all of our family and friends. Even Mason has joined in on getting the place ready. Jenna is driving me crazy with the planning. She's totally into the fall harvest idea, and made me join Pinterest so she could send me the fifty-eight pins she finds every day. If nothing else, it will be decorated to a T.

Despite my bitter attitude about my limited abilities, the gang continues to work to keep me out of a funk. Peyton has played an especially big role in my mental recovery. She's been my sidekick for the past week while Jenna has been tied up in Sacramento. Since my pain medicine won't allow me to drive right now, Peyton's been chauffeuring me around to buy supplies and decorations. Even though she maintains her ties to the Kitty Krew, in the time I've spent with her, I've found she is actually sweet. I have to admit Peyton's insistence on my participation with implementing Jenna's plan is keeping my mind off of swimming, and the other huge list of restrictions I've been barred from while my concussion heals.

CHAPTER 18

MIXING IT UP

```
(102) 004-0807:
Happy Birthday BFF!!!
```

MY BRAND NEW PHONE CHIMES with a text. I'm super excited that my parents gave it to me for an early birthday present. *Yes, no more Dinophone!!!* I think to myself as I hear the catchy new chime coming from my bedside table. I'm thrilled about the new technology; not to mention, I've been going crazy without my old phone that Officer Marnia confiscated to use as evidence against Pistol. The only bright side to that scenario is that it made it much easier to follow the doctor's strict "no texting" orders. Quite frankly, I don't see what texting has to do with a head injury, but what can I say? I'm a rule follower. Finally, my life is falling back into place. I look at the shiny new phone sitting in my hand. Since I couldn't get any of the numbers to transfer from my old phone, I quickly add Jenna as a new contact.

Jenna (BFF):
You'd better get up! The boys are already at the ranch doing all the heavy lifting and dirty work. If we don't get out there fast, they're going to whip out the boxes of decorations . . . I can't even imagine what they'll do with those . . . All my Pinterest searches will be for nothing. WAKE UP!!!!

I try to sit up so I can respond, but my arm is still so stiff I'm finding it hard to roll out of bed . . .

Jenna (BFF):
I'll be there in 10 minutes. And I'm not texting back . . . I'll be driving.

I know Jenna is going to be annoyed with me since I haven't even taken a shower yet. She's a girl on a mission. No amount of fight in me is enough to hold her back when she wants to accomplish a task.

Me:
Hold your horses, Girlfriend . . . I'm just getting up! Now that I'm aging I need my beauty sleep.

Darn that girl wakes up early on weekends. Where does she get all of that energy?

After much struggle, I finally send off a second text.

Me:
Give me at least forty-five. I don't want to look crusty tonight. I've got to take a shower and throw some clothes together to change into after we decorate. Besides, you never know which of those kitties is going to crash my party, and I don't want to look like a scraggly scratch post if they show up.

My phone chimes again. This time, it's from a different number.

(364) 277-4653:
Can't wait to see you tonight. Bet you'll look hot . . . like always.

Awww . . . Brody. He's so sweet.

Ever since the attack, Brody has been extremely cautious. He still likes to joke around and flirt with me, but there's a new softness in his voice and hesitation in his touch. It's almost as though he's checking to see if it's okay with me that he still wants to be more than friends. I smile at the thought of how careful he's been with me lately, as I add him into my contacts.

There's so much pressure from Jenna to get ready, that I don't text him back right away. I set my phone on the sink, and figure I'll text him while I'm doing my hair and makeup.

I carefully slink my pajamas to the ground, and step into the shower. I do my best to wash my hair, but it's still rough lifting my arm above my head. I'm in physical therapy, which is helping some, but I still get light headed when I overuse my arm. I'm frustrated and ticked off that Pistol did this to me. In fact, I'm frustrated and ticked off at life. I used to be able to complete a two thousand meter Fly, and now I can't even lift my arm long enough to wash my hair. I try to subdue the bitterness around my family and friends, but I am so angry inside that sometimes the most innocent comments set me off. I've become the queen of the z-snap and sarcasm.

I've been trying to use my music as an escape, taking the time I've been banned from swim practice, to play my guitar instead. It helps a little, but holding the guitar for too long hurts, and I find myself back in the same frame of mind, despising Pistol, and angry with all that he took from me. At least I haven't had to see or hear from that jerk since the night he destroyed me. The police found him a couple days later at a party on Forest Mountain and served him his restraining order along with a citation for being a minor in possession of alcohol. Lucky bastard. Someone must've found him hog tied to that wheel line and cut him loose.

As I scrub my hair, I imagine shoving a hot poker up his ass. I continuously think of new ways to get revenge on that jerk. I know it'll never happen, at least not to the extent that I hope; but one can dream. My vindictive vision of fiery hot pokers is interrupted by the chime of several more texts, one right after the other. Wow, the phone is blowing up this morning . . . Probably Facebook birthday messages.

I get out of the shower and pull my towel around me. I'm curious about all of the dinging I heard in the shower, so I make my way over to my phone to find several new messages. *Shoot. I don't know who any of them are from. There are just a bunch of unknown numbers.*

```
(364) 539-1212:
Happy Birthday! Hope your day is as
fabulous as you are.
```

(364) 305-0708:
Happy Birthday Sexy Doll.

(286) 774-3563:
Are you really Eighteen today? Wow
. . . my little niece is growing up.

(108) 411-0926:
Grammie and Grampie are sending you
love today, Honey!

(364) 577-7622:
Happy Birthday, you Hamburger!!!
Make a wish to get that arm healed!
I need you back on this team.

1 (997) 426-1025:
I made you another batch of chocolate
chip cookies!!! See you tonight.
Save me a dance.

I start decoding the birthday messages and adding all of the well-wishers to my new contacts. *Hmmm. Not sure who the first one is. I'll have to message them to find out . . . Or the second. That's interesting. Sexy Doll? Hmmmm. Oh, Auntie Lori. I can add her. Grammie and Grampie. That's sweet. Oh, Coach Hendryx. That was nice. And Brody . . . Hmmm. Thought I added him. Must not have saved.*

I re-enter all of my contacts, making sure to save all of them this time. I'm taking way too much time with my new phone, and I know Jenna is going to be busting down my door any second. I decide to chuck the phone into my bag and get ready. I run to the closet and pull on a t-shirt and some yoga pants. Then I choose my Buckle jeans and western boots to wear tonight. I quickly shove them into my overnight bag. I want to stick with the cute country theme Jenna came up with for the party. I throw in my sparkly white, lacy tank top and call it good on my outfit.

I'm struggling to put on my horseshoe necklace when Jenna throws open the door. "Are you ready Birthday Girl?" she shouts.

"Still working on my hair and make-up. Help me with this, will ya?"

Jenna comes over and helps me put on my necklace.

"You know this charm is getting a little old. Aren't you ready to try something new? Maybe something that says . . . I'm eighteen?" she asks as she clasps it around my neck.

"No way. This lucky necklace is a part of me." I lift the horseshoe to my mouth, sliding the U shape over my lip out of habit. I pull it back off and twist it in my fingers, until I finally drop it back to my chest. "I've worn it for every memorable event I've been to since the day Brody gave it to me . . . I can't explain it. It's like a security blanket or something." I shake my head. "Maybe I'm superstitious, but this necklace just makes me feel . . . safe."

"Okay, enough said." Jenna says, raising her hands to show me she's backing off. "Hey, do you need help with your hair? You can't even lift your arm, and we need to get out of here."

In true Jenna fashion, she pulls the brush from my hand and proceeds to help me with my hair and makeup until I look like I just stepped out of a country music video. "There. You look Hot! I hope some of those kitties actually show up, so they can see exactly why Brody's going to ask you to *dance on the hood of his daddy's tractor* tonight,*"* she giggles air quoting the lyrics, as she continues to sing the chorus of Luke's *Country Girl* song.

I finish putting on my lipgloss, grab my bag of party clothes, throw in my make-up, and head down the hall with Jenna. "See you tonight, Mom." I lean in giving her a hug and a kiss on the cheek.

"Have fun getting that barn dance ready Birthday Girl!" my mom smiles, and sends me on my way. "See you in a few hours."

We jump in Jenna's car and she double honks the horn, waving at my mom before we head down the street. It's a brisk fall morning, but the pristine blue sky is the perfect backdrop to accentuate the fall colors that paint the mountain landscape. As we head over the hill toward the valley, I'm glad to see that this part of the forest was left untouched. It was a rough fire season in the area, and hundreds of acres were destroyed by several wildfires. As a matter of fact, the road is still clogged with the traffic of all the workers breaking down the fire camps. Jenna taps her foot impatiently as we get stuck behind a line of Cal Fire trucks heading back over the hill on the one lane highway. "It's okay Jenna. We've got time."

"Not really!" she squeals. "I was supposed to pick up Peyton a half hour ago. Can you call her and tell her we're on our way?"

I grab my phone from my bag, and look at the line of unknown numbers, reminding me, that I no longer have Peyton's contact information. "I would, but I don't have any contacts. I spent twenty minutes this morning trying to decode who was sending me birthday texts."

"Here, use mine." Jenna hands me her phone, and I scroll down to Peyton's name and hit dial.

"Hello?" Peyton's perky, little voice sings.

"Hey Peyton. It's Kaitlyn. We're headed over the hill now. It's a little slow with fire trucks and road construction, but we'll be there as soon as we can, k?"

"No problem, Kait! I'm so excited to spend the day celebrating with you and Caden. Thanks for including me today!"

"After all the creative ideas you came up with, and the time you spent getting this ready, I wouldn't dream of not having you there with us to get the place decorated."

"Awww, I've loved every second of it, Sis. I'm gonna finish my hair real quick before you get here. We'll talk more in the car. See you soon."

We hang up the phone and I turn to Jenna. "You know. I would've never thought Peyton was so sweet. She has been amazing through this entire recovery. Do you know she brought us all dinner the other night just to give my mom a break? By the way, her lasagna is mouth-watering." I pause momentarily, "I think she and my brother are getting pretty serious . . . she just called me Sis."

"Really?" Jenna replies, scrunching up her nose. "Well, just don't go swapping out best friends on me!"

"Never . . . You're my BFF til the end."

We pull up in front of Peyton's house and she comes bouncing out like Santa Claus. She has an armful of gifts, including a shiny box adorned with a big turquoise and white polka-dotted bow. Bouncing blonde hair and a shiny white smile peek out from behind the packages. Jenna looks over at me with a grimace. "Well, Forever BFF . . . I'm still waiting on your present . . ." Jenna groans, looking embarrassed that she's been outdone by my new "sister."

"Got ya something!" Peyton hands the package over the seat as she slides in the car.

"You didn't have to, really!" I squeal, grabbing it out of her hand. "Do you mind if I open it right now? I'm really not good at waiting for surprises . . ."

Peyton laughs, "I know. Caden told me. That's why I *hannnnded* it to you right away."

When I peel off the wrapping paper, I see an adorable polka dotted frame that matches my bedroom. Centered at the bottom, in fancy script, it reads *"Good times, Great friends, Amazing*

Memories." A collage of pictures reveals some of my favorite memories of the gang. As I glimpse across the top, I smile at the photo of all of us standing around a bonfire. Another picture is from late spring when we ditched school and hiked Shackleford Trail. I'm surprised to see one of Brody and me mid-air, holding hands, jumping off Kelsey Creek Bridge. Another is all five of us sitting on the tailgate after mudding in Caden's truck. Highlighting the collage, the largest picture is Jenna and me goofing off after Championships with our high point medals wrapped across our foreheads.

"I got some of the pictures off of Caden's computer. I hope you don't mind," Peyton smiles hesitantly.

"I love it Peyton! This is the cutest gift ever!" I grab her, and pull her through the space in the front seats, for a warm hug. Then she turns to Jenna and pulls out another package from behind her back.

"I hope you like it too Jenna. Cuz I made you a matching one." She smiles, handing it to her.

I'm pretty sure this is the first time I've seen Jenna speechless. Her eyes widen and I can see the glossy tears start to form. She quickly sucks the tears back in, with her tough girl magic, and pulls Peyton in for a hug, "Welcome to the family, Sis!" she laughs. At that, Peyton tears up too.

"So do you guys think Caden will like his birthday gift too? It's a little more manly than yours, but I did my best to highlight the last couple months with him."

"Oh, he's going to love it Peyton. I'm sure it will go right on his wall as soon as he gets home," I reassure her.

"Ya, that kid could never get enough of looking at himself," Jenna bursts out laughing.

"Come on now, cut him some slack, it's his birthday," I interrupt, feeling a little guilty for talking about my brother like that.

"Speaking of cut. I also got him this." Peyton opens the lid to another small gift box, and pulls out a shiny new pocket knife. "I had his name engraved on it. I noticed he collects them."

"I'm sure it will be his new favorite, Girl. It looks like it's a cut above the rest! Ha . . . ha" I slap my knee at my corny joke."

"Oh geez, look at the time. Bring it on in girls," Jenna laughs. And the three of us lean in and hug it out before heading over the hill to decorate for the barn dance.

By the time we pull up to the ranch, the boys have what looks to be a hundred bales of hay, lining the dance floor inside the big, open barn. The boys, however, are nowhere in sight. "Well that should be plenty of seating," Jenna laughs out as we look around trying to spot them. "Where is everyone?"

"Listen. I hear them squabbling. I just can't see them." Peyton snickers.

I start walking around, trying to follow the muffled bickering sound I hear coming from behind the enormous hay stack. "Up there!" I point. Caden is hanging upside down from one of the rafters, trying to twist what looks like a five hundred foot string of lights around the beam.

"I found some camo Duck tape to wrap around it," Caden shouts. "It'll blend right in so no one sees it!"

"No. no. no. I've got baling twine right here. It'll hold way better," Mason counters Caden.

"That is the most hideous shade of orange I've ever seen. You are not using that on those lights!" Jenna commands. Then she turns to us red-faced and snarling. "We got here just in time ladies."

We can't help but crack up at Jenna's incensed response.

"First of all. You need to disconnect twenty of those strings. It's way too hard to wrap five hundred feet of lights around a beam at one time. Reel it out boys. The girls are here to help."

I hear Brody's deep voice boom from the haystack, "Listen up Bo and Luke. Daisy Duke is here to save the day."

"It's more like Boss Hog, Bro." I hear Caden pipe in.

"I heard that Caden! And if you're not careful . . . you're going to land smack dab in the heart of Hazzard County, for sure," Jenna shouts, shaking her fist up at the rafters. Another round of laughter erupts in our small circle. "Now seriously. I have my list here of things we need to get done before the party."

Jenna starts giving orders, and we steadily find ourselves in the rhythm of hanging lights, laying table cloths, and setting out decorations until we've transformed the barn into a magical fall harvest. Looking around, everything looks incredible. There are twinkling baby white lights wrapped around the wagon wheels leading up to the barn. Mason jars, filled with citronella candles, hang gracefully from the rafters. Saddle blankets lay atop the bales of hay lining the perimeter of the barn. Huge water troughs are filled with ice, soft drinks, and adult beverages. At the far end of the barn, near the DJ, Peyton has designed and set up a photo booth with a painted red barn and scarecrows as a backdrop.

"Awww, Photographer Peyton! I love it!" I wink, giving her a big hug. "Thank you so much for everything you did to help." I am incredibly touched by everything our friends and family have done to make our eighteenth birthday so special. My brother and I are so blessed to have this circle of friends. Turning toward the rest of the crowd, I choke out, "Thank you all so much, for everything." I open my arms and take each one in for a warm embrace.

"Happy Birthday, Happy Birthday Twinsies." I hear repeatedly from all of our friends. "You two are so worth it," Jenna says.

"We're just glad you're still here to celebrate with us." Brody smiles shyly, looking down at the ground, shuffling his boots in the hay. I can tell he is still bothered by that night. He doesn't look me in the eyes when he talks about it. I'm sure the image of my lifeless body lying on the ground with blood coming from my mouth is still burned into his memory.

The circle of gratitude is interrupted when Grandma Sandy and Auntie Macy stumble in with two wheelbarrows full of gigantic Gatorade thermoses, the kind you see on the sidelines at football games. Auntie Macy stops just short of the circle and stutters, "I'm pretty sure this is the Spiked Apple Pie Punch." In contemplation, she squints her eyes at the thermos, pinches her lips into a line, and shakes her head slightly up and down. Her tongue clicks just before she quickly cocks her head to the side and grabs a cup from the big bag in the wheelbarrow. We all watch in amusement as she fills the cup to the top, tips it back and chugs it until it's completely empty. "Ya, I'm pretty sure about that. The one Grandma Sandy has is for you kids." She says pointing at the matching thermos. "Here, stick this sign on there to make sure they don't get mixed up now," she giggles, handing Caden a sign that reads, *"Alcoholic."*

I look over at Jenna, and she and Caden are glancing at each other with mischief in their eyes. I shake my head, trying to imagine what they are thinking. "I've got this Grandma," Caden nods and smiles, taking the wheelbarrow out of her hands, and sticking the sign down on Auntie Macy's cooler. "Hey Jenna, would you come give me a hand with this?" Caden whispers.

"Sure thing."

I look at Brody. When our eyes meet, the corner of his lip turns up in a half grin. For some reason, I think this party is about to get interesting. He holds out his hand, "Hey Pip? You ready to go get freshened up?" He moves closer, brushing his thumb against my skin. "You had a little something on your cheek. I'll take you down to the ranch to get cleaned up. I think Caden and Jenna have some stuff to take care of before the party. You and I . . ." he points back and forth between the two of us, " . . . should probably put a little distance between us, and those two hooligans carting the thermoses over there."

"You're probably right," I giggle.

He grabs my hand, and begins to pull me toward the car so I can get my bag. As we're walking, I feel a nudge, and catch a glimpse of Brody looking back over his shoulder. I watch Jenna and Caden peel the sign from the thermos, and end their shenanigans with a high five. I'm pretty sure, I hear Jenna's voice off in the distance, "We really shouldn't label anyone an 'Alcoholic' now, should we?"

We both laugh and shake our heads in amusement. "Those two are something else."

It doesn't take long to freshen up at the ranch. I put on some deodorant, fix my make-up, and throw on my cute birthday outfit. I look as good as new. When we head back to the barn, the sun is just dipping down below the horizon. Country music is flowing from the dimly lit barn, and family and friends are beginning to line the long dirt road. When I glance up into the barn, my eyes are instantly drawn to Jenna and Caden standing up on the hay bales having a twerking contest.

"Oh, my. Look who's already gotten into the spiked apple cider," Brody looks at me and chuckles.

In the background, *Drink to That All Night* by Jerrod Niemann, is blasting. Caden and Jenna jump from bale to bale, playing tag, and twerking intermittently. "You ready to party with me all night?" Brody asks, with a half grin and a wink.

"You know there's no one in this county I'd rather party with til the sun comes up." I mutter shyly, poking Brody in the belly. "Let's do it!"

At that, I feel Brody's hand come around my waist, as he carefully flips me up onto his back. He suddenly pauses, "Wait, is your shoulder okay?"

"Yep, you did good! Now Giddy up cowboy," I giggle, giving him a friendly kick accompanied by a *click click* of my tongue. I set my chin on his shoulder, as he gives me a piggyback ride up the dirt road. Secure in Brody's strong arms, I try to take in everything, every sight, sound, and feeling; the crunch of the gravel beneath his feet, the baby white lights guiding our way up the road, friends and family illuminated by the glow of the bonfire. A smile spreads across my face. I can't believe how much love and care our friends and family put into this party for us. If this can't pull me out of my depression, I don't know what can. This eighteenth birthday party is monumental.

As we near Caden and Jenna, they pause and look at us. Then they look at each other. I swear those two can read each other's minds. I watch Caden wink at Jenna before he yells down to us, "Hey Brody?"

"Ya?" He yells back up to the top of the haystack where Caden and Jenna are now giggling.

"Why did the horse cross the road?"

"Why's that, Cade?"

"Because he was looking for . . . HAY!!!!"

At that, Jenna and Caden pick up huge flakes of hay and begin to pummel us with them. Brody carefully drops me down to the ground so we can defend ourselves. I cover my head and face, as showers of alfalfa come hammering down on our heads. Brody, scampers back quickly trying to dodge the relentless attack, as he backs into the drink trough. It almost looks as though it's in slow motion. I see his arms flailing in circles out to the side. "Whoaaaaa," he neighs, as he hits the ice, perfectly molding it around his body. The mounds of displaced ice knock some of the drinks over the edge. I watch them hit the ground as explosions of soda start spraying everywhere. I can hear shrieks of hysterics as people pull their hands over their heads and run for the big open door. All I can do is laugh, but poor Brody is stuck in a big trough of ice. "Help!!! I've fallen and I can't giddy-up!" he laughs. At that, Caden bounces down the bales and extends his hand to Brody, pulling him out of the trough.

"Here, have a drink. It looks like you could use one." Caden holds out a plastic cup to Brody.

Brody pauses for a second, as if contemplating whether he

should try it. "Hmmm . . . you only live once, I guess." He takes a big swig, chokes a little, and looks up with teary eyes. His eyebrows raise, as he clears his throat.

He looks over at me and says, "Any more of these, and I might be bouncing around those hay bales too. You've got to try one of these Pip," he chuckles. "You wanna get a little redneck rowdy with me?"

I've never actually drank before. It's not something that ever really intrigued me. But I can't refuse an invitation like that from Brody. "Well, you only turn eighteen once! Let's do it!"

"Hey bartender, can I order one of these for your little sister?"

Caden grins mischievously, "Hey Jenna?" he shouts back up the haystack. "We're headed over to get another round of that virgin cider. You in?"

"Heck ya! Let's get this party STARTED!" Jenna shrieks, jumping straight down to the floor. She holds her arms straight out, "Super Girl!!" she yells, as she flies through the air.

"Now that's why she's in my wolf pack," Caden howls, pointing down at her with a quick poke. "Let's go Wonder Woman," he gives Jenna a playful shove, pushing her toward the drink table.

We walk over to the thermoses and make a loud scene, hoping to throw any adults off our trail. "So this is the 'NON-ALCOHOLIC' right Caden?" she says slowly.

"Right you are Jenna! Here's your sign!" he blurts out, with his best Jeff Foxworthy impersonation.

"Got it!"

Jenna leans in really close to the spout, concentrating on pouring the drink to the very rim. "I learned that in science class. It's called polarity! See, I can actually fill it fuller than the rim as long as I do it slowly. All those little molecules stick together. Sip now, my precious friend, sip," she says, holding the cup up to my lips, so I can take a drink before it spills out everywhere.

I contemplate whether I should do this. I wouldn't usually drink, but seeing as how I can't swim right now, I guess it really doesn't matter much. Plus, maybe it will help me forget about all this Pistol craziness, and my messed up shoulder injury for a while. I decide to give it my best shot. After all, it's not my style to half-ass anything. I take in a deep swimmer's breath, and slurp until I have to come up for air. "There, that should put a dent in it." I cough. "Phew! That stuff is potent," I gasp. My eyes are tearing up from the burn still making its way down my throat.

"It'll get easier, trust me . . ." Jenna whispers. "This is already my third cup," She holds up four fingers, zooming them in and out between our faces.

"Well, I'm all about easy. Give me that!" I take the cup from her hand and tip my head back until I've swallowed every last drop. "WINNER!!! I yell out," sticking my tongue out Fear Factor style, "Ahhhhhh," I say, "Check. There's nothing left in there." I wiggle my tongue around my mouth, to prove I drank it all.

Just then, Peyton walks up with her mouth open. "Impressive Kaitlyn," she says, shaking her head up and down. "Don't worry Brody," she turns to him. "I'll watch out for them tonight. You boys go ahead and have fun too. Caden smiles. "Well, that settles it. Happy Birthday, Kaitlyn and Caden! I'm your designated driver tonight."

"Okay DD. You're the best," Caden says, wrapping his arms around Peyton, and pulling her in for a kiss on the forehead.

"Anything for you, Babe."

All the mushy stuff happening in front of me, starts to look a little blurry. Jenna's hand bobs across my line of sight with another plastic cup, blocking the view of Beauty and the Beast. "Don't slow down on me now, Birthday Girl. Take this and let's go dance."

I start to walk off with Jenna, when Brody comes up with another cup. "Got ya something." He says, plopping the cup into my open hand.

I look to my left hand, which still holds a full drink; then to my right. "Wow, guess I'm double fistin' it tonight! Where's yours?"

"Right here, Pip." Brody pulls another cup from behind his back. "Now, let's go dance."

We walk back over to the bales that line the dance floor. Brody watches me struggle to step up on one, but I just can't seem to do it with my two drinks in tow. I feel him close in behind me and slip his hands under my elbows. "Let me help you, Pip." I feel his warm soft breath against the nape of my neck, sending shivers across my skin.

I lean back into him, letting my hair fall off my neck. I roll my head to the side, and whisper, "Whoa, Bro . . . you just gave me goosebumps."

I feel the rise and release of his chest, as he pulls in a deep breath; then his soft lips come down just above my left shoulder. He trails soft kisses up to my cheek. When he reaches the corner of my mouth, he whispers, "Kaitlyn, I'm glad you felt that too. I don't want to keep this a secret anymore. I can't." He shakes his head back and forth gently. "It's time to let everyone know about us." He pulls away, just enough to look at me. His eyes plead with me to reveal our secret.

US. Wow, that's a powerful word. I'm overwhelmed by his sincerity. A cyclone of emotion spins from my stomach through my chest, leaving a lump in my throat. My heart forgets to beat momentarily. Brody smiles at the sound of me trying to gasp for air, then leans back in and whispers in my ear, "Pip, you're the most beautifully flustered girl I've ever seen in my life. I'm gonna kiss you in front of everyone right now, and I need you to be okay with it."

I can feel the smile on his lips resting against the most sensitive part of my ear. My face flushes with heat, and I can feel the butterflies begin to take flight. My stomach flips on their ascent. I can't speak. I can't breathe. The only thing left to do is nod in agreement. From the corner of my eye, I watch the smile grow across his face. His hands come around mine, gently lifting the drinks out of my secure hold. He sets them down on the bale of hay in front of us. Slowly, his hands come back to my waist and he gingerly turns me around to face him. He backs me up to the enormous haystack. "I should've done this a long time ago," he whispers, leaning into me.

I feel his soft, full lips slowly press against mine. Our mouths slightly open and close in unison. The connection sends tingles through my entire body. The tingling feeling, mixed with the buzz of the spiked apple cider, sets my head spinning. When our mouths open again, I feel his soft tongue, barely brush against mine, and I can't help but pull him in closer. I grab onto his muscular arms, and clench them tightly in my hands. His touch disintegrates the world around us, replacing it with visions of his beautiful face, the feel of his strong embrace, and the warmth of his genuine, loving soul wrapping itself around mine.

My senses are on fire. He pulls me tighter and holds me close. I can't help but wonder if he can sense my trembling. Our bodies are so close now, I feel his heart beat. I'm overwhelmed with gratitude and love for this boy. He has stuck by my side through the darkest time in my life. He has been my protector and friend, and now, he is bringing back a feeling I never thought I'd have again. Happiness. Security. At this moment, I realize that Brody Tatum owns me. He balances my fragile heart in his hands. My one hope is that he never, never lets it fall.

Behind us, I can hear the crowd getting lively. People are clapping, cheering, and whistling. I am shuttering when Brody pulls back and leaves a kiss on the bridge of my nose. "Kaitlyn Woodley, I promise you, as long as I live, I will never want anyone the way I want you. I'm yours, for as long as you'll have me. And I hope that's a really, really long time, cuz no one will ever own my heart again. It belongs to you now. I'm yours."

A tear rolls down my face. Brody brushes it away with the pad of his thumb. "Are you okay with this, Pip? Why the tears?" My throat is tight. It stings. I feel like I'm dying. It's so tight, I can't swallow. I take a deep breath, and still can't find my voice.

I know I have to respond, so I pull him back into me and kiss him with everything I have in me. When I'm done, I pull away smiling. "Brody Tatum. I love you so much it hurts. I've loved you my whole life. I just didn't know it til now. I'm the luckiest girl in the world." I think about what he's just said, and want to lay it all out there. "And. . . you will have me for a really, really long time. I know that because you own my heart too. You always have."

Brody smiles at me, throws his head up toward the sky and shouts, "Thank you Lord!!!" He picks me up by the waist, and twirls me around in a circle, until I wrap my legs around his waist, and pull back into him.

Everyone around us erupts in cheers and laughter. Caden walks up behind us, and pats Brody on the back, "Welcome to the family, Bro. I know you'll treat her the way she deserves to be treated. I've seen it now. Take care of her, Buddy. You've got my blessing." Then he turns to me, "Happy Birthday Twin."

CHAPTER 19

TORN

"**L**ET'S DANCE!" CADEN SPINS AROUND and yells to Peyton, grabbing her by the hand and twirling her out to the dance floor. Brody wraps me in his arms so we're both facing the dancing duo. Cradling me against him, Brody guides my movement as we sway to the music.

I feel his warm breath tickle the back of my ear, and quickly scrunch my head down toward my shoulder, as he starts to whisper, "We finally got his blessing, Pip. Can you believe this is really happening? I feel like the luckiest guy in the world." Shivers crawl across my neck and shoulder; his whispers, leave a trail of tiny goosebumps. He plants a tiny kiss on my ear, and pulls away with a little nibble. When he sees the goosebumps he's left, he begins to chuckle, and proudly revels, "Ya, I just did that to you."

My nerves do that little shaken soda thing that has become a frequent reaction when Brody is near. I grab his hands tightly in mine. I'm not sure if it's his words, or that spiked apple cider, but I find it hard to breathe. My dizziness becomes apparent as I watch my brother swinging and flipping Peyton. Blurry streaks of color follow each of their movements. I scrunch my eyes closed, trying to stop the spinning. Just as I thought I've blocked out the world, I hear laughter erupt all around me. Brody is laughing so hard, I feel his firm abs bouncing up and down against my back. I open my eyes, and look up to Brody, "What's so funny?"

"Ummm . . . Look at your brother right now," he laughs. "You think the ice trough was embarrassing? That's nothing compared to the *Kiss me I'm Irish* boxer shorts peeking through that ripped seem in your brother's britches."

I look toward the dance floor to see Peyton holding Caden's pants together at the seam. She shuffles him out the door, through the crowds of laughing parents and friends toward a hysterical Mason, who laughs out in his best Irish brogue, "That's quite an ars, you've got shinin' through your pantaloons. Too bad your luck didn't save your seam that time."

Peyton pushes Caden around the side of the barn and runs back in to me, "Uh, I'm gonna take him to Mason's to go fix this before we pull everyone together to sing you guys *Happy Birthday.* Don't go far, I'll be right back, okay?"

"Why don't you stay here with, Kaitlyn? I've got a birthday surprise, that I left down at Mason's. Besides, I need to have a man to man chat with my new bro-in-law to make sure he knows I have pure intentions with his twin sister." Brody convinces Peyton to stay with me so he can take care of his business.

"Ya . . . um. .sure, Brody. Go ahead and take him. I need to get Kaitlyn and Jenna over to my photo booth anyway. "Well," she giggles, "if I can pull Jenna away from Ty." She throws a quick glance over toward Jenna, who's currently attempting an upside down shot with Ty holding her feet. We turn toward each other giggling. "Let's go get that crazy girl."

Brody comes in and gives me a hug, whispering in my ear.

"You stay out of trouble young lady. I'll be right back with that birthday surprise."

Peyton slips her arm through mine and leads me over to my upside down buddy. "Hey Jenna, come get a picture with Kaitlyn and me before you pop all the blood vessels in that beautiful face of yours."

"Just a second ladies," she snorts, pulling one arm away from her handstand and pointing toward the dance floor. Balancing on one arm, as Ty continues to hold her feet, Jenna continues, "You girls should join me. The Kitty Crew is fascinating from this angle. Chelsea's nostrils are the size of candy corns. Dude! Look at that booger. It's a gold mine in there! She's not so sexy now. And wait . . . wait Lexi has sweat stains under her boobs! Oh gosh . . . Oh gosh . . . Janet's digging hard for those undies!" Jenna works herself into hysterics laughing so hard at her new potpourri of discoveries, that her arm collapses. Ty releases his slipping hold on her feet, and she crashes onto her head into a pile of hay. "Man, that didn't even hurt." She jumps up, throws her arms high in the air, and ends her acrobatic stunt with a dismount worthy of a perfect ten.

Jenna stumbles toward us, looking back at Ty and growls, "Catch ya in a bit Handsome." Then she drapes her arms around both of our necks, and starts to belligerently sing, "We're off to see the Wizard . . . oops," she pauses and rolls her head to the side, looking up at me through her drooping eyelids, "I mean the scarecrow! Hey, who cares who we're going to see? Whoever it is . . . well, they're just lucky to have such HOT visitors," she growls. "It's picture time ladies!" As she begins to sing her song again, we skip off like Dorothy and friends, over to the photo station. On the way, Jenna sneaks one more plastic cup of spiked apple cider and shouts, "One more for the Yellow Brick Road!!! Grab some girls!"

"I'm still designated driver," Peyton interrupts, holding her hands up and giving a slight shake of her head " . . . but Kaitlyn, you go ahead Birthday Girl. I've got your back."

My head is already spinning. I'm so new at this, I don't want to risk drinking any more. I really don't like how it's making me feel. I've never been so dizzy and floppy before. I'm an athlete. I like having control of my body. I'm finding this is not my thing at all.

Before I can respond to Peyton's offer I hear, "Here Kait . . . you have mine. I can get more!" Jenna quickly spins toward me, sending a swirling tsunami of cider all over my shirt. She's in rare form tonight. She is loud, showy, and absolutely hilarious. I know I'm buzzing a little, but poor Jenna. All I can think is, she's really gonna feel this in the morning.

At the photo station, we take a few goofy-faced pictures. In the middle of our third frame, my phone dings. I hold up my hand toward the photographer. "Just a sec. I need to check this." I work my new, oversized phone out of my pocket and see a text from Brody.

Brody:
Hey there Doll. Meet me in the tack room in 5. I have a surprise for you.

That's strange. Doesn't sound like Brody . . . He must have had way too many tonight. I feel rude for the delay, so I quickly jam my phone back in my pocket. "Okay girls. I have like five minutes. Let's get in a couple more pictures." We decide to try some pyramid shots.

"I'm flyer!" Jenna shouts, working to scale up Peyton's and my legs. No sooner does she get to the top, then she yells out, "Snap one mid-air!" Suddenly, with great force, Jenna hurdles off our hips, and jumps toward the camera. At the extensive thrust, Peyton and I collapse to the ground in hysterics. Flashes fly, and so does Jenna . . . right into Chelsea and Lexi, who are standing directly behind the quick footed photographer; who, by the way, instantly scampered away to avoid the collision. Not only does Jenna crash their party, but she knocks their drinks to the floor, and takes them down like bowling pins.

"Watch where you're going!" Chelsea growls. "Out of this entire barn, why do you have to fly right into us?"

"Soooooorrrry!" Jenna snarls back. "I didn't realize I had to file a flight plan and check with Catland Security before take-off!" At her snide remark, claws come out and fur starts to fly between Jenna and the felines. Peyton and I sit in disbelief, mouths gaping, as Chelsea grabs hold of Jenna's hair, twists it around her fist, and starts yanking her like a scarecrow without stuffing.

Peyton untangles herself from me, jumps up, and rushes over to her friends. "Stop that Chelsea! You've gone too far! Get your hands off of her!" She pushes Chelsea back. "It was an accident. You know she's had a lot to drink, and so have you. You should just leave before you're escorted out . . . or worse, someone knocks your prissy ass out!"

Peyton points to the open barn door and yells, "Go!" Without another word, Chelsea and Lexi put their tails between their legs and shuffle out. Peyton reaches down and pulls Jenna off the ground; she helps brush her off and begins picking the hay out of her hair. "Boy Jenna, you're something special in the air. Are you okay my flying friend?"

Jenna laughs, "Thanks for restoring our friendly skies, Air Marshall." Then she salutes Peyton, and heads off to find Ty to escape all the excitement.

"Peyton," I look down at the ground and then back up to her. "Thanks for taking care of my buddy. I know that must've been hard on you cuz those are your friends." I'm still buzzing, and feeling all warm and fuzzy inside, so I give Peyton a genuine hug.

"Awww . . . Kait, you two have been better friends to me than they ever were. Besides, I think I love Caden. And that means you're like my sis now. I told you I've got your back, and I meant it. Speaking of Caden, they should be back here any minute."

I realize I'm pushing it on time. Brody said to meet him in five minutes, and it's probably been ten.

"Ya, I need to go meet Brody really fast. He texted a few minutes ago. Do you think you can hold off on that birthday song til I get back?"

"Make it snappy, or I'll have to come hunt you down." Peyton giggles.

"Ok, I'll be back in a flash," I grin and run off to the tack room.

As I run down the gravel road, the music begins to fade behind me along with the twinkling lights. Whoo, I've had a lot to drink. I'm winded and dizzy by the time I get down to the tack room. I bend over and put my hands on my knees trying to catch my breath before I pull back the heavy wooden door. It slowly creaks open and I peek inside. "Peek a Boo," I sing playfully as I peer in trying to spot Brody. I can't see a thing through the darkness. I jump when I hear the sudden flitting of wings swoosh up toward the rafters. *It's just a bat. The opening door must have scared the creepy little bugger.* It's a good thing I have a little liquid courage flowing through my veins right now, otherwise Brody's surprise would have to wait. I look around again before stepping inside. I thought he would at least be out front. He knows how creeped out I get by dark, scary rooms. Maybe he wants to surprise me in private. "Brody," I whisper. "I'm starting to freak out here. Where are you?" I feel my way along the wall of hanging tools. "Come out come out wherever you are," I giggle in a half drunken stupor.

I stop for a second to give Brody a chance to reveal himself. Out of nervous habit, I grab at my necklace while I wait for him. I don't feel it there. *It must've twisted off to the side.* I pat around my chest, searching for my charm. *My necklace . . .*

it's not there. A spike of adrenaline shoots through me as I think back on putting it on earlier. *I know I wore it. Jenna helped me with the clasp. Emptiness begins to fill the pit of my stomach.*

I'm pulled from my racing thoughts when off in the corner, a small light appears. From behind the wall of saddles, I hear a muffled voice float toward me. "Didn't think you'd actually show up Doll."

My heart stops and the blood in my veins turns to ice when I realize this is not Brody's voice. I hear the slow shuffle of boots across the old wooden floor, and begin to make out the blurry silhouette of a cowboy that I've grown to fear so intensely over the last six weeks. Lit, by the glow of his phone, the shadow that's cast along his face, makes him look hard, rough, and angry. "Why did you call me Brody?"

Slowly I begin to stumble backwards, trying to feel my way back to the wall. "Answer me Babydoll! Why?" His words come out angry, hurt, and slurred. The fear begins to wrap itself around my senses, sobering my mind to the realization that I'm in great danger. Pistol is drunk again, and I know that's when I get hurt.

I work to break through the drunken barricades blocking my senses. My thinking is slow. *How can I get rid of him? What can I say to make him leave? Think Kaitlyn . . . Think!* I desperately blurt the first thing that comes to mind, "Because Brody texted me and asked me to meet him here." *There. Now he knows Brody's coming.* My breathing picks up as the adrenaline begins to course through my chest. "He . . . he's going to be here any second. You'd better leave." I shake my head and reach in my pocket for my phone. *My phone. Oh no. It's not in my pocket.*

"Really?" Pistol sneakers. "So you think Brody is going to meet you here in the tack room? That's odd. Cuz about ten minutes ago . . . I texted you and told you to meet ME here. You must be confused."

"What? What do you mean YOU sent me that text? I . . .

I . . ."

My mind fumbles. *I only got one text. How could that have been Pistol? It said Brody in my phone. . . my new phone. Oh my Goodness. I didn't . . . I couldn't have added his contact as Brody this morning, could I have? Do I have two Brody's in my phone?* The alcohol in my system starts to churn. I begin to feel nauseous as my mind hits overdrive searching for an escape. *Think Kaitlyn . . . Think! How am I going to get out of this?* My cheeks begin to quiver from the nausea. I back further along the wall, but I'm clumsy from too much alcohol and the wall is endless. I can't find the opening anywhere. I hear his footsteps closing in on me. I can feel his energy invading my space.

"You know you want me Kaitlyn. Why are you backing away from me? Though I am enjoying this little game of cat and mouse." His devious cackle fills the room.

"Stay back. I'm gonna get sick." I hold my hand out to stop his advance. I feel his movement pause, when I double over. The burning, spiked apple pie cider forces its way up my throat and splatters all over the ground before me. I wretch and vomit, while he waits. *Darn it . . . I hate throwing up more than anything else in the world. Now I know why I don't drink . . . and never will again.* The dizziness intensifies with each heave, and I begin to sweat and cry. In between waves I yell, "Leave Pistol! Just leave me alone!"

After three slow clicks of his tongue, Pistols replies, "No can do Babydoll. I've been waiting way too long to hold you again. This is our big night, yours and mine. We're gonna celebrate your birthday in a big way."

His steps come toward me once again, and I shuffle against the wall trying to find my way to the door. As I slide across the wall, I feel a gouge and the rip of my skin. I'm caught up on something sticking out of the wall. I feel the blood begin to trickle down my back, and I hear the tear of my lacy tank top as I pry myself from whatever I'm stuck on.

I hear the crescendo of his footsteps. "Oops, I'll just step around that little mess you made. No biggie Babydoll."

I finally pull away from the wall, but I've lost sense of where I am. Maybe if I don't move, he won't find me. I drop to the ground and try to hold my breath as I cringe in the darkness. Silence fills the air, and an eerie feeling overtakes me. As I crouch on the cold ground, I feel the draft seeping up through the hardwood floor. My legs are ready to give way from the excessive trembling. For a moment the world disappears. I hear, see, and feel nothing. Silence. Unexpectedly, I feel the quick sudden grasp of my shoulders, followed by a speedy swooping motion. Like a rag doll, he has pulled me into him and he clutches me beneath his brutally strong arms. His hand covers my mouth, as he spins me around, and holds me from behind.

Shocked, and mortified, can't begin to explain the terror that seizes my entire body. The blood drains from my face, and I stand frozen and speechless when I realize I have officially been taken captive by one drunken Pistol Black.

I kick, and drag, as he pulls me backward toward the stalls. "Bro . . .," I try to scream until he silences me with his violent hand. He laughs out, "You've got nothin' on a steer Babydoll. I've been wrestling animals bigger than you since I could walk. You might as well stop fighting me."

Pistol's enormous hand has managed to find its way over my nose and I struggle to pull air in through his fingers. I can't get enough oxygen. I'm left with no choice. As my last defense, I bite down on his finger as hard as I can.

"Owww, you little BITCH!" he screams, spinning me away from him and holding me at arms length. He cocks his fist back to his shoulder. Before I can rationalize what's happening, full throttle, he lets it fly into my left jaw. The impact sends me barreling across the floor. I hit a stack of antique milk jugs, which crash down, and scatter all over the tack room floor. The loud collapse sends Pistol into full panic mode. He rushes toward me, grabs a handful of my hair and begins to tug me backwards. "You little Klutz! You just had to go and make all that racket, didn't you? They probably heard you all the way up at the barn! Now shut the hell up or I'm gonna shove my fist down your throat!"

As he continues to pull me by the hair to the back room, I back peddle, and shuffle, trying to use my hands and feet to keep up with him. I collapse from the awkward movement and the pain of putting weight on my injured shoulder. I shriek in agony as my hair begins to rip out by the roots, and though my shoulder is being torn to shreds, I continue to crab crawl to ease the pain of my ripping scalp. Pistol begins to pull me through the back door, shoving me into the room where Brody, Mason, Caden, and I played as kids. It's full of antique farrier equipment. It's dark, terrifying, and there's no way out. I know this isn't good, so I grasp onto the wall and hold on with everything in me. I scream in pain as I feel the slivers of the decaying wooden doorframe spike beneath my fingernails.

"Shut the hell up!" Pistol screams. "You know this is your fault. Why are you making this harder than it has to be?" I feel the painful impact of his boot as it crashes into my stomach. With the crunch, the air is forced from my lungs. I open my mouth to scream for help, but the only sound I'm able to produce is a weak hiss. Searing pain shoots through my ribs, seizing my breath, once again ending my struggle to pull in air. I gasp and wheeze, gasp and wheeze, but too little oxygen is making its way into my parched lungs. Blackness begins to invade my mind . . . *Don't lose it Kaitlyn. Don't pass out . . . You can't pass out. Think! Breathe!*

With a furious yank, Pistol pulls me from the doorframe and drags me to the middle of the room. The sudden movement sends my head crashing into the ground. There is instant pounding and tightening at the base of my skull. As I clench my eyes shut, trying to regain focus, I feel him come down over the top of me, and pin me beneath him. I feel like one of the poor calves he wrestles during rodeos. Dizzily, I writhe beneath him. I kick and stomp my feet, rolling my head side to side, trying to escape. Forcefully, he lays his right arm across my chest, pinning down both of my shoulders. "Shhh, Babydoll. You and I both know you aren't gonna get out of this one. You might as well just relax and enjoy our time together." He grabs my wrists and drags them above my head. I shiver when I see him pull out his piggin string.

A tear streams from my eye and rolls down the side of my cheek. I'm exhausted, I'm in so much pain, I don't know what hurts worse, my head, my shoulder, my ribs, stomach, or slivers shooting up my nail beds. I'm so dizzy, I can't see straight. My world has become dark, blurry, and hopeless. As the light and sound begins to fade, I hear the soft echo of my pastor's voice in my head, "*I will fear no evil, for you are with me.*"

I scream a desperate prayer, "Please God . . . Please . . . If you're with me, help me!" I hear Pistol chuckle, and feel the rope tighten on my wrists. I let out one more scream, "Please!"

There's a momentary pause, and a brief feeling of calm. It's almost as though God himself is warning Pistol not to go through with this heinous plan. The momentary silence allows me to hear a strange scuffle, followed by a loud crunch. The full weight of his body comes plummeting down on me, but not in the way I'm expecting. It feels as though someone has just dropped a two hundred pound corpse on top of me. His dead weight buries me. I can't move. My hands are tied, and I'm being smothered by my drunken stalker.

What just happened? Since there's no movement, I dare to peek over Pistol's slumping shoulder. There stands Peyton, holding a huge antique milk jug over her head, poised to strike him again. She's shaking uncontrollably and I know I need to help her snap out of her state of shock.

"I'm okay . . . I'm okay . . . Thank you God." I gasp. "Peyton . . . help me, Peyton! We have to get out of here!" I cry. It's as though Peyton is staring beyond me, and not seeing my struggle. *This must look horrifying. She's still in shock.* "Peyton . . . Look at me, Peyton. I'm tied!" I give one last kick, trying to roll a milk jug her way. As it rolls into her leg I yell, "Peyton, I'm down here!"

Suddenly, she drops her head, and her eyes meet mine. She drops the jug to the floor. "Kaitlyn. I've got you!" She reaches down and tugs Pistol's torso from mine. He's out cold, and too heavy to budge. "I can't do this by myself," Peyton's voice shakes with fatigue.

"Get my hands," I cry.

She unties my arms so I can help push the rest of his body from mine. When I'm finally free, we both kick at him violently, and work to roll him into the corner. I take the piggin string lying on the ground, and fumble nervously to tie his hands together. I have no strength, and I'm so dizzy I'm not sure how well I did, but I can sense we don't have long.

"We've got to get out of here Peyton. Let's go." I get up to run, and fall right back to the ground. I'm hurt and dizzy. I need help. Peyton gets me back on my feet. I take three steps toward the door and fall to the ground again. "I can't do it!" I cry. "Peyton! Go! He's gonna kill me! Go get help!" We jump when we hear rustling coming from the dark corner where we left Pistol.

"I will not leave you with him Kaitlyn. He's waking up. Put your arm around my neck . . ." Peyton whispers, moving in under my good shoulder. I stand again, using her for balance. "One step at a time, Sis. Let's go."

Sidled up next to her, Peyton shuffles me through the room and out the door. In a series of baby steps, we move toward the exit of the tack room. I trip and stumble when we accidentally kick one of the many milk jugs scattered along the floor. Again, Peyton catches me. "Here, let's use this for light." She pulls my phone from her pocket.

"My phone? How did you get that?"

"I think it fell out of your pocket when we were taking pictures. It's a good thing too. It's the reason I came looking for you."

We use the light of the phone to make our way out of the little tack house and into the cool night air. Peyton shuffles me down to Mason's and sets me up against an old oak tree to rest while she calls the boys to tell them where we are. As I work to tune out the pain and the world around me, Peyton's voice fades off into the distance. I sit against the cool tree in a state of shock, looking up to the night sky. My gaze catches one of the last oak leaves, drifting on the breeze. I follow its path until it vanishes from sight. Tracking the drifting leaf has left me in a state of delirium. The pain and fear begin to subside. The last thing that crosses my mind as I slip from consciousness is how beautiful and comforting it is out here in the wide open space at the Mason Ranch. The autumn breeze kisses my fresh wounds, and calms my churning stomach. The music off in the distance, lulls me into a dreamlike state. "The boys are on their way," I hear Peyton's whisper. "Oh, I found something else." I feel Peyton set something light and cool in my hand. She gently pushes my fingers around it. "It's your necklace. I found it by your phone. You're safe now Kait." At her words, my mind slips away completely.

CHAPTER 20

TUNED OUT

"YOU KNOW YOU'RE GOING TO have to come out sometime, right Honey?" My mom peeks her head through my doorway and tries to coax me out of my room for the umpteenth time this week. I nod my head and continue to stare down at my guitar, trying to figure out the fingering for the melody that keeps swirling around in my head.

I've barely come out of my room for two weeks. My parents have me on independent study so I don't even have to go to school. My superficial wounds have healed; the knots on my head are gone, and I'm back to normal . . . on the outside. Inside, I'm a billowing mess, and I really don't want anyone to see how broken and scared I am. *Pistol got away.* This fact has haunted me for the last three-hundred seventeen hours and forty-two minutes. Somehow, between the time I drifted off against the oak tree, and the time the boys got to me, Pistol disappeared. Now, he's out there somewhere, and I'm scared as hell that he's going to come back and finish the job that he started.

I jump every time I hear the creak of my floor, or the whipping of an oak branch against my bedroom window. I never realized how eerie the sounds of fall can be. I'm tired from the lack of sleep, and nauseous because I can't shake the incessant nightmare that continues to creep into my thoughts. Every time I close my eyes, the darkness lets him back into my mind, his forceful grip, shadowy, dark face, the smell of liquor on his breath, and his raspy, drunken slur. He broke me that night . . . completely and utterly broke me.

After coming out to the ranch and taking my new report, Officer Marnia warned me about the potential likelihood of his return. They searched for hours with no luck. She promised she and her team would keep vigilant watch over me until they find Pistol; but I know in my heart, it will take an army standing guard at my house all hours of the day to keep me safe. Her warnings have left me anxious and rattled. I live with the new reality that I'm being hunted. I can't even walk down my hallway without looking over my shoulder. I know the minute I let my guard down, Pistol will attack. My home, has become my prison. The only safety I've found, is the corner of my bedroom, where I can face the door. There, at least I know he can't attack me from behind.

The only time I don't fixate on my fear is when I pick up my guitar. It's my release, and helps clear my mind. I begin to play some of the worship songs and ballads that have brought me comfort in the past, but my own lyrics continue to break through each song and sneak their way into my head. Visions of this magnificent fall and the hurt that has come with it beat at the back of my mind. This time of year is so incredible. There's a final burst of unimaginable color and fantastic life, revealing that even in the transition to death there is wonder, beauty, and strength. And even in its glory, this type of beauty is often paralleled by uncontrollable sadness and loss. My vision is a reminder that everything changes, and even things that were once brilliant and lovely, fade away, fall off, and sometimes break.

Why does it have to hurt so badly? Why has this fall left me so broken? This has been the hardest season of my life. Images of being hit, dragged, torn, and broken float through my mind. They are replaced by greens, turning to vivid, reds, oranges, and yellows. Visions of hospital rooms and gurneys change to forested mountains and green pastures. I feel heat turning to cold, and see falling leaves meandering on the gentle breeze. The slideshow is a collage of images swapping back and forth between beauty and pain, comfort and fear, love and hate. The incessant reel rolls through my mind as I strum and strum, searching for words to describe this crazy kaleidoscope of imagery. Finally, in one magical moment, there is an intermingling of all of my senses, images, and words, and it hits me . . . This is exactly what the world becomes *"When fall breaks."*

The images surging through my mind have been trapped for weeks. They've been clawing at me, setting my nerves on fire, and tearing me apart. The only way I can think to release this haunting metaphor, is to write it down in words and pour it out in song. Talking with the therapist hasn't seemed to help. Hiding shamefully in the corner at the teen support group hasn't done a thing for me either. It's time for a new approach. I'm going to do this situation some poetic justice. Besides, I've often thought about how great it would feel to get revenge through a song. It seems to work for Taylor. *That's it . . . I'm gonna Taylor Swift that asshole!* My mind has cleared, and for the first time in weeks, a smile emerges. I take out a piece of paper and begin to write.

When Fall Breaks

Sittin' on the tailgate of his daddy's truck;
baskin' in the bonfire's glow
He holds me tight and twirls my hair
as the wind begins to blow
He pulls me close and holds me tight;
my heart jumps for goodness sake
There's nothin' quite like a country night
with him~
When fall breaks

And just like that the winds of time
unleash the bitter cold
His love grows dim, the colors die;
to him we're growin old
I watch them dance around the floor
tears roll as my heart aches
There's nothin' quite like a broken heart
from him~
When fall breaks

Chorus

And with the change of seasons——

I'm jumping the gun here . . . I need another verse before that chorus . . . I begin to scratch out the next line, when my door swings open and I'm interrupted by my mom.

"So Kiddo, Dad and I have been talking with Brody's and Mason's grandparents. We want to get you kids away for Thanksgiving. We thought it would be fun if we all went to

Salmon River for vacation this year. There's plenty of room for everyone to stay at their family cabins and we know how you kids love it over there. We were thinking, we could even go Christmas tree cutting the day after Thanksgiving. There are beautiful Silver Tips up in the Marbles." I pause and look up from my songwriting when my mom pops back in my room with her newest ploy to try to get me out of the house. "Of course, we'll go with the Baileys and the Tatums. Cinda and I are going to have to miss some of our adoption stories on TV, but you know we'll bring our wine glasses," she laughs, jokingly trying to lighten the mood. "Caden will bring Peyton too. I know how much all of you kids love to hang out together. What do you think?"

Well, the first thing that runs through my mind is, *Is it safe?* But that's not what comes out of my mouth. What I actually say is, "Can we bring the guns?" The look on my mom's face reveals that, that was wrong thing to say. Her mouth is practically hanging to the floor and I know I've shocked her with my unsettling thoughts. I know I should say I'm just joking; but I'm not. There's no way I want to be that far from civilization without some kind of weapon capable of blasting a few holes through my relentless predator. I do not want her to stick me in any more therapy. I've got to throw her off the trail, and make her think I'm not still scared about Pistol. "Mom, I've taken hunter's safety. I shoot with Dad all the time. It's just a precaution. You know, for bears and stuff. They're really bad right now cuz of the fires. You know we even had three bears in our neighborhood this week . . . and that's right in town. If we're going to be out in that forest scouting for a tree, I'm at least taking my 22." *Yep, that was the right thing to say.*

I know I'm over rationalizing to her, but she seems to relax as she reasons, "I see what you mean, Dear. It's always a good idea to be prepared for the unexpected. Oh, you may want to take a shower. Brody called, and whether you want to see him or not, he's headed over here."

"Dang it! Mom, you can't let him see me like this! I really wish you would have told him I was busy." I haven't let Brody visit me since the day after the barn dance. I can't handle seeing the pain in his eyes when he looks at me. He keeps texting me that he's sorry, he let me down again . . . I don't want him to feel bad. He can't be my protector every minute of every day. Odds are, if he's in my life, he's going to be dealing with a lot more of the kind of disappointment that comes from me getting hurt. I'm a walking danger magnet. I know it's just a matter of time before Pistol comes for me again. And I'll be darned if Brody is going to feel responsible when he finally kills me. If I can just push him away long enough, maybe he won't feel like I belong to him anymore. I have to end this with Brody. He doesn't deserve to have my burdens . . . and I don't want to put him in danger. I'm not good enough for him anyway. Brody deserves safety, happiness, and a future. I'll just hold onto him in my songs and in my dreams. *That's it. When he comes over today, I'm ending it with him for good.* Even as I'm thinking these thoughts, I'm falling apart inside. There will never be anyone who treats me like he does. Even in my dreams, I could not have pictured a boyfriend as perfect as him. How will I go on without the greatest guy I have ever known? I don't know . . . I don't want to know. But I will have to try . . . for his sake.

"Kaitlyn, I'm not going to lie to him. He knows darned well you haven't left this room. You have been cooped up long enough. You love this time of year. Now, get yourself in the shower, get your butt out the door, and experience the fall as it's meant to be experienced. I hear he wants to take you ice-skating down in Mt. Shasta. It'll do you some good to get out of this dungeon. You've got ten minutes to get in that shower, and then I'm letting him know it's safe to come in."

It's no use. I'm not going to be able to fight her on this one.

She can be very stubborn when her mind is set on something . . . and right now, it's set on getting me out of this house. "Wow, Mom you sure are a dragon slayer, aren't you?"

Chuckling my mom says, "I'm about ready to grab my stinky, little dragon by the tail and throw her into that shower. Now move it Puff. The clock is tickin'."

When I get out of the bathroom, Brody is sitting on my bed waiting for me. He looks down at his hands, twirling a slender, square, silver package back and forth. He doesn't even look up when I hear his soft voice floating toward me. "I brought you your present." He lifts it up a little, so I can see the gift he's holding. "I meant to give it to you on your birthday, but . . . well, you know." I can hear the hurt in his voice, and I hate the fact that I have caused him such pain.

"Are you okay, Brody?" I walk over and take the gift from his hand.

"Just missing you, Pip." He shakes his head, continuing to look down. "You haven't let me see or talk to you for almost two weeks. I'm sorry I didn't do a better job of protecting you. I know I let you down. I know that's why you don't want to see me. Isn't it?" He finally looks up, and I see shame blanketing his face.

"Bro, you didn't let me down." I set the gift on the bed and grab onto the sides of his face. "This is my fault. I keep putting you in dangerous situations where you have to protect me. Brody, this is not fair to you. I don't want to do this to you anymore."

"What are you trying to say, Pip? I don't think I like where this is going."

"I'm saying, I love you Brody Tatum. I love you more than anything in the world, and that's why I'm letting you go."

Brody springs from the bed. "Damn it Pip." He raises his voice, and lowers it again when he sees me jump. "I'm not going anywhere. You are not pushing me away. I won't let you.

You see this Pip?" Brody pulls the gift from the bed and opens it in front of me. He holds a CD, with his writing scrawled across the label. "This is us." He brings it up next to his face and slightly shakes it back and forth. "You listen to this, and tell me we're not meant to be together. I've put every song that ever reminded me of us on here. This is our story, and I'm not letting it end now, not like this." Brody drops to his knees in front of me. "I love you Kaitlyn Elizabeth Woodley. The thought of losing you kills me. You can try to push me away, but it's not going to work. I was made to love you. I was made to protect you. That's never been more clear to me than it is at this moment. So go ahead and fight me on this. But I'm not going anywhere."

He drops the CD at my feet, "I'll be out in the front room. Meet me out there when you're ready to let me love you." He stands up and slowly moves out the door. I am so confused. I don't know what to think. I love him, and I don't want to hurt him. But sometimes the only way to protect someone you love is to keep them out of harms way. And to me, that means, keeping Brody in the safety zone . . . away from me. I pick the CD up off the ground and read the label.

> To the one who hung my moon,
> sparked the flame in my heart, and
> painted my country nights beautiful.
> Happy Birthday Babe.
> Love Forever & Always,
> Brody

I slide the CD into the computer, plug in my headphones, and listen intently to each and every word on that album. Even though I can sense Brody is still at my house, I don't leave my room. I don't know what time he leaves that night, or if he does at all. All I know, is this is the best darned CD I've ever heard in my life, and as long as I'm plugged in, I reside in another world; a place where I feel safe, calm, and at peace. Word after word and tune after tune, wrap themselves around my soul. My heart begins to soften. The heartbreak of fall begins to chip away. It's replaced by happy childhood memories, good old fashioned country fun, an evolving friendship, and a growing love. I love this cure . . . almost as much as I love the boy who made it.

I don't know how much time has passed when I take out my phone to text Brody.

Me:
Brody? Where are you?

About three seconds lapse between the time I hit send, and the time I see the little bubbles come up on my screen.

Brody:
I'm still in your living room . . . waiting. I told you I'm not going anywhere.

Me:
But it's been like three days???

Brody:
I'm only eighteen. I figure I have a few good years left in me to wait for you.

At his words, I rip my headphones from my ears, throw my phone on my bed, and run down the hallway to the living room. Brody has obviously been home sometime in the last three days, because he looks unbelievable. He is so hot, he darn near glistens! I can see the outline of his abs through his tight

Oregon State Beavers T-shirt and his calves look amazing in his matching basketball shorts. His face lights up when he sees me running at him. I grin and throw myself into his lap, wrapping my arms around his neck. "I thought you were signing on with the Ducks?" I giggle, pulling at the Beaver on his shirt.

"Well, that's still up in the air. And, you were awfully convincing about me joining Beaver Nation with you. Naaa . . ." he shakes his head, " . . . the Ducks do have a better football team," he smirks. "I just wore this lucky Beaver shirt, hoping this would be the day, you'd decide to come out of your room."

"I'm sorry for making you wait so long . . . I've been listening to this really great CD someone gave me for my birthday. Brody, those songs were exactly what I needed to get up and find my way back to you. You're right, they told our story. They made me realize you've been by my side all along . . . and when I was losing my feelings for Pistol a couple months ago, it's because my feelings for you were trying to knock my butt out, and wake me up to who I was really meant to be with. I mean, by the time we left the Homecoming dance together, I could barely breathe in your presence. I had so much electricity flowing through me, I felt like I was going to blow a circuit."

Brody, chuckles, "I knew you felt it too. For a while there, I thought I was going crazy . . . especially on Homecoming when you totally threw me into the lion's den with Chelsea," he laughs. "That's when I thought this thing between us was all in my head. But then later that night our first kiss set me straight. I knew after I held you in my arms and felt what you did to me, I was done for. There was no way I was going to be able to stay away from you, even after Caden's warning. I had more than one sleepless night wondering how I was going to save my manhood. I looked over my shoulder for weeks. But I'll tell you what Pip, you are worth every bad date I had to get through and every sleepless night I had to endure to bring us together."

"I'm sorry I put you through that. I should've just had the

guts to open up to my brother and tell him what I was feeling. Maybe it would've helped if he'd known these feelings between us weren't one sided. I just didn't know how to let myself have you as more than a friend. There was a raging battle inside my head. I tried to push you out of my mind, but no matter how hard I tried, you kept breaking down the walls. I couldn't stand feeling disloyal to Pistol, even though I knew he wasn't right for me anymore."

"He was never right for you Pip. I saw it from the beginning. I just didn't realize how wrong he was until it was too late. How could I have let this go so far?" Brody shakes his head in disbelief. "Why didn't you leave him Pip? Why did you let him treat you that way? You're so much better than all that."

"Maybe I was scared. I don't know if I was more afraid of what he would do to me, or about giving my heart over to my best friend." I shake my head, pausing to think through what I need to say to Brody. "Now that my mind is clear, I realize, that in my heart, it's always been you. You're the one I want, and the one I need. And I know now that I can't send you away from me; you're a part of me. There's not a good day of my life that doesn't have some part of you embedded in it. All of the best pieces of me have you tangled inside of them. I've finally realized that if I let Pistol ruin my life, he's also ruining yours. I'm still really scared and I have some issues I need to work through . . . like ever leaving the safety of my house again, but it helps knowing you're there to pick me up if I fall."

Brody leans in, "Pip, don't be scared. I'm not going anywhere and I won't let him hurt you again . . . and, don't ever try to push me away again you little pip squeak," he pulls me in closer and kisses the top of my head. He holds onto me like his life depends on it. After twenty minutes of holding me in silence, I begin to wonder if he's ever going to let me go. Then he whispers, "You need to trust me to take care of you. I'm right here with you every step of the way. I'm stuck to you like glue."

"Hot glue . . ." I laugh.

He bites the inside of his cheek and raises his eyebrows. Then with a smirk he replies, "Even better."

CHAPTER 21

STUFFED

"THAT'S THE END OF IT," my mom says as she stuffs the last of our luggage in the car. "We'd better hurry so we can catch the caravan at the Bailey's."

"Hold on, I've gotta grab my guitar."

"I'm not sure that's going to fit Sweetheart," my mom looks speculatively at the minimal space left in the backseat. It's filled to the brim, and there is barely enough room for our legs. It's a good thing my dad and brother are taking Caden's truck, so Peyton could ride with them.

"I'll carry it on my lap, Mom. I'm kinda working on something, and I want to finish it during vacation."

"Is it really necessary?" she says as I try to pull it onto my lap. The neck, pokes back through the opening in my headrest and pins my head to the side so my seatbelt saws at the exposed skin by my collar.

"Umm, yes, Mom. It's necessary," I huff. "It's this, or another five hundred dollar therapy bill."

"We'll make room, Honey," she smirks, and turns the ignition. We fall into line behind my dad, and make our way through the rainy streets, up to Bailey's Vineyard.

When we pull up at the vineyard, Mr. Bailey comes out with a large crate. "Thought we'd try out some of this season's new wines," he winks toward my parents. Then turning his head toward our crowd of friends, he shoots us a stern look, "Adults only kids . . . no signs needed. If it's in a bottle, stay away from it!" He lifts his eyebrows and presses his lips into a straight line.

Our parents have been on us ever since the barn dance. They were not too impressed with our Apple Cider sign swap fiasco, and the dangers that ensued that night.

"Don't you think we've learned our lesson by now Dad?" retorts Jenna. "We've all been grounded for three weeks . . . not that we'd ever pull a stunt like that again anyway."

"Ya, we were all scared shitless, Mr. Bailey."

"Ahem . . . language Son," my dad replies smacking Caden upside the back of the head.

"We'd better get going guys," Mr. Bailey warns. "The road report says a storm's headed our way around eleven this morning. We want to make it to the cabin before it gets icy, not to mention, we need enough time to cook that turkey." Mr. Bailey pats his belly and lifts his eyebrows. "And you know how this ole boy loves his leftover turkey sandwiches."

"Good idea Honey," Cinda claps her hands together, "Chop chop kids . . . time to go." At that, we all shuffle into our respective vehicles and take off toward Dotty's hamburger joint where Mason and his family are waiting to lead the way to their cabins at Forks of the Salmon.

When we finally pull up at Dotty's, Mason is sitting on the picnic table in the parking lot, huddled next to his and Brody's grandparents. The temperature has dropped and the valley skies are beginning to show signs of snow. Everyone is super excited for the first snowfall of the year.

"You got those chains ready for that little BMW Bad Boy,

Bailey?" my dad puffs out his chest, ready to take on the potential challenge of hazardous driving.

"Ya, how 'bout you Woodley? Got yours?"

"No need my friend," my dad beats his chest like Tarzan. "Only four-wheel drive for this ole country boy. But if you need help putting chains on your little beast, the boys are still needing to work off the rest of their punishment from the barn dance."

"Oh ya," laughs Mr. Bailey, "It was really great getting all that free labor the other weekend. And I really enjoyed watching them work off those hangovers. The vineyard looks amazing and I'm pretty sure I have enough kindling for the winter now."

"Way to beat a dead horse into the ground, Dad," snarls Caden. "Are you ever going to let us live that down? The girls were in on it too, you know."

"Well that settles it then. If it snows today, the girls get to put the chains on."

Everyone laughs but us.

Jenna and I turn our heads and look at each other. Then we look up at the sky. *Crap.*

Jenna bursts out, "What are we waiting for? It's time to hit the road!" She snaps her fingers and we all load up. Mason, his Dad, and his grandparents lead the way, followed by Brody and his parents. My dad, Caden, and Peyton, take up the third position. We are at the tail end of the pack, sandwiching the Baileys snugly in between us. Our five vehicle caravan is quite a sight. There are sleeping bags, pillows, air mattresses, luggage, grocery sacks, and all kinds of unimaginable supplies, shoved up against the windows and poking through seats. I search intently, through the tiny non-obstructed openings in the windows of the cars in front of me, and can see some of my travel mates, bobbing their heads and whipping them around, back and forth. They're fidgeting in their cramped seats, just as much as I am. I think they are searching for each other too. Every once in a while, I catch a wildly waving hand, and know that my friends

have made contact. It's a fun way to stay in touch on such a remote road, where cell service is hit and miss.

The road to the cabins is desolate. Outside of our caravan,
there's not another car in sight. The road is long and windy,
and curls through the steep, heavily forested cliff sides. Drops
of rain begin splattering the windshield, and draw my attention
upward. I strain to see through the grey mist, and I can barely
make out the sliver of sky peeking through the giant cedars, and
intersecting mountaintops. Dense, grey clouds, begin to float
downward with the increasing winds. My gaze follows them
as they sink below the road, toward the valley floor. It's always
been so strange to me to sit above the clouds, but on this kind
of road, where the ravine is hundreds of feet below us, it's quite
common to see at this time of year. The odd placement makes
me feel like I'm trapped in a child's three-dimensional view
finder.

As we get closer to the cabins, I notice the heavy, green
gates are still open to traffic. In a few weeks that will no longer
be the case. As soon as the first heavy snowfall comes, the Forest Service will come and close the roads off to traffic. A bit of
an eerie thought overcomes me "Mom, could you imagine getting stuck out here? What if they shut the gates and didn't know
there were people staying back here? That would be creepy."

She looks over her shoulder at the back seat and laughs,
"Well it's a good thing we brought enough food to feed an army.
It's a pretty good possibility that we'll be getting enough snow
to keep us here for a while."

"You're joking right? I mean Thanksgiving break is only
five days, and my independent study is up at the end of it. I cannot miss any more school."

"Oh Honey, we wouldn't have brought the entire crew
down here if we thought there was a chance we couldn't get
back out. We all have four wheel drives or chains, we'll be fine
. . . Hey look!" my mom points at a crazy, gnarly bend in the

road. "It's Jump Off Joe!"

"What is Jump Off Joe?"

"Oh wow, I have never told you the story about the cowboy named Joe?"

"Not that I remember."

"Do you see that turn right there? Decades ago, a local cowboy was down here looking for his stray cattle. It was just after a big snow storm. Well, he found darned near all of them, and at the end of his successful day, he was trying to pull his overstocked trailer around that sharp turn. Sadly, he lost his brakes when the cattle truck hit ice and he slid off the road, plummeting down that precipice back there. It's been told, that on snowy nights, along this stretch of road, people have spotted a man who fits Joe's description, just wandering around. I guess if you listen very carefully, you can also hear the sound of cow-bells off in the distance."

"Holy hell mom! You know how much I hate ghost stories." I am livid that my mom just freaked me out with that. "Thanks a lot!" Goosebumps creep their way down my spine, as I try to shake the thought of dead Cowboy Joe's spirit clinging to the side of my car. The drizzling rain and low clouds add to the eeriness of this section of road.

My mom chuckles when I draw in closer to the center console, "Well, that's the way the old timers tell it. You know, it's probably not even true. I bet Joe was driving a logging truck and didn't even own cattle."

"I don't care what he was driving! Now I'm going to be freaked out the rest of the way to the cabin." Suddenly I feel like I'm riding in a car at Disney's Haunted Mansion. I check the side of me just to make sure Joe's not sitting next to me. "I wasn't really up for an invisible hitchhiker today."

"Don't be ridiculous Kaitlyn. It's just an urban legend." My mom shakes her head and dismisses my phasmophobia.

"What are we doing?" I cry, as my mom begins to slow to

a stop.

"Look, the Bailey's are pulling over. We can't just pass by without seeing what's wrong."

"Don't stop here! Don't stop here . . . What are you doing Mom?" I cannot believe she is pulling over with Cowboy Joe haunting this hillside.

One by one the cars pull over and stop on the side of the road. When we come to a halt behind the Baileys, anxiety begins to fill me. If there's one thing I know about myself, it's that my greatest fear is ghosts, and I'll be darned if I'm going to let myself see one right now. I pull my pillow over my head, as my heart rate accelerates and the adrenaline courses through me.

When my mom rolls down the window to see what's going on, I pull my head out from under the pillow to find Mason doubled over on the side of the road. Caden and Brody are standing at his side pointing at the ground, and chuckling with each gagging noise. *Seriously . . . now puke?* I have two phobias in my life. The first is ghosts, and the second is puke. Now I'm dealing with both of them simultaneously. I bury my head back under my pillow, and in a muffled tone, say, "Mason is not staying in a cabin with us, right?"

"You've got to get over your Germaphobia Kaitlyn. Last time I was sick you barricaded yourself in your room for three days. You wouldn't even respond to my texts for help. Did you think my germs were going to transmit through the phone or something? Auntie Cinda had to bring me soup and crackers." My mom shakes her head and laughs at my ridiculous phobia. "How are you ever going to be a mother when you can't even look at a little vomit?" My mom criticizes.

"I don't even want kids . . ." I rapidly dismiss her comment as soon as it leaves her mouth. "So is he?"

"Is he what?"

"Staying in our cabin?

"No Dear, Brody's and Mason's family are staying in the

cabin next door. We're staying in the same cabin as the Baileys. Obviously, Caden will be staying the night with the guys, since Peyton will be in a cabin with us. No stinky teenage boys in our cabin," she laughs. "Does that sound like a plan?"

"Sounds great mom, as long as I'm not dealing with any bacteria or viruses."

"Oh Kaitlyn, it's only car sickness. He will be fine as soon as we get to the cabin. We'll be there in about fifteen minutes. Looks like he's doing better already. They're all loading up."

The rest of the ride is uneventful. We travel several miles down a long gravel road, past some green meadows, grazing cattle, and a small Forest Service camp site. As we continue back into the forest, the trees begin to close in and the road narrows. The ride grows slightly darker as the trees begin to drown out the light from above. Finally, we come to a stop. Gazing up to the left of the gently sloping hill, I see four cabins set no more than fifty feet apart from each other. With the exception of the cabin off to the right, which has been screened in and looks as though it's been sitting vacant for a few years, the area is just like I remembered it.

I open the door, and step down onto the gravel road. The brisk mountain air opens my lungs, and I breathe in the refreshing mist. The roaring sound of water draws my attention down the hillside, and I can't help but follow the short trail of moss covered rocks. I stop a few feet below the road, where I look down through the manzanita to see the rushing Salmon River. Standing on the rocks, and glancing over at Mule Bridge brings back so many childhood memories of fishing with the family, splashing around in the pristine swimming hole, and playing hide and seek between the giant evergreens.

"Kaitlyn," I hear my dad's voice. "You need to get back up here and help us unload. We've got to get that bird in the oven so we can eat at a decent hour!"

"Sorry Dad, just checking out the water level." And I am.

It's raging compared to the Scott River. The drought must not have hit this part of the Marbles quite as hard as it did on the other side of the mountain range. "Coming!" I yell, as I trek back up the hill to the car.

The guys work to unload every last bit of food, luggage, and bedding, while we prepare the turkey and pies in our cabin. When we're finally settled and the food is prepped and in the oven, Jenna, Peyton, and I go over to the boys cabin to see what they're up to. When we walk in, they're giggling like school girls.

"Just go over there Dude. Act like we need something and go talk to her." I see Mason pressed up against the side of the window trying to peek through the shutters, while Brody and Caden try to convince him to go to the cabin next door.

"What's all this?" Peyton laughs. "Do we have a mystery girl in attendance this weekend?"

"Oh she's more than a girl. She's a goddess," Mason replies distractedly.

"He won't peel his eyes away from that window. He's been standing there for at least twenty minutes," Caden shakes his head. "None of us have actually seen her, and who knows about this guy's taste in women, but it sure is fun to watch him drool."

"Guys . . . guys . . . psst . . . get over here . . . I see her," Mason frantically whispers.

We all run to the window, and crowd around, trying to pull the shutters back slightly, so we won't be seen.

"Hooollllyyyyy crap," Caden slips as he's instantly backhanded on his shoulder by Peyton.

Brody simply nods his head for several seconds, mouth closed, and finally turns toward Mason. He draws his eyebrows together as an amused grin grows on his ever bobbing head, "Yep, good taste runs in our genes." He turns his head and wags his eyebrows at me.

I narrow my eyes at him and with a sarcastic smirk reply,

"Nice save, way smoother than my brother over there."

Walking down the path to her car, I spy the beautiful country stunner the boys are salivating over. She flips her long, loosely curled brown hair over her shoulder, revealing a hot pink quote plastered across her camo sweatshirt.

"What do you think that says?" Brody asks.

"What?" Mason and Caden reply in unison.

"Right there on her chest," Brody squints.

"Why are you looking at her chest?" I growl.

"Kind of hard not to." Mason drools. "Wait, she's coming closer . . . Let me try to figure it out. Slowly he slurs, "*I . . . Love . . . Big Trucks . . . Mudding . . . Bonfires . . . and Country Boys. Hot Damn!!!*" He jumps up excitedly and gives the boys high fives.

Dang, she is gorgeous. That's it; Brody's not going to want to be with me if he has her to look at all week. It's like CJ all over again. I feel all the insecurities Pistol planted creeping back into my mind. She's what every guy here wants. She really is a ten.

"Ya, she looks like she's right up your alley Mason. Why don't you grow a pair and go meet her Dude," Caden jokes.

"She's not that pretty, geez. Look at her booty. She needs a doublewide to haul that thing around."

"Looks pretty dang good to me . . . like it's been handcrafted by a Brazilian surgeon . . . You jealous or something?"

"I'm not jealous and her rack practically blocks her smile. I bet it's stuffed," Jenna says straight faced, nonchalantly.

"Well I am," Peyton quips, "especially since my boyfriend can't seem to keep his mouth closed over here."

"Me too," I add, staring at Cowgirl Barbie sauntering back up toward her cabin.

"Awww. Come here Babe, she doesn't hold a candle to you." Brody holds his arms straight out for me to come to him.

"You either, Sexy. Come here." When Peyton gets to Caden, he grabs her butt. "and . . . damn girl, I'd stand behind you any day."

"You're nuts," she giggles.

"Speaking of futures, I've got to figure out a way to meet mine before this night is over," Mason interrupts Caden's playful banter.

"Well, it's gonna have to wait, cuz we've got to get out there and find some wood while this storm's still holding off." Brody reminds the boys. "Do you girls want to come with us?"

"We'd love to, but we've got cooking duties over at our cabin," I sigh in disappointment.

"Do you all have to go? It's a pretty small kitchen."

"No. Peyton can go with you guys. You probably want to show her around anyway, since she's never been over here before."

"You wouldn't mind? I feel bad. Shouldn't I help?"

"We've got this covered. Go have fun Peyton. Explore. This place is full of surprises."

"Don't worry Jenna. We'll show her what poison oak looks like. We're not gonna let anyone else make the same mistake you did with your magical firewood."

Brody takes me by the hand, "I need to talk to Pip before we head out."

When we get outside on the porch, he pulls me into a close hug and whispers in my ear, "You know I was just messin' around in there about that girl . . . trying to look cool in front of the guys. I meant it when I said she doesn't hold a candle to you."

His words are soft spoken and sincere. He maintains his gentle hold on me, as he pulls away from my ear and rests his chin on top of my head. "Since the barn dance, I've had a lot of time to think about what my world would look like without you. And . . . it would break me Pip. Your smile, your laugh, your smell, those beautiful blue eyes, your feisty little spirit, everything about you . . . You are a masterpiece, handcrafted by God himself. You're beautiful from the inside out. So you've got to know Pip, that even if I look at another girl, I will never see her . . . not the way I see you. I don't see with my eyes, I see with my soul, and you own it . . . completely."

His words are not just words. I can feel them wrapping themselves around my heart, igniting a fire that warms me from the inside out. Bundled in his strong embrace, and captivated by his warmth, I find myself at peace. For the first time, I feel completely secure with another human being. I cannot describe this overpowering feeling. It's like I'm weightless, yet anchored all at the same time. My soul is tethered to Brody's; I actually feel his emotions. I've said I love people before, but I'm not sure that I really knew what that meant . . . until now. A smile plays on my lips as I look up into his eyes.

"I love you Brody Tatum . . ." I shake my head searching for more meaningful words, but I come up with nothing more powerful than those three words. "That's all."

"I love you too Kaitlyn Woodley. Now go cook me some turkey Girl." He pats my butt and lets out a cute chuckle.

Brody kisses the top of my head, gives me a slight wave, and leaves me with a wink and a dimply smile. After he makes his way back into the cabin, Jenna steps through the door and we head back over to our place and get to work. When we finish our kitchen duties, we decide we need a little down time. Jenna heads up to the clearing on the hill so she can text Ty for a while, since there's no service down here in the basin. In the silence of the cabin, so many emotions and words play on my heart that I pick up my guitar and finish the song I started.

When Fall Breaks

Sittin' on the tailgate of his daddy's truck;
baskin' in the bonfire's glow

He holds me tight and twirls my hair
as the wind begins to blow
He pulls me close and holds me tight;
my heart jumps for goodness sake
There's nothin' quite like a country night
with him~
When fall breaks

And just like that the winds of time
unleash the bitter cold
His love grows dim, the colors die;
to him we're growin old
I watch them dance around the floor;
tears roll as my heart aches
There's nothin' quite like a broken heart
from him~
When fall breaks

And then one day, out of the blue
Another looked my way;
He sparked a flame inside my soul
brightened my darkest day
He came around each time I made
the worst of life's mistakes
There's nothing like a helping hand
from him~
When fall breaks

Chorus

And with the change of seasons
He brought a change to me
He pulled me from a fiery hell
and set my spirit free

He gave me wings to fly again
and soar to unknown heights
He put the color in my day
and stars into my nights

How could I know at eight years old,
that you would be the one
To pick me up each time I fell,
each time I came undone
You taught me how to love and trust
You're the heart that fit my key

And now I know that all because of you;
Fall won't break me. . .

~I'll always love you, yes I will, oh yeah
my sweet Brody~

I strum and strum, replaying our story over and over on a constant loop. I feel empowered and lighter with each verse I replay. With the vibration of every string, another sliver of pain is released, and replaced with images of Brody. Happiness begins to consume me. One day I will play this for him, and he'll know just how he saved me. But right now, it's time for Thanksgiving dinner. I hear everyone starting to gather out in the front room. I set my guitar down and rejoin my friends and family.

CHAPTER 22

TRUTH OR DARE

THANKSGIVING DINNER IS INCREDIBLE. THERE'S something about sharing a delicious turkey dinner in the remote wilderness with your closest friends and family that makes for a very special and memorable evening. I glance around the room and take in the beauty of the holiday, working to create a lasting memory. As they watch the fluffy snowflakes gently float through the sky, the lighthearted adults are gathered around the kitchen table pointing out the window and telling stories about the crazy snowstorms they endured at the Forks during the good ole days.

All of us kids lie in front of the crackling fire nestled together like a litter of puppies, laughing at our own jokes and stories. I use Brody as my cozy backrest while he leans against the couch. I look down to see Peyton lying across Caden's lap, holding his hand while he twirls her hair through his fingers. Mason sits right beside me, entranced by a picture he took earlier of the boys in front of the river. It seems his mystery girl slipped into the background unnoticed. He delights in his discovery.

As I watch the smiles, and hear the laughter, I can't help but reflect on my many blessings. I am thankful that despite everything I've been through this season, I am sitting here among my family and dearest friends. I'm thankful for my parents never-ending love and support, for my brother and friends, who stuck by me and protected me, and lastly, I'm thankful for the safety and peace I've found in this beautiful place we call Forks of the Salmon. I hope we can carry on this tradition for many, many more years.

I'm drawn from my state of thankful bliss when I see Mason stand and stretch, "Well, I'm stuffed. How 'bout we take this little rendezvous outside for a bit." He pats his full belly, throwing his head over his shoulder with several quick snaps like he's trying to get us up and moving toward the front door.

"Did something bite your neck? Your less than subtle twitching is creeping me out." Caden smirks. "Kidding . . . But Dude, it's freezing out there. I'd rather stay inside and play with my Legos." He continues to joke with Mason.

I've been watching Mason stare at that picture for ten minutes, and I know perfectly well that he is on a mission to close the distance between Country Barbie and himself. I laugh silently when desperation paints a grimace across his face as he struggles for another excuse to get outside. "I thought we might want to walk off some of that dinner. And didn't the girls want S'mores earlier? There's a great fire pit right outside our cabin." Mason never was good at subtlety, but I'm quite entertained by his effort, so I keep quiet to see what he'll come up with next.

"There's one right out here too!" Jenna points.

"Ours. Is. Better!" He snarls through his clenched teeth.

When Mason narrows his eyes at her and purses his lips, a light bulb comes on over Jenna's head. "Oh. . . I get it." She pokes up her index finger and shakes it next to her head. "You're trying to get a good view of that Sexxxy girl, mmmhmm," she drops her hands to her hips, waggles her eyebrows, and whistles a fox call.

"It's not going to hurt us to help him out guys. Let's go build that fire and see if we can make something happen for our single friend," Peyton interjects in her soft, sweet voice.

"Okay, but bundle up kids, the snow is starting to stick," Brody and Mason's grandma chimes in.

We bundle up in our Carhartt jackets, snow boots, hats, and gloves, and head down to the boys' cabin to build a fire in the pit out front. We huddle close, trying to keep in the heat. The six of us stand in silence listening to the crackle and pop of the flames.

Caden finally breaks the silence, "Well, this is fun. Do you guys want to actually do something? Or just stand around and stare at each other's boots all night?"

"We can sing campfire songs," I suggest.

"Or we can tell ghost stories," Brody chuckles, as I slug him in the side and tell him to shut up.

"I've got it. Let's play Truth or Dare," Jenna suggests.

"Last time I played Truth or Dare, I ended up in a closet with Bethanie the Beaver. I'll be *damned* if I'm gonna do that again," Caden chuckles.

"Oh come on, that was like seventh grade. This will be fun. Besides, there are no beavers around here." Peyton laughs.

"Hey, I'm a Beaver!" I raise my hand and shout out without thinking.

"Why yes you are!" The boys start cracking up.

"You really had to go there, didn't you?" I drop my head and lower my hand slowly. "Not that kind of a beaver." *Boys.* I roll my eyes and shake my head subtly. "Just forget I said that."

"Okay, okay. Enough of this business. It's settled. We're playing." Jenna begins the game. "Peyton, you go first. Truth or Dare?"

"Truth? I guess . . . at least til I see what kind of dares you guys are into."

"Okay, Peyton, when did you start liking Caden?"

"That's easy. It was sophomore year when I watched him cheering for Kaitlyn during the Sharkfest. I thought it was super cute how he got right up behind the blocks and yelled, 'You've got this Sis! Make 'em eat your bubbles now . . . ' like no one was watching. He didn't even care if the other girls' fans were right next to him. His support and loyalty toward Kaitlyn kinda melted my heart."

"Sophomore year? Wish I had've known. I would've asked you out a long time ago." Caden smirks and puffs out his chest, "I didn't even have all this till last summer." He drags his hands down the front of him, running them over his abs first, and then to his thighs. He squirms in a slow fluid motion from side to side like a sidewinder, pulling in a deep, proud breath and audibly releasing it with a grin and eyebrow pump.

"Oh, give me a break. I think I just threw up in my mouth a little." Jenna laughs, " . . . Next question."

"Let me ask you one, Oh Bossy Truth or Dare Hostess," I pipe in. "Jenna, tell me the truth about what you were doing on the computer the night of the bridge. As soon as we got up to the pool, you shut it and acted really odd."

"Oh, um, just reading a weird email from some guy claiming to be my Russian brother. It was the first one I got, so it kind of tripped me out a little. Since then, I've gotten tons of them from random people, so now I know they're just some scam."

"Ohhh Jenna, be careful about that, please."

"Oh, I am . . . I just bounce them all to spam," she grins and cocks her head to the side. "Let's move along. Peyton you get to ask someone something."

"Okay, Mason, if you could have any wish in the world, what would it be?"

Mason gets quiet for a moment as a solemn look crosses his face. Without looking up, he answers, "I wish I could have my mom back."

The circle grows quiet, "Oh . . . mmmm . . . sorry."

I whisper quietly in Peyton's ear. "Let's drop this one."

"Okay, my turn," Mason clears his throat, and in a loud voice, he works to change the subject. "Brody, truth or dare?"

"Enough of this heavy crap. I'll take the dare," Brody grins.

"Okay, I dare you to go hang off of Mule Bridge for one minute. Right out in the middle. No cheating and dangling from the side either."

"No problem. You guys want to come with me to make sure it's legit?"

"Brody, you don't have to take that. The bridge is high, and the water is really rushing right now," I try to convince him not to take the dare.

"Oh girl, I've done this before. One minute is nothing. Come with me. You can watch."

We all walk down the trail to the bridge. The rocks are slick with a thin layer of fresh powder. Each time I lose my footing, I cling onto the bushes to avoid falling to the ground. Finally the trail evens out and stretches out toward our destination. I feel the unevenness of the soft wood beneath my feet as I step up onto the bridge. I turn on my phone's flashlight so I don't trip. Two by two, we walk across to the middle. I drag my hand across the metal rail, and feel the roughness of chipped paint beneath my fingertips. I shine the light onto the rail and see initials, hearts, and memorials scratched into the rusting, green paint. "Oh look. That's sad. It says *R.I.P ~ S.F.*" I point at the scrawled goodbye to a recently lost classmate. "Oh and look there's *Sean + Holly.* That's funny. I didn't know they came all the way over here."

For several minutes, we wander the bridge, reading the carvings, until we decide it's time for Brody to get on with his dare. "You ready Bro? Be careful, the snowflakes are probably making it slick." I say, shivering.

"As ready as I'll ever be," he laughs. "Besides, bridges don't scare me . . . they scare you." He gives me a playful poke in the shoulder. "Here I go."

Brody swings down over the side of the bridge. I can hear him shouting, "Woo Hoo. It's sweet down here! Cold, but sweet!"

"Hang on tight, you big monkey! You can do this! Don't let go!" I screech nervously.

As Brody is finishing his dare, I look over at my brother. He's standing in back of Peyton with his arms wrapped around her. He has her snuggly pressed against the rail of the bridge. His hand curls gently around hers. I watch them closely as they work together, dragging his pocket knife through the chipping paint. When the motion comes to a stop, she rolls her head up and looks him in the eyes. I watch intently as a tear rolls down the side of her face. It's a happy tear. She's smiling. "It means even more that we carved that with the birthday present I gave you."

He reaches up to wipe her tear away, whispering, "It's true Babe. You make me so unbelievably happy."

When Peyton turns into him I take the opportunity to shine my light on their carving. Written inside of a heart, I read, "*Caden Loves Peyton.*" I am thrilled for them. Caden does not take that word lightly. I don't think my brother has ever told anyone he loves them before. Seeing my twin gushing over Peyton touches a new part of my soul. It's like I can feel his love for her. I'm in awe at the sweet story unfolding before me. I love seeing the glow between them as he holds her close whispering in her ear.

I'm pulled from my reverie when Brody suddenly jumps up from behind. "Did it!" he cries. I'm startled by the freezing hands he's just slipped below the bottom of my shirt. He pulls them out quickly, knowing that I'll never be able to warm up after his brutal assault on my belly. "Let's get back to the fire, Pip. It was freezing down there, and I'm kind of wet from the overspray," his chin chatters with his wild shivering.

I draw my arms up to my chest, and pull them in as tight as

I can. With praying hands I chatter, "Okay, it's really cold out here." I turn to my friends who are still watching the snow fall on the water as it flows beneath the bridge. My teeth clatter as I plead to the group, "Hey guys, let's not do any more dares for a minute. We need to go stand by the fire so Brody can warm up." Everyone agrees that the best way to make this night last as long as possible is to stay warm and comfortable. We head back to camp, tromping our way through the deepening snow. As we settle around the toasty crackling fire, I gaze at my friends and recount my blessings. Our little group has me feeling pretty lucky. I can't believe that after all I've been through this month, I'm able to share a Salmon River Thanksgiving with the people I love most in this world.

Again, I focus hard, trying to burn this memory in my mind. This weekend will go down as one of my all time favorites, and there's no way I want to overlook even one minor detail. I watch Jenna and Mason adding more wood to the dying fire as Brody huddles close to the ground, moving his hands back and forth over the flames. I slide behind Caden and Peyton who are snuggling in an oversized chair. I want to get to my Brody, to wrap him in a big bear hug. Maybe that will help warm us both up. As I pass behind them, Caden leans in to whisper something in Peyton's ear. It must have been something really sweet, because I watch her eyes light up, and she melts into him even further. They can't seem to get enough of each other. They have become so connected I can barely tell where one starts and the other begins. I'm overjoyed that Caden has found someone that completes him.

I make my way past Cayton and toward my little bridge monkey. When I finally reach him, he scoops me up in his arms and wraps me around his waist. "You warmin' up Pip?" He gives me an eskimo kiss and tucks me under his chin. I cling to him for several minutes, enjoying the feeling of the thrum of our hearts beating back and forth. The rise and fall of his chest calms me and my eyes begin to flutter closed. Our racing hearts, mixed with the sound of the crackling fire, has us all in a bit of a trance. Enjoying nothing but the sounds of nature and each other's silent company, our tiny group has reached a state of repose. No one is speaking, but I can feel the serenity flowing through our circle.

"That's enough of that! I'm going to fall asleep here." Jenna pipes in. "We need to liven this place up. Who can handle a truth question?" she asks. "Peyton, Mason, Brody, and I have all been on the chopping block. That leaves you two." She points to Caden and me. Well, Kaitlyn, you suck at truths, and Caden, you need a dare, which we're not allowed to do right now, so I'll let you off the hook for a minute. Who wants to ask me another one?"

"Since I just put my butt on the line, I get to ask this question," Brody pipes in. "And I've been wondering about this for a long time . . . Jenna, what can you tell us about the Jefferson High Itching Scandal?"

Jenna and I look at each other and start busting up laughing. "Do you agree that what's said at the Forks stays at the Forks?"

"Hell ya, let's hear it!" Caden says.

"Soooo, remember when we had our little bonfire problem . . . that night you boys were baling . . . when you left us in charge of the fire? Well, I kinda borrowed a baggie of poison oak to show my parents. Yaaaa. Let's just say it came in handy at a certain little boutique downtown when we were trying on Homecoming dresses."

"You didn't??? I ended up with it! That was horrible you turds! The whole cheerleading squad got it!" The shock is evident on Peyton's face.

"Well, you weren't exactly the target. We just had to make sure we got to Chelsea's and CJ's dresses. They were in there shopping together, and we overheard them talking about us. It made us so mad, we just went for it, and let's be honest, if you don't stand with us you stand against us." Jenna grins and raises her eyebrows apologetically. "I wish we'd have known we liked you back then. We might have helped you out."

"Well, remind me not to get on your bad side in the future . . . And seeing how I feel about Chelsea these days, you're forgiven . . . I guess."

As we warm up next to the fire, we throw several more truth questions around the circle. "Well, Dude, I think it's time for a few more dares. Mason, you've been awfully quiet over there for a while. I've got a dare for you."

"Great . . . hit me with it."

"I dare you to go down to the cabin next door and meet that little hottie that's been turning your head all day," I say.

He takes a deep breath in. "Aww heck . . . if I do this, I'm coming up with a really good one that's equally worthy of getting your heart pumping . . . And I mean like to the point it's going to blow out of your chest . . . Do you agree?"

Well, what can he make me do around here? The bridge dare is already done. "Okay, go for it Mason. Let's see your smooth moves."

We stay frozen in place around the fire and stalk Mason as he stands up and moves toward the glowing cabin. We sit in awe as we watch him knock on the cabin door. When it opens, a tall, balding man comes to the door. A few seconds later, he disappears from the doorway and is soon replaced by the cute, wavy-haired brunette. We watch the back of Mason's head bob up and down, and spy the side of his face as his hand suddenly gestures toward us. Then he drops his arm, slips his hands into his pockets, and shrugs his shoulders.

"Oh crap, oh crap . . . he's going for his phone." Jenna laughs. "Holy crap . . . Are they taking a selfie together?"

A few minutes later, Mason returns, holds up his phone, and shows us his new contact. The picture is a selfie of him and the country princess. "All in a hard days work ladies and gentlemen. Meet Miss Marissa Matthews. She'll be over later," Mason winks, "Which brings us to the final dare. Let's go out with a bang."

Nerves well up inside of me. I don't know what this guy is thinking, but his tone is ripping me up inside. I take in a deep breath. "I never go back on a dare . . . so what've you got Mason?"

Mason looks up and off to the right. "See that abandoned cabin that sits just above yours?"

"Ya, I see it."

"I DARE you to go in there and climb that ladder to see what's up there."

"Creepy cabin? You want me to go sneak into creepy cabin at night? You're kidding me right?"

"You made a deal Kaitlyn. Okay, just so you think I'm not a huge ass, I'll let you take the girls with you."

"Fine," I suck it up and stand up. That cabin has been freaking me out ever since we pulled up this morning, but if I can take the girls with me, I think I might be able to do this. I release the deep breath that I've been holding for the last two minutes. "Jenna and Peyton, will you help me out on this?"

They hesitate for a moment, and I think I'm going to have to go it alone, until finally, Jenna says, "I'll go with you."

"Me too," Peyton grabs onto my left arm, and Jenna grabs onto my right. I take out my phone to use its flashlight app, and we slowly begin to make our way toward creepy, screened-in cabin. We walk slowly up the hill, over some mossy, lightly powdered rocks. Then we make our way around a few pine trees, through some soggy leaf piles, and up to a squashy trail. Our boots slosh in the mud, and we stop abruptly when we hear a nearby squishing sound. "Is that you?" I jump.

"What?" Peyton replies.

"Nothing, well, I thought I heard something." I shake my head, and we continue on.

As we get closer to the old rotting cabin, another wave of unrest slinks over me. "This is really getting creepy. I feel like someone's in there."

"Oh stop," Jenna whispers. "There's no light . . . there's no way anyone is out here in these conditions without at least a fire. Come on, we can't wuss out now. The guys don't think we'll go through with this. Let's prove them wrong."

"Okay," I tug them forward. A few steps farther up the hill, I feel a thud against my big toe, and hear a ping as the object I just kicked ricochets from my boot. When we hear the crunch of glass in front of Peyton we all jump.

"What was that?" Peyton shrieks. "My foot is soaking wet!"

I shine the light in front of us. "I think I just kicked that beer bottle, and you stepped on it." We look down and see the frothing bubbles seeping into the ground, and melting the surrounding snow.

Peyton looks back down at the ground, "Do you think the adults were drinking over here? That looks pretty fresh. It's still foaming."

"No. They don't drink beer. Holy crap, let's get this over with." We huddle back together and continue on the path, walking past the front of the old screened in porch, and over to the far side of the cabin, where we find the entrance. I shine the light at the old wooden steps, and we squeeze in close so we can take the stairs together. We jump at the first creak, and freeze.

"What was that?" Peyton whispers.

"It was just us. The stairs are creaky. Let's go." Jenna whispers back.

"That creak was not below us. It was over there!" Peyton squeaks back.

"It's all connected. You can step here and cause a creak over there. Now let's go!" Jenna starts to become aggressive at Peyton's jumpiness and questioning.

I can't even talk right now. I am petrified with fear, and gripping my phone so tightly that it's molding itself into my skin. We finally pry ourselves from the stairs, and step onto the porch, when a strong breeze comes up through the floorboards, chilling me to the bone. Leaves begin to fly from the ground, plastering themselves against the screen. We're pelted by the small bits of dust and fragments that make their way through the holes and various rips in the screen. The howling has us on edge as we proceed toward the rickety ladder that leads up to some sort of open loft.

"I can't climb that," I shiver.

"I'll do it," Jenna replies.

"No I have to or I'm going back on the dare."

"Okay. I'll go up first and check it out, then when you know there's nothing to be afraid of, you can go."

Oh my dear Jenna; she's always been so brave. I am thankful for her willingness to sacrifice herself for my dare. When it comes to best friends, she takes the prize. She always has. "This could be bad Jenna. I don't like the feeling I have right now. There's bad energy in here. What if there's something dead up there or something? Are you sure about this?"

"I'm sure." Jenna says as she begins to climb the ladder. She looks down at me, "I've got this girl," she continues to climb. When she reaches the top of the ladder, she looks back down, "I think I see something Kait. I need light. Give me your phone."

"Jenna you don't have to go through with this," I squeak as I begin to climb the ladder with my light. "Come back down." I tug at her leg.

"No . . . Give it to me Kait."

When I hand her my phone, she takes it and shines it up into the opening. I swear I hear breathing. "I hear something Jenna." I reach to tug her back down. However, she's too far out of my reach, and I just miss her foot. No sooner does the light hit the loft, then something flies into her hand, knocking the phone to the ground. We both scream, and drop to the floor. Peyton grabs my phone.

"Run!!!" I shriek. All of us join in screaming. We sprint all the way down the hill, screaming at the top of our lungs, jumping over rocks, darting around trees, brushing through buckbrush. My heart is darn near pounding out of my chest.

When we get back to the fire, the boys are laughing hysterically. They are holding their stomachs, doubled over, snort laughing. When they finally come up for air, Mason laughs out, "Scared much? I told you I'd make your heart pound out of your chest. What happened up there?"

I bend over and put my hands on my knees. "What the hell flew at us Jenna?" I force the words through my shallow, jagged breaths.

In just as forced a reply, Jenna answers, "I don't know guys, but I saw a mattress and blankets. I think someone's in there."

Continuing their hysterics, Mason laughs, "It was probably a raccoon or a bat. That place hasn't been touched all year." The boys try to calm us down and reason with us, but I'm not of a mind to be reasoned with.

"You keep thinking that. I swear I heard breathing up there. Then something flew out at us guys. It literally knocked the phone out of Jenna's hand."

"Bat! I tell you," Caden replies.

"Na, Coon," says Brody.

"I call Horsecrap," I reply, raising my eyebrows. "You guys know just as well as I do that bats and raccoons don't throw things." I swallow the lump in my throat. "I'm just glad I convinced mom to bring the guns."

"Whoa, calm down Sis! If we thought there was someone over there, we'd go check it out right now. T, you're letting your imagination get away from you. You think if someone looked over here and saw all this muscle," he raises his clenched fist toward his face and pumps his bicep, "they would even dare hang around here? I mean, just look at this crew. I wouldn't mess with us."

"Yep, Kaitlyn, judging by the size of those arms, I'm glad you brought the guns," Jenna laughs. "Now if Ty was here to help out, it might be a different story."

"Stop goofing around you guys. Let's be serious for a minute. Don't you think you boys should go check it out?" Peyton questions.

Caden shakes his head and giggles, "No Peyton. Don't worry. You girls should just settle down. It's easy to get freaked out in these dark canyons. Brody, Mason, and I have seen all kinds of critters hanging in and around the cabins. I promise, it was nothin'."

I'm still shaking when Brody walks over and pulls me in for a hug. I stand stiffly with my fists clenched and arms pinned to my sides. I'm so mad at the boys for laughing at us and disregarding our fear, that I don't return his embrace. "Come on Kaitlyn, everything's okay. This is just a game in the dark. The whole point is to do crazy things and laugh at ourselves for it." Brody continues holding me with one arm and rubbing his hand up and down my back with the other. After a few minutes of him trying to comfort me, he whispers, "Pip, you're really scared aren't you? Oh Babe, relax. I'm right here with you. I'm not going anywhere. I've got you. Besides, I know how to be a whole lot scarier than anything out there. I'll take care of you."

In my mind, I know there was something in that loft. But Brody's reassurance is beginning to calm me down. After all, he is here to protect me, and maybe the boys are right. It could be any kind of critter. I do know one thing. Being in Brody's arms makes me feel safe. I start to relax as I put my arms around him.

"That's my girl. You know I won't let anything happen to you."

"Okay Brody, but I really don't want to end this night with

the fear of a Cabin Creeper looming in my head. And I also know we need to get this fire out cuz our parents are going to want us back in our cabins soon. So, I have one more dare for you."

"Ya, what's that?"

"I dare you to sneak over to my cabin tonight to check on me."

Brody stops in contemplation. After a minute he replies. "I'll do it under one condition . . ."

"What's that?"

"That you play your guitar for me while I'm there. I overheard you working on something earlier, and I want to hear it. Besides, I know that playing your guitar always seems to get your mind off things and makes you feel better."

I'm not sure if my song is ready. Can I do it? Can I play and sing for Brody? Sometimes you need to just take a leap of faith and lay it out there. I think I'm ready to do this. I can at least try. "Deal." I pull away from Brody and put my pinky out. "Let's seal it." He grabs my little finger in his strong hand and pulls me into him.

"That's not how I like to seal a deal with my favorite girl." He leans into me, gently pressing his lips to mine. Brody knows just how to time his sweet kisses. I don't know how I have any butterflies left inside of me after all of the ones that have escaped, but they sure have managed to find their way back.

He pulls away smiling down at me, "There, now that's a deal."

"A deal that can't come soon enough," I whisper with a smile.

I look up to see Mason and Caden smothering the fire and packing up the chairs. "Guess it's time to get back to our cabins," I give Brody a wink, excited about our little secret.

He gives me one more squeeze and lets me go.

The girls are asleep when Brody comes crawling up to the side of my bed. He knows how skittish I've been, so he's careful not to scare me. "Pip . . . Pip . . ." he whispers. "I'm here to check on you."

I'm glad he's finally here. I haven't been able to fall asleep thinking about the crazy game of truth or dare. My nerves calm the moment he wraps his strong hand around mine. I feel him sidle up next to me, and I lean in close so we can hear our whispers. "I'm so glad you came back. I couldn't sleep. You got past my parents okay?"

"Ya, everyone's asleep. I asked your brother if I could use his key. I told him I wanted to check on you, but I didn't want to wake up your parents or scare any of you girls by crawling through the window. He was cool with it."

I'm glad my brother has come to his senses about us. It was really nice of him to help Brody out like that.

"Ok Pip, I held up my end of the bargain, now I need you to come with me so you can sing me this song of yours."

I forgot about that part. I have to play for him. *How can I get out of this?* My stomach begins to tie up in knots. "You know . . . if I play for you in here, we'll wake everyone up."

"Oh, you're not playing in here, Girl. Bundle up and grab your guitar."

Hesitantly, I slip on my extra warm ski jacket, scarf, and cozy boots. I feel my way to my guitar that I left standing against the doorframe. I need to be cautious. Jenna is sleeping on an air mattress just a few feet away. Careful not to wake her, I bend down and grab my guitar by the base of its neck just as Brody takes me by the other hand and tiptoes me through the doorway.

We sneak through the main room of the cabin and Brody slowly creaks the door open, guiding me out to the front porch with his hand on my back. When I look up, I see flames dancing in the fire pit in front of our cabin. The oversized chair sits right beside it with a big fuzzy blanket waiting for us.

"Thought we could do a little star gazing while we're at it. The cloud cover just cleared and you can see Orion right now. Come here." Brody gently tugs me down toward the crackling fire. He takes the guitar from my hand and props it against the chair. Then he sits himself down and pulls me onto his lap. He spreads the fuzzy blanket across us, tucking it in behind him. I feel his criss crossed arms close in on mine. It feels comforting to be wrapped up in his arms. Calm comes over me as we sit silently gazing up at the crystal clear sky. "The snow is beautiful, but I'm glad the clouds have passed for a bit. See, Orion Pip? He's up really high right now." He pulls one arm out of the blanket and points into the night sky. "Right there. Look for his belt."

"Awww, that's my favorite constellation Bro. The Mighty Hunter."

"I know. I remember how you used to look for it all the time when we were kids."

"You remembered that?" I scrunch my face up in disbelief.

Brody tucks a strand of hair behind my ear and pulls his head in close whispering, "When you really care about someone, the little things they say and do tend to stick with you." The warmth of his breath spreading across my skin, sends shivers through me.

"You're an amazing boy Brody. I don't know how I can ever repay you for getting me through this fall."

"Pip, you don't owe me anything. You're my girl. It was selfish, really."

"What do you mean?"

"What I mean is, I need you in my life. And now that I

know what it's like to have you as my girl, I couldn't get through another minute on this earth if you weren't the one beside me. If I can keep you safe, I save myself too. See . . . selfish."

"Brody Tatum, I don't know what I would do without you." I stop and shake my head. *I wish there was a way to show him how much he means to me. Words just don't seem to be enough.* "So the song you heard me strumming on my guitar earlier?"

"Ya?"

"It was for you."

"Really Pip? You wrote that song for me?" I hear the flattery sneak into Brody's voice.

I take a deep breath, gathering my nerve. "Ya . . . It actually has lyrics. You ready to hear it?"

"That's why we're here Babe. Well that, and so I can see the stars twinkling in those beautiful blue eyes." He tickles my belly until I curl over laughing. "I know that was cheesy . . . just had to say it."

I regain my composure, and take in another deep breath. "Okay, here I go."

I pull my arms from beneath the blanket and pick up the guitar. Sitting up straight I inform him, "Brody, this is a fair warning . . . I don't sing in front of people."

"Well in that case, I feel really special." He grins, raising his eyebrows. "No judging here. I promise." As I sit with my back to him, he slips his hands across my lap, tucking them gently behind the guitar.

"I'll do it for you . . . but this is a once in a lifetime deal. You hear?" It takes me a second to tune my guitar before I clear my throat and start strumming the intro. Everything feels so right sitting here cuddled up in front of the fire with my sweet Brody. His head rests against my back, and for some reason, I can sense him smiling as I begin to sing. Like a snuggling puppy, his head gently moves up and down against my back. As I play into the song, I'm captured by the lyrics. I almost forget

I'm playing for an audience, when the emotion comes out and my voice grows stronger. I close my eyes, and imagine every word coming to life. I want him to know I'm singing it to him, and I want him to feel every last word of it.

As I hit the final verse, Brody's arms tighten around me.

When I finally strum the last line, I hear, "Wow, Pip . . . Your voice is beautiful. I'm the heart that fit your key?"

I set my guitar down on the ground afraid to turn around and see his reaction. "Yes, Brody." I take in a deep breath. "And I've realized something . . . YOU are the reason this fall didn't break me."

A moment of silence settles in between us. "Look at me Pip," he whispers.

When I slowly turn to face him, I see a tear rolling down the side of his cheek. "Look what you do to me. I didn't know I could want another human being as much as I want you right now. Snuggle in closer. I need you right next to me." He pulls me into him, tugging the blanket up over our heads. He whispers in my ear, sending shivers across my sensitive skin, "I love you . . . so much my little Pipsqueak." I feel him trembling beneath me as he presses his soft lips to mine. I don't know how long we're under there, holding and kissing each other, sharing an unforgettable night under the stars, before we see the light of the fire go out. When the crackling dies and darkness invades our tented blanket, Brody picks me up and carries me back inside the cabin where he tucks me into my bed, kisses me on the bridge of my nose, and sends me off to dreamland. As I close my eyes, I hear his whisper, "I'll see you in my dreams Pip, I always do."

CHAPTER 23

THE HUNT

"RISE AND SHINE GIRLS!" BRODY'S voice wakes me from my deep sleep. "We're going hunting for our Christmas trees this morning, and we need to get an early start." He jumps on my air mattress and starts tickling my stomach. I curl up in a ball and try to turn my head to the side, so he doesn't catch a whiff of my foul morning breath.

"Give me a minute Brody. I'm coming, I'm coming." I groan into my pillow as he continues his relentless tickle assault.

"Why are you hiding under that pillow Pip? Come! Out!"

The tickling finally ceases when I hear the patter of feet, followed by swooshing and thumping noises. I peek out of my pillow to see Jenna and Peyton attacking Brody. He has both arms wrapped around his head, trying to cover his face with his elbows. He's hunched over the top of me chuckling, as the girls bat their pillows at him mercilessly.

"You know, you really shouldn't come creeping into a girls cabin at six in the morning!" Jenna snarls as she wallops him upside the head once again.

"Ya . . . what she said!" Peyton pops him from the front.

"Okay, okay. I'm sorry. But we've got to get going, and Mason was kind of hoping you girls could convince Marissa to come along. She came to our cabin for a while last night and played some poker with us boys after that obnoxious game of Truth or Dare. Mason really wants to hang out with her some more, and we thought it would be good to get her away from those stiff parents of hers. You've got to hear this one. They set her phone timer to make sure she didn't stay longer than forty-five minutes! Geez, you're only a teenager once." Brody shakes his head in disbelief. "It was so funny though, she left her phone on her front porch and pretended she forgot to bring it. She stayed for an hour and fifteen minutes, til her dad came knocking at the door to get her back."

A contemplative look spreads across Peyton's face. "Well it sounds like she was a lot of fun. Seems like she could be a bit of a rebel if you ask me . . . despite the fact that her parents keep her under lock and key." She looks at us, "What do you think girls?"

Jenna shakes her head in agreement, "We'll give it a shot . . . for Mason."

"Okay," I agree. "Let's get dressed and see if we can pry Miss Marissa out of her parents' clutches for a few hours of back country fun."

After we're dressed in our snow gear, we head down the hill to Marissa's cabin. We spend nearly a half hour convincing her parents that we know these woods like the backs of our hands and we're up to nothing more than finding the perfect Christmas tree. Finally, with some hesitance, the Matthew's agree to let her come with us on the hunt. Mason, Marissa, Peyton, and Caden climb into Caden's truck, while Brody, Jenna, and I jump into my dad's truck.

"We just got word that the main road is closed until they get the snowplows out here, so we're going to take our time driving the back roads. Is that okay with you girls? We can wait until tomorrow if you don't want to risk getting stuck." Brody asks our opinions before we begin our ascent up the winding, snow covered road. We shake our heads and reassure him that today's the day, and we're up for anything as long as we're not the ones who have to drive in the snow and ice. I trust Brody completely. He knows how to drive in these conditions better than any of us, being he has to help Mason feed cattle on the family ranch during the winter. He's constantly driving over Forest Mountain when the roads are blanketed with snow.

At our okay, Brody pulls out behind Caden, and we make our way back along the river toward an old logging road. The fresh snow blanketing the trees and bridges has me in awe of the natural beauty of these mountains. The light shines through the trees, making the snow glisten. It lights the hills along the roadside, giving it a gorgeous aqua glow that radiates through the crevices in the mounds. The beauty and stillness of it all, has me feeling as though I'm traveling inside one of Thomas Kincade's Winter Wonderland paintings.

As we climb higher up the mountain, the wind begins to pick up. It howls across the roadway, and blows the fresh powder up onto the windshield, causing just enough moisture to streak the glass with grime as the wipers work to swipe it away. It's making such a mess that its difficult to see Caden's truck ten feet in front of us.

Nervousness brought on by the treacherous conditions, fills the cab, and I know we're going to need to break the tension soon. "You girls might want to stop breathing so hard, I know I have a tendency to do that to women, but you're fogging up the windshield and it's already hard to see," Brody watches from the corner of his eye, with a turned up smirk on his face. I can tell he's trying to elicit a smart aleck response from one of us.

In true Jenna fashion, she comes through with a witty reply,

"I'm not the one full of hot air Bro."

"Ya, I guess I set myself up for that one, didn't I?" he chuckles

"Uh huh," I giggle. "Just watch the road Hottie, the snow's getting a lot deeper. Are you sure we can make it all the way up to our spot?"

"We've got this Babe. Just hold on tight."

And I do. Brody shifts into four wheel drive, and begins to barrel into the narrowing gravel road. It's getting a little dicey, as we begin to climb off the road, through trees. At one point I cover my face with my hands, peeking through the crack in my fingers. We barely clear the trees on each side of us. The truck bounces to the left and right, and the wheels spin, trying to catch hold of the slick, uneven road beneath us. At one point I think we're stuck. I giggle nervously as we bounce and spin up the hill.

Jenna sits next to me slapping the seat, yelling, "Giddy up Monster Truck! You got this!"

"Shhh, Jenna, not now!" I screech nervously. "Brody needs to concentrate."

Brody laughs. "No Pip, I'm fine. We're fine. Look at Caden up there. If he can make it pulling all those crazy stunts, then we're all good." He points up at Caden's truck making its way up the hill in front of us. He's fishtailing, spinning out, throwing mud, and taking the sides of hills like he's skiing Mt. Shasta.

"My brother is a crazy man!" I shake my head.

"Yep, that's why I let him run in my wolf pack!" Jenna winks at me. "Why won't anyone let me drive?"

Brody clears his throat and shakes his head back and forth. "Well, Jenna, being as how you can't even drive a Go Kart, do I really need to answer that? Tell me you didn't forget about the time we went to the Family Fun Center and you completely jumped the track and ran into the side of the hotdog stand. That was some funny stuff right there."

"He does have a point Jenna. I mean, they almost revoked your license for that one." I laugh.

"Man, I'll never live that down, will I? Do you guys really have to keep bringing that up?"

"Only when you ask to drive," I smile. "But we'll let it die for now."

Just as I've had about as much four wheeling as I can take for the morning, we reach the top of the hill, and tuck ourselves into our secret spot where we traditionally hunt for trees.

"That looks like a good place to start our fire," Brody points to a flat clearing as he jumps out of the truck. "Help me grab some firewood from the back of Caden's truck."

"You've got it."

We all work together to unload the wood, set up a small circle of chairs, and build a fire. Marissa sits close to Mason. They must've connected a bit on the truck ride up, because they're looking very cozy. I sit on Brody's lap, enjoying snuggling in his warmth while I finish up my hot cocoa. Jenna cracks jokes, keeping everyone entertained as usual. And then there's Caden and Peyton. When I look over, I see that they've taken the bag of marshmallows we used for our hot chocolate. They're playing a silly game called "Chubby Bunny."

They have us in hysterics. They've both got at least seven marshmallows shoved in their faces. With cheeks stretched to maximum capacity, drool and goop runs from their mouths and traces its way toward their chins. "One more," Caden mumbles, as they shove an eighth marshmallow in and try to say "chubby bunny." On the eighth one, the marshmallow pops from Peyton's mouth, plopping onto Caden's lap. It's followed by a river of creamy, white, sticky drool. Caden jumps up, and laughs as the blob of disintegrating marshmallows fall from his mouth to the ground.

"Guess we should get cleaned up, huh?" Peyton asks Caden.

"Let me help you guys with that." I intervene. "I always carry wipes in the woods," You can never be too prepared for germs and messes. I walk over to the truck and help my brother and his girl get the sticky mess off of their pants and fingers.

When I turn around, I see Mason and Brody pointing up the hill. Yep, they are already scouting for the perfect Silver Tip, I just wish we could get a little higher in elevation so I could get a Noble Fir. They're my favorites. I'm just waiting to see what happens with this year's final choices. It seems like we always end up with the Charlie Brown tree, while the Tatum's make out with the most beautiful tree on the mountain. Well, not if I can help it. Since last year's tree was so ugly, today, I get the final say. Mom and Dad are behind me one hundred percent on that one, especially since we had so many catastrophes last year. The needles fell off in less than a week, and the limbs were so small and frail, they couldn't even hold up the ornaments. Every night as we sat watching the Hallmark Channel, we could hear a few more ornaments slip through the branches and crash to the ground. We picked glass out of the carpet for days.

"Pip, I'll make sure to help you get a beautiful tree this year." Brody slips behind me and whispers in my ear. "I spotted a patch of trees up that hill, and I want you to come with me to take a look at them." He takes me by the hand and walks me up the hill. Dang he looks good from this angle. I don't know another guy who can look that hot in snow pants. I can actually make out the cut of his muscular thighs through them. I'm mesmerized by Brody, when my foot sinks further than I anticipate, causing me to lose my balance. Sunken into the snow on all fours, I laugh at my clumsiness.

"Help me up!" I reach out to him.

"Oh sorry Pip. You're just so darn cute struggling down there. I wanted to take it all in for a sec." He reaches out for me. I grab his hand and give him a good tug, pulling him down next to me. We roar with laughter, as Brody grabs a handful of snow and shoves it into my face, "Brain freeze!" he yells.

"I'll show you brain freeze!" I begin to climb on top of him so I can shove his head down in the snow, when I notice a trail of fresh footprints. "Hey Bro, I didn't see any other cars up here. Did you?"

"No, why?"

"There's a trail of footprints here." I point to one of the footprints under my hand. "I'm pretty sure, that's what I fell into."

"You're right Pip . . . there are!" He says in a sarcastic voice. "Maybe it's Sasquatch!" he jokes, starting another tickle fight.

"Stop Brody. Don't you find it a little odd?"

"Pip, just because it's our secret spot, doesn't mean it's a secret to everyone. People come up here all the time. It's a logging road for crying out loud. But if it's bothering you, let's hurry up and get that tree, so we can get back down to the truck."

"Thanks Brody. I guess I'm still a little jumpy about, well, you know. I know you're here to protect me. Let's take our time picking out that tree."

Within an hour, we are pulling a gorgeous Silver Tip down to the truck. As we make our descent, something feels off. When we get closer to the gang, everyone is frantic. They are shaking their heads in disbelief. They've just returned from the hunt with their trees too. As we approach the trucks, we see the windows have been smashed out of Caden's truck and our stuff is strewn all over the ground. "Oh no!" I whimper.

"What is it?" Brody asks.

"I left the rifle under Caden's seat so Mom wouldn't see me take it. Please tell me it's still there!" I cross my fingers and say a silent prayer that the gun has not been stolen.

Brody bends down and drags his hand along the floorboard as he searches for the gun.

My face goes pale, and the blood rushes from my body,

when he pops back up from under the seat, shaking his head, "It's gone." From its place, Brody pulls out an empty bottle of Jack Daniels.

He shakes it in the air, "Son of a Bitch!" he shouts, as he throws it to the ground. "Load up! We have to get out of here. Caden, are you okay to drive your truck like that?"

"Ya, I can make it Dude. It's freezing out there; try to fit as many people into Dad's truck as you can. Brody walks to my brother, leans in close, and whispers something. The look on Caden's face tells me there's more to this than someone sabotaging Caden's truck. Caden yells, "Hurry Guys! The storm is getting worse. We need to get out of here!"

We throw the trees into the back of our truck. Jenna, Brody, and I squish into the front seat, while Mason and Marissa get into the back. They scoot over to make room for Peyton. Caden tries to help her in, but she's hell bent on going with him. "I'm not letting you go alone Babe. I can handle the cold. I've got you to keep me warm," Peyton grabs onto Caden, pleading with him to take her.

"Babe, you know it's gonna be one helluva ride, right?"

"I don't care. I want to go with you. I don't want you driving alone. I won't feel safe if we're in different trucks."

"Alright. Come with me." Caden finally gives in. "But you're wearing my Carhartt jacket."

Brody pulls up next to Caden and rolls down the window. "Caden, we need to stick together. Don't lose sight of our truck!"

"You've got it Dude."

As we take off in the howling wind, I feel sorry for my brother and Peyton traveling in the bitter cold with no windows. Brody acts strange, almost shaken. He is silent, and looks intently forward with his arms held straight out from the steering wheel. His white knuckles grip so tightly that the pressure nearly has his bones piercing through his skin. "Brody, what are you not telling me?" I ask him with a shaky voice. He shakes his head slightly but doesn't answer. "Brody, are we in more trouble than I think, here? Answer me!" I raise my voice frustrated from his lack of response. "Please tell me we aren't going to keep secrets from each other after everything we've been through. I need to know what we're up against. Please talk to me, Bro."

"I wasn't going to say anything, Pip, but that Jack Daniels . . . That's the same shit I found by your car the night you were attacked after Championships. That's the same shit I found out in the barn after you were attacked at the barn dance. Kaitlyn, it's Pistol! I'll be damned if those weren't his footprints you fell into. This is a game to him. He's hunting you!"

Shaking uncontrollably I grab onto Brody's shirt, "Bro, I'm really scared! Pistol doesn't react like a normal person when he's been drinking Jack. He's a violent drunk. We aren't safe. You know that, don't you? We can't hide anywhere. He's going to find us. Can't we go faster?"

"Pip, I wish I could say yes . . . but I have to stay in four wheel drive and we're already in high gear. It's really slick. Besides, if we speed up, we could run Caden off the road. He's having a tough enough time without the windows."

As the fear and panic build in me, tears begin to stream down my face, and my shaking intensifies. Jenna's hand comes up over the back of the seat and she rests it on my shoulder. "We're going to be okay."

Just as those words leave Jenna's mouth, I see Caden begin to fish tale in front of us. "What's going on? Look at Caden!" I point and yell. I can't see more than ten feet in front of us, but my heart jumps out of my chest when I process the narrowness of the road versus the width of Caden's swerving.

"Oh Lord NO!" Brody screams. I hear a popping sound "Duck Pip!"

Screech.

"Are those gun shots?" I stutter.

"God No! He's headed straight for Caden."

I hold onto the dashboard, and peek over it just enough to see Pistol's oncoming truck ready to collide with my brother. I'd recognize that truck anywhere. Brody pulls his foot from the gas to avoid running into the back of Caden's slowing truck. I can hear Brody yelling at me to get down, but I'm frozen. I can't even scream. My blood runs cold as I hear the shots and watch Caden spin toward the embankment. As he spins out of control, he wraps into the side of Pistol's truck, pulling him over the embankment with him.

"NO!!!!" I shriek, as I hear the crashing and crunching of metal. I cover my ears to block out the piercing sounds coming up from the canyon.

Brody slides to a stop. I can't process it all. I hear screaming, more crunching, and then the blackness begins to overtake me. For a moment, I am in a dark tunnel. There is no sound but that newly familiar buzzing that fills my ears. I feel weightless, like I'm in a dream. My face is cold. Really. Really. Cold. My cheek is pressed up against something hard. As I focus on my freezing face, the buzzing begins to fade away. My ears tune into a new sound of panic.

"Help Pip, Help!" I feel Brody shaking me. "I need you Pip! Wake! Up!"

When I open my eyes, I see Brody's tear stained face. He's gasping for air. "You've got to come with me Pip. They're down there." He reaches out for my hand. "I found Caden. He needs you. You're a lifeguard Pip . . . you know CPR and first aid. Quick Pip Quick. I can't do this alone! I need you to be strong! Caden needs you to be strong!"

I'm out of my mind with fear, and still struggling with the dizziness from my fainting spell. I can't catch my breath. I can't even focus. The fear in Brody's voice is pulling me back in. It's then that I realize. *My. Brother. Just. Flew. Over. A. Cliff!*

I'm trying to catch my breath. It hurts to pull in air. My hands are trembling as I try to gather my strength. I know time is working against us. I grab Brody's hand and let him pull me to my feet.

I'm terrified to look over the side of the hill. I know that I will never be able to unsee what I'm about to witness. I take in a deep breath, and ask God to help me, and then I dare to look down. The first thing I see is Jenna and Marissa, hunched over a large rock at the bottom of the ravine near the river. Off to the side, sitting in the river, is Caden's truck. The cab is crunched in, and the water flows all around it. It is submerged in water, with only about six inches sitting above the surface. My friends are peering in at the truck screaming for us to get down there. Mason is standing in the river hunched over, calling up for Brody.

Mason's panicked voice echoes up the canyon, "I can't do it Dude! I can't get the door open. I can't get my footing and I'm not strong enough! Get down here Brody! Hurry!"

Brody grabs my hand tightly. "Kaitlyn, don't let go of me! We have to hurry down that hill. Be careful, the snow is pretty deep in some places. Follow the path Mason made."

We bound down the hill as fast as we can, staying on the path. I stumble a few times from fatigue, but Brody pulls me right up and we keep going. I'm sweating and out of breath when we reach the riverbank. Mason is shivering and shaking as he tries to reach into the cab of the truck through the window. "Hold on Peyton, hold on . . . try to keep your head up." I hear him shivering.

Caden is lying on the riverbank shrieking, in pain. Every few seconds he grunts, "Help her! Help Peyton!"

I gasp when I see his condition. He looks blue, and his face is covered in blood. His pants are torn and bloody. Someone has tied a tourniquet around his arm. I'm horrified when I instantly recognize he has a compound fracture. Jenna is trying to place pressure on his wound to stop the bleeding. As I get closer, I hear his labored breathing. It's raspy and crackling. I'm terrified as I kneel beside him.

"Caden, hang in there brother. I love you. I'm going to try to help Peyton."

"Please Kait . . . go now. It's really bad." He cringes and holds his breath, then let's out an agonizing shriek.

We need more help. I'm starting to panic. "Has anyone tried their cell phone?!?" I scream.

"I tried, but there's no service!" Marissa cries.

"Run to the top of the hill and try again! Sometimes you can get service if you're high in a clearing!"

Quickly, Marissa starts running up the hill. She yells over her shoulder, "If I'm not back right away, I'm finding help. Please God! Get Peyton out of that truck!"

I run toward the river where Brody has joined Mason. They're taking turns trying to pry the door open. "It's so damn cold, my hands won't work! Son of a Bitch!" Brody screams.

I lose my breath as I step into the icy river for the first time. The freezing water severely constrains my movement; I slowly wade in up to my hips and scream at myself to get out there faster. "Move Kaitlyn! Move!" I cry. I lean forward and dig at the water with my arms to push myself closer to Peyton. When I finally reach the truck, I grab onto the doorframe and steady myself in the current. "The cab is crushed. You're the only one small enough to fit in there Kaitlyn. See if you can get to her. We need to see what's holding her in there!" Mason yells.

Brody shakes his head, "Mason, it's too dangerous! What if she gets stuck. I won't risk Pip!"

"Brody, I have to try to save her. I'm going down there. Don't stop me." I take a deep breath, and pull myself in through the window. The shock of putting my head under, rips at my skin and punches me in the stomach. I almost lose my breath as

I shiver beneath the frigid water, but work to pull myself into the crunched cab. When I feel the seat beneath my hand, I open my eyes. I look in, and spot Peyton. Her face is up against the roof of the truck. She's found a small pocket of air at the top of the cab. She bangs desperately at the passenger door as the water continues to rage around her face. When I can hold my breath no longer, I reluctantly claw back up to the surface.

I gasp desperately, and screech to the boys, "She has a little air. Not much, but some." I wheeze for breath. "I'm worried about the water temperature. She can't be down there much longer!" Choking and spitting, I pull in another breath and dive down again. Already knowing my way, I get in more quickly this time. I hunch down, and pull myself closer to Peyton, opening my eyes to see that she's still locked securely in her seat belt. I pull wildly at the clasp, trying to unfasten it from her waist. It won't budge. The air pocket gets smaller, as a sudden bobbling movement shifts the truck beneath me. I hear a small moan, "Kaitlyn, help." Peyton's cry is strained and barely audible. The movement startles me, and I reflexively give a swift kick, hitting the gear shift with tremendous force.

A split second later, a hand shoots down through the window and clamps onto my shirt. I hear Brody's garbled voice permeating the surface of the water. "It's gonna go!"

As I feel myself being pulled back through the open window, I try to reach for Peyton, but she's just too far away. The truck begins to slip from beneath me. The strong tow of the sinking truck, tugs at my legs, while Brody pulls me back to the surface. With a terrifying wheeze, I pull oxygen into my parched lungs.

Screams pierce the air around me. I stand shivering in the water, looking on in horror. I'm caught in the middle of a horrific nightmare. Before my eyes, I watch Caden's submerged truck bob down the raging river. Cries and screams continue to wail out around me.

"Oh my God!" Jenna screams.

"No!" I hear Mason, cry.

Along with the terror of Peyton being swept away with the truck, something more is wrong. I don't hear my brother's voice among the screams. When I whip my head around to check on him, I see Caden, motionless on the snowy sand. Jenna is bent over him crying, and patting his face. "Wake up Caden, wake up!" she sobs.

Brody, Mason, and I drag ourselves out of the water and fall to our knees before him. With the vision that lies in front of me, I shake uncontrollably. A thousand fears shove my face to the ground, and anchor me in place. I shake violently, huddled in a ball. I pull my arms around my head and hold on tightly, rocking back and forth, trying to escape the nightmare. An ear piercing, unfamiliar growl escapes my searing throat.

"Not him too!" I cry hysterically.

Peyton is gone. My brother is unresponsive. My friends wail in horror around me. Frozen and drowning in the pain of this Jefferson fall, my heart breaks.

To Be Continued . . .

Coming in 2015
The Seasons of Jefferson Series
Book 2: The Dead of Winter

A Message from the Authors

Being a teen is one of the most difficult times in a person's life. There are a couple of commonly faced issues that we wanted to address when we were writing this book. The first issue is underage drinking and substance use. We hope it was clear, that underage drinking is never a good idea. Drinking in any situation clouds a person's judgement, leads one to take risks that they wouldn't normally take, and causes great obstacles for getting out of those dangerous situations. Readers, here is a great example from the story. Had Kaitlyn not been drinking, would she have ever entered that tack room alone at night? Also, think about when Pistol attacked her. Was he sober?

If you know of a young person who needs help, *The Pathway Program* is available. You can call Toll Free at 1–877–921–4050 or visit them on the web at www.thepathwayprogram.com. If you are a teen and find yourself struggling with drinking or substance abuse, please reach out to a parent, school counselor, teacher, youth pastor, or friend. As teachers, we are always open to help our students get the help they need. It doesn't matter if you were a former student, current student, or didn't even have us as a teacher. We care about all of you!

A second issue that many teens and young adults struggle with is domestic violence. This can happen to people of any race, age, sexual orientation, religion, or gender. Sometimes it starts out subtly, and intensifies without the victim realizing how bad it has become. If friends are warning you that they see signs of control, verbal, or physical abuse, please listen. Many abusers are masters at manipulating their victims and making them feel like THEY are the reason for the incident. It's NEVER okay. It is NOT your fault. If you or someone you know is in an abusive relationship, there is confidential support out there 24/7. Please visit the National Domestic Violence Hotline at http://

www.thehotline.org. Teens can go to www.loveisrespect.org, or call 1–866–331–9474 to speak with someone privately. It's a confidential online resource available to help young adults prevent and end abusive relationships.

WHEN FALL BREAKS

PLAYLIST

"Cruise" by Florida Georgia Line

"You Know I'm Here for the Party" by Gretchin Wilson

"Party Rock Anthem" by LMFAO

"Can't be Tamed" by Miley Cirus

"Really Don't Care" by Demi Lovato

"Pop, Lock, and Drop It" by Huey

"My Eyes" by Blake Shelton

"Country Girl Shake it For Me" by Luke Bryan

"When You Say Nothing at All" by Keith Whitley

"Drink to That All Night" by Jerrod Niemann

"When Fall Breaks" by Julie Solano

ACKNOWLEDGEMENTS

Ancient Chinese legend tells us that there is an invisible red thread that connects two people together, that are destined to meet regardless of time, place, or circumstance. Those people meet either to help each other in a certain situation or in some way. The thread may stretch or tangle, but it will never break. If there's a thread of friendship, we've certainly been blessed with it. After a series of near misses over a several year span, we finally met as teachers in a middle school in far Northern California nearly two decades ago. Since that time, there has been a common fascination that has kept our friendship entertaining and adventurous. Along with our fabulous personalities, it was our love of good books. Late night phone calls, big city adventures, and even color runs, were often fueled with character analysis, plot deviations, and talks of what would make a great story.

Inspired by our love of literature and our fascination with the people who create it, we began reaching out to some authors whose books made a huge impression on us. One of those incredible authors decided she'd "let us win" a trip to the Indie Girl CON in South Carolina in February of 2013. That trip provided us with many fulfilled bucket list items, like meeting our favorite Indie author and spending time with several others at late night clubs, almost being kidnapped by a crazed taxi driver, missing a flight out of Chicago O'Hare, and running through the streets of Chicago singing the theme song to Laverne and Shirley. We had so much fun in this new author world, that we decided the next time we would attend an author convention, it would be to fulfill our newest bucket list item. We'd already had scenes written and scattered haphazardly throughout our computers, but used them solely as therapy, with no thought to turning them into a novel. However, all that changed when we got back from Indie Girl CON. Encouraged by several authors who took us under their wings and became our friends, we decided to take the leap and begin writing a novel of our own.

So here we are. Nearly a year later, our first novel is finished, and we're ready to thank those who were instrumental in making that happen. First and foremost, Alison G. Bailey, our BAFF (Best Author Friend Forever), this novel would not have happened if we'd never met you. You're the one who pulled us into this Tweet world with those tickets last February. Your kindness and kick butt personality made us want to dive into this author gig. Thank you for your willingness to overlook our nutty personalities and for not hiring security guards to haul us off before we got our signed paperbacks of Present Perfect. To Riley Mackenzie, thank you for filling us in on the perks of writing a novel together. It was basically the most fun thing we've ever done in our lives.

Thank you to our Moms, brothers, sisters, and close family who put up with our lame excuses and didn't pry our secret out of us, even though we know you questioned our children on more than one occasion. Now you know why we missed Fourth of July parties, hid in our hotel rooms at swim meets, missed more than one Sunday at church, and skipped out on summer camping trips. We weren't lying when we said we were working on a literacy project. Thank you for taking our kids and not knowing why. Once you all found out about what we were doing, you gave us the courage we needed to actually publish this. All of your sweet, encouraging texts and comments have helped us stay brave. We love you Moms. We love you too Grampie and Papa. And to our Dads; we thank you for teaching us about country living, blessing us with half of our goofy personalities, our humor, and creativity. Though you're no longer with us, you inspire us everyday to make you proud. We wish you were here to see us reaching for the stars and making our dreams a reality. We miss you!

Thank you to our students who endured cranky, tired teachers on those nights we put in extra hours. Sometimes when an idea hits, you have to go with it. Follow our example and live the dream. No one says you can't live a double life. Now you know why we have our horseshoe necklaces. It gave us luck on this journey. To our principal who didn't question why we were hiding in our classrooms at all hours of the day, and to our colleagues for enduring the code talk in the hallways, out on the playground, and during collaboration meetings, we know you think we're crazy, but we like you anyway. A special "thank you" goes to Mrs. Vianna Bailey who kept our secret and helped us with our technology. Thank you for designing our beautiful webpage and playing on our side of the court with the code talk.

To our friends, we hope you enjoy reading this book. Some of you may see similarities in your personalities, ya, it's probably based on you. Stacey Lee, that scene when Kaitlyn flipped over the horse backward and landed on her head, well, you remember how that all went down. We had to give you a small piece of this, didn't we? Marnia, you asked for it and we delivered. Mr. Hendryx, we couldn't help it. You have the strongest personality of any teacher/coach we ever had! Your nicknames will live on in infamy. Thank you for being that teacher that will forever have a special place in our hearts.

Thank you to Taylor Himbert who didn't think twice about giving us her permission to use the beautiful picture on our cover. You are an incredible photographer, and we hope to use more of your pictures in the future. Thank you to Larry Butcher for letting us use his picture on the back cover of the book. You have captured the Forks of the Salmon's beauty like no other.

Thank you to all who are willing to pick up this book and give it a chance. We love our area, and the country life we live. Southern Oregon and Northern California is one of the most beautiful places on earth. We hope you see the true spirit of the State of Jefferson! Wait until you see what we have planned for the second book in the Seasons of Jefferson Series, *The Dead of Winter.*

More than anyone else on this earth, this dream would not have been possible without the support of our husbands and children. They listened to our crazy idea about writing this book and instead of laughing at us, they encouraged and supported us all the way.

A special thanks goes out to our children who kept our secret and inspired the personalities behind our characters. Thank you for willingly letting us steal your personalities, and even loaning us some of your real life experiences. Thank you for feeding us dialog when our writer's block got the best of us. Thank you T, for being brave enough to let us put your picture on the cover. T, you know this picture shows your beauty inside and out. You are such an incredible young lady. Your personality shined through in this novel. And to that boy of yours. He knows who he is. He deserves a big thank you for inspiring some of the sweetness that made Brody the perfect novel boyfriend.

To our husbands, thank you for taking us on road trips to research the geography and sharing with us some of the local legends written into our story. Thank you for the countless four wheel rides, trail hikes, rivers, bridges, and bonfires. From the very beginning, you helped put the country in us. Also, a huge thank you for all the days you took the kids so we could work, and all the nights you had to go to bed with the light on. We love you guys more than you'll ever know! Because of your support and belief in us, you made this dream a reality. Thank you for encouraging us to follow our dreams.

Julie Solano has lived in far Northern California, nearly her entire life. She graduated from CSU, Chico, where she majored in Psychology and minored in Child Development. She later went on to Simpson University where she obtained her multiple subject teaching credential. Julie enjoys life in the "State of Jefferson" where she lives with her husband and two children. As a family, they spend their time tromping around the Marble Mountains and Russian Wilderness. They also take pleasure in rafting, skiing, snowmobiling, off-roading, campfires, and living it up in the great outdoors. When she's not with her family, Julie spends her days teaching next door to her co-author, fellow prankster, and partner in crime, Tracy. The most recent of their crazy adventures was to take on the challenge of writing this silly, little novel about life in their neck of the woods. They hope you have fun reading this story which was inspired by their small town, rural upbringing, and the personalities of their four children.

Born and raised in Northern California, Tracy Justice is a wife, mother, and full-time teacher. She graduated from CSU, Chico with a Bachelor of Arts Degree in Liberal Arts. One of her fondest memories growing up was herding cattle in the Marble Mountains with her family. She enjoys spending time with her family and friends, riding horses, running, hiking, swimming, and of course reading. After some encouragement from Julie, she decided to add "Co-author" to her ever growing bucket list. She never knew how much fun it would be to write a book with her best friend. She hopes you enjoys reading this story as much as they enjoyed writing it. Remember to visit Julie and Tracy on Facebook at JT Authors and on the web at www.jtauthors.com.

Made in the USA
San Bernardino, CA
01 March 2015